THE HALF TURN

STEVEN BARTHOLOMEW

First published in paperback by
Michael Terence Publishing in 2023
www.mtp.agency

ISBN 9781800946651

To Kate, Chloe, and Mia

The Grid

The grid, with its twenty zones, which Joe uses to instruct the players on their positions and movement in relation to each other, their opponents, and the location of the ball.

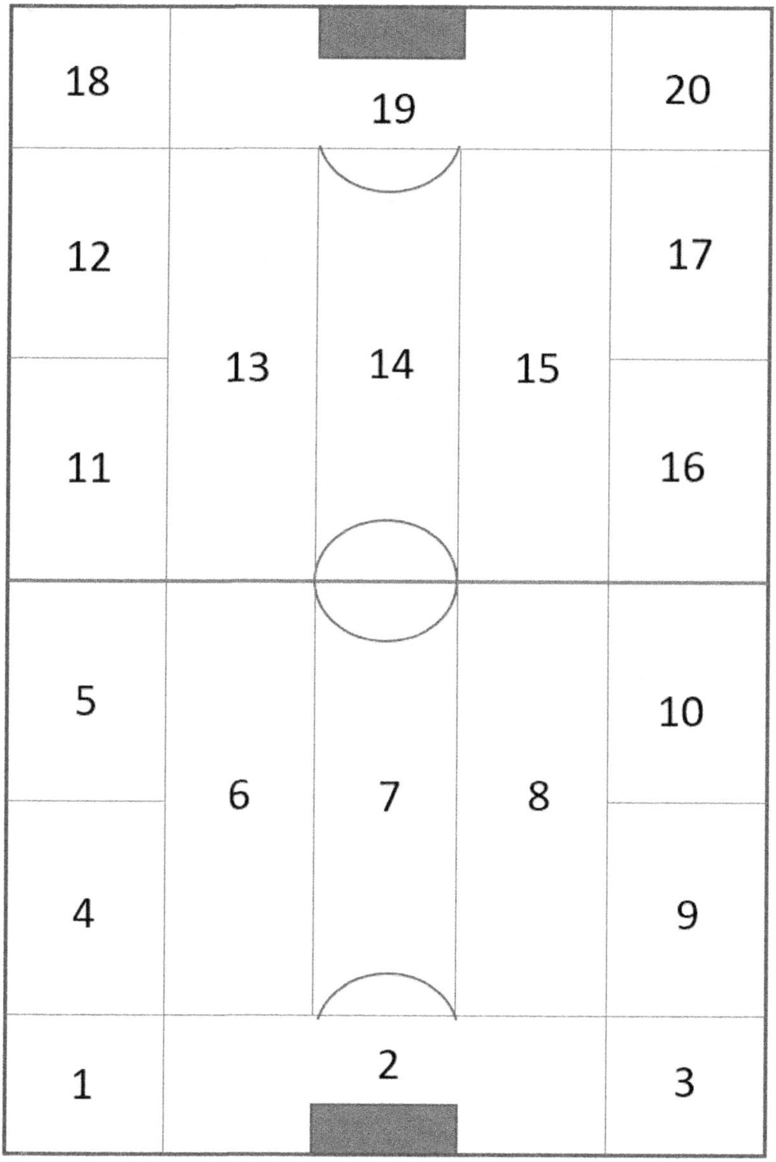

18
19
20
12
17
13
14
15
11
16
5
10
6
7
8
4
9
1
2
3

1

Manor Road was a hard place to visit. A bear pit of a ground with stands tight to the pitch and a tough, hostile crowd who were onto the players before the game had even started, hurling coins and cigarette lighters as they warmed up. Baiting them with taunts about their wives or children, anything to get under their skin. But it was also a crowd that could turn on their own if things did not go their way and we had taken control under the lights that February evening with a performance full of courage. The players looking for the ball. Daring to take chances, to be creative, when everything was on the line. Pinning the crimson shirts and white shorts in their own half and showing the willingness to work and suffer as a team when out of possession. Pressing in units high up the pitch and devouring the second-ball.

Collingham could not cope with our shape or movement, our ability to conjure space between the lines. The tireless running in the channels or Vlado Stolar's willingness to drop back and create overloads in the central third. And they were not prepared to match our work rate. The star studded front three, with their pass-by-on-the-other-side disdain for defensive duties, refused to track the runs of our fullbacks as they powered up the line, or press our central defenders when they built play.

A cloud of red smoke from yet another flare drifted across the pitch and away into the night sky, leaving behind the aftertaste of burnt rubber. Stefan Fryc twisted and turned to elude a challenge and broke Collingham's second line with one of his forward leaning passes, a low spun ball that skimmed across the wet grass and took three players out of the game. With his shaved head and ramrod straight back, Fryc looked like he had just stepped off the parade ground. The young Pole was the fulcrum of the team. The intermediary between defence and attack. The out-ball for our defenders in the first phase of play and the instigator of our attacks. To this day he remains, pound for pound, the best signing I've made.

Our supporters had also brought their A-game that evening. Once again, they opened and closed their arms above their heads in their own take on the Viking thunderclap. The deafening noise rung out around the stadium.

'BOOM. BOOM. *HUH.*'

The game was won in the wide areas (zones 5, 11, and 12 on the left and 10, 16, and 17 on the right). Collingham's forwards' distaste for the grubby side of the game left their teammates outgunned in the middle of the pitch. We pulled the midfield three from side to side and then Knežević and Ružic switched play with raking cross-field passes into the open space on other wing, isolating the fullbacks two v one.

We doubled our lead with one of these cross-field diagonals. It was a sequence of passes, a flurry of interchanging movement that we had practiced and perfected in hundreds of sessions on the training pitch overlooking the Adriatic. After a turnover in possession near our box, we bypassed the first disjointed press with an isosceles triangle of rapid short passes. Boban Knežević played the ball forward and wide, out to Sarić on the left wing. While Sarić exchanged passes with Stolar, our wide forward on the other flank moved to the interior dragging his fullback with him. The ball was then switched to Theophile Mboma, our right sided attacking midfielder, who had arrived in the vacated space. The young Cameroon controlled the ball with his chest and then played it across the box to Sarić who stroked the ball into the red and white striped net from eight yards out. Sarić ran behind the goal, cupping his hand to his ear for the benefit of the baying home fans, and then threw himself to his knees, sliding to a standstill in front of the corner flag where he was engulfed by a downpour of plastic bottles and paper cups.

The goal killed the tie. You could see it in their players' body language - shoulders slumped, arms waved at each other after a misplaced pass - and the lack of discipline. The needless fouls and frustrated backchat. They knew there was no way back. That no substitutions or tactical adjustments could turnaround this deficit. The crowd knew it as well and began to stream out with fifteen minutes to go, not sticking around to witness our third goal, a crisp first-time strike from Stolar into the top left corner. It was a goal that sealed the victory and cost Alec Forsyth in the neighbouring technical area his job.

The semi-final against A.C Montichiari three weeks later was a war of attrition. Once again, the boys rose to the occasion, playing with the perfect balance of tactical discipline and creativity in the final third. The Italians assumed a low block from kick off. Content to soak up the pressure, they lay back on the ropes absorbing blow after blow, like Ali in Zaire. It was a level of organisation and discipline we had not encountered before. A Roman legion holding firm with its triple line.

Just one man stepping out to press at a time, the rest shuffling across to fill the gap as they defended the edge of their box. And for all our pressure, all our dominance of the ball, we barely left a dent in their armour. Montichiari were in no rush to attack, happy to wait for the chance they knew would come their way. And sure enough in the second leg, with the tie still goalless, they floored us with a sucker punch. A cleverly worked corner to the back post was bundled in at the second attempt, after an outstanding reflex save on the line earned us the briefest of reprieves. It was a reminder of the harshest of truths: no matter how well you play, how hard you work, every competition ends in defeat for all but the eventual champions. Montichiari were themselves beaten in the final, departing with the medals that no one wants. But it was these floodlit contests, when we matched the level of the best in Europe, that gave me the opportunity to test my ideas on a bigger stage.

2

Nine months later...

'Welcome aboard. You can sit wherever you like,' said the young stewardess dressed in a floaty white dress and sandals. The cabin was the length of a penalty area with a handful of seats in different configurations. It smelt of freshly baked bread and cut flowers. Balearic beats drowned out the hum of the engines. I walked past a sculpture made out of vintage games consoles and chose a leather swivel chair facing the cockpit. Across the aisle, stood a pair of The Owner's turntables. He was, by all accounts, a terrible DJ, usually too wasted to match the beats, but this didn't stop him headlining Dionysus' legendary Manic Monday or Thirsty Thursday staff parties or using the company's sponsorship budget to bag warm up sets at the Super Bowl and the Burning Man festival.

By the time I had plugged in my laptop and opened the slides setting out my stall, the door had closed and we were taxiing onto the runway. No waiting for other passengers to board, no jostling for overhead locker space, and no waiting for a slot, the jet accelerating down the runway like Mbappé onto a through-ball.

The Cathedral and old town shrank beneath us as the jet banked to admire the skyline. In the east, the stadium with its two crescent shaped roofs was no bigger than a Subbuteo set. As it slipped from sight, I felt a flicker of guilt. I had not missed a session in eight years and the boys would know something was up.

We broke through clouds of rippling goal nets into sky blue sunlight. The stewardess flipped up the shelf beneath the window and folded out a table with a heavy wooden top. The small, light Gulfstream flew at a higher altitude than commercial airlines, avoiding congested air space and adverse weather she explained, and so the flight to London was the length of a match plus stoppages, half the time it normally took me. I turned down the offer of a glass of champagne from The Owner's estate in Epernay and she glided back down the aisle, giving me a chance to take some photos to show Emily.

A portrait of Kurt Cobain stretching from floor to ceiling was sprayed across the wall dividing the cabin from the galley. The singer looked pale and gaunt, his hair dirty and matted. He wore a white medical bracelet around his left wrist and held a handful of pills and a bottle of Whisky. A shotgun lay at his feet next to a small wooden box containing a syringe, a spoon, and a lighter. Em would have loved the edgy rawness, the anguish and the torment, but the glorification of squandered talent made me want to hurl. On the other wall The Owner was hanging out with Javier Medina and Elisha Raisman, the ultimate Californian power couple. Raisman taking a break from plundering personal data, Medina cultivating a beard for his role as the tortured genius in *Fusion*. The three of them, and one of The Owner's ex-girlfriends sipped sundowners on the deck of his super-yacht.

There was no sign of the notorious in-flight entertainment. The golden shower game where The Owner and his entourage sprayed naked escorts with champagne and then took turns to lick them dry. The eating competitions where The Owner offered $1 million to anyone who could beat *Cool Hand Luke's* record of fifty hard boiled eggs in an hour. The speedball session that ended with a cardiac arrest and an emergency landing in Reykjavík. The Owner calling his childhood friend a fucking lightweight when he collapsed.

A gleaming tumbler filled with iced water and a small plate of smoked almonds and salted cashews, warm from the oven, appeared a few moments later along with a menu written in Japanese calligraphy. Beautiful brush strokes in a bold black ink swished across cream card with English translations on the reverse.

'Jiro-San has designed the menu just for you. High on protein, low on carbs to give you a slow release of energy throughout the day. And then on your flight back with us this evening things will be a bit more indulgent. Freshly prepared sushi and sashimi, which is Out. Of. This. World. Plus, these amazing little crab tacos. Or we can rustle you up a Wagyu steak, Tataki style. Unless, of course, you have any special requests?'

'No, that sounds incredible.'

While my breakfast was being prepared, I took a closer look at the hologram trophy cabinet at the rear of the cabin which showcased the spoils of The Owner's investment in Athletic and his partnership with Paco Valbuena. Five silver replica league trophies, the club's gold and maroon ribbons tied to each handle. Three intricately engraved FA Cups, and towering above them all, the European Cup with its two giant ears. Paco hung up his tracksuit and note pad after winning this last elusive trophy, declining the offer to move upstairs as director of football. When Em and I visited his place in Begur a few weeks later, he told me he had no intention of becoming a *futbolista de sofá*, that Kevin Dalton had to be free to win things his own way. He must have known then that Dalton wasn't up to the job. Did he warn The Owner and Lord Rigg? Point out how much the game had moved on since Dalton left Tufnell Park in 2003? Or did part of Paco want the club to flounder after he retired, to show the world he was irreplaceable? Did no one tell Dalton he would spend his afternoons in transfer committee meetings and discussing performance metrics rather than playing golf? Or did they press ahead regardless? Blinded by the feel-good factor and the lure of the photo opportunity? Two other unsuccessful head coaches had followed, each bringing their own ideas and principles, and adding and subtracting different names to the group. What was left was a confused muddle. An unbalanced, demotivated, ageing squad. A team that was far away from being able to compete with the very best.

I thought again about who else Lord Rigg would be talking to and how to stand out from the crowd. The plan was to present a concise analysis of Athletic's failings and a strategy to save their season, without criticising The Owner or Rigg - even if the pair had been ball watching for the past couple of years. After finishing my eggs, I re-read the articles I had found on Rigg. According to a profile in *The Sunday Times* ('The Lord on the board'), Cecil Rigg was the son of an ageing stockbroker and the family's young Swiss au pair. Unlike his older siblings, Rigg did not attend Charterhouse. Instead, he was packed off to a minor fee-paying school in Bromley - boarding for bastards as his tormentors in the Bullingdon club called it - where he excelled at mathematics and cricket and captained the debating team. Upon turning eighteen, Rigg dispensed with Cecil, a name he had always loathed, and rechristened himself Robert, after Redford, De Niro, and the first Earl of Gloucester. An ex-girlfriend, there were many, described Rigg as a social climber who was more interested in a leg up than a leg over. *The Guardian* focused on Rigg's time at Oxford, from where he graduated with a First in Politics, Philosophy, and Economics and a taste for the finer things in life. The article included a grainy photo of Rigg and Nick Cole celebrating their graduation, Cole slumped against Rigg at sunrise on Magdalen Bridge. The *FT* picked up the story. Rigg stripped assets for a few years, long enough to buy himself a house in one of the quiet backstreets close to the Palace of Westminster, then carried red boxes for four Chancellors of the Exchequer (the Conservatives made a double substitution in the 1989-

90 season), jumping ship a few months before the Labour landslide and reinventing himself as a non-executive director. When Nick Cole mounted his leadership bid a few years later, Rigg was one of the Sherpas and the Lord North Street house with its fifty new phone lines, served as base camp. Cole re-paid his old friend with a peerage when he entered No 10 and Rigg now divided his time between the House of Lords, chairing Athletic, and sitting on the board of various companies (Caribbean Tobacco, Arctic Gas and Oil, and Apical the US defence contractor.)

The final cutting, an article from a diary column, revealed that researchers in Conservative Central Office played a drinking game when Rigg delivered his annual tub-thumping party conference speech. One-shot for every reference of hard-working families, de-regulation, or asylum seekers. Two shots when he made his customary call for the reintroduction of the death penalty for paedophiles and sex offenders ('Castration is too good for them!' he would cry to rounds of applause.)

We landed in heavy rain at a small private airport an hour south east of London. Home to The Few in the Battle of Britain, it was now used by wealthy executives and celebrities who wanted to avoid the queues and camera phones at Heathrow. The stewardess opened the door and pressed a button to release the retractable stairs. As we waited for the hydraulics to drop the steps into place, she passed me a umbrella. The sky was grey, the colour of Daventry United's strip the day the players couldn't see each other, and the wind and rain lashed my face the moment I stepped out.

The border patrol officer waiting on the runway gave my passport a brief cursory glance as water dripped from the peak of his cap, and then dived back into his car. A jet-black Tesla with dark tinted windows was parked in a dirty puddle next to him. The driver introduced himself as Rex and handed me a bottle of water. He was in his early sixties, with thinning grey hair, and a spare tyre around his waist from a lifetime of sitting in traffic. We spoke about Athletic's difficulties as we crawled through the sodden streets of South London. Rex was in no doubt about who was to blame.

'Archer is a wrecking ball, smashing his way through the club. He was a top, top player, but he's got no experience of building a squad.'

I had heard stories about drivers and receptionists being part of the vetting process at some clubs, so I maintained a diplomatic silence, refusing to be drawn. Rex carried on regardless.

'He's all over the shop. He let Gotsmanov and Bruno Chelot go for free and look at them now, both tearing up trees. He signs Thomas Dekker, the only footballer in the whole of bleeding Belgium who's not any good. He brings in Slaney and Varallo on crazy money, torching the wage structure… WAKEY WAKEY PAL, LIGHTS ARE GREEN… and then he panics and gives Mats and Bailey long-term deals. It's a shower of shit.'

'I picked him up from his home the other day – he kept me waiting for forty minutes – and then took him into Knightsbridge for lunch. You should've heard him on the phone to Gonzalo Ortega, taking his orders. "Yes Gonzalo. No Gonzalo. You're right Gonzalo." I've never heard anything like it. Completely arse about tit.'

Like everyone else, I knew the history. Ortega was a surrogate father to Archer. The man who had planned and shaped his career meticulously. Who saw the potential others overlooked, and through force of character, turned Archer into a one-man brand, brokering a series of blockbuster transfers and endorsements.

'Ortega has run Archer's life since he was a kid. Told him who to sign for, when to hand in his notice, what products to stick his face on. It's not easy to shift the dynamics.'

'I get that but there's no independent thought process here. No plan for the long-term… DON'T WORRY ABOUT SIGNALLING I'M A BLEEDING CLAIRVOYANT… Just Ortega trying to flog whoever happens to be available. And it gets worse. Archer then agrees to buy a player we don't want, after Ortega promised to steer some big names our way in the next window. You should have heard Archer. "You won't screw me over on this will you Gonzalo?" Course he fucking will.'

The conversation petered out as we crossed Chelsea Bridge. Rex turned on the radio just in time to catch the headlines:

'…is finalising his long-awaited reshuffle. Iain Porter has already announced he is returning to the back benches and Michael Harris is expected to join him, while Health Secretary Michelle Danjuma and Culture Secretary Claire Nicholls are tipped for promotion.'

Outside The Tate gallery a teacher fought a losing battle, attempting to marshal a large school party into groups. The kids wore different coloured bibs and again I thought about the boys back in Split and the massive game at the weekend. A chance to tighten our grip on the title or stumble and be reeled in by the chasing pack.

'As many as seven hundred thousand homes in Essex, Suffolk, Norfolk, and Lincolnshire are still without electricity almost a week after Hurricane Norma battered the East Coast of England.'

An unmarked police car parted the traffic on the other side of the road, blue lights flashing in its front grille.

'And in sports news, the BBC understands that Athletic…' With this Rex turned up the volume '…are in advanced discussions with Massimo Suppici about him becoming the club's new head coach. The Italian, who has won league titles in Italy, Spain, and Germany, is believed to have been offered a three-year contract.'

Rex glanced at my face in the rear mirror but said nothing. Why, we both asked ourselves, was I on my way to meet the club's Chairman if he was about to appoint someone else?

We continued in silence, past Millbank Tower and the Houses of Parliament. Past the gates to Downing Street and a solitary, placard wielding protester. Past the Cenotaph with its display of ceramic red poppies, and the bear skinned Guardsmen standing to attention in their sentry boxes, and onto Trafalgar Square. The way Rex drove, with his hands perfectly positioned at ten and two, threading the wheel through as we turned each corner, reminded me of my grandad. Darryl and I used to stay with him and my Nan in their small terraced house in Chelmsford during the school holidays, when he would drive us out for picnics in the countryside or trips to the coast in their old Ford Cortina. He always had a football book on the go but had no interest in the modern game. For him, the 1950s was the golden age. Every mealtime he would dip into his back catalogue of stories, not realising he had told each anecdote many times before. He would wax lyrical about the great Real Madrid side of Di Stefano and Francisco Gento that lifted the European Cup five years in a row, with Di Stefano scoring in all five finals. How Gento, 'the storm of the Cantabria', played in eight European Cup finals, winning six, and scoring the winner in the 1957 final in the Bernabeu in front of a crowd of 124,000 adoring Madridistas. How Real Madrid and Barcelona bought Di Stefano together - splitting the transfer fee 50:50 as if it were a restaurant bill - to resolve a dispute over who would sign the Argentinian, and how Barcelona sold their share back to Madrid after a handful of underwhelming performances.

About Johnny Berry the outside right who helped the Busby babes to win three league titles but was kept out of the England side by Stanley Matthews and Tom Finney. And most of all, countless stories about his hero John Charles. How Charles single-handedly lifted Leeds out of the second division into the first. The thirty-eight goals he scored in forty games in his one season with Leeds in the topflight. And how *Il Gigante Buono* took Italian football by storm forming the 'Holy Trident' frontline with Omar Sivori and Giampiero Boniperti, and firing Juventus to three Scudetti.

After Sunday lunch, I would be watching a game on TV, trying not to think about the long car journey home and school the next day, when he would say 'I remember when this lot…' (by which he meant the Spurs team of Hoddle, Ardiles, Villa and Perryman. Ray Clemence, Steve Archibald and Graham Roberts, a team of proper players) '…were good', and then go back to one of his books. He was referring to Arthur Rowe's team which won back to back championships, the old second division in 1950 and old first division in 1951. It was Rowe, as my grandad told me many, many times, who invented the one-two - or *Push and Run* as Grandad insisted on calling it - and laid the foundations for the Spurs Way.

My favourite story was Di Stefano's abduction from his hotel in Caracas on a pre-season tour of South America by Venezuelan revolutionaries. How he was released unharmed after two days of smoking cigarettes and playing chess with his captors and how he still had the nerve to play the final game of the tour.

The only time I can remember him showing any grudging admiration for modern football was when he heard about Mark Hughes playing two matches in one day for club and country. ('I should think so too given how much they all earn these days.')

I am under no illusions. I know this will be me in thirty years time, droning onto Em's kids about the Dutch masters. Dennis Bergkamp's improvised wonder goal against Newcastle in 2002. How, with his back to goal, he flicked the ball around one side of the defender and in the same movement spun around the other side. The control, the pirouette, the strength to hold off the defender, and the calmness, after a moment of genius, in the finish. About Clarence Seedorf, the only man to win the Champion's League with three different clubs. How Ruud Gullit and AC Milan bossed Europe in the late 80s. How Johan's dream team of Zubizarreta, Ferrer, Koeman, Nadal, Guardiola, Laudrup, Begiristain, Romario, and Stoichkov won four successive league titles. How Laudrup, the ultimate players' player, adored by teammates, then moved to Real and won his fifth consecutive La Liga, the only foreign player to do so.

We came to a halt on the western side of Trafalgar Square. I glanced across at the Yodas and Gandalfs hovering in the rain outside the National Gallery. We passed through the stone archway, the one that looks like the Arc de Triumphe, and onto the Mall. Metal crowd barriers lined either side of the road, stretching all the way to the black gates of Buckingham Palace. French flags and Union Jacks body popped in the wind above us.

'Just as well you're doing this today. The French President is here on Thursday, and it will be mobbed.'

Half way along the Mall we turned right, worked our way through a couple of side streets, the car pausing every now and then to gaze at shop windows, until we reached our destination, a tall, grey stone building set back from the street. I stepped over a fat cigar, discarded in the gutter after only a few puffs, and bounded up the stairs. The receptionist had the air of someone who had been interrupted in the middle of an important task. He ran a finger down a list of names in a battered old book and sighed.

'You're rather early and Lord Rigg has a number of appointments today. I suggest you wait in the reading room until he's ready. And here, you'll need this,' he said handing me a tie. 'Club rules.'

I found a seat by the window. The room was cold and the waiter, for all his 'I'll be right with you' nods and hand signals, too busy to take my drinks order. There was time to clear my inbox, fire off some questions to the under 16's coach about the dip in performances, and tinker with my presentation on the 1-3-3-1-3 formation for our monthly technical review meeting. Midway through a slide on the importance of inverted fullbacks, one of the murmuring black jacketed attendants asked me to accompany him. We walked through a gloomy hallway, past the billiards room and the cards room, past a noticeboard advertising the club's fencing tournament, and up a flight of stairs lined with old portraits.

'The Churchill Room. Lord Rigg's favourite,' said the attendant when we reached the end of the corridor. He knocked once and then entered. Rigg was sitting in one of two sea green armchairs making a call.

'Please, he doesn't know the meaning of the word,' he said motioning for me to take a seat.

'Every time the conceited prick opens his mouth we lose another thousand votes. Offer him something half decent and see how quickly he forgets about his bloody moral compass… I don't know, what's available?'

The room was small with a view of the bald oak trees and waterlogged lawn, the size of a five aside pitch, in the walled garden below. Churchill glowered defiantly at us from above the mantelpiece. There was no screen to present on or any other evidence of the twenty first century.

'High Commissioner to South Africa should do it. Tell him the time zone means you can sleep overnight in first both ways. And if that doesn't work you're going to have to dip into the black book… I know, no one does, but what would The Lady do?…Exactly.'

Rigg's voice was as smooth as Ralgex, as deep as a ball to the far post. His thick white hair, cut rakishly long at the back, smacked of generations of good breeding. He needed glasses but was too vain to wear the pair that sat on the coffee table.

'…Home Office is a good idea for Danjuma. Give her enough rope to hang herself. What about Harris?… Yes, I agree, his time is up. The officials have been running rings around him.'

A sparrow touched down on the windowsill, took a drinks break, then launched itself into a diving header.

'…Yes, I'll be there. You know me, any excuse to break out the black tie. I'm coming straight from the Landmark… No, I wish. It's another sodding league meeting. What's the collective noun for a roomful of overweening egos?'

Rigg roared with laughter.

'…Yes, very good, or A *CABINET*.'

He slapped his thigh in delight at his own joke.

'…Yes, me too. OK, I'll see you there. And Nick, remember, this is not about you or them. It's doing what's right for the country and the party… Good man. Illegitimum non carborundum,' he said ending the call and levering himself out of the armchair.

'Sorry to keep you. I've been juggling balls like a ruddy circus clown this morning. Have you come far?'

He wore a pin striped suit and a gold sovereign ring on his left hand. His tanned skin bordered on orange.

'Split.'

He gave me a blank look.

'Croatia.'

'Ah, yes of course. I hear it's very nice. Excellent sailing. And how was the flight?'

'Very good thanks.'

'Did you enjoy the food? We poached Tatsuo from The Owner's favourite place in Yokohama. The man is a miracle worker. You lose thirty percent of your taste and smell when you're in the air due to the lower oxygen levels, and yet his sashimi is still the tangiest you'll ever taste. The only problem with the jet is that it spoils you. Trust me, you can never fly business again.'

He poured two teas and then dived straight in, exuding the easy confidence that comes from being surrounded by people who always do what they are told.

'Afraid I've not had a chance to look at your CV and to be honest you weren't really on my radar.'

Great.

'That's OK. I can give you're a quick summary. And I've prepared a presentation,' I said passing him a printed copy. 'A three-year plan to get Athletic back where it belongs, competing for titles.'

Rigg's phone buzzed three times as a hat-trick of messages landed in his in-box.

'It's a manifesto for change, setting out early priorities - how to reboot the playing style, shore up the defence, increase fitness and stamina, with some longer-term structural changes like restoring the pathways from the academy to the first team, overhauling recruitment—.'

'Look I'm terribly sorry,' he said staring at the ream of paper in his hands. 'I don't have time for this right now. We have a division at twelve and it's a three line whip, bloody animal welfare, and all hell has broken loose with the reshuffle. Every Tom, Dick, and Harry wants the inside track. But I'll take a proper look at it later, Scout's honour.'

Rigg's phone buzzed again. He held it at arm's length, squinted at the screen, and then started to tap out a response. Without looking up he said 'Let's get down to brass tacks. Why do you want the job?'

If this is just some box ticking exercise I thought to myself, then I might as well go down swinging.

'Right now I should be leading training with the best group of players I've ever worked with. Committed professionals who've won multiple titles and would run through fire for each other. Even thinking about walking away from them and what we've achieved together is a massive decision for me. But this is Athletic. A club that is loved and respected around the world.'

Rigg looked distracted, preoccupied by events taking place elsewhere. If he was one of my players, I would have told him to focus. That winners are always present in the moment. Instead, I used a verbal cue to drag him back into the room.

'So, the pull of the badge, that's the starting point, but the main reason is the scale of the challenge and the opportunity to make a difference. To make an *impact*.'

With this last sentence I was paraphrasing the theme of Rigg's own maiden speech in the House of Lords. He nodded his approval.

'Yes, yes, that's exactly why I went into politics. The opportunity to serve. Carry on.'

'We're not talking about a poor set of results here or a bad season or two. This is structural. The game has moved on and Athletic has been left behind. Fading away, weaker by the season. Financially outgunned, with an unbalanced squad. Half the players don't want to play for the club, they've checked out mentally. The other half aren't good enough. It's like a swimmer that's been swept out to sea, the tide taking them further and further out, pulling them down for the third time. Only a superhuman effort can get you back to the shore. And that, *that's* what I'm here to offer.'

'Well, that was very—' said Rigg.

If he thought I was finished, he was mistaken.

'Because no one has a god given right to win trophies. Look at Nottingham Forest and Aston Villa. They were European Champions forty years ago. Where are they now? Everton won the league in 1985 and 1987, won the European Cup Winners' Cup. What have they done in the past thirty years? Leeds, Spurs, the list goes on.' I paused and then pushed the old Tory's Thatcherite hot-button.

'So like Britain in the 1980s you have a choice. Are you willing to accept slow decline is inevitable? Or do you face your challenges head on? If you're happy to bump around in the top eight, win the occasional cup, then I'm not the right person for you. But if you want to knock City off their perch, play exciting football, attract the best players, you need me.'

'I'm all for shaking things up Joe. Always have been. The question is how would you do this? Anyone can throw around big promises. What matters is delivery.'

'Firstly, we have to re-build team spirit and get the winning mentality back. For too many of the players this is about the pay cheque. They're just going through the motions, maintaining a lifestyle.

But playing for Athletic isn't a job. It has to be a way of life. Total commitment, nothing less,' I said.

Rigg snapped a shortbread in half, dunked one piece in his tea and ate it, and then inserted two fingers into his mouth up to the second knuckle and sucked off the sugary crumbs.

'It's about setting the highest standards. Embedding a different mindset, where the players are looking for continual improvement, constantly asking themselves how they can become a better player, what they need to do to win the next game. And if they can't give us that, we move them on. Secondly, we need to—'

'We'll come to that. But let's rewind a second. You mentioned style of play. What's your preferred formation?'

'Formations are a smokescreen.'

This grabbed his attention.

'What do you mean?'

'They're an oversimplification, whose significance is exaggerated by the media and the pundits.'

He gave me a sceptical look.

'Is that so?'

'Yes. My teams don't play with a static system. We are much more fluid, adjusting our shape depending on the phase of play, game state, availability of players, or the opponent's strengths and weaknesses. So, we line up in a 1-4-3-3 for kick-off but from the moment play begins we are constantly moving and altering our shape. We build up in 1-3-5-2. Attack in 1-2-3-5. Press high in a 1-3-3-4. If they play through the press we drop and re-arrange ourselves into a 1-4-1-4-1 mid-block. Principles, not systems is what matters most—.'

The sound of Rigg's ringtone severed the final threads of his concentration. He squinted at the screen and frowned.

'I'm very sorry but I'm going to have to take this.'

For fuck's sake.

'That's okay.'

'Would you mind waiting outside?' He pointed to the door. 'It shouldn't take long.'

I stood in the wood panelled corridor scanning the notes on my phone, fighting to keep my temper under control. I told myself it wasn't meant to be. That every knock back, every bad experience, has an intrinsic value. I just needed to suck up what was left of this fiasco and get back to Split where I could harness the torrent of emotions. Use it to motivate the boys to destroy Gradanski at the weekend. I could hear the low murmur of Rigg's voice but not what he was saying. After a minute or two, his end of the conversation grew louder as he approached the other side of the door.

'…I'm not going to sugarcoat it, there's bound to be a reaction from some quarters. The usual stuff, human rights, sportswashing, Yemen, blah, blah, blah. But it will blow over… No, I'm entirely relaxed about that. For HMG it's all about bringing our friends in Tehran back in from the cold… I'm with the PM at a fundraiser tomorrow night. I'll square it with him then… Yes, you're right that's the biggest hurdle. Anders is a slippery shit, and he has his eyes on the FIFA job, so he won't want to do anything to upset the Saudis… I'll speak in the margins of the league meeting. See what it takes to make the objections go away. In the meantime, let's hope they don't hang any more dissidents… Yes, I know… OK, no problem. Good talking to you too Anita.' He chuckled. 'Will do my best.'

He opened the door and beckoned me back into the room.

'I'm sorry. I wish I could say it's not always like this but sadly it is. Now where were we?'

'Systems and principles.'

'Ah, yes, that's right. You were saying?'

'That systems are fluid and principles are more important than formations.'

'Principles? What sort of thing?' he said still toying with his phone.

'My teams play proactive attacking football, with and without the ball. We look to establish superiority in every phase, and control games by creating and constricting space. Building from the back. Always having a spare man in the first phase of possession. Routing the ball through the third man to break the lines. Overloading the channels between the fullbacks and centre backs. Pressing high to score not just regain possession.'

Another message flashed up on his screen. Rigg held up a finger.

'Just a second Jim.'

Enough was enough. I snapped my fingers.

'OK TIME OUT.' Rigg looked up, startled.

'Here's the deal. We either end this right now or you put your phone down and give me five minutes of your full, undivided attention. Your call. I'm happy either way.'

Rigg fiddled with his device for a moment and then set it down on the table between us. He reappraised me with his bluey grey eyes. Eyes that had laid sight on prime ministers and presidents. Dictators and oligarchs. Big tech messiahs and Wall Street whales. Eyes that saw through bluster. Recognised strength and weakness, ambition and greed.

'Clock's ticking,' he said pointing to the timer on his phone.

I ripped a page out from my pad.

'Let me show you how it works.'

I sketched a couple of diagrams illustrating how we alter the number of players at the back to take account of the opposition's press.

'If they press with two attacking players we build with a back three, with the fullbacks pushing up and the pivot—'

'Pivot?'

'The defensive midfielder. He drops in here between the two centre backs.'

'I see. And if they press with three forwards?'

'We shift to four across the back and then the number eight drops to join the pivot here, to increase the passing options. No matter what, we always have an extra man.'

'Very interesting. Do you mind?' He picked up the diagrams. 'Tell me more about raising standards.'

'Standards and culture are the most important aspect of any football club. I will set the very highest standards and hold every player, every member of staff to them. No exceptions. Competition for places is a big part of it. This team has picked itself for too long. No one should feel they are guaranteed to start. There needs to be two high quality players in every position, minimum. So we bring through some of the academy players, have them join first team training. We strengthen the squad over successive windows. A new striker, a central midfielder - someone like Mohamed Jarir who can play through the lines – and a new centre back to play alongside Valon. Put some steel in the spine. Finally, we need to re-establish the connection between the team and the supporters. Get the stadium rocking again. And I've got the energy and communication skills—'

There was a knock on the door and the attendant entered.

'Your car is here Lord Rigg.'

'Thanks Markham. I'll be there in a jiffy.'

Rigg looked at me. Giving nothing away.

'Well, that's it from me. Do you have any questions?'

Why are you wasting my fucking time? Is what I wanted to ask. Instead, I simply said: 'Is it true you are going to appoint Suppici?'

I thought I caught a momentary flicker of surprise in his eyes.

'I like you Joe and I'm going to pay you the biggest compliment a politician can give.'

'What's that?'

'An honest answer to an honest question. The Owner has been wooing Massimo for years. We've had several meetings and someone, either Archer or Massimo's agent, has leaked it to move things along. But benchmarking your preferred candidate against whoever else is on the market is good practice for any senior hire. Besides, there's many a slip twixt cup and lip. Now I really must go. Time and the division bell wait for no one.'

He picked up his phone and glasses case.

'Make sure you have the Martini with Sake and green tea on the way home. One is splendid, two is too many…' He stood up, flashed me a crooked smile. '…and three is never enough.'

3

As a kid, I was the best player on the estate, captain of the school team, the scorer of countless goals for the borough, but nowhere near good enough to get a contract. The closest I came was a trial for Leyton Orient, stuck out of position on the left wing, the ball and my big chance passing me by. It wasn't for a lack of effort. I spent hours, whole afternoons, flouting the no ball games rule down by the garages at the foot of our tower block working on my close control. Playing one touch passes off the wall, alternating from my stronger right foot to my weaker left. Heading the ball against the wall from five metres, then ten metres. League matches on a Saturday afternoon and again on a Sunday morning with two different clubs, both for the age group above. Training sessions three times a week. Interval sprint training on the way back from my paper round: jogging the distance between two lampposts and then sprinting to the next. Repeating this for thirty minutes at a time.

Thanks to a couple of amazing teachers, I somehow made it to university where a degree in Sports Science taught me about bio-mechanics, how to speed up the body's recovery after intensive exercise, and sports psychology. My dissertation was on marginal gains. How microscopically small improvements in sporting performance can cumulatively add up to a significant advantage. The concept is common practice across all sports now but was groundbreaking and exciting at the time. An underground movement with only a handful of disciples. Ridiculed and dismissed by the sporting establishment and then embraced by visionaries like Clive Woodward, Arsene Wenger, and Alex Ferguson.

After graduating, I headed off on a pilgrimage. A tour of the aristocracy of European football. My friend Neil and I visited Ajax (Danny Blind, the de Boer twins, Jari Litmanen); Bayern Munich (Matthäus, Scholl, Klinsmann, Papin) AC Milan (Maldini, Albertini, Costacurta, Desailly, Kluivert, Weah); Juventus (Conte, Deschamps, Del Piero); Monaco (Barthez, Collins, Henry, Trezeguet); Real Madrid (Carlos, Guti, Seedorf, Suker) and Barcelona (Guardiola, Figo, Stoichkov, Rivaldo). We slept on trains to save money. Discussed reunification over glasses of cold helles lager with the Ultras in Munich. Hung out with the guys behind the biggest fanzine in Madrid and were shot down in flames by a succession of hot Italian girls, living proof that persistence doesn't always pay off. Basking in the autumn sunshine outside a café on Piazza della Rotonda, we channelled James Richardson from *Gazzetta Football Italia.* We sipped our cappuccinos and munched pastries, while trying to decipher the headlines in *Corriere dello Sport* and the pink pages of *La Gazzetta dello Sport* and replayed our favourite Richardson one-liners.

To break up the journey, we stopped at some smaller clubs along the way: Standard Liege (waffles at half-time), FC Cologne (drinking Kolsh from paper cups on the terraces), and Basel with its eye wateringly expensive tickets. Before we left England I had no idea what I wanted to do with the rest of my life. In fact, being able to postpone any decisions about my future was one of the attractions of the trip. But after watching training in Munich and Turin, touring the Bernabéu and the San Siro, I knew I had to work in football. I just didn't know how to break into this world.

Barcelona proved to be the last leg of my tour. In those days, long before the opening of the new Masia complex, training took place on a small pitch next door to Camp Nou and security was half-hearted. Standing on a large crate I was able to peer over the fence and watch the players at work. I stood there for two days scribbling notes, drawing diagrams, and taking the occasional photo – camera film was a precious commodity for an unemployed football-spotter. On the third day I was standing at my usual spot, enjoying the warmth of the gentle winter sun and watching the now familiar pattern of box drills, when one of the assistant coaches came over and asked if I was a spy for 'Los Merengues'. I laughed and told him about my trip. About the compact lines of AC Milan, something you could never appreciate when watching on TV. George Weah's wonder goal against Verona. How Ajax spent an hour fine tuning their intricate set pieces the day before they played.

He flicked through my note pad. 'You do this for every game?' he said pointing to the hand drawn target tables showing all shots on and off target, and the passing maps with the dots and lines recording the direction and origin of every pass and cross into the final third. Black lines for successful passes, red for assists. Blue dots for shots, gold for goals.

'Every time I watch a new team for the first time.'

He studied the charts with interest then handed the note pad back and clapped me on the shoulder.

'Muy bien. And what have you learnt about us *el espía*?'

I summarised what I had seen in those two full throttle sessions.

'Everything you do is with the ball. All the drills, the fitness work, the positioning exercises – everything. And the tempo is so high. You move the ball around fast. It's all just one or two touches, with everyone moving in relation to the ball. And with the emphasis in the small sided games on keeping possession and playing through tight spaces.'

'You're a fast learner hombre.'

We discussed Johan's midfield diamond, with the four men inside. How his team constantly rearranged itself into a network of triangles, so that each player always had two passing options, no matter where they stood on the pitch. The short distances between players to enable quickfire ball circulation. Laudrup's role as a false nine, dropping deep to disorientate opposing centre backs and create space for Txiki Begiristain and José Mari Bakero to advance into.

The next day Johan himself came over. He was wearing shorts, a polo shirt with a yellow bib over the top, and a deep tan. He smelt of cigarettes and success.

'Paco told me about your book,' he said holding out his hand. I passed it to him and watched as he examined my notes.

'This is not right,' he said pointing to a sketch of the rondo drills. 'Here.' He snatched the pencil from my hand, made the correction, and then turned to the shot tracker and passing map for Real Madrid v Rayo Vallecano.

'You did this?' he asked, pointing at the picture of the goal with the blue and gold dots.

'Yes,' I said beaming with pride.

'You need three different kinds of circles to show the power of the shot. Solid for full power, shaded for medium, an empty dot for weak or mis-hit shots. And this,' he said puffing out air. 'This doesn't tell me what foot they used to shoot.'

He turned to the passing map on the next page and shook his head.

'Where is the space? You need to show the space. Space is *everything*,' he said shoving the book back into my hands.

'Come see me tomorrow. I'll show you how to do it properly.'

4

The training ground in Split was a sight to behold. Freshly dried lines of fleet paint, as white as snow, applied earlier that morning with an electric pump marker. Turf the colour of a rainforest. We had watered it ourselves during the hosepipe ban the previous summer, each of us sprinkling twenty large watering cans three times a day. Toblerone shaped advertising boards dotted around for the benefit of the fans who gathered to watch each session. And twenty-two of the best lads you could hope to work with. All willing to suffer for their teammates. How many Athletic players could say the same?

It had been three days since my meeting with Rigg and neither I nor my brother Darryl, who acted as my agent, had heard anything since.

'Did you hear about Suppici? asked Feli Reyes, one of my two assistant coaches, and a man who had been with me since the very beginning. Together we had taken the squad I inherited apart and remoulded it bit by bit into a high tempo, high pressure, possession based attacking force. A team built in Johan's image, which swept aside everything that stood in its way domestically and punched well above its weight in Europe.

Feli was more than just on the same wavelength, he had become part of me. A second brain. We shared the same relentless drive, the constant pursuit of improvement, the unquenchable thirst for victory. We made each other better. Picked one another up and spurred each other on. And I could not have imagined working anywhere without him. We first met while studying for our badges at Ciudad de fútbol, the Spanish federation's training centre on the outskirts of Madrid. At breakfast on the first morning, he plonked himself down in the next seat. Before I could mumble a shy *hola*, he began to admonish me for eating a cheese, tomato, and jamón tostada, words that would still be a heresy for many Spaniards today.

'You can't eat that shit,' he said wagging his finger. 'Junk in, junk out. Here, try this.' He handed me a Tupperware tub, similar to what my nan used to use to store her all-bran.

'Overnight oaks. Yoghurt, nuts, and berries. It's what we make all our boys eat for breakfast.'

Before I could say anything, he pointed at my name badge.

'So you're Valbuena's analyst, right? *El espia.* The guy with the spreadsheets?'

Between mouthfuls of oats, Feli pumped me for information about Paco's methods. The structure of training sessions, pressing triggers, the positioning of various players in defensive transitions. Fitness conditioning. Was it true, he asked that, Paco, like Johan before him, encouraged the players to coach themselves, placing them in scenarios in training - the slowest forward pitted against the fastest defender - which forced them to think about how to improve aspects of their game? By the way he spoke and carried himself, I assumed this loud, brash guy was with one of the other big clubs, so I did not give much away, limiting myself to the comments I had heard Paco make in press conferences. It was only later, that I found out Feli had a part time unpaid role coaching the under 15s for a non-league side in his hometown of Sagrajas. Sensing my reluctance to open up, Feli switched tack, and began to outline his game ideas. His belief in applying constant pressure against the ball, with players leaving their lines to proactively press and harry their opponents. How to build overloads from the back and counter-press high up the pitch with inverted wingers and full backs. It did not take long to realise we shared the same philosophy, even if we differed in our approach in certain areas (like Paco, I believed in covering spaces in the counter-press, whereas Feli was in favour of going man to man) and over the years we fused these principles into a winning combination.

'Yes, Massimo has landed on his feet again,' I said to Feli.

By now everyone had heard about Suppici's appointment.

'Ruthless huh?'

'That's football,' I said tersely, trying to close down the conversation.

Suppici and his agent had used Athletic to engineer his appointment as the new head coach in Turin. The Italian champions had been in discussions with Suppici for some time and moved swiftly after the media linked him with Athletic. He would take over at the end of the season, replacing Jens Olsen, who had won several trophies but not the supporters' hearts.

'Neeskens has ruled himself out of the Athletic job. Can't blame him. Who's going to want to go down with that ship?'

'It's a massive club,' I said a little too quickly. 'Someone will want to take them on, especially if the Iranians get the green light.'

The day before, Athletic had announced a proposed investment in the club by IPIV, the Iranian sovereign wealth fund. In an interview with Athletic TV, Rigg stressed that it was only a minority stake and that the club would continue to be controlled by its current owner Chris Cato. While for their part, the Iranians made all the right PR friendly noises. The goal, they said in a short-written statement, was for Athletic to be back where it belonged, winning titles. They pledged to provide funding for new players and to revitalise the academy. As well as a stake in the club, IPIV also appeared to have acquired Rigg. The peer would Chair the fund's newly established European advisory board and become an ambassador for Iran's bid to host the 2030 World Cup. But despite all the well-crafted, smoothly delivered messages, the news had ignited a firestorm. Rigg and The Owner were criticised for allowing the Iranians to use Athletic's brand and history to launder their reputation, while NGOs and politicians lined up to condemn Iran's human rights abuses, its censorship of the media, and support for terrorist activity across the Middle East. It was a different story, however, with the supporters. A few protested outside the ground, threatening to cut up their season tickets, but most welcomed the investment and the chance to catch up with City and Bury with open arms.

'Not if the Iranians are picking the team.'

'Yeah, I don't know what they were thinking there,' I said with a shake of the head. The club had also announced the signing of Hamid Pezeshkzad from Hoffenheim. It was a curious piece of recruitment. The 27-year-old Iranian had contributed just the one goal and two assists in 46 appearances across four seasons in Germany, and from the limited amount I had seen, did not possess the pace or guile required to make it at the highest level.

Later that evening, while watching Dortmund v Mainz and Lens v Auxerre on the big screens at home, I received a call from Darryl. He was speaking fast, the excitement rising in his voice.

'You've got to hear this bro. I'm just gonna put my phone on speaker.'

I heard a rustle and then a soft thud.

'What is it?'

'That my man, is the sound of your future. The sound of a seventy-two-page contract from Athletic literally landing on my desk. Do you want to hear it again?'

'You're shitting me.'

'I've never been more serious. It's all here in black-and-white. You just need to sign on the dotted line and you'll be in the dugout on Sunday. You should see the package. Jeez, it's another level. The basic is seven million a year, pro rata'd, with a two million bonus if you finish in the top four. Then there's—'

'Why's it pro rata'd?'

'I'll come back to that in a second, let's go through the rest of the package first.'

Something wasn't right.

'There's a relocation allowance plus your own suite at the Four Seasons. A car and a driver. Stock options. One point five million Athletic shares which vest in two years' time, shit, they've even thrown in a seat on The Owner's first space flight next year.' He let out a short nervous laugh. 'I told them you'd probably prefer the second flight. And that's not all—'

'Darryl, why is it pro rata'd?'

'Here's the thing. The initial contract runs until the end of the season when there is an option for renewal.' He said this casually, as if it wasn't a big deal.

'No one said anything about an interim deal. You need to push back.'

'Believe me I tried. I'm dealing with Anita Fang. She's as tough as everyone says, I mean really fucking hard, and she's refusing to budge. It's take it or leave it and get back to us in the next hour or the deal's off the table.'

All the excitement drained way, as if the assistant referee had raised the flag after a brilliant goal. I sat back down, took a deep breath.

'It's not personal. Alain Bescond has just trousered fifteen million. They can't afford another expensive pay off if it doesn't work out with you.'

'No. They have someone else in mind for next season.'

Darryl worked alone, representing me and a handful of my players and few others in the English lower divisions, but he was always on the lookout for the deal that would catapult him into the big time, and I had the feeling he was more interested in his own future than mine.

'Maybe, but possession's nine tenths of the law bro. You get in there and you'll make this job your own, yeah? And if not, fuck'em. We'll find something better. Either way you can't lose.'

'No, you can't lose. I've spent eight years building this club up, and they're asking me to throw it all away to keep the seat warm for a few months.'

'This is *Athletic* we're talking about. Jobs like this don't come around very often. But it's your call, I'm just the middleman here.'

He paused for a moment before continuing.

'You've got to ask yourself though, where do you want to be in twelve months' time? Do you want to be working at one of the biggest clubs in the world. Measuring yourself against the best? Or do you want to be rebuilding your squad, *again*?'

He was right about that. We were running out of road in Split.

'Now I can call them straight back, tell them the deal is off, but I don't think you really want that. Am I right?'

The decision to offer me the role was hard fought I later found out. As their options diminished, Rigg convened an emergency executive meeting to discuss the way forward. It was a heated, bad tempered discussion over fish pie and Chablis in the boardroom at Preston Park. Paco went to the wall, making an impassioned case for my appointment. His central theme was the need for a long-term plan. He cited my track record of operating within financial constraints and improving players and bringing through youth as proof I was the right man to lead the project. David Archer, however, was angling for the job himself, and spoke against my appointment. Paco dealt with his objections one by one and then reminded the board of the difference between playing for a big club and running a big club, making an enemy of the Ulsterman in the process. He invoked his own experience in Spain. How the President had taken a chance on him, and made a decision based on personality and principles not politics, when the media and supporters were demanding a big name. He didn't mention the three trophies he won in his first season. He didn't need to.

'OK, I'm on,' I said.

Moving on an interim basis and sacrificing everything I had built up was a huge gamble, but Darryl was right. I had to back myself to succeed.

'For a dude who's just struck the jackpot you don't sound very happy J. You got to see the big picture here. This is going to be the making of you. Now there's a couple of clauses you need to know about. Something I've not seen before. The first prevents you from poaching players when… if you leave Athletic.'

'Fair enough.'

'The second prevents you from taking performance data and information about the players' fitness levels.'

'I can live with that. Anything else?'

'Just those two, the rest is standard stuff.'

'What about staff? I want to bring in Feli and Bojan.'

'I spoke to Anita about this.' Darryl was all super casual again. 'She said they've got a great team in place and don't feel the need to bring anyone else in. Terry Locke will be your number two. He's been there forever and will ensure there's continuity.'

'Continuity is the last thing they need. Have you seen the run of results they've been on?'

'You know what I mean. He's someone who knows what makes the players tick and how the club operates. A bit of Ying and Yang ain't such a bad thing. Besides you can always link up with Feli again in the future.'

5

We arrived early at Preston Park, and I asked Rex to drop me outside the West Stand so I could walk around the ground and soak up the history. The stadium sat in the heart of a residential neighbourhood, jostling for space alongside rows of small red bricked Victorian houses. It was Archibald Leitch's final project and masterpiece. Leitch, the Frank Lloyd Wright of football stadiums, drew upon the experience he gained from designing Anfield, Old Trafford, Highbury, and countless other grounds across England and Scotland. You could see the influence of his earlier work. The steep single tiered Hill End was the largest Spion Kop in England, dwarfing its older sister on Merseyside. Over thirty thousand supporters swayed and surged on its terraces until the move to all-seater stadiums in the early nineties. The West Stand's marble interiors, intricate patterns of steel, and famous Art Deco façade, with its beautiful concrete carvings, were lifted from Highbury. I looked up at the etching of Alf Hart's winning goal in the 1932 Cup Final. All new signings posed for a photo beneath it, scarf held aloft. A scene hundreds of fans recreated and shared on social media every match day. Hart hanging in mid-air above them for all time, poised to head the heavy leather ball past poor old Harry Millichip. I passed the statue of Jonny Ellis and rubbed his worn away right boot for good luck, another match day tradition, then turned into the narrow bottle neck behind the East Stand. Turnstiles to my right, high brick walls to my left, only a few metres between the two. This tight space was where the Cowper Hill Firm would ambush unsuspecting away fans back in the seventies and eighties. Like a kill zone in a Medieval castle, there was no space to advance or retreat as they steamed in with their skin heads and Stanley knives.

On the other side of the wall, gardens sloped up to the houses perched on Cowper Hill. The back bedrooms with their prized view of the pitch were as good as any executive box. If you ever looked up during a match, you would see faces pressed against the glass, framed by flags and scarfs, or necks craning out of the windows when the ball was in the corner.

The East Stand served as a mortuary during the Blitz. A bronze plaque on the wall next to the disabled toilets listed the names of the men, women, and children who died in their beds or huddled together in the false security of Anderson shelters. Towering above me at the corner of the ground was one of the four floodlights installed in the late fifties to end the embarrassment of having to play European ties under the lights at Stamford Bridge.

I reached the Milton Road gate, the club's stage door, where fans hung out after every home game hoping for a photo with their favourite player. The iron bars alternated between gold and maroon, and the paintwork was chipped and flecked with rust, a symbol of the decline in fortune and standards. The security guard was chatting to one of the women who worked in the club shop and was in no hurry to let me pass. Eventually the conversation wound up. He stared at her swaying arse until she disappeared around the corner and then turned to me.

'You've got the wrong place mate. It's the Cowper Road gate for all deliveries,' he said pointing to his left. Waiter, shoplifter, and now delivery man. I've been mistaken for them all.

'I have an appointment with Lord Rigg.'

'Oh, I'm sorry sir. And what's your name?'

'Joe Hendricks.'

'Ah yes, here you are,' he said looking at his list.

'Can I see some ID?'

I showed him my passport and he pointed towards the reception on the other side of the small car park. On a match day it would have been full with the players cars – Valon's Mercedes G Wagon, with the child seats in the back, parked bumper to bumper with Slaney's flame red Lamborghini Aventador and Zharnell's Audi e-tron – as well as broadcast trucks, a St John's ambulance or two, and a steady flow of corporate hospitality guests, but it was half empty on that wet Tuesday morning. I passed through two glass double doors into the famous marbled hallway where I was greeted by a wall mounted sterilising gel dispenser and a sign saying 'Germs cost games. Please clean your hands.' At least someone was doing their job properly.

Lord Rigg was running late and had left instructions for Scott 'Scooter' Wheaton, the club's Chief Commercial Officer, to greet me. Scooter blew into reception, a hurricane of energy and empty flatter. He wore one of the club's long sleeve training tops with his initials on the front and a smorgasbord of sponsors' logos on the back.

'Here he is. Our saviour!' he said loudly, bowing before me with his arms stretched out in a 'we're not worthy' gesture.

'The best young English coach you've never heard of. Not my words…'

He slapped me on the back. 'How's it feel to be playing in the big leagues? No buyer's remorse I hope? Because it's too late to change your mind now buddy. Come this way.'

We walked through the bowels of the stadium, narrow stairwells and corridors decorated with photos of players past and present. Each image accompanied by a short quote describing the player's favourite Athletic memory. Scooter stopped from time to time to point out a photo or tell an anecdote, as if I was another potential sponsor to impress before we talked terms. He showed me photos of The Valentine's Day massacre. Athletic drubbing their rivals six - one in the West London Derby back in February 1954. The last gasp winner in the 1977 FA Cup final, Frank Ridley hooking in a second ball from a corner. The photos were fantastic. You immediately felt part of something special, a club with a glorious history and rich traditions, but those who live in the past, die in the past, and anyone who followed this route could only come to one conclusion: Athletic's best days were well behind them.

By now we had travelled from the Hill End to somewhere under the West Stand. We climbed some more stairs, with views through narrow slit windows of the turnstiles and toilets below. Scooter moved fast for a heavy man but was out of breath when we reached the top of the staircase. He paused for a second resting his weight on the banister and then barrelled into a short corridor. The first of the four doors was ajar and led into the boardroom.

'Forget about the dressing room Joe…' said Scooter, still puffing and panting. '…this is where all the real decisions get made around here.'

Floor to ceiling windows on one side of the room looked out across rows of terraced seating to the pitch. Even in the winter gloom it looked magnificent. Scooter took me by the arm and steered me through a glass door out to the best seats in the house.

'Welcome to the theatre of bad dreams,' he muttered.

The unmistakable stench of liquid garlic hit me between the eyes. This was not the sweet smell of juicy prawns frying in garlic. Not even last night's garlic bread on the breath of a beery colleague. No, this was industrial, mega-watt, nostril stripping garlic. The most powerful weapon in the hundred years' war between groundsmen and nematode worms. The microscopic parasites weaken the playing surface by eating away at the grass roots, restricting the supply of water and soil nutrients. Liquid garlic is their Kryptonite. Large grow lights, dotted around the pitch on wheeled rigs, were busy performing their confidence trick. The gullible blades of grass only too happy to be duped into thinking it was a warm April afternoon rather than a cold wet January morning. The turf was a hybrid. A combination of dwarf perennial ryegrass - genetically modified to harden it against the winter frost and the afternoon shade from the roof of the Hill End - and eighteen million artificial grass fibres. It sat on a bed of sand with only the smallest amount of soil. The sand accelerates drainage - the pitch could handle six inches of rain an hour before any puddles started to form - but doesn't provide the stability of traditional soil. The artificial fibres, sunk twenty centimetres into the ground, compensated for this, strengthening the playing surface.

Before we re-entered the boardroom Scooter pointed to a mark in the red brickwork next to the windows.

'Some Trot took a potshot at Ramsay McDonald for selling out the left. Tried to start a revolution, but he missed and the bullet lodged here.'

'When was this?'

'August 1934.'

Not even the garlic could block out the smell of this bullshit.

'I don't remember learning that at school.'

'Deep state Joe. That's how it works.' A knowing look. 'They didn't want to give the plebs any ideas.'

The cover up of the attempted assassination of the Prime Minister in front of eighty thousand people did not, it seems, extend to filling in the masonry. Back inside the boardroom a timeline stretched around the maroon-coloured walls with golden silhouettes of each of the trophies the club had won since its first league title in 1963. The large empty space to the right of the 2015 Community shield, a taunting reminder that pride comes before a fall.

We moved next door. Like its owner, Scooter's office was large, irregular shaped, and going through a mid-life crisis. Wooden beams set into the sloping ceiling matched the oak panelling below. Two circular stain glassed windows yielded minimal natural light. A standing desk was positioned in the far corner, away from the eves, to provide maximum headroom. A sofa and two chairs made of concrete and copper were grouped around a rectangular coffee table in the middle of the room. Artfully arranged copies of *Shoe Dog* and *Blink* and the latest edition of *The Harvard Business Review* sat on the table. The books were pristine props, unskimmed and unread. The chairs deeply uncomfortable, a hangover, Scooter explained from the past.

'Before I moved to focus on just commercial matters…' Before Dave Archer stole half of your job. '…I'd negotiate contracts in here. The agents would agree anything to get out of those chairs.'

'What do you do when you meet sponsors?'

'I prefer lunch in town. Ply them with moonshine.' He gave me a wink. 'But if we have to do it here, we use the boardroom.'

Behind the smiles and jokes and flights of fancy, Scooter was a money machine. A human calculator. We went out for dinner one time. Before we sat down, he had counted the tables and seats and calculated how many covers they served across the week. He scanned the menu and wine list and estimated average spend per customer (or ASPC as he called it) factoring in people spending less in the first half of the week, and then multiplied covers by average spend to estimate the restaurant's annual revenue and profit. All within a matter of seconds. While the waitress stood there waiting to take our drinks order, he told me how he could add another fifteen percent to the bottom line by pooling the tips and removing three items from the menu.

'It's the Pareto principle Joe,' he explained. 'Eighty percent of all outputs come from twenty percent of inputs. It's true in every walk of life. Business, finance, gambling, relationships, and sport. We saw it at the Chiefs when the guys analysed wins above replacement.'

The Chiefs were the Kansas City Chiefs, an under the radar, second tier baseball team who Scooter had transformed into one of the sport's most profitable franchises before he was lured to London.

'A small group of players were responsible for the majority of wins.'

'I've heard of the concept, a few people have tried to use it for recruitment, but the principal doesn't apply in my teams. Everyone has a part to play. They have to defend and attack as a unit, sacrifice their needs for the greater good. Work together to control and exploit space. Establish numerical and positional advantage in every phase of play. And it only works when it all works.'

Scooter sat down on the sofa and consulted his iPad.

'Right, let's see what the folks have organised for you. Eleven thirty you're meeting…' he switched to the voice of a ringside MC '…the bruiser from Bogside, the master of disaster, a three-time winner of the Ballon d'Or, five-time player of the year.' He jabbed the air three times in quick succession, alternating between both fists. 'The only man to be sent off in the FA Cup final for fighting with a teammate. Athletic's very own Pol Pot. The one, the only DAAAVID ARRRCHER.'

He turned serious for a moment.

'Word to the wise buddy. You need to watch out for Dave. He wants your job, feels it's owed to him, like some sort of birthright. He made a play for it at the board. Banged on about how he is the best qualified sporting director in the league, and he had it in his little stubby fingers for a moment or two.'

Scooter had this way of making people feel special. Trusted. He spoke openly about the other executives, as if he was confiding in you, and did it with such charisma that you never questioned what he said about you behind your back. And when he needed something, he morphed into a super attentive listener. Leaning forward, maintaining eye contact, and sucking the words right out of you with a flash of his whitened teeth and vigorous nods of the head.

'You could see the chairman toying with the idea, how it would play with the fans. Glossing over the lack of experience, the anger management, until Paco spoke out and then Anita killed him with kindness. Anyway, if you come out of that alive you're in with Lara Tait who heads up comms, marketing and supporter relations. She'll walk you through the plans for the unveiling. Then you'll film a piece to camera for Athletic TV to give you some practice in a safe environment – we'll push it out via the app to more than four hundred million subscribers. After that it's the photo shoot and then we'll film some B-Roll. Press conference is at two. Straight after that, you'll do one on ones with some of the friendly press – there's still a few – then it's a town hall with all the non-playing staff based here. Lara will prep you for that.'

'When do I get to meet the players?'

'They're over at Datchet. You'll see them tomorrow morning. We need to film you after the town hall for a bit of spon-con we're doing with Anselm. How their washing machines give us the edge. You know the sort of thing. They're pushing it out next week to support a new product launch in Tokyo and it'll give our brand a much needed boost in APAC. We filmed Alain before Christmas. We just need to reshoot that segment. It'll only take an hour or so.'

'OK. Let's get the boys together after that.'

'No, you have drinks with some of our biggest partners. Tungsten, KP, Scratch. They're all coming in.'

Fighting hard to keep my temper, I told Scooter I needed to get to work with the boys immediately, that there was so much for them to get their heads around.

'Listen bud. I hear what you're saying, but I need you to zoom out, see the bigger picture. We are in a financial nosedive.' He motioned downwards with his hand. 'The ground is rushing towards us by the second and it's not going to be a soft landing, you know what I'm saying? But if we can convince Herald and Villain to sign on the dotted line we might just be able to pull the wheel up before we're all smashed to pieces. The trouble is no one wants to align themselves with a failing brand. *Fact.* But getting in early on a turnaround, the rebirth of a famous club under the leadership of a new young charismatic coach. Well, that's a different proposition all together. So, it's all hands on the flight deck. Capeesh?'

Athletic's balance sheet had been ravaged by a perfect storm of rising costs and falling income over the previous five years, squeezed by a surge in transfer prices, a wage bill spiralling out of control, and the unexpected loss of European football. And The Owner was no longer in a position to prime the pump. What was left of his finances after the divorce was tied up in his space programme, so instead he began to dip his hands in the till, awarding himself a series of dividends. Scooter was recruited by Anita Fang - the club's chief legal counsel and The Owner's closest advisor - and tasked with turning water into wine. Together with an army of consultants, he and Anita reviewed the club's commercial activities and pulled every lever, trimming fat and boosting margins. New and evermore ingenious ways of taking on additional debt were devised. The club borrowed against future TV rights, brand licensing revenue, and other potential future earnings. Preston Park was sold to a property investor (an Athletic fan with designs on having a stand named after him) and leased back on generous terms. Anita and Scooter built a network of wholly or partially owned affiliate clubs around the world (Rigg loved to boast that the sun never set on The Athletic Football Group). Existing clubs were bought and rebranded - names and team colours changed, logos jettisoned – and new franchises acquired. The idea was to develop a worldwide scouting operation and a global pool of players, underpinned by increased sponsorship and merchandise revenues, and complex tax avoidance. Nonplaying staff rotated through, sharing best practice on youth development, coaching, and sports science. Rigg brushed aside any concerns about the scale of the borrowing when pressed at a supporters' association meeting. ('Our aim is to put the club on an independent, self-sustaining financial footing. And you must remember, we are living in an era of historically low interest rates. Frankly, it would be remiss of us not to take advantage.') This period of exuberance was costly but short lived. Slaney, Varallo, and Rafiq joined on eye-watering deals. Contract extensions and pay rises were handed out to Valon, Mats, and Schnellinger, and then a surge in interest rates turned the cheap debt into a pair of concrete boots, pulling the club under the choppy financial waters. Austerity followed. Ticket prices rose. New signings were placed on hold, and Valon, Fabio, and Mats agreed, against their agents' better judgment, to a wage deferral. Rigg and Archer repaid this loyalty by offering the three men to other clubs without their knowledge and by briefing against them in the media ('The bed blockers need to do the honourable thing and free up space for those who will write the next chapter in this great club's history.')

And all the while, City and Bury pulled further away, taking it in turns to shatter transfer records as they assembled squads with two world-class players in every position.

I gave Scooter a long hard look. He stared back through his oversized glasses.

'Okay it's grip and grin this afternoon but that's it for the rest of the week.'

'My man. Now, let's take you down to your office.'

We re-traced our steps down the stairs and back into the main corridor. From there we headed away from reception, past the old indoor sports hall, out of which came the screech of trainers on polished wooden floor and the sound of children having fun.

'Lara invited the local schools in to use the sports hall when we opened Datchet. Part of Athletic in the Community. We do it every day. Then there's a reading club in the afternoon three days a week. Some of the players drop in from time to time, the one's that can read that is.'

He waited for me to laugh but fuck that. Most players I know speak two or three languages and have passed more tests than Scooter had ever had to. And while I'll won't hesitate to tell them what they need to hear, I never ridicule the boys behind their back. So I ignored this remark and we resumed our journey in silence. Dust and silvery cobwebs decorated the equipment in the mothballed gym next door. We turned a corner and dropped down a short flight of steps into the pitch side area. My office was at the mouth of the tunnel, next to the home changing room. I stood by the tactical board drinking in the history. This was the room where Paco plotted back to back domestic doubles and commiserated with opposing managers during those long fortress years. Just the one home defeat in six seasons. The room where promising young players were handed their debuts and loyal servants let go. Where some of the best to ever play the game unloaded their innermost doubts and fears as they struggled to come to terms with a loss of form or a yard of pace. The room where Bob Mackie shared bottles of scotch with Matt Busby, Bill Shankly and Don Revie.

'Here she is, the most important person in the club,' said Scooter. I turned to face the doorway. 'Joe, meet Caroline.'

Caroline, my new executive assistant, started to speak but Scooter talked over her.

'Caroline knows how everything works around here. She'll manage your diary, intercept the hate mail, and take care of your travel arrangements and expenses - basically run your life. So be nice to her.'

I asked Caroline how long she had been with the club, and she told me she had joined straight from school back in 1993.

'Tell Joe how many head coaches you've worked with,' said Scooter. Somehow, he had missed his calling as a diplomat. Caroline glanced at me, hesitated and then replied. 'Twelve. You're number thirteen.'

'Unlucky for some hey buddy?' Scooter said slapping me on the back. Caroline turned to him. 'And you're the eighth sponsorship director.'

Scooter laughed but didn't like this reminder of his own mortality.

'But the first Chief Commercial Officer. Right, I'll leave you kids to it. Remember Joe keep hammering the turnaround message in the presser. You can't say it enough.'

I sat down at my desk and Caroline pulled up a chair. 'Where would you like to start?' she asked resting her pad on one leg and brushing a strand of chestnut hair back from her face.

I outlined the programme of meetings I wanted her to schedule.

'The top priority for me is to spend some time with the players. What time does training start?'

'Alain liked to start around ten and finish at twelve. The players drift in from nine thirty onwards. Some have breakfast in the restaurant, but most eat at home first, especially the ones with kids.'

'That's going to have to change.'

She gave me a look as if to say: 'Good luck with that.'

'I'll get there for seven fifteen and hit the gym. Then I'll say a few words. Where's the best place?

'The changing room could work, or there's plenty of space in the indoor sports hall but I would go with the presentation suite. There's a screen if you want to show slides or video.'

'Perfect. Is there a WhatsApp group for the players and coaching staff?'

'No.'

'We'll need one. Do you have their numbers?'

'Yes, I keep a list. I'll stick them in your phone when you go into to see Lara.'

'And then I'd like one to ones with each of the players. I'll do six a day until we have worked through the whole squad. Three before training and three after. The first six I want to see are Fabio, Valon, Bailey, Slaney, Mats, and Dekker. In that order.' She nodded as she scribbled, filling the page of her pad with dots and dashes.

'Then I want to sit down with the sports science team, and book me in to watch a couple of the academy sessions.'

I looked around the office which was still full of Bescond's photos and belongings. It was as if the guy had died. The magnetic counters on the tactical board still arranged in the 1-5-4-1 formation that cost him his job.

'And we need to do something about this place. Box up all Bescond's stuff and ship it back to him.'

I stood up and moved across the room. 'Over here I want a planner with all our fixtures for the remainder of the season. First team, reserves, under 23's, under 18's and the women's team. Colour coded. With a column to show the scorelines of each of our opponent's five preceding games. Like this.' I showed her a photo of the wall chart in my old office in Split.

'No problem. We'll have that sorted by tomorrow.'

Caroline, as I quickly came to learn, was one of the most results-oriented people in the club. Taking responsibility for improving the facilities for disabled supporters was just one example. Long before the establishment of the Disability Liaison Team, she noticed how supporters with wheelchairs had no protection from the wind or rain in their spot at the foot of the East Stand. She badgered the then Chairman to do something about it, and after wearing him down, oversaw the installation of a low covered roof and heating. This was just the start. She then pioneered the introduction of a free audio description commentary service, with headsets available for visually impaired home and away supporters, and every December she hosted the Disabled Supporters Association's Christmas Party in the boardroom, ensuring the players dropped in for photos and autographs.

'Can you fix up a call with the performance analysis team for this evening. I want to go through the analysis for Sunday's game. Get them to send me a copy of the presentation. I'll take a look while I'm in the car.'

'Sure.'

'And can you get me a room at Datchet? I'm going to check out of the hotel tomorrow.'

'Yes, of course. We keep a few spare for parents visiting the academy but it's dead in the evening and you're in the middle of nowhere.'

'Don't worry about that.'

There was always a game to watch, analysis to review, sessions to plan. A player who needed a quiet word. I picked a DVD up from the shelf. It was the *Pink Panther*.

'What's with this?'

She sighed and shook her head.

'It was a secret Santa present from one of the players. They all called him Clouseau behind his back.'

Bescond's time at Athletic was a long hard slog. A two-and-a-half-year trudge through waist deep snow. It was Bescond's first job in English football and he continually butted his head against the language barrier, failing to get his ideas across on the training ground or in the media room. It wasn't long before the players began to mock his broken halted English, openly impersonating him in the dressing room or in the canteen, whilst the reporters sniggered at his mangled syntax. His style of play, with the ponderous, glacially slow build up, was an anathema to Athletic fans who had been conditioned to expect free flowing, high scoring football. But comparisons with Paco were unfair. Unlike his illustrious predecessor, Bescond did not have full control over signings. Instead, he had to live with, and publicly defend, Archer's incoherent approach to recruitment. The playing field had also been tilted away from him by the arrival of the sovereign wealth funds who stole some of Athletic's best players and pushed the prices of suitable replacements beyond the club's reach. The murmurs of discontent from the supporters in his first year in charge erupted into a full-blown revolt midway through the second season. For the final home game, a group of fans clubbed together to hire a double decker bus which they placed outside the Hill End. Posters on either side read 'Stop parking the bus at home.' Lineups and systems continually changed but results remained poor and Bescond was widely expected to leave at the end of his second season. And yet he was still there in the dugout three months later with the same defiant smile, the epitome of grace under pressure, after Rigg and Anita blocked Archer's attempts to replace him. Their motives were unclear. Some speculated the Frenchman had been rewarded for holding the line publicly over the lack of investment in the squad. Others suggested, perhaps more accurately, that Rigg and The Owner could not afford to lose their lightning rod. A positive start to Bescond's third season at the helm bought him further time but sunlit victories in August and September gave way to rain washed draws and defeats in October and pressure began to mount again. A few weeks before Christmas, *The Sun* reported that Bescond would be out of the club by the time the January transfer window opened, quoting an unnamed club executive as saying the Frenchman was a dead man walking. The article was written by Doug Molloy, who co-wrote Archer's autobiography, and was met with the most half-hearted of denials. Seeing what was coming, Bescond sought to salvage his reputation and prepare the ground for a return to Ligue 1. In an interview with a French newspaper, he spoke about his frustration with the club's refusal to back him in the transfer market, listing one by one the transfer targets the club had vetoed. When the end finally came it was swift and brutal. The final straw was a toothless home defeat against Goole on New Year's Day, the culmination of a dismal run of results and performances. The players no longer playing or running for the manager but ambling back after every turnover in possession. Rigg fired his human shield by text message, accusing the Frenchman of an unspecified breach of contract in an attempt to avoid paying any compensation. Bescond did not return to the club to say goodbye to the squad or staff and was last seen leaving the Four Seasons, his home for the previous two years, in the early hours of the morning.

We wandered back through the corridors to Caroline's office to pick up my new iPad with the custom-built app containing all the players' performance data. The screensaver on her PC showed two kids on top of a sand dune, the sea stretching out to the horizon behind them.

'Where's that?'

'Pyla near Bordeaux. The largest sand dune in Europe. It's amazing. The wind from the Atlantic blows sand off the sandbar at low tide and so the dune is constantly growing and changing shape. It's doubled in size in the past hundred years. We went there last summer. Alain lent us his house. He has this place right on the beach. You can cycle along the coast to the bakery in the morning for bread and croissants. Fresh fish or crab for dinner. Wine and cheese. It was bliss.'

'Is that where he is now?'

'No, he and Luna have gone to South America.'

Luna was Bescond's third wife.

'He asked me to make the arrangements before Christmas. He knew it was only a matter of time. I sorted out tickets for Vasco de Gama versus Flamengo at the Maracaná.'

Sunshine, Caipiroskas and the Clássico dos Milhões, the biggest Derby in Brazil. Not a bad way to lick your wounds.

'Then it's a couple of games in Montevideo followed by Independiente v Palmeiras in the Copa Libertadores in Buenos Aires.'

'Good for him. How old are your kids?' I said pointing at the screen.

'Millie is eleven, Ethan is nine.'

She blushed as she caught me doing the mental arithmetic.

'We didn't think we could have kids and just when we'd given up, Millie came along, and then Ethan followed two years later.'

'It's a lovely age.'

Small talk is like football. There are plenty of well-rehearsed pre-set moves you can rely upon.

'Yes, we're in the golden years. We've done the sleepless nights and tantrums, and we have a little bit of time before they no longer want to be around us.' Her face came alive as she said this, eyes glowing with pride.

'I missed those years with Emily. They grow up so fast.'

Another preset move.

'They sure do. It's not that I don't want them to grow up but if I could just slow things down, make it last a bit longer. How old is your daughter?'

'Seventeen, eighteen in March.'

'Doing her A-Levels?'

'Yes, maths, biology, chemistry and…' I replied, struggling to remember the fourth subject. Was it physics or economics? Caroline, sensing my embarrassment, moved the conversation on.

'She sounds like a bright kid. What University is she hoping to go to?'

Again, I was a bit hazy on the details.

'She's applied to a couple. It depends on the grades.'

Now it was Caroline's turn to resort to platitudes.

'There's a lot of pressure on them these days.'

'I know, now I need your help with something. Give this to the ground staff at Datchet.' I passed her a diagram. 'I want it marked out on one of the practice pitches by tomorrow. Tell them it's drawn to scale, and they must use the exact measurements.'

6

A South American commentator was in mid-flow, a tremble of excitement building in his voice, as I approached David Archer's office.

'Dorado, Scarone, Dorado, NASAZZI.'

And then he detonated when I entered the room.

'GOOOOOOOOOOOOOOOOOOOOOOOOOOOOOOOOOOOOOOLLLLLL.'

Archer sat with his feet on his desk, hands clasped behind his head. He wore dark trousers and a crisp white shirt buttoned up to the collar but no tie. Without taking his eyes off the screen, he held up the palm of one tattooed hand and motioned for me to stay quiet while he watched the next clip on the large screen on the wall.

Carlos Andrade burst through the lines, jinking past two challenges, and then arrowed a shot towards the top left corner. Miguel Encina soared to his right and palmed the ball away with two hands. I had watched Andrade at the Lat Am Sub23 in Colombia the previous year. He had everything Athletic needed. The speed of thought and technical ability, the calmness under fire, to build play and control games from the base of midfield. Hard running out of possession, and the character and energy to lift the dressing room, to demand that the others matched his level.

'What do you think?'

'He's a top, top player. Quick feet, fantastic technique. Plays with his head up. Energy and aggression in the counter-press.'

'Not him, the goalie. Fabio's past it. We need to make a change in the summer.'

'We can do better. Encina's not good enough on the ball. He always wants an extra touch, especially if it's played to his left. He would be shredded by a high press. Szabó is a better option. His pass appreciation—.'

'Do you know what's the most important thing for a goalie?'

Archer gave me a sharp look which made it clear he wasn't interested in my answer.

'It's bottle. There's no coaching courage. You either have it or you don't. And this lad's fucking got it. You should see the way he throws himself at a striker's feet. How he deals with a high ball in a crowded box. More bottle than a milkman. That's what we need.'

He pointed to the sofa, signalling the discussion was over.

'Take a seat.'

Three framed shirts, all with the number ten on the back, looked down from the wall facing me. Sandwiched between Maradona's Aegean blue Napoli top and Zidane's zebra stripes was the green jersey Archer wore when he dragged Northern Ireland to the final of the 2006 World Cup. The message was clear and designed to intimidate: Archer belonged in the company of the greats. He pushed back his chair, walked round to stand in front of me, and leant on the arm of the sofa to reverse the height advantage. I smelt his Cologne and was immediately reminded of all those adverts they used to run at half time. Archer playing up to his bad boy image, exiting the casino at dawn, bowtie untied, jacket slung over one shoulder, a beautiful woman in tow. The wolffish smile as he turned to the camera to tell us you make your own luck in life. Or the one where he vaults over the railing of the speedboat as it pulls into a Mediterranean harbour at sunset, ready to hit the town.

He sat down on the edge of the sofa and contorted his body to encircle me. His left arm lay behind my shoulders across the back of the sofa. His legs stretched past my feet at right angles, and his right arm formed a barrier as he reached across to grip the arm rest.

'You might as well know, I was dead set against your appointment,' he said, his face inches away from mine.

'I told the Chairman to go after Lukasz Wyszkowska, do whatever it takes to land him. I called Lukasz myself. Ran him through our plans for the next couple of years. The deals Gonzalo and I are going to put together. The quality of the facilities. The special history of this place. But it wasn't to be,' he said philosophically and then squeezed my shoulder. Overly friendly all of sudden.

'And you're here now and I want you to do well. No matter what anyone says. You understand?'

I nodded.

'We've got to stop the rot. That means working as a team. We'll talk first thing every morning, and you can message me any time night or day, no matter where I am in the world.'

Unlike some coaches, I had never had a problem working alongside a sporting director. Modern football dictates the separation of powers, with the coach focused on winning the next game and the sporting director taking care of the club's long-term interests. The demands are simply too great for one person. There's far too much complex information to process. Too many heads to manage. Too many decisions to call. And in the end, it's all about opportunity costs. An hour spent negotiating with agents, reviewing the club's approach to soft tissue injuries, or travelling to watch a player in Belarus, is an hour less on the training ground preparing for the next game. A good sporting director puts order and structure in place. Establishes the conditions for success. They embed a common philosophy and playing style which informs every aspect of the club, from how the first team - and every age group below it - play and train, to where to send young players on loan. They serve as a bridge between the first team and the other football departments, ensuring that the recruitment team speak to the academy before making a new signing. The very best are a link and a buffer between the coach and the board, managing an owner's unrealistic expectations, and buying time to deliver success. Per Knudson was the perfect example. After Lothar Steck's difficult first season in England, Knudson convinced Chester City's trigger-happy Chairman to give the German two more windows and the pair worked together to rebuild the squad. Selling Kimura at the peak of his value, moving on Pereira and Coulson and bringing in players who possessed the tactical discipline and relentless energy required to operate Steck's Gegenpress. And the rest is history, with City setting new standards on their way to three titles in four years.

Archer picked an apple from the bowl on the table in front of us. He began to eat it, his mouth millimetres from my ear.

CRUNCH 'Like I say, I'm here to help, share the benefit of my wisdom.' *CRUNCH* 'We'll talk through how the boys are performing, your tactics and selection plans. Where we are with injuries.' *CRUNCH* 'Two heads are better than one, right?' He gave my shoulder another squeeze. 'The other thing to be clear on is what's outside the scope...' *CRUNCH* '...of your role. It's simple really. Everything off the pitch – recruitment, contract renewals, loans, staffing appointments, the academy, sports science, conditioning - is my responsibility.' He mapped out each piece of his territory with a jab to my chest. 'As long as you remember that you can't go wrong.'

If you look hard enough on YouTube, you can find a video of a ten-year-old Chris Cato juggling a ball while wearing a shirt with Archer's name on the back. And so, it was no great surprise when the Ulsterman was appointed as an honorary director, a largely ceremonial role, a few months after Paco's retirement. Archer used this sinecure as a bridgehead to grow and expand his influence. He sat alongside The

Owner in the executive box, wearing a different suit each week, and passed him notes or whispered in his ear. It was not long before he acquired a new job title (Special Adviser to The Owner) and a seat on the club's football board. The ill-defined position, which gave him the license to meddle in and second-guess every aspect of the football operations, soon led to conflict with Yotam Klein, the new director of football. Archer used his status, and regular training ground appearances, to turn the players against Klein, while his friends in the media agitated for him to replace the Israeli. But if Archer was savvy enough to accumulate power, he lacked the skills and experience to wield it. He was incapable of communicating a vision or setting measurable goals. Budgetary spreadsheets may as well have been written in Mandarin. Instead, he spent his time casting around for quick wins or putting out fires. Micromanaging first team affairs and recruitment but providing no leadership or co-ordination to the rest of the football operation.

'I take part in training whenever I can. The boys love having me around and I'm still the best on the pitch, you'll see.'

'You're welcome to join the box drills and small sided games at the beginning, but we're going to spend a lot of time working on positioning in and out of possession, where to be in relation to each other in every phase of play, and we'll keep that to just the group.'

Archer glowered at me for a long awkward moment. I let the silence grow, bracing myself for the eruption. And then he surprised me.

'That's grand. Organisation is just what those fuckers need,' he said matter-of-factly.

Now...' *CRUNCH* '...what do you want to know?'

'Tell me about the squad.'

He let out a long sigh.

'Some of them are not with us. It's as simple as that. We've still got a few who're only here for the money or because their wives wanted to live in London. You don't see them hurting when we lose.'

I found myself thinking about the World Cup final in Berlin. The look of disgust on Archer's face when he received his runner's up medal. The story of his 'second is nowhere' rant in the dressing room. How he tossed the medal in the bin before boarding the bus and refused to speak to or play with his countrymen again.

'They've hidden behind the manager for too long. Bescond was never cut out for Athletic. But it doesn't matter how bad the coach is, you owe it to yourself and the fans to perform. Tambroni was a jumped-up kit man but that didn't stop us winning the title when I was in Madrid. We took responsibility, figured it out on the pitch. But this lot…' He shook his head. 'There's no shortage of talent but they want to be spoon fed everything. Bailey is a talented fucker, but he doesn't understand the value of hard graft. Costa has the concentration span of a goldfish. Mats needs to get over himself. The World Cup was four fucking years ago, what he's done since? Kuipers is lost, completely lost. And other teams know it. They keep targeting him. Talaat is an honest lad, but he's not an Athletic player.'

Encina spread himself and blocked a close range shot with his thigh.

'What's the story with Kuipers?'

'Bescond never wanted him. He kept pushing us to sign some skinny little French kid from Nantes.'

'Diarra?'

'Yeah, that's the one. So, when I brought in Kuipers he didn't give him a chance. Made a point of playing him out of position and then complained about a lack of impact.'

'He's an eight or a ten, not a wing back,' I replied.

'This is what I kept saying but Bescond didn't want to hear it. He was so stubborn, especially towards the end. It was as if he'd rather get the bullet than admit he was wrong.' Archer shrugged. 'His fucking funeral.'

He smiled as Encina smothered a low skidding shot.

'Kuipers is a confidence player.'

'Yeah, one hundred percent. A total fucking bedwetter but he'll do a job for you if you can get him going again.'

'We'll build him back up.'

Archer signalled his approval with a faint nod of the head. 'Grand. He's got goals in him. You've seen what he's like when he plays for his country. That's the player we signed. You've got to light a fire under him.'

Encina conceded a soft goal at his near post after a momentary lapse of concentration. He beat the ball away with one fist in frustration. I didn't like the way he then remonstrated with his teammates rather than take responsibility for his own error. Archer turned the TV off.

'Is there anyone we can bring through?'

'Nah. Now is not the time for kids. I've spoken to Crofty. We'll start to integrate two or three next season. Take them with us to the States in July. In the meantime, you are going to have to make do with what we've got, unless I can work some more magic in the market.'

'What's the plan for the window?'

'We'll have to sell one or two before we can bring anyone in. His Lordship's sodding golden rule.'

Rigg had introduced new financial restrictions the previous year, forcing the club to finally live within its means. Net transfer spend was capped at £115 million across the three most recent windows and the squad's salary bill index linked to the club's revenue.

'There must be a few we can move on. What's the score with Slaney?'

Ryan Slaney was obsessed with burnishing his legacy as he approached the end of his career. He spoke publicly about what he expected to achieve at Athletic when he joined the club the previous season: a tenth golden boot. One last European Cup. Another Ballon d'or. But instead, he found himself feeding off crumbs from Athletic's stilted build up and sitting at home watching other teams play in Europe. And so, he and his agent Pascal Fidalgo were trying to engineer a move to Chester City.

'Fidalgo is pulling all the usual tricks behind the scenes, but Slaney's too scared of the pond life on social media to force the issue.'

Archer plucked a piece of fluff from his trousers. 'So we just need to sit tight and hold the line for a few more weeks.'

'Is it true about the break clause?'

According to the press Slaney had an eighty million release clause.

'It's all bollocks. Fidalgo put it about to stir up interest. Ryan and I had a conversation, never anything more than that. They're all playing games. Did you see this?'

He held up a newspaper, folded open at the sports pages.

'That shit van Meegeren has been tapping him up through the media again.'

City's director of football had spoken to reporters about his ambition to sign Slaney. Archer read aloud:

'A player of Ryan's quality deserves to be competing for titles.' Can you believe the nerve of the man? No fucking class. And it's not just that gobshite, their players are at it to.'

He held up his phone so I could see the screen. James Ellis, City's holding midfielder, had tweeted a photo of him and Slaney swigging from drinks bottles at an England training camp with the caption 'Why drink water in economy when you can sip champagne in business?'

'In my day we used to whip busy cunts like him with towels. Lock them in the clothes dryer and sweat some respect out of them. You make sure someone smashes him when we play them next,' he said slamming his hand down on the arm of the sofa.

I chose to ignore this.

'How much are they offering?'

'They're lowballing us. Opening bids of sixty and then sixty five million.'

'How far could you push them?'

'He's not for sale,' Archer said angrily.

'I know, but how much could you move him for if he was?'

'Double or more,' he boasted.

'Then we should take the money.'

Archer gave me the look again.

'I wouldn't sell a dummy to that mob.'

'Come on Dave, one hundred million or more for a thirty-two-year-old. We take the money and use it to rebuild.'

'We are not caving into them again. Not after the Mwanawasa deal. You don't strengthen your rivals. I'd rather sell him to the Spanish for less.'

'Then let's play the two off against each other. There's no point hanging onto a player who doesn't want to be here. Look at what happened to Durazi at Bury.'

'He's staying put. End of story. We build around him and generate money elsewhere. Gonzalo and I are putting together a deal for Valon but we are miles off on valuation and personal terms. We're also trying to pension off Schnellinger to Qatar or China but he's not interested. Told us he's going to run down the clock and then move back to Paris next year. Bag himself a big signing on fee. I want you to change his mind. Tell him you're only interested in players who are committed to the club's future. That he's going to get zero fucking game time between now and the World Cup. That should do the job.'

I shook my head. 'I'm not freezing him out. My priority is to build trust with the group—'

'You need to show them who's boss. Schnellinger doesn't play or you and me are going to have a major problem.'

I didn't go looking for an argument with Archer on my first morning, but it was better to set the boundaries rather than duck the issue and let it fester.

'You told me your remit Dave. Selection is mine,' I said calmly, resisting the temptation to jab him in the chest. Archer leapt to his feet and threw the apple core across the room in a sudden violent movement. This was my first sighting of his famous temper. The inner rage that drove every team he played in and sparked countless confrontations on and off the field.

'You do what I tell you son,' he said, his eyes boring into me. I held his gaze for several seconds, as if staring down a wild animal, and then slowly repeated myself.

'Selection is my area Dave. Decisions will be based on form and winning football matches. Nothing else.'

I braced myself for the meltdown but then the strangest thing happened. Archer closed his eyes and began to breathe slowly and deeply, taking a long breath in through his nose and exhaling through his mouth. He rolled his shoulders a few times. After ten seconds or so he opened his eyes and the anger had drained away.

'I feel like you are trying to provoke me,' he said slowly and deliberately, carefully enunciating each syllable. 'But I'm willing to forgive you.'

He took three more deep breaths in and out and then went on: 'This is Athletic not FC Toytown. You should expect input from everyone, especially from those who've been in the game longer than you. But you'll see for yourself. He's not the player he was. Too many miles on the clock.'

He pulled his lips back over his teeth and gave me another disconcerting smile.

'You need to get ready for the presser. Have they prepped you?'

'Not yet. I'm seeing Lara next.

'You've got to watch your back with them, especially Mike Duff he's a weasel. He'd sell his baby's organs to get an exclusive. Oli Hopper is just as bad. He'll be all 'I'm-your-only-friend here-Joe' and then knife you in the stomach at the first opportunity. Bob Andrews is harmless enough, but a complete tool. Always drawing comparisons with his Sunday league team for Christ's sake. I had to tell him once, 'Bob, it's not the same game, not even close.' He looked at me as if I had shat on his bed after doing his wife.'

'Dougie Molloy is OK. Aye, I've got a lot of time for Dougie. But the rest…' He shook his head in disgust, his voice trailing away.

'And whatever you do, don't criticise our signings. I won't have anyone trash my record. No one. You tell them Davie Archer has worked miracles. You got it? No one else could've convinced Ryan Slaney to sign for this club.'

He looked at his watch, a chunky Swiss number, and another endorsement.

'Now I'm off for lunch with Gonzalo. See if we can pull something out of the bag again.'

7

I ran into Lord Rigg in the corridor after leaving Archer's office. His grey, lifeless hair had been trimmed for the cameras, and I could have sworn his eyebrows had been plucked.

'I'm sorry I couldn't be here this morning. Urgent matters of state,' he rasped. 'On your way to the Ministry of Truth?'

It took me half a beat to understand what he meant.

'Yes, Lara and the team are going to put me through my paces.'

'Excellent. You're in safe hands. Tell Lara I'll be down in a jiffy.'

The media room was a game of two halves. Everything that could be seen on screen was in pristine condition. A desk painted in the club's colours sat on a raised platform. Sponsors logos jostled for attention on the chequerboard backdrop behind it. Three heavily branded tumblers, mugged to the camera like scene stealing extras. But off camera it was a different story. The room was tired and cluttered and hadn't seen a fresh coat of paint since Robbie Fowler was banging in twenty goals a season. Cables ran across the floor in every direction, snaking their way between the rows of plastic chairs. Lara was hunched over a laptop at the front of the room. Her younger colleague spotted me first, and nudged Lara gently with her elbow.

'Welcome to Athletic Joe,' she said rushing over to greet me. She quickly introduced me to six or seven of her team – gone were the days when a local journalist ghost wrote the program notes and the press spoke to the manager direct. Lara had built Athletic's very own content factory with - I was astonished to learn - three writers, videographers or designers for every player we had on the books, including a network of regional production hubs in Asia, Africa and Latin America producing foreign language content. They churned out videos, GIFs and podcasts, news articles and feature stories for the club's TV channel, website, official app, and social media accounts. This ranged from interviews with the players and the backroom staff, to the 'Access all Athletic areas' behind the scenes series. For Christmas they created an advent calendar with players past and present taking it in turns to give a blow-by-blow account of how they scored their favourite goal. On the tenth day of Christmas, David Archer reminisced about his rocket in the West London derby Cup Final.

'Have you had a chance to look through the pack?' asked Lara.

'What pack?'

'Scooter was meant to give you the lines to take and the Q&A.' A glimpse of frustration flickered across her face and then vanished. 'But don't worry about that. I'll give you the low down.'

Lara was a superb operator with a microscopic attention to detail but also the ability to zoom out and see the big picture.

'The first thing to remember is it's not about the guys in this room. No matter what they think. They're just a channel. Nothing more. The reason we communicate is to connect with the supporters and build our fan base around the world. What they want to hear today – and there will be hundreds of thousands tuning in on the app or watching the playback on YouTube – is positivity. How you're going to turn the season around and get the boys playing again. That's all they care about. Having said that, we do need to reset the relationship with the media. Things got so bad with Alain towards the end. It was trench warfare, both sides kicking the shit out of each other and achieving nothing. So, setting the right tone is vital. You need to show them you're someone they can work with. That you'll give them what they need but you're not going to be pushed around.'

'The key thing for me is the players. They'll all be watching in the canteen or when they get home. I want to create a good first impression.'

'We've covered that,' she said with a smile. 'We'll make sure you talk up the quality in the squad while making it clear they're going to have to work… watch your back.'

One of the facilities team wheeled a large ATV branded camera into position while Lara steered me towards the front of the room.

'In terms of the mechanics, we start with the broadcasters. Athletic TV, Sky, BBC, the league's production company, plus a shedload of foreign media - NBC is as important as the BBC when you're growing the brand. The dead tree brigade sit in on this but have to stay shtum until the broadcast portion is done. They then get fifteen minutes with you. Enough time for eight or nine questions and then we call it a day.'

'TESTING, TESTING, ONE, TWO, THREE,' boomed the speakers. Followed by a blast of:

'LOWE… LOWE HAS DONE HIS HAMSTRING AGAIN. OOH LOWE… LOWE HAS DONE HIS HAMSTRING AGAIN.'

'Thank you Raz. I think we can safely say it is working,' said Lara.

She lowered her voice. 'The print guys are a tricky bunch. They like to hunt in packs. Three or four of the senior reporters, those have been on the beat the longest, coordinate with the others about who gets to ask what questions. They call themselves the cartel. At the same time, they'll all compete to see who can get the best line out of you. Steph has taken a couple of soundings to see where they are coming from.'

'I got hold of Paul from The Mail first thing—.'

'Onions,' I replied pronouncing his name like the vegetable.

'No,' said Lara speaking fast. 'Don't ever call him that. He'll flip. It's Oh-nye-ons.'

Steph continued.

'He's pleased to see an English coach get the job and described Hadjuk as one of the best coached sides he's seen in the past few years.'

'I feel a but coming,' said Lara.

'Afraid so. His editor has told him to monster Joe over his lack of experience.'

'We're talking Arsene Who?'

'Yeah… on steroids.'

'The Chairman and the Mail's editor have history,' Lara said to me. 'Lord Rigg and his cronies made his life a misery at Oxford. Made him pick up their bar bill for his first two terms and then black balled his application to their club.'

'Don't look so worried Joe,' she continued. 'It's only when they liken you to a root vegetable that you have a problem.'

She handed Steph a print out covered in marked up edits.

'You crack on with the black notes. He'll be with us any second.'

She turned back to me. 'The Chairman has asked for some last minute changes to his speaker notes,' she explained.

'He wants us to put back in the words he asked us to remove yesterday,' said Steph over her shoulder.

'And he can be a bit of a Diva if he doesn't get what he wants. But enough about him. We've got a good idea what they're going to ask you about: can you manage this dressing room? Who are you going to bring in? Do you want the job on a permanent basis? None of which you're going to want to answer. The trick is to make a bridge between what they want to ask and what we want to say, without looking evasive or robotic. You give them plenty of super crisp messages on the things we want to talk about and then keep it short and tight on any tricky stuff. It's like how your teams play. Open and expansive when in control. Nice and compact when on the defensive. Got it?'

I could see why Rigg and Scooter rated Lara so highly.

'Will you be sitting there?' I pointed to the desk.

'No, Ali will chair. I prefer to watch it from the back of the room, to see what the cameras can see. We won't go to anyone on the shit list, but if you do get any questions about the Iranians or the SEC investigation or any of that stuff, the Chairman's riding shotgun, so just leave it to him.'

'Got it.'

'And you mustn't say a word about Lantsov, the whole thing is sub judice. The judge will throw the book at you if you say anything.'

Vladimir Lantsov, one of only two recognised pivots in the twenty-four-man squad, was on remand at Pentonville Prison charged with rape, sexual assault, and supplying class A drugs at a party at his home while his wife and children were away.

'We'll wait until Sky are back from the ads, so they don't miss the start, and then we'll come in through there,' Lara said pointing to an entrance off to the side of the desk.

'Motherfucker,' said Steph.

'What?' said Lara looking over to her.

'Archer has shafted us again. Here take a look.' She passed her laptop to Lara.

'Every time we have some good news he has to wreck it. Every fucking time.'

She showed me the screen. Dan Stevens, one of Archer's former teammates, had tweeted: 'Am hearing that the club have dropped another bollock and appointed a nobody. #Clueless.'

She scrolled to the next Tweet.

'Can't understand why they won't give Davie Archer the job. #legend.'

'Someone is bound to lead on this. Steph, Ali, can you cook up some comebacks. Something short and snappy to defuse it. I'll review them once I've prepped the chairman,' said Lara.

She gave me a smile that said 'nothing is ever easy here' and then regrouped.

'Now, time for the important bit: make up.'

She hollered across the room at a flame haired woman standing by the door.

'Liz…! We're ready when you are sweetie.'

'Liz'll make sure you look good in HD and then we'll do a full stagger-through.'

8

Paco was waiting with a stepladder when I arrived at the training ground wall the day after my first encounter with Johan.

'*Venga el espía*. Today you watch the session with us,' he said with a lopsided grin and offered me a hand as I clambered over the wall. 'Let's go. You don't want to be late for *El Jefe*.'

We dashed across the pitch - everything took place at full throttle in Johan's sessions - towards the circle of players warming up in the shadow of the stadium next door. Two or three gave me an amused look or a friendly smile, but most were too busy with their stretches. They crossed their legs and touched their toes, one, two, three, four times. Then bent in half, hands on knees, and flexed their calves and hamstrings. Lifted and twisted their knees high and across their trunk. Jogged on the spot, then two paces forward and two steps back. Into the centre of the circle and back out again. Then across the width of the pitch in pairs. After this they began ball work with groups of three in triangles, stroking the ball backwards and forwards. After five minutes or so Johan added an extra ball to each triangle. The players upped their intensity, receiving the second ball a split second after passing the first.

Sunlight glinted off the windows of the old farmhouse, home to fifty or so of the youth players, and I raised a hand to shield my eyes. Paco murmured in my ear: 'You're going to see something special today. You see him over there?' He indicated towards a short Spanish kid – five foot six or five foot seven – with floppy hair and a baggy oversized shirt tucked into his shorts. He could only have been fifteen or sixteen.

'Forget about the rest. Just watch him. He's everything we stand for. A future captain.'

Training started, as always, with rondo, the ball zipping around the small boxes at warp speed. This was followed by a series of quick-fire small sided games. Three v three and four v three. The players throwing themselves into challenges as if their lives depended upon it. Johan took part, manipulating the ball with the silkiest of touches, and when he wasn't playing, he barked instructions non-stop, drowning out the thrum of the city around us.

'Control with your left. The *left*.'

'FASTER. You need to win the ball back faster than that.'

Paco was right about the kid in the baggy shirt. He had unbelievable vision and awareness, conjuring passing lanes out of nowhere. The tactical intelligence and anticipation to know when and where to move to to receive the ball, and near faultless control and distribution off both feet.

'Look at how he protects the ball. These guys are ten, fifteen years older than him. Champions. And they can't get near him.'

We watched as he received the ball under close pressure from two players and turned full circle to throw both men off balance and create space for himself, before calmly sliding the ball forward. The turn was a thing of beauty, a swirl of grace and dexterity. So good that I laughed out loud. The only question mark was his lack of height. Paco must have read my mind.

'He wouldn't get a game in England or Germany, but here we will build a team around him.'

Johan was as good as his word. After I had helped bag up the balls and gather the cones, and he had finished speaking to the players, he ushered me into his office deep within the stadium.

'This is how you do it,' he said and thrusted three sheets of paper into my hands. Somehow, between training sessions and press conferences, watching the B team and fending off interference from the President, Johan had found the time to plot Getafe's chance creation from the game against Osasuna at the weekend. He didn't stop there. Instead, he launched into a detailed explanation of his philosophy of positional play, or *Juego de posición.* The concept of using player positioning to create space and numerical advantage, and as a result additional passing options, as the ball is progressed towards the goal. The players constantly re-arranging themselves in relation to each other's position. Maximising the width and height of the pitch when in possession to unlock space in central areas, and then shrinking the playing space in defensive transition.

'How much time do you think a player has on the ball each match?' He didn't wait for my answer. 'Three minutes. THREE MINUTES. That's all you get. And it's what you do for the other eighty-seven minutes that determines whether you are a good player or not.'

'It takes discipline to hold your position,' he went on. 'To sacrifice yourself for the team. To know that you are part of a system and that each part has a role to play. One of the clowns here,' he pointed towards the ceiling of his cramped office, 'said to me Roldós didn't do anything today after our first win in the Classico. Didn't do anything? I said. Did you not watch the game? He spent an hour and a half pinning their fullback and centre back. Took two men out. We would not have scored either goal if he had chased the ball like a child.'

Johan taught me more in that hour than you could learn in a lifetime watching the game. He explained the principles of positional play. Opened my eyes to the importance of disrupting the opposing team's shape by moving them out of position. He used the tactical board to demonstrate how his fullbacks created additional passing options for the pivot or ball carrying centre back by shifting to the interior in build-up. How they stretched the pitch in the next phase of play by advancing high and wide, enabling the wingers to move infield and attack the half-space or create overloads in the central areas. Three or four times he reiterated that short passing lines were the key to maintaining possession and speeding up ball circulation.

'Once you move them out of position, you must move the ball fast. Don't allow them time to regain their shape. You'll need to get that right if you want to work for us. Speak to Victor on your way out. He will take care of the paperwork.'

And with that, my induction into an unspecified role at Europe's finest football club was complete.

9

Nothing, not even media training from the best in the business, can prepare someone for being unveiled as the new Athletic head coach in front of the world's media. The rehearsal, with Laura and her team taking it in turns to fire questions, was not even in the same ballpark. It was the difference between playing a practice match behind closed doors and walking out under the lights at Preston Park for a European cup tie.

After taking my seat I gazed out into the room, trying to hide my nerves. The press room was as crowded as a six-yard box for an injury time corner. The smell of damp clothes and grease from the complimentary bacon rolls hung in the air. Those journalists who couldn't find a seat leant against the wall on either side of the room or congregated in the spill over area at the back, craning their necks to get their first glimpse of me. The photographers crouched on the floor in front of the raised platform, out of shot of the TV cameras, and scuttled from side to side like beetles. An assortment of smartphones and other recording devices lay on the desk in front of me. Rigg leaned over and murmured in my ear. 'How many journalists does it take to change a lightbulb?' and then poured us both a glass of water.

Scooter gave me a thumbs up from his seat in the front row. Lara stood in the doorway assessing the optics. Between them the hundred or so reporters re-read the embargoed press release or tapped at their keyboards. The release confirmed the terms of my appointment and provided a short biography, listing the six titles I had won in Croatia and the technical and coaching roles I had held in Spain and Italy.

'Afternoon everyone,' said Rigg kicking off. 'I'd like to introduce you to Athletic's new head coach, Joe Hendricks. I'm sure you'll make him very welcome.'

While Rigg spoke, I silently rehearsed the answer to the opening question, and when he finished Ali, the club's Head of Press, took over.

'You know the drill. Raise your hands if you wish to ask a question. One per person and please keep them short so that we can get through as many as possible,' he continued. 'Right, who shall we start with?'

The reporters, who all knew the answer, groaned and jeered good humouredly. Ali brought a hand up to his eyes and peered out into the room. 'How about the lady in the black jacket.' The Athletic TV reporter played along, looking to her left and to her right, and then mouthed 'Me?' with mock surprise. 'Yes you. Please state your name and organisation.' It was the silkiest of touches, poking fun at the club's reputation for control freakery.

'Vicky Wilcox, Athletic TV.'

Wilcox cut the ball back to me for an open goal, two yards out.

'Welcome Joe. How does it feel to be joining one of the biggest, most successful clubs in Europe?'

'Thanks Vicky. How does it feel to be joining Athletic?' The other broadcasters would edit Wilcox's question out, so Lara had instructed me to repeat the question. 'I'm very excited and very proud. Athletic is a massive club, with an incredible history, and a talented group of players. I can't wait to get to work.'

As I spoke there was a loud rat-a-tat-tat of camera shutters.

Wilcox followed up with a second question. 'And do you have a message for the fans?'

'Yes, the fans are the special ones at this club. They've supported the club through good times and bad. We really need them to get behind us on Saturday. Give us some energy to feed off.'

This was greeted by the sudden click clack of a hundred keyboards. The plan was to leave it there but with my confidence growing I began to ad lib.

'It's easy to forget what it is like to be a supporter. How much they look forward to the game at the weekend. How much stick they take from their mates if we lose. The amount they spend on tickets and travel each year. And so results are crucial but I also want to entertain people. To play attacking football that gets the fans out of their seats and puts a smile on their faces.'

'Stick to the script,' Lara mouthed from her spot at the rear of the room, as Ali invited Rajan Lanjwani from Sky Sports News to ask his question.

'Hi Joe. What are your targets for the season? Is top four achievable?'

'The same targets that led me to be sitting here in front of you: win games and help the players perform to their level,' I replied, ducking his question. Now was not the time to be putting unnecessary pressure on the players.

'Mike Baxter, BBC. Welcome Joe. You've got a massive job on your hands to turn the club around. Where do you start?'

'Confidence and spirit is everything in football Mike. We've got super talented players here. I want to get them believing again. Believing in themselves and each other. And I want to see more energy, more aggression and more intensity. We get that right and then we build from there.'

'Are you going to be signing anyone before the window closes?'

'I'm really happy with the players I've got here. As a coach it's my job to get them playing to their potential.'

'How important is it that Ryan Slaney signs a new deal and commits his future to the club?'

'What can I say? Ryan's a top, top player who would improve any side in Europe. I remember the game against Sporting, how he tore them apart that evening. So I hope it gets sorted soon.'

One of the reporters coughed, drowning out the first part of the next question.

'…coaching staff?' I shot Ali a puzzled look.

'Can you repeat the question please.'

'Will you be bringing in any additional coaching staff?'

'No, we've got a strong team here, good football people, and I'm looking forward to working with them to get the club back up the table.'

Rigg and Archer had continued to block my request for Feli to join the coaching staff. Paco and I had discussed it by phone and agreed there was some logic to their position. Wholesale clear outs are always a mistake, he told me. 'You lose so much knowledge. A new CEO would never fire his entire leadership team on the first day in the job, no matter how bad the business is performing. You manage the transition, take time to assess who adds value and who doesn't.'

The rest of the broadcasters took it in turns to ask variations of the questions Lara had predicted, then after fifteen minutes or so Ali signalled it was time to move to the print media. My throat felt dry from the heat of the lights and all the talking, and the jumper under my blazer was a big mistake. I could feel rivulets of sweat running down my back. I muted the microphone, coughed to clear my throat, and then gulped down a mouthful of water while we waited for the TV crews to leave.

'Do you want the job on a permanent basis?'

'Yes, of course,' I said, ripping up the script. 'Who wouldn't want to help this club get back to where it belongs? But that's a conversation for another day. The priority is improve performances and win games. That's all I'll be thinking about for the next four months.'

At the back of the room, Lara's face turned to stone. During our rehearsal she had drilled me to sidestep this question, but no player responds well to a lame duck.

'Hello Joe, congratulations again on your appointment. You mentioned confidence and belief earlier on. Were you referring to Fabio Bacigalupo?'

Mistakes in the first few months of the season had sapped Fabio's confidence. He had the worst xGoT in the league, conceding nine more goals from shots on target than the algorithm would expect. The go-ahead-punk aura was long gone, replaced with a thousand yard stare.

'No, I didn't have any individuals in mind. Every team needs to walk ten foot tall, to feel as confident as Gerd Muller in the penalty area.'

'So will Fabio be your number one?'

'It's a fresh start for all the players. The past is the past. Ancient history as far as I'm concerned. Mistakes or achievements, it all counts for nothing. I'm only interested in the players' mentality and their performance in training and on match days. As for goalkeepers, we've strong options, but Fabio has been the best keeper in the country for the past eight years. A few mistakes or a bit of bad luck doesn't change that. He's a strong character and I'm sure he will bounce back.'

'Doug Molloy,' said Ali pointing at Archer's ghost writer and co-conspirator.

'Dan Stevens has slammed your appointment, calling you a no nothing in a smart suit.'

Molloy spoke with exaggerated Estuary English, dropping his 't's and 'h's, to conceal an expensive private school education. 'He thinks the club should have appointed David Archer and a quick poll shows that eighty percent of our readers agree. How does it feel to be so unpopular?'

'If dripping poison is what Stevens has to do to still feel relevant then good luck to him,' is what I was itching to say, but instead I opted for the pre-agreed, safe sideways ball.

'News travels fast,' I deadpanned to polite laughter. 'And as someone once said, you can't please all of the people all of the time.'

Molloy wasn't satisfied with this and held onto the microphone, ignoring the outstretched hand from the press officer and Ali's one question per person rule.

'What about David Archer?'

It was a tough choice. Anoint Archer as my successor on my first day or call him out in public for being unfit to do the job? Again, Lara and the team had come up trumps.

'I'm sure he'll get his chance when he's ready.' The implication being he wasn't there yet. 'In the meantime, he's got plenty to keep him busy.'

Ali swiftly moved onto the next reporter before Molloy could ask a third question.

'Coming back to transfers. If the club does bring people in, will you be involved in the process?'

'Of course—'

Someone sneezed twice in quick succession.

'Bless you. I'm here to help the team improve. The focus will be on working with the group we have but I'll have a view on where we need to strengthen and who to bring in. At my old club they used to call me The Stalker because I was always following someone.'

I felt Ali tense up beside me. He scribbled in his notebook and then slid it across the desk to me, taking care to ensure the cameras couldn't see what he had written. The note said: 'Stick to the line on transfers.'

'Bob,' said Ali gesturing at the clump of reporters at the back of the room. While we waited for the microphone to reach him, a young reporter in the second row stood up.

'Cara Reeves, The Guardian. Amnesty International has criticised the proposed investment by the Iranian sovereign wealth fund, citing the regime's appalling human rights record. Are you comfortable being the face of this sports washing exercise?'

Rigg muted my microphone and murmured, 'I'll take this one.'

There was a howl of feedback as he moved his microphone closer to him.

'As we have said ad nauseam in recent days, the consortium is a purely commercial venture, entirely free from political control and we're confident that the proposed inward investment into this country's sporting infrastructure will pass the league's owners and directors tests with flying colours. More generally I think we should celebrate not denigrate the rapprochement with Iran, one of the world's oldest civilisations. The birthplace of chess, algebra, even the concept of taxation that your newspaper is so fond of. A country that made profound contributions to the advancement of medicine, science, and astronomy. What could be better than bringing them back into the fold? Next question.'

'Going back to what you said about the squad—'

The question was cut short by a loud hum of interference from the speakers. A split second later one of the phones on the desk in front of me began to vibrate. I held the phone up and pointed to the screen. 'Shall I answer it?'

'I'm sorry… yes please,' said a reporter in the third row sheepishly.

The opportunity to pay Archer back, to show that I could not be pushed around by him or Dan Stevens, was just too tempting. I declined the call and then pretended to answer it.

'This is Joe Hendricks from Athletic… Oh, hi there Dave. I'm in the middle of the press conference… OK… Uh-huh… Yep, will take a look later.'

I placed the phone back down on the desk and paused for a second and then said:

'That was David Archer. He just wanted my thoughts on a player he's looking at.'

The reporters roared with laughter.

'Now, where were we?'

More questions followed, the probing and the inane. Eventually, deep into added time, Ali brought the press conference to a close.

'That, ladies and gentlemen is I'm afraid, all we have time for. We'll see you same time, same place on Friday. In the meantime, I look forward to seeing your fair and balanced coverage.'

I followed Rigg and Ali out of the room. The Chairman pulled me to one side as soon as the door was closed behind us. He was furious.

'That was gratuitous, totally uncalled for.'

'What?'

'You know full well what I mean,' he said in an icy tone. 'All that transfer claptrap and poking fun at David. Trust me Joe, this is how major conflicts start. A skirmish on the border and before you know it, it's Def Con One.'

Ali studied his phone, pretending not to listen.

'We don't want to go down that road again. Get your tanks off David's lawn, pronto,' he said and then stalked off.

Later that evening, after the town-hall event, where I did my best to dispel the gloom, and a dreary drinks reception with the sponsors, I finally returned to my office. An email from Archer was waiting for me. The message, headed 'FUCKER, was copied to Lara. It said:

'What's all this shit about transfers? I told you this is MY AREA…!!! Lara put out a statement to clear this up.'

Lara had responded immediately to reject Archer's request:

'A statement will only make matters worse. We'll end up with *club at war* headlines. All our media followers know you lead on transfers and we can use the comms around any signings to reiterate this.'

The sensible thing would have been to ignore it or wait until the following morning, but instead I fired off quick response.

'I was stating a fact. I will have a view on who comes in and who goes out.'

Next, I sent a short message to the players and technical staff in the new WhatsApp group telling them how much I was looking forward to working with them. I then sent personalised messages to each of the players, starting with the spine of the team and the problem cases. Fabio was the first to reply, thanking me for my comments in the press conference. The others, with the exception of Ryan Slaney, all replied over the next hour or so, all saying the right things.

10

Uninvited guests were not welcome at the Athletic Performance Centre. There was no postcode to guide Sat Navs, no signs in the narrow Berkshire lanes that wound their way to the main entrance. Anyone stumbling across the security gates would assume it was just another Oligarch's weekend bolthole. The outer pitches bordered the M4 motorway just before the junction for Windsor. A row of trees guarded the perimeter like a well organised wall, preventing passing motorists from seeing the academy players at work.

Athletic were still sharing training facilities with a West London rugby club when Paco was appointed. One morning, a few months into the job, he called an additional session only to be told the training ground was already booked for an under 15's rugby tournament. That evening he sketched out the first plans himself and this wish list was then transformed into a work of wonder by the same firm of architects who designed Dionysus' campus in Mountain View. When new signings approached by helicopter they saw a giant football made up of five hexagonal slate topped buildings, each identical in size, separated by hexagonal courtyards of snow white paving stones, all encircled by a covered walkway. The Kelso building, the central panel of the ball, contained the first team changing rooms, a presentation theatre, meeting rooms, and offices for the coaching staff and performance analysts. The Glass sports centre, named after Hugh Glass, the club's all-time leading goal scorer, had a physical conditioning room, a large sports hall with two indoor running tracks, two swimming pools - one for stamina training, the other for hydrotherapy - a Pilates studio, offices for three onsite doctors, treatment rooms and the rehabilitation centre. The ground floor of the Fenner building was home to the laundry and boot room. Upstairs was the players' restaurant and games room. It's neighbour, the Gueran building, had twelve classrooms - the academy players had maths, science, English, and ICT lessons every afternoon – and sixty en-suite bedrooms for academy players, parents, and other visitors.

Beyond the buildings, stretching out to the motorway, lay twenty-nine full size pitches, all with undersoil heating and cut to slightly different lengths to simulate different playing conditions. Deep below the ground an artificial reservoir recycled and stored rainwater to irrigate the pitches. When Paco gave the media a guided tour a few days before the official opening, he highlighted three aspects which were particularly important to him. Firstly, he wanted to break down the barriers between the first team squad and the academy. The two would train at the same site, and apart from the dressing room and lounge, there were no first team only areas. This closer integration was intended to help the academy players make the transition into the first team squad and keep the first team hungry and motivated. For them to see firsthand, that a talented crop of players were coming through and they had to work even harder to hold onto their shirts. Secondly, the club had a poor record with injuries and so Paco wanted to overhaul the sports science and medical facilities. An emphasis was placed on prevention and health management with the close monitoring of the players' individual fitness levels and performance indicators. Thirdly, before moving to Datchet the players had no access to a canteen. After training they either went their own way or headed to the local Nando's for lager and fried chicken. Neither was ideal. A restaurant and dining area where the players could bond over a nutritious breakfast or lunch was essential.

Datchet was a bellwether of Athletic's status and success. In its day, back when the club was the dominant force in Europe, the performance centre was revolutionary - another example of how Paco raised the bar on and off the pitch with his laser like focus on the smallest detail - but over the previous ten years the competition had taken his blueprint and built upon it, adding their own enhancements. Chester City's new multi million-pound campus, for example, had a 20,000 seater stadium where they played crowd noise through a sound system to replicate match day conditions. The coaching staff could even target individual players with boos and other sound effects every time they touched the ball. Back in Split we had a better hydrotherapy pool, more cryotherapy tanks, and an anti-gravity treadmill (originally designed for astronauts, it enabled players returning from an injury to rebuild strength whilst placing less weight and strain on their lower body). Athletic, meanwhile, had underinvested in the facilities at Datchet, Archer siphoning money away to meet the clamour for wage increases, and by the time I arrived, it had become a symbol of the club's lapsed ambition. Its maddening contentment to run with the field rather than lead the pack. A thick fug of mediocrity - the acceptance that just enough is good enough – hung about the place and after ten minutes I wanted to give everything and everyone a good shake.

My first meeting was with Terry Locke, my new assistant coach. At fifty seven years old, Terry was the great survivor. The grizzled Sergeant who nurses wet behind the ears Ivy League officers through their first tour of duty, dodging bullets and side stepping landmines. He was also late. I watched as he crossed the courtyard below, stopping to share a joke with the ground staff, his appearance as sloppy as his time keeping. A spare tyre hanging out over the top of his crumpled tracksuit bottoms. A bird's nest of a beard. I thought to myself, 'how the fuck do you expect professional athletes to take you seriously looking like that?'

Terry joined Athletic from Dagenham and Redbridge in the mid-eighties and made forty-nine appearances, often from the bench, before rupturing his ACL in his third season. Several abortive comebacks followed until he finally listened to what his body and the specialists in the US were telling him and retired from the game at twenty-four. Chas Macdonald looked after him, always grateful for the scuffed equaliser against Palace in the Milk Cup semi-final that saved his job. First there was a scouting role, clocking up miles on the motorway to keep tabs on transfer targets in the lower divisions. Then once he had gained his badges, five years coaching the under nineteens, bringing through Dan Stevens, Hector Regueiro, and Ethan Doyle. From there he rose to reserve team coach and when Chas Macdonald retired six years later, he stepped up to become assistant first team coach, a role he had held under six managers and head coaches. To his surprise, Terry was kept on when Paco and his close-knit team of Spanish assistants and players (*Los Conquistadors* as the media called them) arrived. And while Terry was never truly part of the inner circle, Paco soon came to value his knowledge of the English game. The inside track on opposing teams and players. Who would go missing if they took a couple of early whacks. How far you could push certain referees. The dimensions and topography of each ground. Which end to kick towards in the second half if you won the toss.

Terry was also, as he told his support group every Monday evening, an addict. A recovering alcoholic, who sat at the very back of the wagon, legs dangling over the side, and had a tendency to tumble off at the first bump in the road. He was also a compulsive gambler who had blown his life savings, money set aside for his kids' university fees, with a string of bad bets. ('I'd bet on anything – anything. You name, it I've lost money on it. Kite surfing world championships. MotoGP. Second division games in Macedonia. It's cost me marriages, friendships, millions down the bleedin' drain.')

He ambled in with his mug of tea. There was a friendly greeting but no apology for being late. Punctuality is the hallmark of a high-performance culture, so I told him straight.

'You're late.'

For a second he thought I was joking. Then the smile vanished from his face.

'Steady on gaffer, it's not even five past,' he said checking his watch.

'I don't care if it's five minutes or twenty-five minutes. From now on we operate on Lombardi Time. Ten minutes early for all meetings and training.'

He looked at me with his hangdog face, the bags under his eyes stretching down towards his nostrils.

'Yes, boss.'

It was not how I wanted to kick off our relationship, but you have to set high standards and ensure everyone sticks to them. Rule number one.

'How did the lads react to the news yesterday?'

'We caught the tail end of the presser as we were coming in. Let's just say they weren't pulling cartwheels. Some of the boys came to see me later. Moaning about how The Owner has chucked in the towel. At least for this season. No signings in the window. A caretaker coach with no experience...' His voice trailed away.

This didn't faze me. All players, from the kid in the park to the Galatico, want the same things. To win, to improve, and to enjoy their football. If you can give them all three, and demonstrate you've got their backs, then they will play for you. Kick their ways through walls for you. No matter who you are or what trophies you have or haven't won.

'And what's the mood like in the group?'

'Ugly. Fucking horrible. People liked to pile on Alain, god bless him, but the problems go a lot deeper than him.'

Rigg had said something similar as we killed time waiting for the press conference to begin the day before. 'I may not grasp the tactical minutiae Joe, but I understand people, always have done. Forget all the lions led by donkeys nonsense, there's something rotten in that dressing room.'

'Basically,' Terry continued 'we've got more divisions than Norman Stormin' Shwarzkopf. We've got a bunch of players who are not playing to their level. Either their confidence has been shredded, they're in their armchairs, or pissed off because Archer hawked them around Europe last summer.'

He shook his head in despair.

'Christ, he might as well stuck them on eBay. Then we've got a group of players who've got the hump because they ain't getting enough minutes and don't believe those who start are better than them. You'd think they'd be fighting for a spot but none of them are giving it. They don't want to leave, though, because that would mean a pay cut or moving up North. So they hang around like a bad smell. Whining to each other in the canteen or on WhatsApp. Sniggering on the bench like kids when we make mistakes. And Alain handled these boys badly. No communication. Some of them would go weeks without talking to him.'

He ran a hand through his beard.

'Then you've got the dedicated pro's – and there's not enough of them – Vallo, Fab, Kuipers who are cheesed off with the others taking liberties. You can see it affecting them. Plus, there's the usual factions you get in any dressing room. The Spanish speakers are tight and keep themselves to themselves. The younger boys, Bailey and Zharnell spend all their time blowing each other up on Xbox. The defensive unit hang out with their families. But the main faultline, the San fackin Andreas, is the beef between Slaney and Valon. Slaney likes to drip poison in Archer's ear. First, he says the armband has become a distraction and he should take over as captain while Valon recovers his form. But it doesn't stop there. A couple of games later he's telling anyone who will listen that the big man needs to be taken out of the firing line. Getting his pals in the media to say the same. V went nuts when word got back to him, and they had this almighty barney. I've never seen V so angry, effin' and jeffin' as he reminded Slaney you defend as a team not just with four at the back and then delivered a detailed anaylsis in front of the other boys of the weaknesses in Slaney's game. Withering it was. *Withering*. And now Slaney refuses to speak to him, won't even pass to him. It's not so noticeable, because they play at the other end of the pitch, but if you watch corners and set pieces, Slaney never puts it in Valon's zone. You can see it in the stats too. V hasn't scored for almost a year but before that he used to average three or four a season. And this has affected V more than he lets on. He's used to being the main man. You know, treated with respect by the other lads. To have someone like Slaney, with everything he's done, the players he's played with, say you're not good enough has gotta hurt.'

We discussed various members of the squad. Fabio's issues with shots from distance. Jose Costa's tendency to switch off. Kuipers loss of form and confidence. How he would benefit from a fresh start. How Valon's reading of the game had compensated for the decline in his recovery speed. I highlighted the lack of intensity out of possession, especially in midfield, and how this would have to change.

'Football is a running game. Any team which comes last in yards covered can't expect to win games,' I told him and then outlined the training block to boost their fitness levels.

I asked about Bailey. Terry slumped back in his chair. 'The kid's a baller, got serious silks, but he's lost the eye of the tiger. Had his feet up since the last deal. It was too much, too soon. When I was his age we'd scrub the khazi and the bath after training. Clean boots until the skin on our knuckles was raw. Paint the stands. Muck out in the laundry room. Go down the bookies and place bets for the senior pro's. You name it we did it. But Bailey will be off to film some advert or play with his toys at home. Never sticks around to eat with the others. Alain wasn't interested but I tried to get a tune out of him. You name it I tried it. An arm around the shoulder. Targets. A bit of tough love. Even had him and his old man over for dinner. But his heart ain't in it. Archer and Alain talked about offloading him last summer but we needed another body to meet our quota.'

The league stipulated that each club must have a minimum of eight homegrown players in their twenty-five-man squad.

'I'll give it a shot, see if I can get him going.'

'I hope you can, I really do, but the kid's a lost cause. Honestly, you're better off not wasting your time.'

I talked Terry through how we were going to play and explained the grid. His biggest concerns were the high line and building from the back.

'Playing out won't work. We ain't got a six to link play.' He looked at me. I stared back, saying nothing. 'There's not enough time to work on it. We'll end up giving too many cheap goals away.'

He didn't get it. Building from the back and establishing an overload in the first phase was central to everything. We would do it or die trying.

'Listen Terry. The only problem with playing out is that mistakes are more visible. What people don't see is the control it gives you. Kick long and you have a fifty-fifty chance of winning the second ball, less against some teams. But play it out on the floor and you take control.'

I rearranged the magnets on the tactical board. 'Look at how it stretches the space between the lines as their front two or three are drawn closer to our goal. There's so much more space for us to operate here,' I said pointing to zone seven, a rectangle of space ten yards from the D to the edge of the centre circle. 'One of the fullbacks comes inside to occupy this space, giving the Pivot who has dropped back and the centre backs, who have moved out wide, another passing option.' I moved two of the blue magnets forward. 'And if their midfield step up to close down the fullback it opens up passing lanes to the front three here and here,' I said tracing two lines on the board with my index finger.

He gave me a look that said, 'it might work in Croatia but over here you need to play our way' but then smiled so wide I could see his breakfast stuck between his teeth.

'Whatever you say gaffer, let's give it a bash.'

Terry stared out of the window, eyes on stalks, at Natalia Castillo, the first team physio. She strode past with one of the masseurs. Both had wet hair after an early morning swim.

I asked him about Bescond. He sighed. 'Alain was a strange fish, very cold. He liked to keep his distance. The boys would come to me and say they didn't know where they stood with him. And he was always looking to assert his authority. Command and control. But it doesn't work like that anymore. You have to bend a little, especially with the bigger egos. I played under George Steel. He was a hard man George. A stone-cold killer. He would monster you the minute you stepped out of line. But that's just how it was in those days. You took your lumps and moved on. Worked that bit harder to get back on his good side. But you try throwing a tea cup now. They'll be off crying to their agent or bleating to Anita or the Chairman.' He took a slurp of tea from his mug and then continued.

'The first thing he did, the very first thing, was single out Sorensen. Told him he didn't figure in his plans and gave his squad number to Zharnell. This was two days into pre-season. Two days. Well, the boys didn't like that. Not one bit. Sorro was a popular lad, did a lot for the club. He deserved better. So less than a week in and he's pissed away any goodwill.' Terry took another swig of tea. 'But Alain didn't see it this way and then last November he decides to take on Slaney.'

'What happened?'

'He called Slaney in here. Told him he was too selfish and needed to start playing for the team. To lead the press. But Slaney wasn't having that. There's no way he's sprinting thirty yards to recover the ball. All he cares about is scoring goals. He'll be in a foul mood if we've won and he's not scored, and buzzing after pulling one back when we get stuffed, lording it over the rest of the boys, accusing them of not pulling their weight. Anyway, that's when the willy waving started. Alain dropped him against Macclesfield. He didn't tell him, just leaked it to the press. Problem was they caned us. So Archer and Anita came down hard on Alain and told him to put Slaney back in the team.'

'But Bescond was right. Slaney needs to do more than preen in the box.'

'Maybe but it was a fight he was never going to win.'

This was true. Some players are bigger than the club, no matter what they say, and Slaney was one of them. Unfortunately for both parties, he was a square peg in a round hole. A luxury Athletic did not need and could not afford. Archer was railroaded into buying him by The Owner and the fans. Recruitment by headline, rather than part of any plan. He had joined the club eighteen months earlier, after six hugely successful seasons in Germany. Slaney's agent pressurised the club to waive the usual due diligence, warning that FC Haarlem were about to hijack the deal, and so Archer and Scooter rushed it through, blinded by the chance to make a statement signing and the lure of image rights. But they had bought at the top of the market and a correction was coming. Age and an accumulation of injuries had robbed Slaney of pace and movement. The dynamic first five steps and slaloming runs had vanished and the large physical frame, an asset for most of his career, had turned against him. Weighed him down. Where once he crackled with irrepressible energy, constantly taking up different positions, now he changed direction like a supertanker. Hanging around the box waiting for the ball, no longer coming deep or attacking the channels. He fed off penalties and cut backs, tap ins and crosses. Still averaging a goal every 2.4 games. Enough to hold down a spot and convince himself and his friends in the media that the fault lay elsewhere. If only his service improved, the fanboys argued, everything would be OK. But the goals were a roll of shiny paper over a cracked wall. Athletic were one dimensional, slow in the build-up and on the break. Too easy to defend against, and too easy to play through in the first phase, Slaney having given up any pretence of leading the press. Instead, he looked on as opposing teams routed the ball through to midfield.

'Who's he close to?'

'No one. There's respect for what's he done, the things he's won, but no one likes him, especially after the Christmas party last year.'

This was good. Most players have at least two or three close friends in the dressing room, so if you take on one difficult individual you risk falling out with nucleus of your side.

'What happened?'

'Things got out of hand the previous year.' He was referring to the footage of Bailey staggering through Soho eating a kebab, dressed as a suicide bomber. 'So I suggested we invite the WAGs to stop it getting messy. Slaney moved the place cards so he could sit next to Pablo's girlfriend and spent the evening trying to grope her under the table. Pablo was not happy, had a right go. So Slaney glassed him in the thigh. Severed a fackin artery. Thankfully Natalia was there, otherwise he wouldn't have made it.'

'Christ.'

'Yeah, serious shit. Anyway, the lads try to stay on his good side, laugh at his jokes that sort of thing. No one wants to be the next target. But you should see the lengths they go to avoid sitting near him on the coach.' He switched accents. 'It's all, after you Claude, as they board.'

He drained his mug with a loud slurp. Wiped his mouth with the back of his hand. I looked away in time to see one of the grounds staff ride past on a grass cutter, towing a trailer of equipment and plastic tubs.

'And it has got worse since he opened his legs to City. Making it clear in training that he doesn't want to be here. Finding fault with everything and everyone. Running down the club.'

'We need to get rid of him.'

Outside Ken Fenton – or half dead Ken, as Slaney called him – shuffled along the path, pushing a trolley with that day's kit. The wind whistling between the buildings blew his few remaining strands of grey hair on end. He stopped to take a breather as he neared the entrance to our building. The cold weather played havoc with his arthritis and he bent lower to rub a knee with one of his liver spotted hands.

'Damn right. The thing is The Owner still has a hard-on for him. Won't hear a word against him. And Archer knows he won't get your job if he sells him.'

'It's only going to end one way. We have to take control of the process. Make the most of the opportunity.'

'You know that. I know that. I suspect even Dave knows it, but The Owner doesn't want to hear it.'

The alarm on my phone interrupted us. 'Time to go. I want to be down there when they arrive.'

11

The ground staff had marked up two of the practice pitches to create perfect, life size replicas of the grid – painstaking but important work – and we used this to hardwire positional play into the team. For the boys, used to a relaxed knockabout, the hours of practice were dull and repetitive, but shape and movement improved hour by hour, day by day.

'STOP.'

The players slowed to a halt amidst a few groans. I pointed to Dekker, Kuipers, and Zharnell who were bunched together in the central zone.

'Dekko look where Kuipsie is. Remember, never more than two in a vertical column. When Kuipsie moves inside you switch to zone 11 or 12. Right let's go back to the first phase.'

'Again?' said one of the players.

'Yes, we do it again until you get it right and then we keep working at it until its muscle memory, a fast twitching reflex.'

A couple of the players near me exchanged looks. On the opposite wing, out of earshot, Varallo and Bailey muttered to themselves. Out of the corner of my eye I caught Terry checking his watch.

'Come on, you've got this. Your distances are already better,' I said and then kicked the ball back to Terry.

'Let's go, let's go, let's go.'

'COME ON BOYS, YOU HEARD THE MAN,' shouted Valon, throwing his considerable weight behind me. 'MOVE IT.'

Archer watched from his covered golf buggy on the far side of the pitch, his phone clamped between neck and shoulder, typing note after note on the iPad balanced on his knee. He wore a shiny black parka over his training kit and a large Russian fur hat. He had arrived midway through the box drills, grunted hello to Terry, blanked me, and then ejected one of the younger players from a 4 v 2 Rondo, telling the rest of the group to watch how it is done. It was hard to take your eyes off him. He still had the gossamer touch and hypnotic hold over the ball. Still moved with the loose-limbed easy grace and knowing confidence of a circus conjurer. While he flicked the ball around the box, he bragged about receiving a blow job from a shop assistant in a clothing store in Milan. 'She was a greedy bitch. Guzzled it all down. Then begged me to stick my fingers in her married pussy.'

Johan introduced boxes or 'rondo' to Barcelona when he returned to save the club in 1988. It was central to his vision of how football should be played and works on three of the most important elements of the modern game: finding space, keeping possession, and pressing to win the ball back. It's the drill that changed football. Without it, there would be no Iniesta, no Xavi, no playing out from the back. Two players stand in the middle of a ten by eight metre box and have to win the ball back from the other four players who stand around them. The players with the ball can only use one touch to pass it to each other and must keep the ball within the box. Whoever loses possession swaps places with the player in the middle who made the interception. There's nowhere to hide in the box with the ball zipping around at high speed in a tight space. A player with poor technique is quickly found out, and the boys loved embarrassing each other by keeping someone in the middle for a long time, or best of all, nutmegging them with a pass between their legs.

I moved from box to box keeping a close eye on the players' movement and ability on the ball. There was laughter in the third box as Bailey and Chela were run ragged, twisting and turning and moving at speed as they tried to get the ball back.

'Fancy a go?' said Archer, flicking the ball up and catching it in one hand.

'Yeah, come on gaffer, show us your moves!' said one of the players.

I never take part in drills or practice games. Some head coaches find it useful, or like to make a point by reminding their players how good they were, but I prefer to watch and analyse.

'Another time boys. I don't want to destroy you on my first day.'

Rondo was a standard drill according to Terry, but I was surprised to see it treated as a quick, fun warm-up. For me box work is a guiding philosophy underpinning everything that takes place on the pitch. And it is called a drill for a reason. With all my teams we practise rondo until what is uncomfortable becomes routine and natural. It's about building good habits. Players automatically looking to take the ball when under pressure, maximising the space available to them and making the split-second pass.

To increase the intensity of the rondo session I told the players to count their touches out loud and see if they could reach thirty and added a new rule. If one of the two players regained the ball in the first five touches then they both moved out of the middle, but after five touches only the player who made the turnover re-joined the other players. I shouted instructions and encouragement as I paced between the boxes.

'TRIANGLES, looking to create angles all the time. YES, ZHARNELL LIKE THAT.'

'Keep going, don't let go of the ball.'

'Come on you two where's the pressure? You're making it too easy for them. *Faster*.'

'Body shape. BODY SHAPE! HEAD UP, LOOK AROUND YOU.'

I stopped the drill and spoke to Thomas Dekker about adjusting his body shape to receive the ball.

'As the ball comes towards you turn your body forty five degrees. It gives you a wider view of the pitch ahead and it's easier to play the quick pass. I'll send you some clips of Scholes and Pirlo. Take a look. Watch how they play with their heads up.'

We resumed the drill, the players struggling to complete more than nine or ten passes. This was piss poor – my old squad would almost always manage more than forty.

Zharnell flicked the ball to Bailey, and he hit a firm volley towards Slaney on the other side of the box, just out of the reach of Jose Costa who was in the middle with Mats. Slaney mishit his pass and Jose Costa blocked it back towards him. Slaney picked up the ball and threw it at Bailey's head.

'What the fuck was that scrote? You hit it too hard. You can go in the middle. You need the practice more than me.'

Terry didn't say a word, just looked at me, so I stepped in.

'Come on Ryan you know the rules, in you go.'

Slaney glowered. I smiled back.

'Show me your hustle… LET'S GO BOYS,' I said clapping my hands. The other players hesitated for a second and then started to move the ball around again at speed, counting out loud. Slaney gave pursuit, moving like an arthritic crab. The pass count ticked up quickly as Slaney struggled to get close to the ball, until one of the boys, fearing the retaliation that would follow, gifted him possession.

'GOOD WORK BOYS. TEN MORE MINUTES AND THEN WE'LL WORK ON POSITIONING,' I shouted giving Slaney the thumbs up. He returned it with a look of pure hatred. Archer was watching and just for a second, I thought I caught a glimpse of approval on his face.

I jogged across to the neighbouring pitch to check out Fabio. As with all English clubs, at Athletic the goalkeepers trained separately with the goalkeeping coach for the first hour before taking part in an eleven-a-side game or defence v attack. Each keeper had their own individual programme. Marc Juppé, the goalkeeping coach, took Fabio through his training block, while the number two and three keepers worked with his assistants. Juppé began with alternating high and low balls kicked from hands. Next Fabio stood on the goal line facing the net and spun one hundred and eighty degrees as the ball was kicked towards him. After five minutes of this, Juppé lined up four balls in a row, and kicked each at Fabio in quick succession from close range, repeating the drill ten times. I then added two drills to assess his mobility and recovery. Juppé did not attempt to hide his annoyance at this. Ignoring him, I held one ball and kicked the other low and hard from ten yards. As soon as Fabio blocked or smothered it on the ground, I threw the second ball at head height. He had to spring up to catch it or tip it over the bar. We repeated this for a few minutes and then moved to the next drill. Fabio knelt near one of the posts and was not allowed to move until I began my two-step run up, when he had to push off the ground and launch himself at a medium paced shot aimed at the centre of the goal. He looked sharp.

Juppé switched it up, moving onto five minutes of one on ones and claiming high balls. Only then did they work on shots from distance. It's a sensible strategy, one I've used many times. Groove the player's strengths to build confidence and then address the problem area. Juppé stood five yards from the D and fired ball after ball at the goal. Fabio dealt with them all comfortably, the smile on his face growing with every save, but this was not a real match play scenario. There was no one in the box to obscure Fabio's view and the shots lacked the pace, dip, and swerve of what he would face in a game. I made a note to make it more realistic by involving the attacking unit. When Fabio went to retrieve the balls he had tipped over the bar I took the opportunity to speak to Juppé.

'He's in great shape. Quick, strong, great recovery.'

Juppé gave me a sullen look. 'Of course. We know what we're doing.'

I raised the issue of shots from distance.

'Have you checked his eyes?'

'He has a test every four weeks,' Juppé said defensively and then pointed in the direction of the sports science building. 'They're happy, kept his contact lenses on the same prescription.'

'So what's the problem?'

'It's the reflexes. Your nerves deteriorate long before your muscles. Happens to everyone in their mid to late thirties, but it's more prevalent in keepers. They play on longer and are more exposed if they make a mistake. I published a paper on it a few years ago.'

I didn't buy it. Fabio had the reflexes of a panther.

'I want to see his performance data.'

'It's all in the app,' Juppé said over his shoulder as he started to walk away.

'One more thing.'

He stopped and turned around, screwed his face up at me.

'From tomorrow the keepers will join the rest of the boys for rondo and positional work. You get them at the end of normal training.'

'No, no, no,' he said waving his hand. 'That doesn't work. I need more time and I need them fresh.'

Johan always used to say the goalkeeper was not just the last defender, they are also the first attacker, and I wanted Fabio involved in building play and sweeping behind a higher line.

'Ball control and passing under pressure is the priority now. Besides, too much training in isolation isn't good for them. They need more game-based scenarios.'

There's a reason why keepers are late developers, often only establishing themselves in their mid to late twenties. Training away from the rest of the squad stunts their growth, depriving them of the experiences that inform decision-making.

'This is bullshit.'

I took a step towards him, lowered my voice.

'We're going to do it my way now.'

For the final thirty minutes, when the boys' concentration began to slip, we worked on regaining the ball. Closing down players, cutting off their passing options, and forcing an error is nothing new. Ian Rush would defend from the front for Liverpool in the 1980s, playing defence in five-a-side training matches to improve his tackling. What has changed is the intensity. It requires fitness, discipline, and teamwork. There's nothing more dispiriting than being the only player to press, running yourself into the ground, only to find your opponents have men in space because your teammates aren't willing to put a shift in. You have to press as a unit, moving fast to block the passing lanes.

'When we lose the ball, you've got five seconds to win it back. I want to see bodies around the ball, pressing as a unit to close down the angles. If we've not regained possession after five seconds, we revert to our defensive shape with the pivot dropping deep to shield the back four.'

We worked on winning possession higher up the pitch, with two teams of ten playing against each other. Terry or I fed the ball to one team and they had fifteen seconds to move it from their back three through the thirds and score, whilst the other team pressed aggressively. We awarded three points for regaining possession in the first five seconds and one point for a goal and kept a tally for each individual player. The players with the lowest points tally at the end of the week did the post-match tour of the hospitality suites.

Terry wandered over while the boys took a final drinks break. He glanced at Archer who was still tapping away at his iPad.

'What the fack do you think he's up to?'

'Writing his shopping list for the window. How to stiffen the spine.'

'Dream the fack on gaffer.'

I had mixed feelings as we filed back into the building at the end of the session. The scale of the project was clear. Fitness and ball work needed to drastically improve. It would take time to get the level I wanted and some of the players would never get there. But more than this, I was shocked by the lack of intensity in training. The sight of elite athletes going through the motions rather than giving it their all. The lack of bite in their tackles. The weary resignation when they lost possession. No shame or anger at their failure to land a trophy for years. You train as you play, I told them over and over again, words that became a mantra in those difficult first weeks.

My three biggest concerns were the Slaney-sized hole in the first line of our counter press. A right back who lacked the pace to hurt teams going forward. And most of all, the absence of a ball playing six. Thomas Dekker, the only deep lying midfielder in the group, was a passive shield, accustomed to reacting to incoming threats, but not equipped to take the ball on the half turn and move it forward under close pressure. Unfortunately, there were no easy solutions. Slaney was all but undroppable and we were short of natural replacements in the other two positions.

On the plus side, there was real quality in the group. Valon was still the best ball playing central defender of his generation. Mats had unbelievable tactical intelligence, switching and rotating positions, always in the right place in relation to his teammates and rarely missing a pass. Kuipers had responded well to our conversation that morning. I had assured him he would be back in an advanced central position and encouraged him to take risks, to attack defenders one-on-one. And Zharnell Wilkins, the last player to step up from the academy two years before, stood out with his perfect blend of hustle and technical ability. He drifted effortlessly between the lines, manufacturing time and space for himself. He had an intuitive awareness of how to maximise his passing angles and kept running and moving, throwing himself into full-blooded challenges and sprinting to close down opponents after every turnover in possession. If only every player mirrored his intensity and commitment.

I spoke to Emily that evening, the first time in almost a week. I told her about the first couple of days in the role. How the players had responded well to the messages I gave them in our session, but that their confidence was shot to pieces from a bad run of results and a lengthy barren spell without a trophy. How some had succumbed to imposter syndrome, doubting their own ability to play at the highest level, while others were past caring. Emily ate as we spoke, a habit I hated but tolerated for fear she might end the call. I told her about Terry, and how I was beginning to suspect he hid a sharp footballing brain behind the barrow boy act. About the strange phone conversation I had with Anita Fang, the club's lawyer and one of The Owner's closest advisers. She had called to tell me The Owner was unhappy with the negative comments directed at him in social media by the supporters.

'He wants you to placate the crowd,' she instructed. 'Give them what they want: more open, expansive football. More goals.' This, she empathised, was non-negotiable.

I didn't mention to Emily that Slaney badmouthed me as we trooped back into the building after three hours working on the grid. It was neither the time nor the place to confront him. I didn't want Slaney to define the first day or distract the rest of the group from what we had been working on. So, I pretended not to hear him and continued to explain to Zharnell the importance of taking shorter steps when defending close to the box and how this makes it easier to quickly change direction.

'Have you met David Archer?'

'A couple of times. He joined in training this morning.'

'Seriously? What's he like?'

'Everything you've heard and then some.'

She laughed.

'Has he shown you any of his paintings?'

'Not yet.'

Archer had taken up oil painting five or six years before, during one of his post-retirement stints in rehab. His agent had milked it until the udders were cracked and bleeding. A TV documentary. Exhibitions in London, Paris, and Milan. A coffee table book. Calendars for charity. His work, as Archer said on TV and in multiple fawning interviews, was an output for his anger. A stick to beat off the black dog of depression.

'Where are you staying?'

'Above the shop for the time being.'

'What at Preston Park?'

'No, here at the training ground in Datchet. We've got our own hotel.'

'How long are you planning to stay there?'

'For the foreseeable. It's the perfect set up. A five minute walk to my office. No time wasted in the car.'

Emily clammed up when I asked how she was doing, deflecting my interest with a series of 'yeahs' and 'nahs.' When she was like this, she reminded me of the old war movies my grandad watched at Christmas, where the POW blinked into the spotlight and stubbornly repeated his name, rank, and number. For whatever reason, she didn't want to let me in, and before I could break out the thumbscrews, Em steered the conversation back to me, asking about my first meeting with the squad. I told her it had gone as well as I could have hoped given the mood of the group and the obvious scepticism about my track record.

We gathered together in the presentation theatre with its rows of tiered seating. On Fridays the room doubled as the venue for the pre-match press conference. It was a lot smarter than its counterpart at Preston Park, but like much of the training complex, it felt clinical and soulless. If Preston Park was stuck in the past, Datchet was entirely divorced from it. There were no photos of past glories, no memorabilia on display. Even Paco had been airbrushed out of history: the mural in reception of him holding the league trophy and the European Cup had been replaced by one of Archer's Jackson Pollock knock-offs.

A billion pounds of misfiring footballers drifted into the room clutching protein shakes and staring at their phones. There was little noise and no banter. I greeted them individually with a smile and a handshake. On my first day in Hadjuk I had impressed the squad by memorising their names – with the correct pronunciation – in advance. But this was not necessary at Athletic. Everyone knew who they were, and they knew it. A handful of young, eager to please players occupied the front row, pens and pads at the ready. The defensive unit - Valon, Jose Costa, Mats, and Javier Varallo – formed a narrow, compact block in the third row. The floating voters came next. They had their doubts but were open to persuasion. Unlike Bailey, Chela, and Reece Hughes, the cynics and the disengaged, in the row behind them. And then slouched at the back on his own was Slaney. Arms folded, feet up on the seat in front, transmitting bad vibes.

'Morning all. It's a privilege to stand in front of you guys. I have huge respect for this club and what has been achieved in the past. But I'm not going to lie to you. Something has gone wrong. Levels have dropped, standards have slipped, results have not been good enough. The media say you are past it. The fans used to call your names… now they're calling for the squad to be broken up. The club tried to move half of you on last year.'

First impressions are like shots on goal, you have to make them count. I held up a couple of the back pages from that morning's papers.

'As for me, I'm the guy no one's heard of. The know nothing, out of his fucking depth Joe-ker.'

The room was silent, all eyes on me. I screwed up one of the articles and tossed it into the bin.

'I don't know about you but I'm not going take this shit,' I said setting light to the bottom of the page of another article.

'I'm going to prize open their jaws and ram every last word down their throats. The question is, what are you going to do? Are you going to coast along to the end of the season and see what happens? Or do you want to show these fuckers how wrong they are?'

The flames spread across the page, heat radiating towards my hand and chest.

'Because that's what I'm going to be doing every minute of every hour for the next four months. I'm going to show them they were wrong about me and wrong about you. Remind them you're a team of winners.'

The flames were now close to my fingers, and it felt as if I was holding my hand over a candle. I couldn't take it much longer.

'I'm going to show you how I want us to play, then we'll hit the grass and get down to work. And you'll each show me whether you're a winner or a quitter.'

With that I dropped the paper into the bin. It was siege mentality 101, straight out of the Paco playbook, and if nothing else, it grabbed their attention.

'Superiority, position, intensity,' I said, holding up three fingers. 'These are the three things that matter the most.'

Communication had always been an afterthought until I started working with a media trainer in Split. Diane Waldegrave, a former BBC World Service correspondent, opened my eyes to the importance of clear, simple, and consistent messages. 'Repetition Joe,' she would say. 'At the point when you're sick of saying it, when you never want to hear the words again, *that's* when you are getting through to them.'

She introduced me to the rule of three, a device used by Shakespeare ('Friends, Romans, countrymen'), Lincoln ('government of the people, by the people, for the people'), and Churchill ('Blood, sweat, and tears') to make messages more memorable. After speaking to her I installed screens throughout the training ground complex displaying three simple messages about our opponents in the days running up to each match.

'Our aim is to gain superiority through positioning and movement. Every player has a role to play, no matter how far away they are from the ball. From Fabio all the way through to Ryan, we work together to manipulate space, move the other team around, and find the free man.' I paused. 'Space is everything.'

Johan taught me many things. But above all he taught me about positional play. To control space by expanding the pitch when you have the ball and compressing space when you don't. Moving the other team around to achieve superiority. Lure one or two players out of position and space suddenly opens up and their team-mates face a dilemma. Do they move across to cover, and in doing so free up another space, or do they hold their position? Take the two centre backs. Ever since their academy days they have been taught to occupy a position between the width of the goal posts. This is their comfort zone. But if a forward moves to one of the half-space channels - the corridors between the fullback and the centre back on either side of the pitch - they have to follow or trust that their fullback will move inside or a midfielder drops deep. Either way space opens up somewhere on the pitch. In the centre of the box, on the wing, or in the space previously guarded by the defensive midfielder. To achieve this every player has to be in the right position and to understand that these positions change as the ball and their teammates move.

In addition to setting out my principles, I also wanted to gauge the players' reaction. To see who was with me and who I would have to look out for. Diane always encouraged me to build a connection with the audience by drawing them into the conversation. Valon was studying for his coaching badges so I singled him out.

'Azem, name me the three types of superiority.'

'Numerical, qualitative, or positional, boss.'

'Well done coach,' called one of the players. Valon raised both hands and nodded his head in ironic acknowledgment.

'Numerical advantage is the most important of the three. We're always looking to create an overload and using the ball as bait. We invite the press and then spring the trap, quickly working the ball to another zone where we have an overload and space for the free man to drive into.'

I showed them clips of Xavi and Iniesta. 'Watch how they sucker them in, waiting for the maximum number of players to arrive, and then suddenly switch play. This is what we want to achieve. Any questions?' Silence. I was about to move on when Zharnell spoke up.

'This is a stupid question—.'

'There's no such thing.'

'You obviously haven't met Zharnell,' said Slaney through a mouthful of gum. I ignored him.

'Go on Zharnell.'

'What's qualitative superiority boss?'

'It's finding ways to put your strengths up against your opponent's weaknesses. Creating mis-matched one v ones, where your fastest player goes up against their slowest, or their worst defender is left isolated against your most dangerous forward.'

Zharnell nodded.

'Like when teams target Jose,' said Slaney.

'I'd like to see you target me. You'd be in here,' said Jose Costa tapping his shirt pocket.

'That's enough,' I said before Slaney could respond. 'Save your aggression for the grass. Now take a look at this. It's important.'

The next slide was a diagram of the pitch divided into zones, ten in each half, with four vertical and five horizontal lines. My blueprint for positional play. It ensures the players know where they need to be, when and where to move, and which zones to target for an overload. The angle and direction to make for a run, and where their teammates will be at any given time. When a player breaks the lines with a no look pass to meet a teammate's run, it seems as if the two share a paranormal understanding. But there's no sixth sense in football. This is a pre-set positional play, rehearsed until it becomes instinctive.

'Guys, this is the grid. We'll use it to maintain our shape as we progress the ball higher up the pitch.' Ezekiel Mwangi held up his phone to take a photo.

'The single most important thing to remember is there should never be more than two players in any of the vertical corridors, and no more than three in any of the horizontal rows. Otherwise, we cut down the passing angles and do the other side's job for them. When someone moves into your row you rotate into a different zone. Like this here.' I played an aerial clip. 'Watch the player circled in red, see how he moves out of the wide corridor and takes up a position in this interior zone here.'

Slaney yawned and fiddled with the zip on his tracksuit top. I responded by increasing my volume and energy.

'Then whenever we have the ball there must always be a player in zones 13 and 15,' I said pointing to the two half-space channels. 'This is where we do the damage. You can play the wide forward in behind the fullback, slip it through to someone in the central area, or take a shot. Watch how Henry uses the space here.' I showed them a montage of Thierry Henry cutting in from the left-wing, using the half-space channel to fire off shots towards the far post. Or drawing players towards him and then slipping the ball behind the back line.

'To ensure the half-spaces don't become congested we have to stretch the pitch. There should always – *always* - be someone in each of the wide areas, to pin their fullbacks and prevent them from moving across. Is that clear?' A handful of nods.

'The wide player only leaves the zone for three reasons. If they have the ball. To attack a ball played into the box, or to rotate places with an overlapping fullback or the player in the half-space. Got it?' I said looking at Bailey and Varallo. Bailey looked away, Varallo gave me the thumbs up.

'Good. Any questions?'

Schnellinger was the first to speak. He leaned forward in his seat. 'But it's a lot of work, Ja?' he said and shook his head doubtfully. 'You need so much time to get it right.'

'You're right. It's tough and will require a lot of work on the training ground. And that's the easy bit. You also need maximum concentration during games. Constant awareness of space and positioning.' I paused. 'There's no mental breathing space, not even when the ball goes out. But this is how we improve. This is how we win games. This is how we take teams apart.'

Slaney lifted his head and spoke next.

'It's easy to come up with clever ideas and pretty pictures, to talk data, but you're overthinking it. Get the ball to me in the box and I'll put it away. Job's a good'un.'

You've been thinking about the game wrong all your life, I wanted to say. You move the opponent and then the ball. Instead I held Slaney's stare, made him wait for my response, and then flicked the ball through his legs.

'Don't worry Ryan, clever lad like you'll soon get your head round it.'

The first flash of steel, just enough to remind them who's in charge. Slaney shrugged his shoulders, as if to say, 'Whatever, I'm out of here.'

'Remember, none of you will have the ball for more than three minutes in any game. What you do for the other ninety-four is where matches are won or lost,' I continued. 'A run to pull a man out of position and open space is as important as any action with the ball.'

Valon, as he did many times over the coming weeks, came to my aid, urging the boys to get behind me. 'Come on Schnelly. You've got to do the hard yards if you want to achieve anything.'

'Too right,' said Kuipers. 'I'm in.'

'That's good to hear. But just so we are clear, this isn't optional. Anyone who doesn't follow the rules, doesn't play.'

Johan liked to say, what you see on the pitch mirrors what happens around it. His teams played aggressive, attacking football, and he insisted the players always performed at a high tempo in training. How they ate their lunch afterwards was an important test. He wanted to see the boys eat quickly. This, he said, showed an aggressive mentality.

'And you can only play this way if you have maximum intensity and aggression. Let me show you what I'm talking about,' I said.

I pressed play on the clicker. Steve McMahon and his red Candy shirt tore across the screen, sprinting thirty yards in pursuit of a ball that was running out of play. He kept it in with a backheel on the touchline, but his momentum carried him off the pitch. He bounced off the advertising hoarding, leapt back on the pitch to pick up the waiting ball, side stepped a tackle from Martin Hayes, slid a pass to Peter Beardsley. Beardsley's low shot was parried into the path of John Aldridge who put away the rebound. Pure, controlled aggression and a goal out of nothing. There were whoops and cheers from the players as the ball went in. 'THAT'S SICK,' said Zharnell. I paused the video.

'This is the level of intensity I want to see from you in everything we do, because quality is never enough. The one thing the best teams – Michels' Ajax, Dalglish's Liverpool, Guardiola's Barcelona - all had in common is work rate. They worked like bastards on and off the pitch and I am going to demand the same of you.'

I paused for effect and looked around the room, making eye contact with as many people as possible before continuing.

'You have to want it more than the other guys. When they leave for the day, we'll be training. On their day off we'll be training. When they are playing video games, you'll be studying clips. If you are up for it, you will play the best football of your careers.'

I left the stage and walked to the door without saying a word. I opened the door, and swept the room with a hard glare before saying:

'If not, you can leave before the window closes. No hard feelings.' And fuck you Archer.

After telling Emily all about this, I shared my concerns about Javier Varallo. By now I could sense she wasn't really listening. I pictured her scrolling through Instagram. Watching Netflix with the subtitles on. Or Snap-chatting her friends. So I wrapped up the call, not wishing to outstay my welcome any longer, and took another look at the recording of the first day's work, frowning again at the poor quality footage. I selected some team and individual clips and added on-screen comments in the captions tool. A mix of positive reinforcement and areas for improvement:

'Good distances.'

'Look at the angles.'

'Watch how Kuipers receives the ball with his back foot.'

'More aggressive, be more aggressive!'

'Hold the line or match the run.'

'You dropped too soon.'

Then I turned my attention to Fabio's difficulties with shots from distance. Working with data is like digging for buried treasure, each stat a grain of sand to sift through your fingers. You don't always know what to look for, or where to look, and for every clue there is a red herring, but perseverance is rewarded. The answer revealing itself to you piece by piece, as the raw data slowly morphs into information.

Using HUDL I created a heat map of Fabio's positioning for all shots from outside the box for the past six seasons, with different colours for each year. The contour of red dots for this season showed Fabio had retreated 1.5 metres closer to the goal line since Williams' twenty-five-yard screamer. The question was, why?

After this I waded through my inbox. The sports science team confirmed what I suspected; several members of the team had exceeded their target weights in that morning's weigh in. I wrote back with a new rule. From the following week, anyone whose BMI was above the agreed limit would train with the academy until they were back in shape.

12

Miguel forced his way through the crowd, like a centre half attacking a set piece, and caught the barman's eye. A moment later we each had a cold glass of Alhambra in our hands and a complimentary tapa to share. We moved away from the crush at the bar and found a spot to stand near the kitchen door where we rested our long-stemmed glasses and the plate of ham croquettes on an upturned Sherry barrel. The bar was in the old Jewish quarter of Granada, down a backstreet off Calle Berrocal. Although he didn't say, I had the impression Miguel had been here many times before.

He stubbed out his cigarette on the barrel and lit another. It had been a long day. Up before the sun rose over La Sagrada Familia. An eight hour car journey, hugging the coast until Valencia and then inland and a slow, climb up through the snow capped Sierra Nevada's, stopping just outside Lorca for petrol, strong coffee, and three packets of cigarettes for Miguel. High up in the mountains, we passed an empty bus on the other side of the narrow windy road. The driver flagged us down, leant out his window and accepted Miguel's offer of a cigarette. The two men spoke about that evening's Classico, a game the whole country was talking about, and one Miguel and I would have to watch on TV. Once he finished his cigarette, the bus driver wished us well and continued on his journey. We reached the stadium in time to see the first warm up, ninety minutes before kick-off. Studying these unguarded moments was one of Miguel's rituals. He gauged a player's character and professionalism on how they interacted with each other and the coaching staff, how seriously they took their drills. 'Never think about signing a player who gives less than one hundred percent in warm-up or training,' he told me.

Miguel also liked to stand among the fans and listen to the chatter from the regulars. To hear who was playing well or which players they couldn't abide. This was before the Internet and social media, when information was harder to come by. Only a couple of games were televised each week and there were no analytics. A good scout could only go by what they saw with their own eyes, what they read in the sporting papers - which focused almost exclusively on the top two sides - and any nuggets they could pick up from their network of informants.

Miguel cautioned against being too reliant on the wisdom of the crowd. Listen to what you hear but never take it at face value he warned me. 'It's a start, nothing more. Often they will be wrong. But every once in a while you will learn something useful. A young player in the reserves who is worth a look. A player who is carrying an injury or who isn't willing to work for the team.'

We watched the game in silence. I made detailed records of shots and passes in the final third. Miguel, who didn't appear to own a pen or notebook, only took his hands out of his pockets to light a cigarette.

Miguel washed down a croquette with another glug of the cold beer.

'*Di-me*,' he said in his gruff Galician accent. I launched into a detailed exposition on Granada's system and playing style, listing their strengths and weaknesses in each area of the field. I highlighted their preference to progress the ball through the central zone. Referenced Leon's tendency to play lateral rather than vertical passes. Ramundo's poor record on one v one duals, on the ground and in the air. I noted the smaller pitch dimensions, and how we would be playing the crowd. Miguel was inscrutable. He gave no hint of what he thought about Granada's performance or whether he agreed with my analysis. I removed my shot map from the match programme, where it was tucked away for safe keeping, and laid it out on the barrel, beaming at Miguel proudly.

'Too much. Far too much. You've got sixty seconds. After that the players stop listening, I promise you. Tell them what they need to know as quickly and simply as possible. Two or three things maximum.'

He waved a hand dismissively at the shot map.

'You're too busy making notes and drawing pictures to watch the game. Anything you can't remember isn't worth writing down,' he chided. 'Try again.'

'They're compact at the back, very narrow—'

'My *abuela* could have told me that and she's been dead for twenty years,' he snorted. 'Focus on what matters: where we can find an edge.'

I thought for a few seconds. Rehearsed a sentence, then pared back the words.

'They'll show us outside down the left, give us space, but an inverted winger like Verges will struggle to cross the ball on his left. He needs to switch sides with Tejada.'

Miguel gestured towards his empty glass as the waiter past.

'Better. What else?'

13

Paco was an early adopter of data and analytics, the first to use ProZone, but performance analysis had stagnated in recent years, the team marginalised and ignored by Alain Bescond and Archer, and football is like a running machine: stand still and you go backwards. The energy was low when I walked into their office, another part of the club needing a jumpstart, so I dialled up the enthusiasm.

'Here it is. The nerve centre,' I said, dishing out smiles and backslaps.

The room was small and cramped, just enough space to accommodate six desks, each with two or three monitors. Infographics and charts taped to the wall like a prisoner's pin ups. Match fitness, with a breakdown of total distance covered by each player in the most recent game. Sprint distance, metres per minute. Possession and distribution numbers: passes per match, pass accuracy, key passes per match, goal scoring actions created. The stats told the story. Not enough energy on the pitch. Not enough regains in the final third. And not enough control, with too many loose passes or long balls going astray.

Jordan Allen, the head of performance analysis, introduced himself and the three other analysts. Jack Grierson zigzagged along the thin line between confidence and arrogance. Tom Ross AKA The Sloth (another of Slaney's nicknames) was the office cynic. A huffing, puffing energy stealer with an aversion to hard work. Kyle Fernsby, a cripplingly shy Mancunian, was the quietest of the lot. He had a pasty white complexion and short thinning hair. Allen was in his late-thirties. The rest were ten years younger than him. All four wore Athletic training tops and tracksuit bottoms and hid behind an excessive amount of jargon and acronyms.

'I know everyone doesn't value what you do but I'm a believer. Together we are going to use analysis to take the boys to another level and take teams apart.'

Every team needs an identity, a philosophy that runs down through every level of the club, but you also have to be aware of who you are up against. Map the threats and flaws, understand the set patterns of play and how they can hurt you. Unearth hidden vulnerabilities.

Because even the strongest chain has a weak link. Look hard enough and you will find something or someone you can target.

I told them I wanted to discuss each person's role, how I work, and their analysis for my first game in charge.

'OK,' said Allen, starting to relax a little. 'It's pretty straightforward. I look after performance analysis for the first team squad, Kyle takes care of the under 23s, and Grierson and Rossy take care of all oppo work.

'What about the academy and players on loan?'

'We don't have the bandwidth.'

'Transfers?'

'I had to cut two heads in the last re-org. All recruitment is agent led these days.'

'Archer doesn't consult you at all?'

He took a moment to select the right words.

'Dave prefers to act on instinct.'

I looked at each of the analysts in turn. 'So, here's how I want to work, starting with oppo analysis. I focus on two games at a time, but you need to work three games ahead.' They nodded their agreement. 'Presentations should be with me as a pre-read first thing the morning after we play. I'll send you a template. Then I want to sit down with you for two hours and crunch through the analysis. We'll agree three points to share with the group – never more than three – and any other items to cover with each of the units. Make sense?'

'Sure,' said Allen. The others nodded their agreement.

'We'll do three meetings with the boys. The first at nine thirty every Monday.'

'Before we all get together?' said Ross, looking puzzled.

'No, we do ours first so we can agree the themes and edit the presentation.'

Ross and Grierson exchanged looks.

'That's right guys. We start at seven thirty, every Monday. And it's our job to make the complex simple, OK? Everything has to be really visual. And where we use text, keep it short and simple, no jargon. If it's not easy to understand and memorable we won't use it. After the team meeting, we'll upload the presentation to their iPads so they can go through it at their own speed when they get home. We'll do sessions with the units on the Tuesday morning, and then pick off every player one on one over the rest of the week to make sure it's gone in. We'll split that between us.'

'Individual meetings will eat up a lot of time,' said Ross, voicing what the others were thinking.

'I know, but it's worth it. None of them will want to admit they don't get it in front of the others. Then we'll get back together as a group on Friday morning, go through it all one more time.'

Fernsby scribbled fast in his pad.

'We'll run the clips on a loop wherever the players spend time during the week. In the restaurant, in the sports science department, in the dressing room. All clear?' I looked at the four of them.

'Crystal,' said Allen.

'Good. Let's run through match days. You'll have a better view of the big picture than me, so send anything you spot during the game to my iPad, and then message Terry to let him know.'

Allen and Grierson exchanged uncomfortable looks. Something was bothering them.

'What is it?'

'We lost our room last season. We used to have a really good spot, right next to the press box, but Scooter was after another hospitality suite and traded it with Archer.'

'So where do you watch home games from? The press box?'

'No, we tried that. Lara told us to do one. We've got a room with a screen—'

'The broom cupboard,' muttered Ross, throwing his arms up in annoyance. Ross was out of shape, not as bad as Terry, but still out of shape. The bulge around his waist strained against his tracksuit top, threatening to break loose at any moment. I pictured him home alone at night eating takeaways from the carton while he played Football Manager.

Allen gave him a sharp look. 'We've got a room next to the ground staff's—.'

'It was a bloody store cupboard,' said Ross laughing with exasperation. He seemed to have no problem undercutting his boss.

'It does the job,' said Allen defensively.

'Anyone afraid of heights?' I asked silencing the bickering.

They all shook their heads.

'Good, I want someone up on the gantry with a wide-angle camera for every home game.'

'I know just the person,' said Grierson, slapping Fernsby on the back. 'A flask full of tea and pigeons for company. What could be better eh Ferno?'

'You'll take it turns. One team,' I replied. 'Do you have access to the tracking data?'

'Yes, we piped it in,' said Allen.

Twelve cameras dotted around the stadium tracked the position of the ball and the players throughout the match, capturing twenty-five frames a second, and generating a data set of one and a half million events.

'What coding software do you use?'

'Sportscode.'

This was something. Sportscode is the best video analysis software on the market. When I was in Spain in the early 2000s all of the analysis work would take place before or after the match. I would spend six hours every Monday watching a re-play of the game on VHS and editing clips for Paco to share with the team while the players enjoyed a round of golf. Now all this took place during the match, with three or four thousand events digitally indexed in real time in every game. Shots, passes, tackles, turnovers, presses, positional mistakes, set pieces, and a hundred other different actions. These can be easily shared with the coaching team on the bench and with the players, either at half time or with a word in the ear of the nearest player to the technical area.

'We'll meet in my office at half time. We won't have much time so I want you all in there when I arrive. Anyone who is late won't be let in.' Ross laughed. 'I mean it. I'll lock the door. Jordan, you'll talk me through what you think we need to share with the boys. Maximum five things. I'll have my own. We'll choose three, no more, agree the clips then I'll go next door and brief the group. We'll then go through any points with the players separately or in their units. It's got to be maximum insight, minimum information. Keep it simple. OK?'

'No problem boss. We try to make things as visual as possible. You have to with all the different languages.'

'Exactly. Is there a tactical screen in the dressing room?'

'Yes,' said Terry, who had been sitting quietly until then, no doubt thinking about his lunch.

'Paco installed one about ten years ago, but the touchscreen has been on the blink since Archer cracked it with a boot when we lost to Goole.'

All you need to know about this club in one sentence.

I looked at Terry. He nodded his head wearily.

'Mr Motivator likes to come in after every home game.'

'We'll need to fix the screen. Who's going to take the action?'

No one met my eye until Grierson finally broke the silence.

'Leave it with me gaffer.'

Finally, someone taking ownership.

'Good man. Do we have Coach Paint?'

'No, we use MatchIt,' said Allen. 'It's cheaper, but a bit clunky.'

'The UX is awful. Completely counter-intuitive.' said Ross.

'Alain vetoed the upgrade to Coach Paint. He and Archer agreed that every spare penny should go into recruitment or salaries. It's not so bad really, you just need some practice,'said Allen.

'Book me in for a test drive once the screen is working.'

'Will do.'

We had already reviewed the analysis for my first match, so over the next hour we went through the analysis for the Aldershot game, discussing their 1-5-4-1 system and how to breakdown the low block by pinning their fullbacks. Then Ross presented his report on set pieces for the following match away to Chirk. He read from a script he had scribbled in the margin of his printout.

'I've been through the corners for the last four matches and the…'

'How many?'

This threw him. 'Sorry…?'

'How many corners have you watched?'

'I don't know… they average five a game so about twenty,' he said re-gaining his balance a little.

'It's not a big enough sample. From now on we go back over the last fifty.' Ross exchanged looks with Allen and then continued. 'I noticed something interesting. Four out of five corners are in-swingers aimed at the front post or the back post but when Karlovic comes on they just stand it up around the penalty spot, let him attack it.

I bit my tongue, resisted the temptation to say: *Is that the best you can do? Rigg could have told me that.*

'Okay good what else? Do they play it short or on the ground?'

'No, never.'

'Never?'

'Well, not in the past four games.'

'Exactly. Look at fifty corners before you start talking about trends. Which side do most goals come from?'

He thumbed through the printout. 'Sixty four percent left… thirty six right.' He didn't need me to tell him he had fucked up. But I did anyway. Standards.

'So, they're almost twice as likely to score from the left and you didn't think that was worth highlighting?'

Ross went to say something and then stopped himself.

'What about goal types?'

'It's in here somewhere… here we are. Forty six percent with the head, fifty two percent with feet. Two percent other.'

'They get a lot from the second ball?'

'Yes.'

It's a common mistake to assume most goals from corners are headers.

'OK. That's something we can work with. Terry, let's talk zonal marking and covering the rebound zone tomorrow.'

He gave me a thumbs up. We were still missing something but I couldn't put my finger on it.

'Give me a heat map of player positions.'

'Corners taken from the right or the left?'

'One of each. Let's start with the left.'

The arrowhead darted around the screen, bouncing off various icons. It didn't take long. We stared at the graphic for a few seconds. The blotches and swirls of red, yellow, and green always reminded me of the paintings Em used to bring home from nursery. Chirk's default was to overload the front post with a group of players and draw the defenders to this congested space, leaving one player isolated at the far post for a one on one.

'Who is that at the back post?'

'Weber.'

'How many has he scored?'

'From corners?'

'No, from fucking goal kicks.'

'Two already this season,' he stuttered. 'Seven in total over the past three seasons.'

'What do you think Terry?'

'We double up on him.'

I nodded. 'One man marking, the other zonal.' Terry scribbled a note on his pad.

Ross must have assumed his ordeal was over. Or perhaps it was wishful thinking. He closed the lid of his laptop. Shuffled his papers. Anything to avoid eye contact with me or his colleagues.

'Tell me about the corner area.'

He coughed twice to clear his throat.

'What do you want to know?'

'Everything. How tight is it? Will Slaney need to adjust his run up? Is there a slope? If so what's the angle of the gradient?'

His jaw tightened and eyes widened. He looked from me to Jordan Allen and back again.

'Do you have a photo you can show us?' said Allen, trying to bail him out. We sat and waited, watching the large screen, as Ross trawled the internet, eventually settling on a close up of one of the corner flags.

'This is the corner between the West Stand and the North Bank.' He coughed again but still his larynx wouldn't play ball. 'There's plenty of space for a decent run up,' he said almost in a whisper now.

I stood up and walked over to the screen. 'The problem is the pitch turf ends here, a metre from the corner flag. All of this is astroturf,' I said pointing to the dark green contour at the bottom of the picture. It messes with your head when you move from one to another so Slaney needs to practice taking only two or three steps.' Ross hung his head. I looked at the others. They had grown fat, dumb, and lazy under Bescond. And who could blame them. If no one is listening, why do the work?

'Listen guys. I'm going to push the boys to their very limits over the next four months and I am going to demand the same of you. Now one last thing. I didn't see any cameras on the training ground?'

'We make do with GoPros. Rossy and me wear them in training.'

'So no wide view cameras?'

'No.'

'No drone? Tell me you've got a drone?'

Grierson shook his head. 'But I've heard good things.'

'They're game changing.'

Like a hawk stalking a field mouse, the drone hovers above the pitch, adjusting its position to focus on certain players, or take a closer look at one of the thirds, or to zoom out for a wide angle, or move behind the goal. The aerial view decodes the blur of moving bodies, revealing shape and formations and the space in different zones. Decoy runs, passing lanes, and the ball that breaks the lines all become visible. We used it every day in Split. From time to time, I would stop mid-session and the boys would gather around a four-metre outdoor LED screen to watch the footage and take the insights back onto the pitch. The instant feedback loop accelerated their learning dramatically.

'This is what we used in Split,' I said holding up my phone. 'Buy one today. I want it up and running by Friday.'

14

Forwards win games, defenders win titles, as a wise man once said, and Athletic's back line was haemorrhaging goals. Bescond had singled Fabio and Valon out in his on-camera meltdown after the Flixton game, but the two veterans were symptoms of the illness, not the cause. The white blood cells fighting a losing battle as the infection spreads through the body. The systemic faults in the way Bescond set up his team – too much space in and between the lines, no pressure on the ball – had left Valon, and Fabio behind him, isolated on the transition, fracturing both men's confidence. Archer had touted the pair around Europe, only to discover that shop soiled players on high wages are hard to sell. And when he did put together potential deals, both men turned him down flat, insisting they would rather see out their lucrative contracts. All players crave approval and find it hard when they are not wanted. Some try to prove a point, using the grievance to fuel an upturn in performances, but most fall into a slow tailspin of decline. Rebuilding their confidence and motivation was high on my list of priorities.

Fabio took a seat. He was anxious to impress, to show me he still had what it takes, even if he didn't quite believe it himself. He wore a sleeveless vest and a forced smile. The crucifix, which he kissed after every penalty save, hung over his collar.

'Thanks for what you said at the presser boss.'

'I meant every word,' I replied, fixing him in the eye. 'You're a great keeper Fabio and you're my kind of keeper. Strong with your feet as well as your hands, and that's crucial for how we're going to play. I need you to give us that extra man in defence when we play out and be ready to sweep behind a much higher line. It's a completely different way of playing.'

I pointed to the eighteen-yard box on the grid.

'Here is the source, where so many of our goals will start. The other teams will quickly figure this out. They'll hunt you down, put you under pressure.' He flinched. 'That's good, it free's up another player or two in defence or midfield, gives us the overload. But you need to be ready for it, technically, tactically, and psychologically. The key is to rehearse decision-making and where to pass the ball.'

'I'm good with that but we have to make sure JC doesn't go walkabout, if not it'll all go to shit.'

'Don't worry, he'll get it soon enough. You've got to trust me on this one.'

I asked Fabio about his ambitions. He looked surprised, as if he hadn't thought about this in a long time and took a moment to think before responding.

'Stay fit. Improve my numbers. Play on until my kids are old enough to remember watching me.'

'What about the World Cup?'

He shrugged and gave me an ironic smile. 'Ain't gonna happen.'

'Come on. Canfari only has the shirt on loan. It's yours whenever you want to take it back. The question is do you want it?'

'I'd give anything,' he said quietly.

'Then that's our goal,' I said with a clap of the hands. 'Everything we work on for the next four months is a step towards it. Deal?'

'Deal.'

I told him the best way to achieve any big goal is to break it down into small parts, and that there were a couple of things I wanted to look at. I turned the TV on. Rob Meade's scowl filled the screen. Athletic's former captain was mid-way through his latest rant, cataloging everything that had gone wrong since he retired. '…I feel for the guy, I really do. He's got no big club experience. The squad is unbalanced.' He shook his head in despair. 'Recruitment has been poor, really poor. They're a million miles away from City and Bury.'

As he spoke, I searched unsuccessfully for the input from my laptop.

'And something's not right in the dressing room. When I was at the club…'

'Let me have a go,' said Fabio taking the remote from me. Within seconds the heat map appeared on the screen.

'I want to talk about shots from distance.'

Fabio's smile vanished.

'Sure,' he said quickly. Too quickly. The culture under Bescond was driven by fear, and fear suppresses a team's hunger, its appetite for risk and honesty. I needed to strip all that away. Create a safe environment where the players could be open about their feelings and any weaknesses in their game and understand that the pursuit of high standards is not about perfection. Mistakes, big and small - the under hit back pass, the free header glanced wide, the clumsy tackle in the box - are an intrinsic part of the game. And you can't let a mistake define you. It's about stepping up and owning the mistake. Learning from it, not dwelling on it.

'I've looked at your positioning for shots from distance. You're a metre and a half closer to the line than two years ago.'

Fabio was defensive at first. 'It's an adjustment. That's all.'

I pushed harder. 'I want to know why. Why increase the angle? Why give them a bigger target to aim at?'

He ran his hand through his jet-black hair.

'Your reflexes deteriorate as you get older. Goalkeepers curse Marc calls it. Shuffling back gives me more time to react.'

'Did you shuffle back when you won the European Cup?'

'No.'

'The league titles?'

'No boss. But we did the tests. Marc showed me the results.'

Juppé had got inside Fabio's head and filled it full of shit.

'It's confirmation bias Fabio. He just sees what he wants to see.'

Fabio shook his head.

'It's true. I've watched you myself. Your reflexes are still world class. The Williams goal was a fluke, it could have happened to anyone. If you want to get back to your level you are going to have to be brave. Play like you used to.'

I was pleased to see Valon waiting outside as Fabio left for his blood tests and daily weigh in. My message about time keeping had obviously landed. The two men exchanged fist bumps as they passed. Valon walked with exaggerated slowness, as if he was saving every last kilowatt of energy to leave out on the pitch. He was the alpha dog, a leader of men, built like The Terminator, and a case study in marginal gains. Yoga to maintain flexibility and strengthen his hamstring and glutes. A vegan diet to speed up recovery. Ballet lessons to compensate for his high centre of gravity and trampolining to maximise his leap.

We chatted about the match the previous evening, a dreary goalless draw, Eccles suffocating the life out of the game with a defensive pillow to the face. Valon approved of their discipline and organisation, contrasting it with our own problems. He asked me about my time in Croatia. I trod carefully, mindful of old wounds. We spoke about Split and Zadar, sailing in the Kornati islands. He didn't mention his childhood, fleeing the bombs. His dad and fifteen year-old brother taken away at gun point, never to be seen again. The hard years that followed. Then we got down to it. I took him through the grid one more time, reiterating the messages from our team meeting and thanking him for his support.

'You're the boss. I'll always back you in front of the group, but if something's not working I'll tell it straight in here.'

'I hope so. I want everyone to feel they can speak up. That's the culture I'm used to. I've not coached…' I stopped myself from saying *at this level.* '…in this league before. I'm open to input, different points of view, especially from the senior players. But ultimately I'm paid to make decisions, and will live or die by them, so when I do everybody has to get behind them.'

'Damn right. And anyone who doesn't, will have to answer to me.'

The sounds from the training pitches drifted our way. The kids from the academy calling for the ball or laughing at a miscued shot. The whistles and instructions from the coaches.

'So what's on your mind?'

'We lost our way under Alain, forgot how to defend as a team. I love your ambition but when you have a leak you fix the pipes, you don't turn on the taps. We need to concentrate on the basics, keep clean sheets again, get the belief back.'

'Forget about what you might have read or heard, I'm much more defensive minded than people think. But we're going to defend higher up the pitch. Control space and defend with the ball.'

He looked unsure. I moved over to the tactical board.

'Possession is the best defender in the world. Which is why I want you to play two positions. CD when we're defending, then stepping up into this zone when we have the ball to become the second pivot. Looking for the forward pass and no more hitting it long. It's all about short passes and movement.'

'I get it, I know how your teams play. I watched the tapes last night. But Vara and me don't have the speed to get back for the balls in behind. We'll be cut open on the transition.'

In his prime, Javier Varallo was one of the greats, a rampaging right back, and a bull of a man, with thighs the size of tree trunks. For years the Spaniard terrorised opposing left backs, thundering past them on the overlap, chalking up goals and assists but at thirty-six, those days were long behind him. Now he dialled in his performances, making one or two runs per half and then spending the rest of the time recuperating, like a singer who can no longer hit the high notes, cashing in with a Vegas farewell residency. It was hauntingly sad to see teams target him. For players with a sliver of his ability to go past him as if he wasn't there. And now it fell to me to call time on his great career.

'I'm working on that.'

Valon didn't look convinced.

'Here's my promise to you Vallo: I'll make sure you have the conditions to succeed. Protection in front, pace alongside, and structure and order all around you.'

I took him through my idea to replace Varallo. Valon listened without saying a word and thought long and hard before responding. His face was a trophy cabinet, a museum for the spoils of war. A twice broken nose. Scars on his temple and chin. Dental work to disguise broken teeth.

'That could work.'

'It will work. Trust me.'

Valon folded his arms and leant back in his chair, as if to say 'I'll be the judge of that.'

'Jose also has a big role to play,' I continued. 'Give me your honest assessment of him.'

'I'll start with the positives. He's quick, real fast, and tougher than he looks. Good in the air, rarely goes to ground, and he works. But he doesn't want to defend. The best defenders are like submarines, always on patrol but you barely know they're there. They leave no trace, no drama. But JC wants the headlines, the crowd chanting his name. And he lacks concentration. I have to be in his ear for ninety minutes.'

'His pace has stunted his development. He's never learnt to anticipate, because he's always been quick enough to react.'

'Exactly,' he said looking at me differently.

'So, we're going to drill him until he can find his zones in the dark.'

I asked Valon what went wrong under Bescond. He didn't hold back.

'You hear a lot about Alain being a tyrant but the truth is he didn't work us hard enough. There wasn't enough gym based work, no squats or deadlifts, and so the group lost its physicality, just look at the GPS data. In the end me and a few of the boys booked in our own sessions but Alain didn't like that either. He felt we were making a point and told us to save our energy for the weekend. I'm pleased you're putting it right.'

'We've got a lot of work to do,' I replied.

In truth I was shocked by the players' physical condition. The grotesque sight of elite players waving their arms in a windmill motion to cope with a stitch on the training ground. Incapable of getting up and down the line. Physical stats and pressing numbers that were nowhere near where they needed to be. It was nothing short of neglect by Bescond, complete dereliction of duty, and the contrast with my previous group could not have been more stark. Players who earned less in a year than what their Athletic counterparts took home each week, were in vastly better shape and could outrun, outlast, outfight them. And so, on my second day I introduced a punishing new training block to increase the boys' strength and endurance to the level required to play a high intensity, high pressing game. I upped the load significantly: interval training (five sets of three-minute runs where the players had to come closer and closer to their own individual maximum heart rates), running with the ball drills, followed by forty-five lengths of the pitch at a fast pace. The increased exertion proved too much for Thomas Dekker who threw up after his final length of the pitch. He bent double and retched until he could bring up no more, then wiped his mouth on his sleeve, while an ashen-faced Slaney looked like he would pass out at any moment. Several of the other players lay flat on their backs. Bailey feigned an injury ('I've tweaked my Achilles gaffer. I'd better sit this one out.') Valon and one or two of the senior pros leant their hands on their knees, sucked in air and exchanged approving smiles as if to say 'This, *this* is what we have been missing.'

'Right, we go again,' I told the players. They were too weary, too out of breath to even protest. Kenny Walsh from the conditioning team looked on with his mouth open. He said he had never seen the players work so hard and warned me that the increased load was too much too soon. That someone would break down. I brushed these objections aside. Pushed them harder the following day.

'What's the latest with your contract?'

'Nothing doing. They've made it clear they want me out, and even if they changed their minds, I'm done here. It's time to move on.' He spoke with the wounded pride of a man unaccustomed to rejection, a man whose name was always first on the team sheet.

'Anything lined up?'

His jaw tightened.

'A couple of offers but I'm holding out for Milan. The Italians know how to treat old defenders.'

He gave a deep sigh.

'And you know what, I should have gone last summer on my own terms. It's been one season too many. I don't have the legs for it anymore.'

'Bollocks. You're going through a tough period but this is a blip not a decline. You're only thirty-three. The best is still to come. We'll turn things around, and then you'll have the whip hand. And remember no one is looking out for your interests here. Everyone has an angle. The club, your agent, me, so the only advice I can give is do what's right for you and your family. Work out what that is and let me know how I can help. Just don't rush into anything you'll regret. You're in control of the process. Make sure it works for you. OK?'

Valon took all this in but did not respond immediately. Instead he continued to appraise me, his brown eyes scrutinising my features. Eventually he broke the silence.

'That's the plan. I've given this club everything. Now it's time to put me and my family first.'

'That's fair. It's a short career. Tell me about Slaney.'

'He's a parasite.' Valon spat the words. 'He plays for himself, not the team.'

Like all successful strikers, Slaney was a highly functioning addict, hooked on the warm rush of euphoria that comes from goal scoring, the crack cocaine of football. Go a game or two without finding the net and the sweat and shakes start to break out. Then they will do whatever it takes to score the next hit: dive in the box, punch the ball in the net, stick out a boot to deflect a shot that's already going in, even if there is a risk of being offside, put the ball in an area where their team-mate has no option but to play it back to them. You see the cravings bubble to the surface every once in a while. A group of players squabbling over who takes a penalty like a bunch of coke heads fighting for the last wrap. They'll take any help they can get. Some find religion. Others go with superstition. Blessing the pitch with Holy water. Only pissing in a certain urinal before a match. Changing shirts at half-time if they didn't score in the first forty-five.

'A winner improves other players, lifts the team, but Slaney, he…' Valon paused to search for the word. '…he inhibits the others. Restricts them. They make a mistake or they don't pass to him because there's a better option and he goes crazy. You can see Kuipers shrink everything time he shouts at him. If Archer had any sense, he'd get rid of him.'

15

To re-energise a club and get every member of staff moving in the same direction, you have to make time for people. Show them how important they are to you. So while the boys changed for training - the dressing room at Datchet was their space, not mine - I called in on Ken Fenton.

'Everything alright for Saturday Ken?' His smile widened when I remembered his name.

'Yes gaffer. We're wearing the new fourth strip for the first time. It's a bit different,' he said awkwardly.

'But we're at home.' And Aldershot play in chalk white. 'Why aren't we wearing the stripes?'

'Orders from on high gaffer.'

'What does it look like?'

'Let's just say it ain't an Athletic shirt, know what I mean?' he said, scrunching up his face, like a plumber inspecting someone else's handiwork.

I told Ken I would like to see it and followed him through the laundry, past the boot drier, which was blowing warm air into twenty-four pairs of boots, until we reached the kit room. The room was better than any gallery or museum. Row upon row of framed shirts covered three walls, every iteration of the famous maroon and gold shirt. The width and number of vertical stripes varying from season to season. Each frame also contained a photo and a short caption, handwritten in beautiful copperplate. I leaned in to take a closer look at the 1986-87 shirt with its controversial gold pin stripes, an ill-fated experiment that provoked a boycott and a petition, followed by a mid-season climb down. The photo showed Stanislaw 'Stan the man' Pilecki with the ball at his feet. Socks rolled down, no shin pads, the index and middle fingers of his right hand pressed against his temple in a two-fingered salute, a goalkeeper sprawled in the mud bath behind him. The caption read:

'Stanislaw Pilecki salutes the fans in the Hill End before scoring, after running the length of the pitch and rounding Walsall's Keeper. The flamboyant Polish winger was fined two weeks wages for disrespecting his opponents. Pilecki scored six goals for Athletic in twenty seven appearances before moving to Bari. The goal was voted number nine in the Athletic supporters' association's top ten goals of the twentieth century.'

Above this was the 1979 – 1980 shirt, the first to carry a sponsor's name, a long forgotten Japanese electronics company.

'Magnificent, in'it gaffer? We've got almost every shirt going all the way back to 1906. Mr Valbuena bought a shed load at an auction a few years ago to help us fill in the gaps. Some geezer had been hoarding them in his loft.'

Some managers collect fine wine or racehorses. Others ulcers and divorce settlements. For me, it has always been football shirts. It started with the 1986 England top (shadow stripes and a blue V neck with red and white trim) which was a birthday present from my grandparents. I wore it with two white Slazenger sweatbands on my left wrist to imitate Gary Lineker's wrist cast during the World Cup that year. Next was a 1988 Arsenal shirt. Then I branched out. Using money scraped together from a paper round and long Saturday afternoons on the Sainsbury's fish counter, I bought the red and white Monaco top worn by Glenn Hoddle, George Weah, and Emmanuel Petit when they lost 4-3 to Marseilles in the Coupe de France Final.

Another month of skinning cold, slimy fish – darting out the back to catch the halftime scores on the radio – enabled me to buy the 1990 Dutch top, a masterpiece by Adidas. A shirt made up of triangles for a team that played in triangles. From a second-hand shop behind Camden market, I tracked down the Denmark shirt, with its two panels of contrasting pin stripes, worn by Laudrup and Preben Elkjaer when they beat Uruguay 6 – 1 in Mexico '86. Every time I look at the shirt, I am reminded of Laudrup's second goal, a spellbinding mix of control and awareness, which like Negrete's volley, is forever overshadowed by Maradona's slalom run against England. Laudrup, a man with time, ability, and vision to spare, gliding past one, two, three defenders, rounding the keeper and finishing from an acute angle.

'Here it is boss.' I turned to look at Ken who was holding the new shirt up to his chest. 'What do you think?'

From what Ken had said as we passed through the laundry room I was expecting something similar to the Celtic hoops, but this was very different. Three wide horizontal bands, yellow at the top, white across the middle, and green at the bottom.

'I see what you mean. It's not going to work. Swap it out for the home strip.'

'Problem is, Mr Wheaton has told us we have to use it this weekend.'

'Let me speak to him. I'm sure we can sort it out. And I want to change Fabio's strip.'

'Afraid you'll need to speak to Mr Wheaton about that too.'

Scooter was in a meeting but returned my call an hour later.

'Hey bud, what's up? I'm in Seoul.' In the background, I could hear laughter and the murmur of conversation, the sound of cutlery on china.

'What can I do for you?'

'It's the new shirt Scooter—'

'It's beautiful, isn't it? Our best yet.' His words came at me at high velocity.

'It's not right for Saturday. I'm trying to reboot the club, remind people—'

'What better way to signal a change than a new kit? Excuse me Miss, three more Martinis and some more of these.'

'No, you don't get it. I want to re-build the connection between the players and fans, remind the boys what it means to be an Athletic player.'

'You can do that with your team talk. MISS. I'm sorry. Change of plan, can we have a bottle of champagne. Bring us the good stuff.'

'It's not the same Scooter. Pulling on the Athletic shirt should mean something. A hundred years of history and—'

'You're overthinking this one buddy.'

'I'm serious. How can we expect them to play for the shirt when they are not wearing the shirt? Yellow, white, and green has no connection with the club. They could be playing for anyone.'

'It's saffron.'

'OK saffron but—'

'Look bud, here's the deal. This Saturday is Republic Day in India when the whole country comes together to celebrate their independence from the evil Empire. We've spent months coming up with a shirt that looks like the Tiranga—'

'The what?'

'The Indian flag. It's a fantastic opportunity to build brand awareness in a major growth market and with the Indian diaspora.' His voice was revving up, reaching an even higher gear. 'Did you know there's thirty million non-resident Indians around the world?' He paused waiting for a response that didn't come. 'Anyway, there's no question of dropping it now. The contract is in place. Millions of replicas go on sale tomorrow. Sorry my friend but you've got to see the bigger picture. After all it's only one game. We'll be back in the stripes the week after next.'

Eighty per cent of success in football management is knowing when to pick your battles, so I rolled. 'OK, Scooter. I hear you.'

'That's the spirit. Pragmatism will get you everywhere in this business.'

'There's one thing you can do for me.'

'Name it.'

'I want to change Fabio's strip to all-black. Make him look more imposing in one on ones.'

'We never change kit mid-season Joe. You should know that. It's the same with the Tiranga, you end up with unsold stock, and little Johnny who just got a shirt for Christmas won't be happy. But let me speak to the folks in Oregon, see what we can do.'

16

We concentrated on just two patterns of play in that first week. Every morning, after thirty minutes of rondo, we split the squad into teams of eleven. One player from each team stood in each zone, mirroring the positions I wanted them to assume when our keeper was in possession in a match. The teams took it in turns to progress the ball through the thirds, bypassing two banks of fluro yellow PVC mannequins, and attack the opposition box where our third-choice keeper stood guard. As soon as one team completed their shot on goal they ran back to their positions and watched as the other team worked the ball higher up the pitch. Each team alternated between starting with a goal kick or a back pass and had to contend with three of the academy players who pressed the keeper and the centre-backs.

In the first pattern the centre backs split to take up wider positions, close to the space normally occupied by the fullbacks, and the defensive midfielder dropped deep to form a triangle. They exchanged passes to beat the press and then moved the ball on to an inverted fullback in one of the two half space channels just beyond the halfway line. A lateral pass returned the ball to the pivot who had moved out of defence to occupy the space inside the centre circle. He played a quick, sharp pass to a player lurking in the half space corridor between the opposition lines, who then played it in behind for the wide forward to run onto and shoot or feed a teammate in the box. The initial phase of playing out from the back was the same for the second pattern but when the ball reached the pivot in the circle, one of the forwards dropped deep to receive a short vertical pass and immediately played it round the corner to set up a run in behind from an overlapping eight or ten.

Archer watched the session, as usual, from his golf buggy, filming clips and making notes on his iPad. Like all those that followed, our first early morning meeting at Datchet took place in his office. Not once did he make the short journey down the corridor to come to me. Archer used these meetings to manage upwards. To squirrel away knowledge he could pass off as his own or put on record his misgivings about certain selection decisions. The room had been requisitioned from the performance analysis team as part of Archer's land grab. It was bigger than the first team dressing room and sparsely furnished. A venue for an occasional drop-in rather than a place of work. When I arrived, Archer was seated behind his desk poring over the team sheet for my first game in charge, searching for faults to pick at. It didn't take long.

'Javier is on the bench. Has he picked up a knock?'

'Zharnell comes in for Varallo. He's got the speed and energy we need, creates good angles—'

'WHAT?' he spluttered.

I explained my concerns about Varallo's pace and the lack of control at the base of midfield.

'Zharnell gives us both. The legs to get up and down the line and deal with anyone who gets in behind. And he can come inside and give Valon and JC another option when we build play.'

I had experimented with Zharnell in this position in training. There was nothing makeshift about his performances. He used his pace in the final third to go around his man on the outside and play a smart low cutback or a fizzing outswinging cross targeting the zone between the keeper and the defensive line. He struck the ball hard with unerring accuracy, even when running at full speed. And he looked so assured when he came inside in the first phase. He drifted into the space in front of Valon and took the ball on the half turn with his hips pivoted and his body at almost ninety degrees to his ball-playing teammate, creating options for himself with his body shape. Typically, he collected the ball with his back foot, but his positioning also enabled him to let the ball run past him if a pocket of space was available.

'You're making a big mistake here son. *Huge*. Javi is one of my best signings. Do you know how hard I worked to get that deal done? The promises and assurances I had to give him. You don't ditch him.'

As on our first day, I held firm. But this time I tried to play around Archer rather than through him by appealing to his ambition.

'The fans will love it. Zharnell is one of them. We'll sell it as part of a new dawn. A glimpse of a brighter future. And we both get the credit for re-opening pathways from the academy.'

Starting Zharnell would also signal to the rest of the group that selection was now based on merit and work rate in training rather transfer fees or past achievements. And I figured that pulling on the shirt would mean more to Zharnell than any hired gun. He had been with Athletic since he was eight, understood the club's history and values, and would run his body into the ground for the badge.

Archer sat back in his chair and looked up at the ceiling, calculating the odds and trying to establish whether it was a zero sum game. Did a positive outcome for me automatically equate to a setback for him? Or could he spin it in his favour? Eventually he must have concluded that if Zharnell played well he could find a way to take the credit, and if not he was sufficiently insulated against any backwash.

'You could give your man a shot if you think he's ready.' He moved on quickly from this unexpected climbdown to the next item on his handwritten agenda.

'How did it go with Slaney?'

'Not good. I told him I would build a team around him, but he wasn't having it. Made it clear he wants out.'

This was not entirely true. In fact, it was an outright lie. I didn't try to talk Slaney out of a move away. Instead, I told him we both wanted the same thing and promised to do whatever I could to convince the board it was in everyone's interest to let him go. In return, I challenged Slaney to set the standards in the dressing room. To treat his few remaining matches as if they were his last moments on earth. I reminded him that legacy is about more than trophies and titles. 'How you carry yourself defines how you are remembered.' I warned him that Fidalgo's scorched earth tactics would shatter his bond with the fans. The hog's head on the pitch, burnt cars, and death threats that accompanied Harry Virgo's defection to Darlington was nothing compared to what he could expect. 'Handle this correctly though Ryan,' I advised him, 'and they'll still be singing your name years after you retire.'

I told him he must not be seen as the instigator. The only way to protect his reputation was to present himself as an unwilling participant, press-ganged into a move by a cash-strapped owner. 'Let the club' - by which of course I meant Archer – 'take the heat.'

This struck a chord with Slaney. He shook my hand, thanked me for my support, even offered to talk up my methods in his farewell press conference.

'What are you hearing?'

'*Nada*,' said Archer. 'It's all gone quiet. As I told The Owner last night, if we hold our nerve, he'll still be our player come the end of the month.'

'They'll be back with an improved offer. They've invested too much to walk away now. We should put a plan in place for who we would go for if he forces this through.'

Archer rode this challenge and then swerved around the next as if he was back on the pitch making one of those tricky, jinking runs, beating men with balance and control rather than speed.

'No, I don't want any suggestion we are prepared to let him go. You open that door a crack to take a peak outside and they'll flatten you with it as they barge on in. We stand firm, tie him down for two more years, refurb the squad in the summer, and everything will be just grand.'

He paused for a moment, stretched his arms out in front of him and cracked his knuckles. It was a gesture that conveyed more meaning, more nuance, than a thousand words. 'I may have conceded ground on Varallo,' Archer was telling me, 'but don't mistake self interest for weakness. This is my red line and I dare you to cross it.' But I refused to give him the satisfaction of a confrontation I could not win, and signalled as much with a non-committal nod of the head.

'Any other news? he said gathering up his papers.

'I had a good session with the performance analysis team.'

Archer blew air out of his mouth. 'PUTHHH. Rather you than me. They've got a bad case of data diarrhoea. Statistical squits. It just keeps coming and coming. A non-stop torrent of charts and graphs. You can see the boys sitting there thinking "so what?"' It's the Emperor's fucking new clothes and everyone's too scared to call it out. Yards per carry. Mid third regains. NP fucking XG. Jeez, give it a rest. We had none of this bollocks when I was playing. Lukasz Wyszkowsk would just say to us "you're the better team. Go out there and beat them and if you don't you'll have to deal with me." Nowadays it's total fucking paralysis by analysis. All these people justifying their jobs, filling the players' heads with nonsense about how amazing the other team is. That's not what you need. You wanna walk out the door feeling ten foot tall, that you can take on anyone.'

Bailey, with his unmistakable high-pitched laugh, and Zharnell entered the corridor, heading for the dressing room. They fell silent when they reached Archer's closed door, like schoolchildren tiptoeing past the head teacher's office. The laughter and jokes started up again once they reached the safety of the dressing room door and echoed back towards us. 'Beavis and Butthead are in early today,' said Archer. 'You must be doing something right.'

17

The narrow streets around Preston Park were a sea of people making the slow shuffle from the tube station and pubs to the turnstiles, doing their best to avoid the piles of shit from the police horses. Shouting hellos from afar to old friends on the other side of the street, grumbling at people pushing through ahead of them, or indulging in gallows humour about the team's chances. Fans queued to buy a programme, grab a bite to eat from the burger vans, or pick up a scarf or a 'one night in Leipzig' t-shirt from the stalls that lined the pavement. A couple of lads took a leak in someone's front garden. The owner of the house, who had seen it all before, rapped at the window half-heartedly, as the pair made a point of taking their time to zip up their flies.

From their usual place outside the club shop, the Hill End Steel Band shared good vibes, alternating between crowd friendly reggae - Could you be loved; Get Up, Stand Up – and the tunes to popular terrace chants. Songs to commemorate former players, trophies won in the good old days, and ancient feuds with rival clubs. Pockets of fans, a few pints to the good, shouted the words in time to the beat.

Inside the ground the atmosphere was simmering over a low heat as the stadium started to fill up. Atti the eight and a half foot friendly alligator - the result of a Junior Athletic competition back in the 1980s – did his rounds, bumping fists and high fiving kids in the front row, still dining out on his antics against Eccles when he mocked David Luna for writhing in agony at the first sight of a tackle.

Both sets of fans were busy with the ritual exchange of insults.

'SHIT GROUND NO FANS, SHIT GROUND NO FANS,' cried the Aldershot supporters.

Our lot returned fire with a volley of:

'YOU ALL LIVE IN A BOBBY DOYLE HOUSE, A BOBBY DOYLE HOUSE, A BOBBY DOYLE HOUSE.'

Out on the pitch, the players warmed up, like a pianist going through the scales. The grass freshly cropped to twenty one millimetres, no more no less, as I had asked. The sprinklers at work, long after they would normally be, dousing the pitch to create a slick playing surface that favoured a fast passing game. Fabio practising his reaction saves with Marc Juppé and the reserve keeper in a temporary goal in front of the Harold Chambers stand. The rest of the boys, still wearing their training tops, stood in two lines over in the corner by the East Stand, taking it in turns to sprint ten metres then jog to the back of the queue. After four or five minutes they switched to running backwards and then side steps. Digital advertising boards cycled through their neon messages from Athletic's partners. A Tyre company. A Hong Kong based bank. Beer, burgers, and sugary drinks. Gambling and spread betting websites.

Aldershot Town had long overstayed their welcome in the topflight, like the dinner party guest who won't take the hint, pouring themselves 'just one more glass' and uncorking another tiresome anecdote, as you stack the dishwasher and stare at your watch. After thirteen drab years of mid-table anonymity, they had found themselves in one long struggle against relegation, with three successive close shaves, including an unexpected victory against Chester City on the final day of the previous season, pissing on the champion's parade. Rather than undertake the necessary surgery on the squad, the owners preferred the placebo – taken twice a season – of chopping and changing their manager. But you can only cheat the hangman for so long and with just five points to their name, they were now on track to smash the record for the lowest points total. A home banker if ever there was one, and a great way to get off to a flying start.

***

'For fuck's sake. The goal is down the other end you prick,' screamed a voice in the stand behind us, after Zharnell gave the ball away again in our own half as we attempted to play out from the back.

'He's having a fackin beast,' said Terry throwing his water bottle to the ground. He was right, Zharnell was having a horror show. Two misplaced two passes in the first twenty minutes, with only a sprawling save from Fabio and a covering tackle from Valon preventing Aldershot from taking the lead.

Then in twenty third minute Zharnell scored a beauty… in the wrong goal. A diving looping header over the back-pedalling Fabio into the empty net. The own goal was a distant cousin, the one your family never talks about, to RVP's swan dive against Spain.

'Hook him now before he can do any more damage,' Terry urged, but you don't win over the dressing room in your first week by substituting someone before half-time, no matter how bad they are playing. Besides, I had a lot riding on Zharnell's selection - Archer was sure to tell anyone who would listen that he had advised against it - and I wanted to give Zharnell time to turn things around. As one pundit said that evening, it was this refusal to address what everyone else could see was not working, that hurt us the most. Five minutes before the break Zharnell conceded the softest of penalties. It happens all the time. A player makes a sloppy mistake, desperately tries to retrieve the situation, and only makes things worse. After failing to track the flight of a long diagonal pass, Zharnell dived in when all he had to do was guide the player and the ball out for a goal kick. The referee pointed to the spot, waited to see if the video assistant referee agreed, then used both cards to semaphore that Zharnell's match was over.

The mood of the crowd quickly turned ugly, boos and abuse drowning out the smattering of sympathetic applause. A guy in his fifties wearing an expensive Barbour coat screamed racist abuse at Zharnell as he reached the entrance to the tunnel. The two stewards nearby just looked the other way. It didn't seem to even register with Zharnell – he told me later, he had heard a lot worse – but I found myself shouting.

'HEY YOU, YEAH YOU, THAT'S ENOUGH. YOU CAN CRITICISE THE PLAYER BUT LEAVE HIS COLOUR OUT OF IT.'

Barbour Coat turned, and then started on me. 'And you can fucking do one as well, you fucking wanker,' he screamed, jabbing his finger in my direction. 'This is not your fucking club.' Several other fans joined in with calls of 'fuck off Hendricks' and 'zip it you tosser'.

'Get a photo and show it to security. Tell 'em I want him out at half-time,' I said to Natalia Castillo who was seated behind me. The crowd could see what she was doing and didn't like it. A downpour of coins and keys clattered onto the dugout roof. This stirred the stewards into action and they dragged Barbour Coat out after calling for back up.

My heart hammered my chest, like I had just set a personal best on the Beep Test, but I had to re-focus on the game. Two down, a man down, and the crowd on our case, it was going to be a long afternoon. The away fans, surprised and delighted in equal measure, taunted us with:

'CAN WE PLAY YOU EVERY WEEK'

and

'YOU CAN'T EVEN BEAT US'.

Our supporters' programming kicked in and there was a half-hearted retaliatory burst of:

'GOING DOWN, GOING DOWN, GOING DOWN,

GOING DOWN, GOING DOWN, GOING DOWN, *GOING DOWN*'.

But this was soon replaced by a loud collective groan as Kuipers, playing in a more central role, snatched at a shot from a good position on the edge of the box. Supporters on all four sides of the stadium were quick to vent their frustration.

'What a waste of fucking money.'

'You're *fucking* useless Kuipers.'

'I wouldn't piss on him if he was on fire.'

I watched Kuipers shrink after he heard these words. His shoulders dropped a couple of inches. He wiped a hand across his stricken face, glanced quickly, eyes darting left and right, at Slaney and his other teammates before jogging back into position. It was such a shame. He was incredibly gifted, but so fragile. It would take time and the right conditions to build him back up again.

When I entered the dressing room at half-time Zharnell was sitting on the bench, head in hands, not acknowledging his teammates. His socks and shin pads - custom made SAK Pro's, 'fail better' etched across the gold polymer in black tattoo font - were on the other side of the room but apart from that he showed no intention of getting changed. Like many players, Zharnell preferred to wear boots a size too small for greater feel and control and to reduce the chances of a rolled ankle. The only downside is less protection and his feet were a war zone, each digit swollen and bruised, blood trapped under the nails, like a hand caught in a car door. Putting a hand on his shoulder I said: 'Hey Zharnell, don't beat yourself up. No one died.' His shoulders started to heave.

I guided him towards the treatment room. Once inside I gave him a hug, and with that he started to weep on my shoulder. We stood there next to the defibrillator for several minutes until eventually he broke the embrace.

'Do you want to talk about it?'

'Nah boss, you need to get back in there.'

'Don't worry about that I'll speak to them in a minute. What's up with you?'

He looked away and then looked back. 'I'm sorry boss. I was flicking through my phone before kick-off…' He broke down again.

'Take your time.'

'My brother... Dom...' He paused and wiped his tears on his sleeve.

'He was killed when he was seventeen. Stabbed six times on his way home from training. They told us later it was a case of mistaken identity. Wrong time, wrong place they said, as if it would make us feel better.'

His voice trembled. 'The kid who did it was released yesterday. I saw a photo of him on Insta, celebrating with his mates in a pub near where we grew up. Laughing and smiling as if it had never happened. I thought I would be okay but I couldn't get it out of my head.'

I told Zharnell how sorry I was to hear this and offered to speak to the other players.

'Nah, boss. I'm OK. I'll tell them. But I don't want you to tell the media. I don't want to use Dom as an excuse.'

'It's no excuse. People will understand.'

'No, this is on me. I wasn't strong enough and now I need to own it.'

'OK Zharnell. But know this. Your brother would be proud of you.'

The second half was like one of those bad dreams that go on forever, in which you are at the mercy of events or forces beyond your control. Aldershot made the most of the extra man and the confidence that comes from taking an unexpected two goal lead. They found the space inside our reconfigured structure, laying bare the old problems, things that could not be fixed in four training sessions. A lack of control in midfield. No aggression or intensity. Too much distance between the lines. Energy sapping self-doubt at the first sign of adversity. I tried to rally the players from the touchline, but the shouting and clapping, the substitutes warming up, had no affect. Still the players shirked their defensive duties, hid from the ball when we were in possession.

The post-match media conference was a feeding frenzy. A relentless barrage of leading, loaded questions. About my tactics, in particular the insistence on playing out. My suitability for the role. The decision to bench Javier Varallo, and most of all, Zharnell's performance. Respect and loyalty are not automatically conferred on you with the job title. You earn it every day by setting high standards, being fair, and showing the players you will support and protect them come what may. So, I took the opportunity to show the group I had their backs and went on the offensive.

'Zharnell had a bad day today. He knows that. But let me tell you this, I've seen enough in training over the past week to know that he is an exceptional talent. If he wasn't at this club already, I would move heaven and earth to sign him.'

When I returned to the dressing room I was horrified to see that the boys were eating pizza.

'Where's the fucking nutritionist?' I asked Terry.

'We don't have one anymore. She and Dave had a massive barney and we haven't seen her since.'

'So who supervises the players' diets?'

'No one. We treat them like grown-ups. They all understand the basics, carbs and proteins, fruit and veg that sort of thing. Some of them have private chefs to do the cooking at home.'

This wasn't good enough. Nutrition is a science, and no two players are the same. They each have different vitamin or mineral deficiencies. Their metabolisms burn energy at a different rate and the physical workload over the season varies from position to position. At Split we individually tailored each player's lunch based on the training data from their GPS vests. We even introduced lessons on nutrition and cookery classes for the youngsters in the academy. At Athletic they were still eating pizza with processed meat that causes muscle inflammation. It was like something out of the dark ages. I was half expecting someone to light up a cigarette.

'The pizza is going to have to go. There's a golden hour straight after they finish playing when the enzymes in their muscles are still active and better able to absorb nutrients. They need to be eating a proper meal. Salmon, grilled chicken or eggs. Brown rice and quinoa. I'll ask Caroline to sort it out for the next home match and I want packed meals for away games. And we need to hire a full-time nutritionist as quickly as possible.'

'I'm sure Dave will only be too happy to oblige.'

Thomas Dekker licked his fingers clean, picked up another slice, then called out to me: 'You've had your first East Stand shower then boss. You've officially arrived.'

'I've seen worse,' said Terry. When we lost to Barnet they threw kebabs at Alain. Chilli sauce dribbling all down the back of the dugout wall. You could smell it for weeks. Facking awful. I've been in abattoirs that smelt better.'

'When we played Leipzig they always used to throw condoms at us. Fucks knows what was in them,' said Mats.

'Worst I've had thrown at me is a dildo,' said Kuipers, making an effort to join in the conversation.

'That's what happens if you put it in the wrong fucking hole,' said Slaney.

'Well you would know,' Bailey said helping himself to another slice of pizza. Slaney glowered and threw a rolled up sock at him.

'When I was a kid the Inter Ultras stole a scooter from an Nerazzurri fan, took it into the San Siro, set it on fire and threw it over the railings onto the empty seats below,' said Fabio.

'Wow,' said one of the players.

'I've lost count of how many times I have had bananas thrown at me,' said Omari Iretioluwa.

Just then the dressing room door was thrown open. The handle rebounded off the wall with a loud crack and The Owner staggered in. His eyes were wide, pupils as big as the pills he must have taken. He kicked a drinks bottle hard across the room, narrowly missing Valon's head. The big Bosnian didn't flinch. Archer who was standing nearby talking at (rather than to) one of the players averted his gaze.

'What the fucccckkkk was that, you dickless arseholes?' He screamed. 'You're a fucking disgrace. All of you.'

Then he turned on Dekker. 'That was the worst I've seen you play Dekker. The fucking worst,' he slurred.

Dekker ignored him and continued to eat pizza.

'Really? Am I boring you *Thomas*? Because if you're bored I can cancel your contract. Like that,' he said snapping his fingers.

The Owner stared at me as if he didn't recognise me and then slowly the penny dropped. 'Dude you need to get a grip. You can't give these lazy motherfuckers an inch.'

He helped himself to a slice of pizza, took a large bite, replaced it on the platter, and then left, colliding with the door post on his way out.

18

Bailey Price was a faulty lightbulb, flickering in and out of games. There were occasional moments of brilliance - the lobbed winner from thirty yards against City, a cushioned volley assist, drag backs from the gods – but all too often he was a bystander, lacking the fitness and desire to track back or cover when a teammate moved out of position. And there had been a drip feed of bad news stories: late for training, bust ups with girlfriends, banned from driving, smoking and drinking the night before a game.

Bescond persisted with him in his first season in charge, telling the media he would turn the boy into a man, but lost patience after Bailey vanished without a trace against Macclesfield. He laid into him in the post match presser, accusing Bailey of lacking the courage and mentality required to be a top level player and Bailey had now settled into the role of a benchwarmer, spending more time building the playlist for the pre-match sound system than on his fitness plan.

His childhood was a hothouse, a vicarious outlet for an overbearing father. Price senior was dismissive of English football youth development, dismissing it as Neanderthal. He set about doing it his own way, drawing up a sixty-page blueprint for his infant son. Translating French, Dutch and Spanish coaching manuals – in particular, he became obsessed with the French Football Federation in Clairefontaine – and dangling a sponge ball over Bailey's cot, rewarding every kick with a clap of encouragement. Not long after he could walk, Bailey was spending two hours a day working on his first touch and kicking the ball with both feet. Match play was discouraged as much as possible with his father preferring to concentrate on Bailey's technique. School matches couldn't be avoided but requests to play for the county and invitations to trials were politely declined.

I had asked the performance analysts to prepare a short profile of every player detailing their strengths and development areas, the positions they could play, and performance and fitness stats. I also asked Terry and the fitness coach to provide an assessment of their attitude, leadership qualities, and work rate. I flicked through Bailey's file. Seventy-two appearances. Forty starts, twelve goals – eight in his first breakthrough season - and thirteen assists. His progressive yards carried were good but had fallen away. His VO2 max score (millilitres of oxygen consumed per kilogram of body mass per second, a key measure of aerobic fitness and the body's ability to handle high intensity exercise) was fifty-five percent, four percentage points higher than mine, but way off the sixty-five to seventy percent you would expect of a professional footballer in their early twenties. According to Kenny Walsh it was a constant battle to get Bailey to do more than the bare minimum. 'You literally have to stand over him. Turn your back to help another player and he immediately ease offs. He uses minor injuries as an excuse to avoid strengthening and conditioning work.'

I had also scrolled through Bailey's social media posts. He was prolific, posting at all times of the day and night. Bragging about his lifestyle, with photos or video clips of his apartment, his dog, new clothes and jewellery. Sharing content from his sponsors to promote football boots and sportswear, fast food and soft drinks, video games. Even the most anodyne or incidental received hundreds of comments, and over the past few months the tone had turned nasty.

That was shit today even by ur standards.

Fucking useless.

Ever thought about a different career?

Get. Out. Of. Our. Club.

U R shite.

Please, please, please just fucking do one.

Hope you die you waste of space.

OUT

Do us all a favour and top yourself.

I looked across the desk at Bailey. Despite all the attitude and bravado, I already sensed he was utterly lost. He was short, a few pounds overweight, with just the slightest concave of a belly. His hair was dyed peroxide blonde - a fuck you to Bescond for criticising his lifestyle - and his outfit, even by footballers' standards, was extraordinary. Billowy black tented trousers. A black tabard, with gaps slashed in the back and four over-sized chrome zips in seemingly random positions, over the top of a black t-shirt. Pristine black unbranded trainers with silver laces wound around the length of the shoe on both sides. Chunky silver and chrome jewellery on both hands. A ring the size of a golf ball. A sturdy bracelet that looked like a manacle. And an earring that stretched down below his jawline on a silver chain.

I didn't waste any time with small talk. I asked Bailey what was stopping him from being the best player he could be. He blamed Alain's tactics, the other boys, his Dad for putting too much pressure on him. He complained about a toe injury, about having to fund his friends' lifestyles. Media intrusion and the haters online. I told him straight, that he had to look inside, be the leader of himself.

'You own your fitness and form in the same way you own your career. There's a whole support structure here but only you can do the work. You need to take control. Do the conditioning, think more carefully about what you put on your plate and in your body. Work on your acceleration over short distances, get nine hours sleep every night.'

Bailey grunted. 'Uh-huh.' He fidgeted with the bracelet around his wrist and showed no sign of taking on-board what I had told him. I tried a different approach.

'Do you know how cold it gets in Norway in mid-winter?'

Bailey looked up and shrugged. 'Cold.'

'Cold's not the word. It's fucking arctic. Minus twenty-seven degrees or more. So cold you can't open the car door because it's frozen shut. So cold your eyebrows freeze, your eyelashes freeze. The snot in your nose freezes. And the days are short. In December you get four, maybe five hours of daylight. You fancy that? Because that's where you're heading at the moment. A couple of years of chilblains, scrapping around in the frost in Bergen, playing in front of five or six thousand, and then out of the game by the time you're twenty-seven.'

'You think I care? Do you?' His eyes flashed with anger. 'Do you think I chose this life? That I want to be here?' I kept quiet. Let him pour it all out. 'I've been on a treadmill since I was a baby. Living out someone else's dream. I don't need to play for the next ten years. I've got a house in Chelsea. Apartments in Monaco and Dubai. My girlfriend is a model. Do you know what I do while I wait for her to get home? I count my millions. I've got more money in the bank than ninety nine point nine – I've done the maths – percent of people will make in their lifetime. I could walk away tomorrow.'

'Why don't you?'

Bailey looked at me.

'You only get one life.' I continued. 'Why waste it doing something that doesn't fulfil you?'

'You'll never understand.'

'There's a 23s match tomorrow night. I'm going to come along to see how you get on.'

This barely registered with him.

'See it as an opportunity not a punishment. A chance to do what you enjoy.'

'I don't enjoy football. I've never enjoyed it. I hate it. I've always fucking hated it.'

19

Finch Lane was the ghost of football past. A small, uneven pitch. A low, flat roofed seating area along one touchline. Faded, weather-beaten boards advertising local estate agents and motorcycle dealers, Indian restaurants and DIY stores. Four fifths of a waning moon lit up a cold dark sky. Piles of sand stained, compacted ice sat behind the goals, relics from the snowfall at the weekend. Relatives of both teams clustered together, out bidding each other with their exhortations. A guy in his sixties or seventies made slow circuits of the pitch with his black Labrador. A handful of families wrapped up warm, drank hot chocolate from flasks, after paying the five pound entry. And twenty two players, all wearing gloves, competed for the ball and their careers.

Athletic used to take pride in the local character of its sides, with players like Edwards, Bastin, and Whelan all born with a few miles of the ground, and Paco was never happier than when watching the youth team play, telling anyone who would listen how building for tomorrow was as important as success today. That all managers and coaches are just temporary stewards and the true greats are those who leave a club in a stronger position than they found it. Time and again, he convinced parents that Athletic was the right environment for their child to grow and develop as a player and a person, luring them away from clubs closer to home. It wasn't a difficult sell. His track record of improving every player he worked with spoke for itself. Now though, the academy was just another piece of collateral damage in Archer's war on competence. No player had made the step up in the past two seasons. Instead, they were scattered across Europe in season long loans or sold on at giveaway prices to provide the club with a short-term cash injection. As a result, the quality of the kids attracted to the development programme was also in decline.

Restoring the link between the academy and the first team was an essential part of my project. Too many players knew they would start each week irrespective of their previous performances. Younger players, playing without fear, would lift the team and provide competition for places, as well as demonstrating to the supporters that I understood the club's history and traditions. But only one or two - at best - of the players on the pitch that evening would ultimately make it, and killing a kid's dream is the hardest thing in football. To see the anger and tears in their eyes. To know the conversations they will have with their families. All you can do is shake their hand and tell them to go away and prove you wrong. A few filter down into the lower leagues, and a couple might bounce back, making their way the hard way. The rest either try their luck abroad, take up coaching roles, or leave the game altogether.

Bailey moped around in midfield making the occasional halfhearted challenge or showboating step-over, until he was felled by a full-studded tackle. After that he faded from view. It had been an empty, listless performance. Thirty minutes of squandered potential. The only glimpse of his outrageous ability was a gorgeous no-look pass with the outside of his boot. He threaded the ball through the gap between the two centre backs from forty yards, into space for his teammate to run onto. And then retreated back into his shell. Archer and Terry were both right. The pilot light of ambition had flickered out, and Bailey was unwilling, or unable to reignite it.

Despite this, the long journey down the M4 was far from a waste of time. It was, after all, the night I discovered Zito. The Brazilian teenager was a revelation. A tall, lean kid with a bush of straggly dark hair. He wore black compression shorts under his kit and Nike boots with a plain white swoosh. He possessed the raw pace that gives defenders night terrors but also the control and balance to dribble past players in tight spaces and had a wonderful variety of touches. Quick, short movements to bring a player towards him, then a sudden longer touch to push the ball into open space.

I turned to Tim Croft, the under 23's coach, who stood next to me on the touchline, bellowing instructions and admonishments.

'Who's thirty-three?' The under 23's didn't have allocated squad numbers.

'Brazilian kid. Calls himself Zito.'

'Like the '58 World Cup winner?'

'Yeah I guess so,' he said sounding unsure.

The 1958 team was another of my Grandad's favourites - if he had had his way, he would have named my Dad after Didi. He loved to talk about 'Mr Football'. How he invented the dry leaf free-kick with its sudden knuckleball swerve after he injured his ankle and could only kick with three toes. How when Sweden unexpectedly took the lead in the 1958 final Didi slowly walked back to the centre spot and said to his panicking team mates 'Relax! We're better than them.' How he celebrated Botafogo's 1957 Rio State championship by walking the five miles from his home in downtown Rio to the Maracanã Stadium dressed in his kit, accompanied by ten thousand Botafogo supporters. My grandad liked to remind me how Brazil won back-to-back world cups in 1958 and 1962, and that Didi was the standout player at both tournaments, but especially 1962 when he carried the extra load in Pele's absence.

'What's he like? Good learner?'

'Not sure,' said Croft through a mouthful of gum. I looked at him. It's your job to know his stride pattern, his dietary intolerances, his fucking dental problems.

'He's a stand in. Last minute,' he said reading my mind. 'From the twenties. Our left back let us down… CURTIS. CURTISSSSS! HAVE YOU GOT A LEFT FOOT? THEN FUCKING USE IT… had to go back to Girona for a funeral. Xab convinced me to take a punt on him. Been badgering me for weeks.' He jerked his thumb in the direction of Xabi Santillana, the under twenties coach, who stood on the opposite touchline filming Zito with a handheld camera.

At half time the players formed an energy gel slurping huddle around Croft. Zito stood on his own at the back of the group. Croft bawled at them for allowing their opponents to get back in the game as Xabi crossed the pitch. He paused near the centre circle to replace a divot with his heel and then joined me on the touchline. He was around five feet nine, with hair the colour of coal poking out from under his woollen hat, short closely trimmed stubble, and dark overbearing eyebrows that dominated the rest of his face.

'Zito looks the business,' I said to him. 'He's so positive, so good at taking the ball on the half-turn.'

'I've never seen a kid like him. He's got unbelievable ability and a top, top mentality. Always on himself. And a ferocious competitor. Hates to lose at anything. Matches, small sided games, shooting drills…' He laughed. 'Mini golf… he's always pushing himself to be the best. Got that hunger to improve.'

'Good habits?'

'The best. Always in on time, eats well, sleeps well, doesn't drink or party. Watches his clips. Takes it all onboard.'

It sounded almost too good to be true.

'What are his development areas?'

'Decision making could be better. He needs to learn he can't always carry the ball into congested tight areas. The opposition are too good at the higher level. But that'll come. And he's super critical of himself. I try to tell him "go easy on yourself" when he misses, "it's part of the game". But he finds that hard.'

Xabi clapped his gloved hands together, stomped his feet, anything to get warm.

'Football is all about moving on, being mentally prepared for the next action.'

'*Exactly*. This is what I tell him. But I love how much he wants it.'

He spoke with paternal pride about Zito's journey from street football in Belo Horizonte to the Athletic development programme. The courage he had shown in leaving his family and friends behind at fifteen and moving to the other side of the world. The growth spurt the previous year, when he gained five inches in six months. How he had struggled with the language, the cold weather, and the food.

'Got problems with his hamstrings?' I asked pointing to the compression shorts.

'No, just a precaution,' he replied.

Since Scooter and Anita's cost saving program, the club's resources, in particular the sport science and performance analysis departments, no longer trickled down to the under 20s. Not officially at least. So Xabi had used his considerable powers of persuasion to beg, borrow, and build his own sporting infrastructure, charming the medical team into conducting injury prevention assessments in their spare time. One of these reviews had identified an imbalance between Zito's quad and hamstring muscles on his dominant left leg, which meant he was more susceptible to a hamstring injury.

'We've got him on a strengthening programme, plus yoga, to stretch his BFLH.'

All the research suggests that a player with a shorter BFLH - or biceps femoris long head - is four times more likely to have a hamstring injury. Elongation is proven to mitigate the risk, with every half centimetre gain in length reducing the chances of a hamstring injury by 75%.

Croft continued to lay into the players.

'YOU FUCKING GET INTO 'EM IN THE FIRST TEN. NO DICKING AROUND.'

'I wanted him to prove to himself that he could cope with the step up. Play out of position against bigger lads.'

'Where does he normally play?'

I could see my breath in front of me as we spoke, a small cloud of moisture in the cold air, like fumes from an idling car.

'Wide left or as an eight on the left side of a midfield three. We use his pace to get round the outside.'

A throw-in was awarded to Athletic close to the the half way line early in the second half. After claiming the ball, Bailey took a long run up and threw himself into a forward somersault, rotating head over heals through the air. When he landed on his feet he launched the ball goalwards. The small crowd cheered but the referee blew her whistle.

'Aw, come on,' Bailey whined. 'You're kidding me right? There's nothing wrong with that.'

Croft was not amused.

'DO THAT AGAIN AND YOU'RE OFF,' he hollered.

A few minutes later, the ball went out again on Bailey's side of the pitch. This time he threw a deliberate foul throw with a short abbreviated motion, not bothering to bring the ball back over his head. It was an act of unforgivable petulance. The referee blew her whistle and awarded the throw to the other team.

'That's fucking it,' said Croft.

'Get him off,' I replied.

***

Athletic's right sided central defender hit a long clearance which was headed back towards the centre circle. One of Zito's teammates won the second ball and played it towards him in the left half-space. When the ball arrived he spun his man, brushed past another defender, adjusted his weight to cut inside a third, and then used his toes to delicately scoop the ball up and over the onrushing keeper. It was a beautiful goal in appalling conditions. There were no celebrations from Zito. No arms held aloft, no punching the air. He just trotted back to the halfway line, a hint of apology in his demeanour, as if he was apologising to the older boys for showing them up.

The Brazilian was raw, but he had everything. It was as if he had been created in a laboratory. A test tube baller with Ronaldinho's touch and balance, Ronaldo's pace and acceleration, and Kaka's ability to break the lines. Seeing him for the first time that evening, playing on a disgrace of a pitch, was one of the most thrilling moments of my life. Like visiting a ramshackle secondhand bookshop and finding a rare first edition in mint condition in amongst the piles of dusty reprints.

'We have to have him,' I said to Xabi as he gave Zito a double thumbs up. 'Tell him he's training with the first team on Thursday.'

'Yeesss,' said Xabi fist pumping the air in front of his stomach. 'We're doing a de-brief later; I'll tell him then.'

'Remind him this is the beginning of the journey not the end.'

I took Xabi through the plan for the session so that Zito would know what to expect.

'Tell him to stand tall. To not be fazed by the others. I want him challenging them from day one. And make sure he's there early.'

'No problem. Respecting the clock and other people's time is the first thing they learn with me.'

'TARI. MOVE UP WITH THE LINE. UPPPP!' yelled Croft after Athletic had flung another long ball forward.

'You should also take a look at Shan gaffer,' said Xabi pointing at a figure swaddled in a knee length jacket and maroon beanie hat warming up near the corner flag. 'He was one of the stand out prospects when we had him in the twenties. Great vision and game intelligence.'

'Why's he not playing?'

'He's had a couple of injuries and he doesn't suit Crofty's direct style, but trust me, he's a gem. So good in build-up. Never rushed, always played the right pass.'

It was a big call to bring through a player I had never seen, one who had not established himself in the under twenty threes, no matter how glowing the recommendation. I pointed at Xabi's palmcorder. 'You got much footage of him?'

He grinned. 'Stacks. Small sided games. Box drills. 11v 8. Two seasons of match play. I've coded every aspect of his game, with and against the ball. I'll pull together some clips when I get home.'

'Don't give me anything against easy opponents. I want to see how he performs away from home against the strongest sides.'

After the match, while the boys showered and changed in a portacabin behind the goal, I mingled with the parents of both sets of players. I signed a few autographs and repeated my mantra that *hard work beats talent when talent doesn't work hard*. Then Xabi and I sought sanctuary from the remorseless wind in the warmth of the club house. As with the rest of the ground, it was like stepping back in time. Two pot-bellied men played a quiet game of darts, taking it in turns to chalk their scores up on the blackboard. A small group fed coins into the fruit machine at the end of the bar. The speakers played forgotten childhood memories.

Xabi and I discussed our next opponents. Without any notes or charts or video clips, he provided a concise analysis of Fulwood's attacking and defensive shape. Their patterns in transition. The shifting trends in their non-penalty XG and the reasons behind their improvement over the past ten games. We dissected Fulwood's 1-4-4-2 mid-block and their tendency to allow teams to have the ball in the first third. How they swarmed around their opponents when they reached the middle third, weaponising the touchline by forcing play wide. I took him through my plan to isolate Fulwood's fullbacks by pinning their defensive midfielder and central defenders with just two players, creating an overload in both wide areas. After this, Xabi told me about a goal probability model he was working on.

'We evaluate every action, each pass, shot, or turnover, and assess how much this increases – or decreases – the team's chances of scoring,' he said in hushed tones. 'There's a lot of complicated modelling but basically, it's all about calculating and comparing the likelihood of scoring a goal after every touch of the ball. We use it to assess our players decision-making, their impact on a game—.'

'To show them what good looks like.'

'Yes! It's a really powerful learning tool.'

'Where do you get the tracking data from?'

'That's the catch. We can only do it for away games. Some of the other clubs take pity on us and share the data.'

'We've got to get optical tracking cameras at Datchet.'

'Damn right.'

There was a sudden noise as the fruit machine spewed out coins. 'Mine's a pint of Worthington's Alan,' called one of the darts players.

'What about movement off the ball? I asked him. 'Can you measure the benefit of a run that moves a defender away from where they want to be?'

'No, we've focused on actions with the ball but the principle is the same. You just need to code the event.'

What Xabi had described was hugely impressive. Streets ahead of anything we had built in my time in Split.

'Who designed the algorithm?'

His face broke into a wide smile. 'I've got a post-grad from UCL helping me out three mornings a week. The things she can do are unreal.'

20

The Transfer Steering Group met at Preston Park the following afternoon, six days before the window closed. Archer was swilling mouthwash in the executive washrooms when I arrived. After a long gargle he emptied the contents of his mouth and then left without saying a word or rinsing the sink. When I joined him in the boardroom he was seated at the far end of the table skimming through his pack of papers and twiddling his pen. I sat down next to Mike Brooker, the club's head of recruitment, who reported to Archer, and judging by the awkward silence, also had a difficult relationship with him.

Brooker and I discussed Bury's interest in Riz Fittousi while we waited for the other committee members to arrive. The attempt to sign the Algerian goal machine was a direct response to City's move to lure Slaney away. Out on the pitch two groundsmen, one in each half, cut intricate patterns into the grass with their ride-on mowers, racing to see who could finish first. Mick Harding, the head groundsman, monitored their work from the far touchline. He stood with one foot and one arm resting on his pitchfork, impervious to the wind and drizzle. At sixty-three, and with nearly fifty years' service to the club, Harding had seen it all. The rash of trophies in the seventies. The dark days in the eighties: crowd trouble, the descent down the divisions, and the constant threat of insolvency. Revival and resurgence under Paco, and money, status and success frittered away in recent years.

Rigg and Scooter arrived together making the short journey from Rigg's office. The chairman shuffled slowly and stiffly, like a player coming back from a hip injury. The bags under his eyes had inched closer to his cheek bones since I last saw him.

'Boy, fucking howdy, I need caffeine in my veins, right now,' said Scooter pouring himself a cup and taking several quick sips. He placed his right hand over his heart. 'Aaah, that's better. It's pumping again.'

Brooker mentioned Bury's interest in Fittousi.

'Classic game theory,' said Rigg. 'Prisoner's dilemma. Bury are scared witless about City's interest in Slaney, so they are looking to pre-empt it, but they're in danger of making it a self-fulfilling prophecy. If both clubs kept their hands in their pockets, they would save themselves a hundred million each.'

'City won't mind,' I said. 'Their whole model is built around driving valuations up and pricing us and Darlington out of the market.'

'Joe's right, said Brooker. 'Every player we're following has gone up twenty percent in the past week.'

'So apart from waiting for the price of a barrel of crude to go through the floor, what do we do?' asked Rigg.

'Be smarter than them. Find undervalued players and create a whole that is greater than the sum of the parts,' I replied.

'Think small, be small,' said Archer with a snort. 'We need to go toe to toe. Show the world that we are still a buying club.'

We waited for Anita to arrive, Rigg's authority draining away minute by minute. It was ten past two before she made her entrance, safe in the knowledge that no meeting would start without her. The apology was fulsome, but unnecessary. Rigg, the grey-haired frontman wheeled out to reassure investors, and Scooter the commercial rainmaker, liked to kid themselves that they ran the club, but the real power, I quickly came to realise, sat with Anita. She was the Tiger Mum to The Owner's assets, the architect of his complex company structure and opaque tax arrangements. And while she had no seat on the club's board or biography on the website, every major decision required her approval. According to Paco, she grew up in Hong Kong and moved to London to study law in the late 1990s. An affair with her professor, twenty years her senior, was followed by marriage, citizenship, and then divorce. After that, years of late nights and take-out food as she climbed the ladder at a City law firm. It was here that The Owner first formed his dependence on Anita, a reliance which grew with every M&A deal and regulatory complaint. She led the buy-out of potential competitors. Dealt with all the data breach class actions. Personally oversaw the settlements and super-injunctions for several young female employees.

Rigg cleared his throat and kicked off.

'Right, does everyone have their papers? Good, let's get going. Item one. Ryan Slaney.'

He addressed Archer.

'What's the latest Dave any progress in tying him down?

'Slaney's people are using the window and City's interest as leverage, but it'll get done. He's settled in London, the kids are in a good school, the wife is happy. I don't see him upping sticks for a few extra quid.'

Mike Brooker took his life and career in his own hands by contradicting Archer in front of Rigg and Anita.

'I disagree. He's playing us. It's one ludicrous demand after another. The latest request is an escape clause to allow him to leave for free if we fail to qualify for Europe.'

'Martinez has the same clause,' replied Archer, glaring at Brooker.

'It's not the same Dave,' said Brooker. 'Martinez's contract enables him to leave in the event that Catalonia breaks away from Spain and they are kicked out of the tournament. Slaney's people know there's no way we can agree to it. This is how Pascal works. Constantly putting up obstacles and then blaming us when discussions break down.

'How much are they asking for?' Rigg asked.

'£375,000 a week, and a £30 million loyalty bonus. Plus he wants to end the fifty fifty revenue share on image rights, which is worth twenty two million a year to us, and the freedom to endorse our partners' competitors,' said Brooker.

'You know what I think about negotiating with terrorists,' said Rigg. He glanced around the table. 'Any other views?'

Anita remained impassive. She never acted on instinct or emotion. Instead, she held back and processed the data and competing views before expressing an opinion. And while she was very open, very pragmatic up until she made a decision, she could not be shifted once she had made up her mind. So I offered my opinion.

'It would torch our salary structure. Turn every other player against us. We should sell him now, we'll never get a better opportunity—'

'LISTEN,' shouted Archer. Anger contorted the face that had sold a million shirts and broken a thousand hearts, hardening his soft features.

'He's the *only* fucking world class player we have left. If we lose him how do we persuade a Chinyembe or a Morales to join us?'

He threw his hands in the air, a habit acquired from a lifetime of challenging refereeing decisions. His eyes blazed through narrowed lids. Again I was transported back to the 2002 cup final, the disbelief and scorn that flashed across his face when the red card was brandished.

'This is where you've been going wrong,' I said, forgetting that the honesty of the dressing room is not welcome in the boardroom. 'We don't want to be the farewell tour for big name players who can no longer cut it. We need a core of younger, hungrier players who have something to prove and who can be sold for a profit in a few years' time.'

'You want us to become a fucking selling club,' said Archer.

'Every player has their price Dave,' said Rigg soothingly.

'He's a bad influence in the dressing room, a terrible role model for the younger players, and he's going to walk out of here on a free next year,' I continued. 'Think what we could buy with the money. A whole new frontline, more energy in midfield.'

'Guys. Guys, *GYOZA*,' said Scooter. 'Slaney's our tent pole. Our entire commercial strategy is built around him. If he walks half our sponsors go with him. Doc, Sahara, Fluid, HydroFron, Tungsten, KP, they all have break clauses tied to Slaney. That's sixty five mill gone in an afternoon.'

He turned to look at me.

'Do you have any idea how much merch he shifts? How many likes we get when we push out a video?'

He looked back at Rigg and softened his tone.

'We should settle on a figure close to his number, they won't be expecting the full amount, and then milk him to the cows come home, especially in the Asian tour.'

'Anita, anything you want to add before we take a decision?' Rigg asked casually.

'My position has not changed,' said Anita emerging from her Zen-like state. 'The commercial upsides trump all other considerations. So we do whatever we can to keep him - ceilings and structures are there to be broken - but if it's not done by the end of June, we cash in.'

'Well, that's settled. I'll leave it with you Dave. Now item two. Potential acquisitions.' Sitting tall in his chair - back straight, chin held high – Rigg summonsed up all his authority and reminded everyone that net spend had to be capped at forty million to balance the two previous windows. Anita confirmed this:

'That's the maximum spend in this window, but please don't feel you need to spend it all.'

'Quite right Anita. Mike, take it away.'

Brooker began his presentation with a short recap.

'We've focused our search on our two biggest requirements, beefing up the forward line and finding a replacement for Valon. But top quality, low cost, wide forwards and centre backs are not easy to come by. So our recommendation is to focus on a forward in this window, someone who can play off Slaney, and bring in a new centre back in the summer. We've narrowed it down to one principle target.'

Brooker put a photo on screen of Sándor Kocsis celebrating a goal with a knee slide.

'He gives us options. Can play in any shape, any system. Through the middle, wide in a front three, or as a ten. He's versatile and future proof—'

'What do you mean, future proof?' asked Rigg.

Brooker hesitated so I answered for him.

'He'll have no problem adapting if my successor wants to play him in a different role.'

Rigg took a moment to process this.

'I see. Very good. Carry on.'

Brooker continued with his presentation, summarising Kocsis's career. The breakthrough years in Budapest. Keeping Jerzy Galecki out of the team in Rome. The goal to send Portugal home early from the World Cup. His partnership with Slaney in Milan, and how he was available at a good price now he had turned thirty.

'What's our criteria?' I asked.

Archer shot me a look. 'No statistical bollocks if that's what you mean. We have three main questions. Does he want to wear the shirt? How many goals will he bring to the team? And can we afford him?'

'So no character profiles?'

'Well we—'

'Once you start looking for reasons not to do a deal, you'll always find them,' said Archer cutting across Brooker.

Character is as important as technical ability and tactical awareness. You need to know how players respond to adversity. The challenges they have overcome. Do they bend or break under pressure? How they react when the team falls behind or a teammate makes a mistake. Whether they are a leader or a follower. Do they have a winning mindset, that spark of defiance? How likely are they to settle in a different country, to gell with their teammates? Are they married or in a long-term relationship – which generally means more stability in their private lives - or do they like to party? What's their work rate like? Their energy levels and movement during transitions of play?

'What sort of things do you suggest we look at?' asked Anita, showing interest. I summarized the thirty-point checklist we used for all transfer targets at Hajduk, adding that I had vetoed at least two deals after speaking to former teammates of the boys we were looking to bring in.

'A lot of clubs trawl through social media now,' said Scooter. 'Looking for any sign of inappropriate behaviour or intolerant attitudes.'

Rigg stifled a yawn. 'It's just as well Facebook didn't exist when I was at Oxford.'

'I'm sure The Owner would be interested in seeing a profile,' said Anita, folding her arms. Archer slumped back in his chair.

'Yes, it sounds eminently sensible. You should see the level of screening CCHQ does, trying to weed out the fruitcakes and the loonies,' added Rigg, falling into line.

'What's the deal structure Mike?'

'Sixty five million up front. Then there's the add-ons. Fifteen after twelve months…'

There was a sudden scream of 'GOLLLLLLLLLLL ARCHAAAAAAAA!' Brooker didn't skip a beat.

'…followed by another ten after two years. Eight million for every trophy he wins—'

'Every trophy?' asked Rigg.

Archer punched out a reply and then placed the phone back on the table. The lock screen image was his season ticket to immortality. That bicycle kick against Barcelona back in 1998. Archer in low orbit, his Adidas Copa Mundials, with their kangaroo leather uppers, locked and loaded.

'Yes,' said Brooker.

'Have you carved out the community shield?' asked Rigg.

'It's a standard clause now since the problems we had with Banon. They're fine with it.

Rigg nodded. 'Good. Anything else?'

'Another seven million after seventy appearances. They wanted fifty, we said a hundred, so we settled in the middle.'

Scooter couldn't help himself.

'Hate to break it to you bud, but you're a little short of halfway.'

'What's five games between friends?' replied Brooker not allowing Scooter to derail him. Each club has its own way of determining what constitutes an appearance. I asked about our definition.

'Starting eleven or more than thirty five minutes from the bench,' snapped Archer.

'The fee is too high. We should be paying fifty tops,' said Scooter.

'Not a chance,' said Archer. 'I've spoken to Klaus. He told me they can't afford to go any lower.'

'Mandy Rice Davies,' said Rigg. The room fell quiet as everyone tried to figure out what he meant, until Archer provided the assist.

'Come again?'

'Well he would, *wouldn't he*?' said Rigg wearily. 'This is poker Dave, he's hardly going to show you his hand. Scooter's right. You have to push harder and be prepared to walk away. They need this more than we do.'

Archer's face darkened again. 'We're already shafting them. They know it, we know it. Push any harder and the whole thing will fall apart.'

'So be it,' said Anita. 'We send a message to every other club or agent who wants to try it on with us. And I suggest we hear what Joe has to say before we take any decisions.'

'Splendid idea,' said Rigg. 'Joe, the floor is all yours.'

Archer closed his eyes and took a series of slow, deep breaths. It felt like only a matter of time before he snapped.

'The first thing to say is my names are part of a bigger plan to overhaul the squad over the next three windows. I've looked at who is competing for each position today, who has the potential to step up from the academy in the next eighteen months, and then looked outside the club to identify targets for the short, medium and long-term. Who we would sign tomorrow if we had a serious injury versus who we should bring in next year or the year after if their development continues on the same trajectory.'

Archer didn't take kindly to this incursion into his territory and tried to beat me back, first with a metal pole. ('How can we let a guy who's never won a game in this country dictate our transfer *policy*?') And when that fell on deaf ears, special pleading.

'We agreed I have the first and last word on all signings.'

'And that hasn't changed. But the committee exists for a reason.' Anita paused to let her rebuke sink in. 'Carry on Joe.'

'Firstly, we need someone at the base of the midfield who can shield the defence, drop in and bring it out. I've identified three options, different ages, different prices. Of the three, I strongly recommend Dani Linares.'

I played a selection of clips. Linares recycling the ball under close pressure, breaking lines with balls played to feet or into space. A hook turn, the Spaniard bending his knees, transferring his weight, then dragging the ball behind his standing leg, to create space in the tightest of areas. A succession of defensive actions. Then a rapid montage of first touches - Linares bringing the ball under immediate control and moving it away from the nearest man - followed by more passes.

Archer drummed his fingers on the desk, trying to put me off my stride.

'David, *please*,' snapped Rigg. 'Okay Joe, bash on.'

'What I love about him is how he plays with his head up. Watch here how he scans before he receives the ball.'

Linares looked over his shoulder as the ball came towards him, mapping the location of teammates and opponents.

'He's always two moves ahead.'

'Is he on your radar Dave?' asked Anita.

'I saw him against Atlético. Didn't do much.'

They used to say the same about Gilberto Silva until he was injured, only then did people realise how important he was to Arsenal.

'Didn't he have a bad injury?' asked Brooker.

Rigg stifled another yawn.

'Yes, torn meniscus, left knee. That's how I got to know him. One of my boys had treatment at the same place in Lisbon. He was there on his own, no support from his club. We chatted every time I visited. He's a top lad.'

'How's the knee?' asked Anita. She bore into me with her unblinking, dark eyes. It was a stare that cut through waffle or obfuscation, demanded clear and concise answers. Evidence to back up assumptions and assertions.

'Fine. He's made a good recovery and is back training with the first team.'

'Is he looking to move?' Brooker enquired.

'No, but I don't think it would be hard to convince him.'

'How much?' asked Anita, not giving anything away.

'He's only got eighteen months left on his contract. I think we can get him for thirty seven million plus add ons.'

Rigg looked at his watch and glanced impatiently towards the door. I took the hint and moved on to the forward line. I had used StatsBomb to narrow down the field, focusing on non-penalty xG, assists and shot creating actions, pressures and turnovers, and then shortened the list further with a deep dive into progressive passes received and the ability to find space in and around the box. Two players stood out, Ramon Borello and Mansour Senghor. Borello moved to Spain the previous summer after five successful seasons for his hometown club in Buenos Aires but injuries and a change in manager had prevented him from holding down a place. I wasn't overly concerned by this, under-valued players are always attractive, and the data from his time in Argentina suggested he would be a good fit.

I had kept an eye on Senghor since the African Nations under 23's a few years before. He had the energy and work-rate required to play in my system. Pressing was a central feature of his game, not the dirty work left to someone else (his ball recovery stats were among the best of any forward in Europe), and while playing under Lucien Feyder in Germany he had improved his decision making and finishing. Watching Senghor play, the incessant movement, the pulsing veins, was like listening to trance music with the volume turned up loud, and the two men would complement each other well. Senghor liked to operate in the half space channels on either side of the pitch, whilst Borello preferred to stay central.

'How many did he score last season?' said Anita, pointing at Borello's profile on the screen.

'Nine—'

Archer snorted.

'…in thirty-one appearances.'

'And this season?'

'Six so far, but he's outscored his xG for the last three years.'

'xG?'

'Expected goals Robert. It's a metric to understand the quality of goal scoring chances and therefore the likelihood of scoring,' said Anita. 'It tells you how many goals a player or team should have scored given the chances created in a game or a series of games.'

Rigg looked like he was trying to get his head around quadratic equations.

'The fact that Borello has outperformed his xG suggests he is a better finisher than the average striker.'

'He's in the top ten percentile,' I added.

'And so if the model is correct, he would score disproportionately more goals if he played in a team that created more chances,' said Anita patiently.

'To be honest, I'm not so interested in theoretical goals and algorithms,' said Rigg. He wasn't a details person, getting by on quick wits, wisdom acquired through age, and a network of backscratching contacts, and like all bluffers he had a tell. Whenever he didn't know an answer or couldn't understand something he'd begin his response with 'To be honest, employing an extra baritone of gravitas, as if he was disclosing a state secret, and then skate over the facts with some superficial waffle. 'I want to see real goals.'

'Let's take a look.'

I played another clip, illustrating Borello's ability to find space in the box. 'Watch how he takes the step… there.' Borello took one step towards the ball, his marker moved to follow and as he did Borello moved in the opposite direction. 'And he doesn't wait for the ball to arrive, he moves to where he thinks it will go.' Borello met the ball seven yards out and slammed it into the roof of the net.

'But there's a lot more to his game than goals. He's good at dropping deep and pulling central defenders out of position, creating space for others—.'

There was a tentative knock on the boardroom door.

'Eileen, there you are,' said Rigg, with a wide smile. 'I was beginning to think you'd forgotten us.' Eileen, the club's tea lady wheeled in the cake trolley, a weekly tradition dating back to the 1930s. After a lengthy deliberation, Rigg took a slice of cherry cake and another cup of Earl Grey. Scooter opted for coffee and walnut. The rest of us passed. Scooter asked after Eileen's grandchildren and then slipped a ten-pound note into the charity tin next to the plate of scones. Anita and I did the same. Archer tossed in some coins.

'Who do you think we should go for?' Anita asked once Eileen had closed the door behind her.

'If we could, I'd sell Slaney and buy all three.' Archer bristled at this. 'But if I had to select just one it would be Linares.'

'The fans will flay us alive on social,' said Scooter through a mouthful of cake. 'They want names. Stardust. These guys just won't cut it.'

'I'm not so sure,' said Anita quietly. 'And I imagine The Owner would be interested in learning more about all three. Let's prepare physical and video scouting reports and run the stats. Benchmark them against our current players in the same positions.'

'We can do that. What metrics do you… will he want to see? asked Brooker.

'I'll leave you to figure that out.'

'Are we all in agreement?' asked Rigg.

'Yeah that plan rocks,' said Scooter, quickly changing his tune now that Anita had declared her position.

Brooker spoke next, hedging his bets. 'Linares is worth a look. The question mark for me is his knee.'

Everyone looked at Archer.

'Whatever,' he said glowering at me.

'The ayes have it. Next item. Mike can you give us a update on the three players we agreed to track at the last meeting.'

'Thanks Chairman. Maaroufi is continuing to develop and has established himself in the first team at Rennes. I'm going over to watch him play again next week. I'll also hook up with a couple of local agents while I'm there. Sabalenka is doing well at Eintracht and attracting interest from other clubs. It's possible someone may come in for him before the window closes. If so we may want to bring forward our offer from the summer. And Einarsson picked up a groin strain and has been out for the past couple of weeks. He should be back in action by the end of the month so nothing serious. Final reports on all three will be circulated ahead of the May TSG so we can take a decision in time for the summer window.'

'Any other business before we close?'

'Just a quick update on Kang's work permit,' said Brooker. The club had signed Kim Kang the previous summer but had loaned the South Korean attacking midfielder to Athletic Bruges to build up the necessary game time after difficulties with his work permit.

'We are still waiting for clearance. It's been seven months now.'

'The wheels turn slowly in Marsham Street, especially since Brexit. Leave it with me. Danjuma used to do the photocopying when I was at CCO. I'll have a word, see if we can move it to the top of the pile,' said Rigg cheerfully, winding the meeting up.

21

The clips and stats Xabi compiled indicated Shan was a player of considerable but unrealised potential, like a grand building, a stadium or a palace, mid-construction. He was more of an eight than a six, always looking to force the tempo in the final third, drifting into the no man's land between the midfield and defensive lines, rotating positions with the wide forwards, or appearing late and unmarked on the edge of the box for a low cutback. He held and released the ball well under pressure, had great vision for someone so young, and ran himself into the ground in defensive transitions, counter pressing with intensity and tracking opposition runs. There were, of course, some development issues. The tendency to lose the player behind him in transition, to go to ground too quickly. The over exuberant desire to be involved in everything (which is not uncommon among players who have excelled at youth level) that impacted his positioning and decision making, but nothing that could not be coached out of him. And so, he and Zito joined first team training on another cold, windswept January morning. The pair were accompanied by Nathan Cox, a tall, ungainly defender who I had agreed to take a look at as a sop to Tim Croft after bringing Shan through against his advice. Archer had laughed scornfully when I told him this. 'That meat-head couldn't complete a pass if his todger depended on it,' he scoffed.

Valon greeted the new boys with fist bumps and smiles, shining his warmth upon them. He explained the new system of fines and then introduced them one by one to the rest of the squad. Most of the boys were friendly enough. Zharnell swapped stories about the academy staff, while Mats reined in his when-I-won-the-World-Cup routine, asking Zito about his family back in Brazil. A few of the others, however, wary of the potential challenge, asserted their place in the hierarchy. Slaney blanked Zito and made a nasty comment about Shan being here to sell shirts.

'That's enough,' Valon told him. 'The boys have to earn their place in the group but they get our respect from day one.'

'It's alright,' said Shan. He looked embarrassed, unhappy with the attention.

While Pal De Backer took the group through their stretches, Kuipers told a story about the school run. Like the rest of the players, he wore a long sleeve thermal underlayer beneath his short-sleeved shirt.

'I was at the lights at the bottom of the slip road. A guy pulls up next to me in a Mercedes 4x4, two kids in the back. He does a double take, realises it's me and winds down the window. I think he's going to ask for a photo or something so I do the same. He then starts to lay into me, the team, our results. Calls me a fucking disgrace. A waste of money. Hammers me for the missed chance against Flixton.'

'What did you do?'

'The kid in the back was recording it all on his phone and I had Ingrid's girls with me.' Kuipers' wife was eleven years older than him and had three children from her first marriage.

'So I just said we're working hard, playing well and the wins will come. He then leans across the passenger seat and spits out the window. With the gob dripping down the car door he says "I hope you break your fucking leg at the weekend".'

'I trust you chinned the facker,' said Terry.

The boys all laughed at the idea of Kuipers throwing a punch.

'I just complemented him on his parenting and dropped him when the lights turned.'

Sadly this, like endless gambling adverts and FA Cup semi-finals at Wembley, is part and parcel of modern football. Every player has a story. Friends and relatives singled out for abuse by opposing fans seated nearby. Spat at in front of their children while at the cinema. Flares fired at bedroom windows. Parked cars defaced. Endless bile on social media. It's almost as if the more the players earn, the more the public feel they have the right to have a go. And of course, for the players, there is the knowledge that if they react in any way, are human for just one brief moment, it will trigger an outpouring of media condemnation.

A shy, reluctant sun, poked its head out and then thought better of it, darting back behind the curtain of grey clouds. The trees lining the perimeter clung together for warmth. The surface looked good despite the heavy rainfall over night. Zito and Shan started the Rondo in the middle, hustling hard to run the ball down, scuttling side to side. Zito was at ease in the outer circle, redirecting the fast moving ball and evading the close press from the players in the middle. Shan, unnerved by Slaney's running commentary, made a couple of early mistakes and quickly found himself back in the middle, but began to grow in confidence, using the inside of his boot to take the sting out of Slaney's deliberately heavy passes and angle cushioned balls towards his teammates. Nathan Cox, however, wasn't ready to make the step up. He looked out of place and out of time, like a dancer moving to the wrong beat. The misplaced passes and awkward control exposed the limitations in his game. And he knew it. I suspect deep down he'd always known it. You could tell by the stress in his face as he sliced a clearance behind for a corner in the positional drill. The mixture of relief and defeat when he was withdrawn from the firing line of the defensive zone. The premonition that his career was over before it began. Of watching the game he loved - and kids he had grown up with - for years to come and thinking 'that could have been me.

We finished each session with shooting practice. Terry placed five different coloured cones around the D and each player took it in turn to stand at a sixth cone. I called out a colour in random order and the player ran to the cone, received a ball and either took a touch or shot first time, before returning to the starting position, all within four seconds. One point for a goal, a bonus point if the goal was from a first time shot, and a point deducted for every shot missed. On the first morning Slaney hung back, sizing up the drill with his pickpocket eyes, but now he insisted on going first and putting down a marker for the other boys. He started fast, drilling the ball inside the near post, then back across Fabio for the second. 'Top bin Fab' he shouted as he ran towards the third ball, ripping into the top left corner. But the drill is a test of fitness and movement as well as finishing, and Slaney arrived a fraction late to the fifth ball, taking an extra touch before firing home.

'Nine points,' called Terry.

'That ladies is how to fucking score goals,' Slaney said turning to face the players. 'Anyone who beats that gets my motor.'

'Which one?' asked Bailey, from his perch on top of the wheeled drinks chest.

'The Superleggera. Not that you need to worry.'

Jose Costa went next, followed by Dekker. Fabio clapped his gloves, baiting the players. Jose Costa scored a total of five points - a respectable number for a player who had only scored two goals in the previous two seasons - and celebrated as if he had won the World Cup. Dekker registered a duck, his worst yet. Fabio caught the first shot, absorbing the energy with his chest, parried the second, conceded the third and fourth, and looked on as the final effort missed the target.

Bailey looked sharp. Motivated for once. He propelled the ball into the net, one, two, three, four times, reminding Fabio whose side physics and geometry were really on. The chit chat from the other players stopped as he approached his fifth shot. The distant hum of the motorway the only sound. I called 'blue', the closest cone to the starting position and on his stronger foot. Bailey took five paces and chipped the pass from Terry first time, shooting into the ground to generate backspin. The ball's glide path bent towards the far corner as it floated over Fabio. The Italian took three quick steps backwards, pushed off the ground, arched his back, and reached behind his head to flick the ball onto the bar, before making a hard landing on the cold, damp turf.

'Seven points,' said Terry. Fabio, stony faced, picked himself up and retrieved the ball. 'No one chips me.' He launched the ball the length of the pitch. 'Fetch,' he said to Bailey as the other boys laughed and cheered.

Zito was one of the last to go. I watched his movement closely. The stride pattern needed work but quick acceleration insured he was there with time to spare for all five shots, and he struck the ball cleanly, not fazed by the crowd of egos. The shot placement, however, was naïve. Fabio beat away two shots with his gloves, and a third with his legs, conceding just the two goals. This was why they called him The Wall.

'Someone needs to show him where the net is,' said Slaney.

We then moved inside the penalty area, with four cones and two starting positions. Again I called a random colour and the player had to move to the cone, but this time Valon and Jose Costa took it in turns to try to block the shot or intercept the cross, simulating the experience of receiving under pressure. Kuipers registered a personal best. He struck four goals first time, and put a lunging, sliding Jose Costa on the ground with a dummied drag back for his fifth. Zito looked more assured, scoring three times. It was as if the pressure of the extra man in the box made him forget he was up against one of the world's greatest goalkeepers. But he still took too many touches.

At the end of the session I called the three academy boys over. The rest of the group walked back to the dressing room apart from Bailey and Zharnell who stopped to play crossbar challenge. They took it in turns to strike the ball against the bar, starting in the D and moving back ten yards after every successful attempt while Rafiq recorded it on his phone. I told Shan I would see him tomorrow. I'd liked what I seen. The variety of his passes. Clipped short, like his hair, drilled through the lines and to feet, or arced out to the wings, and always forward. It was a different conversation with Cox. 'It was a tough session,' I told him. 'But now you know the level you have to be at. Think about what you want to take away from today and what you need to do to get back here. Talk it over with Crofty and then come see me.'

He looked crushed. But it was the right call. The kids in the academy had to see that progress was possible, but not inevitable. That they all had to redouble their efforts, make the necessary sacrifices. Earn their place. I put my arm around his shoulder.

'This isn't over. Work hard, come back stronger. That's the Athletic way.'

Another icy blast blew across the wide open space.

'Thanks boss,' he said. 'The nerves got to me.'

I slapped him on the back and he headed off to the dressing room, wiping his eyes on his sleeve and spitting on the grass. Zito studied his boots waiting for the verdict. I called over Xabi who had joined us for the final fifteen minutes and then asked Zito for his own assessment.

'How do you think you did today?'

Xabi translated into Brazilian Portuguese and then Zito replied in halting English.

'No good.' He shook his head ruefully. 'No happy with shooting.'

I nodded. 'Let's start with the positives.' I paused to let Xabi translate. 'You didn't look out of place in the group today. You could make the first team bench on speed and athleticism alone, but we need to work on your finishing if you want to be a starter. Your back lift is too pronounced, it makes it easy for the keeper to read. Tomorrow we'll work on a shorter, quicker motion. Like Aguero or Jermaine Defoe.'

Zito listened to the translation, nodding his head in agreement. I told him about Filippo Inzaghi. How he scored more than two hundred times – 68% of all his goals – with first touch finishes.

'When you're in the penalty area - especially in the second six yard box - you've got to hit it first time. At this level you don't have time for the extra touch. Shot placement also has to be smarter. You've got to aim low or high.' I held up my hand. 'Anything at this height is too easy for the keeper. Study Ademir and Stabile. Keep those pictures in your mind.'

22

Early morning sunlight glinted off frosted grass on the outer pitch. The birds chanted from their terraces in the trees, and the corner flags trembled in the wind as the 20s worked on counter pressing and defensive transitions. Xabi and I had split the group into two 9v3 rondos with four teams of three in each box. One group of three pressed the nine in possession. After each turnover, the team of three whose player lost the ball transitioned into recovery with the aim of retrieving the ball immediately, and if this was not possible, slowing the speed and progression of the attack. The drill taught the boys to keep the opposing side close to their own penalty box and to reapply pressure to the ball when the first line of the press is breached. As in every session, my phone was switched off, but I knew something was up when Xabi nudged me with his elbow and pointed towards Terry, who was hurtling towards us in a golf buggy. He parked up behind the goal and made the final thirty metres on foot, half walking, half trotting. I had never seen him move so fast. A ball escaped the confines of the rondo square and made a beeline towards Xabi. Without looking, without *thinking*, he flicked it up with the toes of one booted foot, bounced it off his lower thigh, controlled it with his chest, and then volleyed it lazily with his weaker left foot. A perfectly weighted arc of a pass dropped back in the middle of the box and the drill resumed. Terry reached us, placed his hands on his knees, took several deep breaths, and looked up.

'He's only...gone and... done it,' he panted.

'What?'

'Declared war... an open fackin letter...'

He handed me his phone and I read Slaney's Instagram post on the cracked screen.

'Writing this letter is the hardest thing I have had to do in football but I have too much respect for the fans to go on living a lie. I came to Athletic to win trophies, to help this great club get back to where it belongs at the top of the game. But sadly I now know this will never be possible while the current board is in charge. There is no plan. No ambition. A club with ambition would not have appointed a coach who was out of his depth. A club with ambition would not have passed up the opportunity to bring in top players (players I personally recommended to the club's owner and directors). A club with ambition would be investing in the facilities, not allowing us to fall further behind. As anyone who has played with or watched me will know, I demand a lot from myself and my teammates. I need to spend what time I have left in the game I love in an environment where the ambition and sporting infrastructure matches my own high standards. But instead, I find myself in a situation where my goals and performances are masking a lack of leadership and investment, poor coaching and naïve tactics, and I can no longer be complicit in this deceit. The supporters deserve better. And so for their sake and the sake of my own mental health, I have informed the club I would like to leave. As has been widely reported, there is no break clause in my contract. I never believed this to be necessary. Instead, David Archer and I have a gentlemen's agreement that I can leave if circumstances on or off the pitch change. Sadly, David has chosen not to honour this agreement. In fact, he made it clear he would be happy for me "to rot with the fucking kids and cripples in the reserves" (his words) rather than allow me to pursue my dreams elsewhere. This is not acceptable. But sadly, it is all too common. For too long, we players have been treated as human cargo. Property to be bought and sold. Thanks to my achievements in the game, I am in a position to do something about this once and for all. And so, I intend to use my platform to help all my fellow professionals. To break the chains around our ankles. I will show the money men that they do not own Ryan Slaney any more than they own our sport. I can assure the fans that I will be as professional as ever – they deserve nothing less. I will continue to work hard in training, be an example to my teammates, play to the best of my ability in my remaining fixtures, but one way or another I will leave the club by the end of the January window. And while I am at it, I am also going to challenge head-on the modern slavery of so-called third-party ownership. I have never been subject to such an arrangement, but not all my fellow professionals are as fortunate, so together with my good friends at KP and Sahara I'm creating a fighting fund with an initial pot of $20 million to help ANY player who wishes to challenge third-party ownership in court. We will follow in the footsteps of Nelson Mandela and Gandhi on the long road to freedom. I will be free. We will be free.

Ryan.

'He's rinsed us big time.' said Terry looking over my shoulder.

Xabi kicked the ground in anger. 'Motherfucker.'

I thought back to our meeting two weeks before. Slaney's genuine gratitude at my offer of support. Everything I had done for him since. And how he and his people hadn't hesitated to trash me, in order to get what he wanted.

'Do you want to get back?' said Terry pointing to the golf buggy.

'No, I'll wait until we've finished.'

***

Lara was the first to message in the group chat.

'My phone has gone into melt down. What's our line?'

'We can't be fucking bullied by him. We need to stay strong,' Archer replied.

'Agreed. We can't be held to ransom,' wrote Rigg. 'Keep it firm but dignified on the record. And then hammer him on background. The girls. The fights. The demands. All of it.'

Scooter messaged next.

'The fuckers have got the jump on us with our commercial partners. Fluid, Sahara, KP will all exercise their break clause if he walks.'

'He has to pay for this,' replied Archer.

'Damn right.'

After holding back initially, Anita broke her radio silence.

'I've just got The Owner out of bed. He wants a quick clean divorce but won't countenance a sale to another English side. And he wants us to sever all ties with Fidalgo. Cut him off completely. Make it clear that we refuse to deal with him on this or any other transfer.'

Archer was quick to respond.

'WE CAN'T DO THAT. WE NEED HIS PLAYERS.'

'The Owner was very clear. Make it happen.'

23

Monday, recovery day for the players. A slightly later start to maximise sleep, followed by light exercises in the pool, a deep tissue massage, and a session in the hyperbaric chamber. For the coaching staff, a chance to review the performance at the weekend and build the plan for the week. To go through analysis and scouting reports, and identify weaknesses to target in the forthcoming fixtures. We got together as a group and then sat down with the players to discuss improvements and technical or tactical adjustments. So I was reluctant to break away early but Paco insisted, calling to tell me he had booked a table for lunch in his favourite place down by the river in Putney.

I arrived first and waited at the bar. The zinc counter stretched along one wall until it met the open kitchen. The kitchen staff, dressed in their all-white home strip, operated at warp speed. Clanking pans and sizzling oil fought to be heard over the roar of gas flames. I tend to take a functional view on food - diet, along with conditioning, ball work, and sleep, is a building block towards peak performance - but this was different. Like watching football live for the first time. It was a privilege to witness the unity of the kitchen staff first-hand. Their speed and intensity. The organisation and communication. The highest of high standards. This was Johan's Barca, Sacchi's Milan. Each plate a wonderful team goal. A free flowing move where every member of the team touched the ball. I have never been comfortable handling raw meat or fish, always using tongs or forks to keep contact to the absolute minimum, so I was amazed to see how tactile the chefs were. Manipulating the food with authority, zero compromise, and total fucking commitment to their art.

After a few moments my mind returned to work. Pressure is a constant for a football coach - like oxygen, you can't live without it - but with only two points from twelve this was something else. I could see it in the evasive eyes and hollow smiles from the sports science team and the performance analysts. The receptionist and the canteen staff. They had all wanted to believe, to see me turn the club around, but early optimism and goodwill had vanished, replaced by doubt and defeatism. Dan Stevens and Archer's other friends in the media were calling for him to replace me, and according to *The Times* that morning, I was only two games away from the sack. An unnamed club source (no doubt Archer himself) was quoted as saying 'when a bet is going south you don't throw more good money after bad, you cut your losses.'

The honeymoon with the players had also come to a juddering halt. Slaney was increasingly mutinous, challenging tactical instructions and rolling his eyes during team talks, while those like Varallo and Dekker, who were getting less minutes, became more disgruntled as each game went by. Thankfully a small core were still with me. Only that morning, Valon and Kuipers had come in early, before my meeting with the analysis team, to signal their support. The big Bosnian spoke first, breaking down the improvements he had seen in each unit's performance, and imploring me not to deviate from or dilute our approach.

'We're on the right path gaffer. Stick with it, stick with it. A win is coming our way.'

He was right. Fitness, shape, and organisation had improved from game to game. We were playing with control and aggression, moving the ball faster and smarter. Creating more chances but still not capitalising. It was massively frustrating. Had the results reflected our xG we would have been five places higher up the table. I tried to change the narrative in the media conference after the Bedfont game, highlighting the underlying trends behind the scorelines – possession, ball progression, chances created, number of sprints and distance run, all moving in the right direction – explaining that this was the result of a clearer identity and improved conditioning. I spoke with conviction about how it would soon translate into improved results. A few of the reporters took this on board but for the rest the story wrote itself. It was the old fable of ambition exceeding ability. The inexperienced coach who flew too close to the sun and then slowly tumbled to the ground.

I responded the only way I knew how, working hard late into the night. Going back through the tapes, analysing the squad and our opponents, looking for the smallest clues that would give us the edge. Sleep, like winning, became a distant memory, something I did before taking on the new job. I lay in bed, running through an endless cycle of questions, my mind ignoring the pleas from my body to call it a night. Should I hold my nerve and trust that things would come good? Or did I need to adapt the system? Switch to three at the back, or play with a double pivot? What else could I do to accelerate the group's fitness levels? And I began to question myself. When I first stood in front of the players I was convinced I could get more out of them than Bescond, that my methods were superior to his, but now I was no longer so sure. What if my self-belief turned out to be no more than self-delusion?

And during what precious little sleep I did get my dreams were polluted by our struggles on and off the pitch. Some were reasonably benign, goals ruled out after lengthy reviews, shots colliding with the woodwork, but the rest, in which Archer and Slaney loomed large, were downright malignant. First the three of us were playing up top, Archer refusing to cut the ball back when the goal was at my mercy. Slaney screaming at me for failing to pick him out with a pass. Then after the match, the two of them, along with Barbour jacket man and several other players, began to whip me with towels before throwing me into one of the giant clothes dryers.

I felt a slap on the back. 'Hombre,' said Paco hugging me. He looked five years younger than when I last saw him. We spoke Spanish for a few minutes and then he switched to English. 'Come, let's eat.' He led me to a table by the window overlooking The Thames where we were greeted by the restaurant owner who pocketed the reserved sign and presented us each with a glass of champagne. Paco asked after his children, beaming with pleasure when he heard that the daughter had been promoted.

'The youngest cardiologist in London. We will always be so grateful.'

Paco looked embarrassed and waved away the remark with his hand. 'I'm just happy I was able to help.'

I took a sip of champagne, my first drink since the Martini on the flight back to Split. It tasted incredible, the bubbles tap dancing across my tongue. I gazed out of the window as the two men spoke. The water flowed by on its one-way ticket to the coast. On the tow path runners and cyclists overtook parents with pushchairs. Children in bobble hats and scarves fed the ducks. Across the water, slants of sunlight bounced off Fulham's spectacular Riverside stand. My mind wandered back to the game the previous day. It still hurt like hell. It was our best performance since I took charge, the players really starting to understand what I wanted them to do. Trading positions and finding space. Going around not through Bedfont's Maginot line of expensive but immobile defenders. The XG was 2.3 to 0.6 in our favour. But it was all for nothing, their keeper proving to be a firewall of double reflex saves. Then, like the boxer who's pummeled his opponent through eleven rounds only to be floored by a lucky punch, we let in a goal as soft as cashmere. Jose Costa failed to clear a corner in the closing stages, directing the ball into the danger zone with the weakest of headers, and their centre back was quickest to it, swiveling to hit a mis-controlled half volley past Fabio. The crowd escorted me off with a thrash metal cover of 'You don't know what you're doing.' My thumbs up and applause cutting zero fucking ice.

It was the hardest of defeats. One of those moments when you question and doubt everything you stand for. An unbearable weight on your shoulders for days, squeezing the energy out of you. And to make matters worse, results elsewhere went against us and we had dropped to eleventh in the table.

'How are you my friend?'

'Good.'

'You look terrible.'

Not the pep talk I was hoping for.

'It's been tough… but we'll get there.'

A waitress brought focaccia crusted with salt and rosemary along with a small saucer of olive oil. Paco asked why I had not called him since my first day at the club.

'Would you?'

'Of course. I spoke to Johan every day when I first arrived in England. I wouldn't of got through it without him.'

He tore off a piece of focaccia, dipped it in the oil, and then looked me in the eye.

'Asking for help is a strength not a weakness. This job is too big to do on your own. You should use me, and you should delegate. Trust your staff.'

'That's the problem. Apart from Xabi, I don't trust them. The ship ran aground on their watch.'

Why, I had asked myself again and again, had I agreed to take on the hardest job in football without my number two? What possessed me to think I could do it without him? I should have forced the issue or walked away. It would have made a massive difference to have Feli alongside me on the touchline and in training, working with the players one to one and in their units. He would not have been fazed by Slaney's status or backchat. He would have known exactly how to handle him. We had not spoken since our strained farewell at the training ground but judging by results – Feli had won his first five games in charge – he was coping just fine without me.

'I've never met anyone who wants to do a bad job, Joe. Not once. Terry, Mike, Jordan and his team. These are good people. They just lacked leadership. It's your job to set the direction and then empower your team. Let them—'

'I am.'

'Who leads training?'

'Me. I'm head coach.'

A dog barked at the swans down by the river, straining at the leash.

'That's my point. You need to step back, give Terry the space to do his job. Ayrton and Ramon before him always ran training for me. That way I could observe—.'

'It's too soon. We are going for a total reboot. Positional play. Pre-set moves. Counter-pressing. A higher line. Everything. Give it a few weeks, time to embed my ideas, then I can step back a bit.'

'No Joe it will be too late. You'll have lost them by then. They need to feel it now.'

A rowing boat pulled into the bank and the crew took it in turns to lever themselves out.

'OK, OK.'

'I mean it. A club like Athletic is a different animal. You have to make the machine work for you.'

'When was the last time you were at Datchet? It's not the club you built. Everything's broken. Coaching, analysis, internal talent ID, academy pathways, fitness and conditioning, none of it works. There's no planning, no direction. No co-ordination.'

There was a stir as a familiar face - an actor? an ageing pop star? - entered the restaurant. News of his arrival rippled through the room, diners' heads turning one after another like a Mexican wave. He stopped to say hello to Paco, then offered his thoughts on how to set up the team for our next game. I feigned polite interest. Once he had moved on, I asked Paco what he made of the Bedfont game.

'Aw amigo, so frustrating! They couldn't live with us in the first half. You've got them playing with courage and urgency again.'

Paco ran through his analysis, listing the improved organisation, the increased intensity, before telling me what I knew already: the high line was the right idea but wouldn't work without a high press. We had practiced it for hours. When to hold the line, when to drop. Moving up the pitch as a compact unit with no more than twenty-five metres between the forwards and the defence to avoid space opening up between the lines. I instructed the front three to press as a triangle when the ball was with the goalkeeper or central defenders to cut off the passing lanes and give the centre-back no option but to play the ball to the fullback on their side of the pitch. Then we would attack this zone with a wide forward and a midfielder, establishing a 2 v 1. But if they had not regained possession after five seconds they had to revert to their defensive shape, with the midfield pivot dropping deep to shield the back four. We rehearsed other pressing traps. Deliberately opening up a space in the middle third for opponents to pass or run into and then flooding the zone. The problem was Slaney had no interest in defending from the front, insisting he save his energy for offensive play, so rather than direct the ball into an area where we could force an error or a turnover, we allowed teams to pass short to a dropping midfielder or play over our back line into the space beyond. His departure could not come soon enough.

'Where are we with Slaney?'

I checked who was seated within earshot, lowered my voice.

'City are trying to lever the situation, get him on the cheap.'

'Everyone knows we're past the point of no return now.'

'Yes, but The Owner is having none of it. He refuses point blank to sell to City. So Dave is just stringing them along to push the price up, while working up a deal to send him back to Germany.'

Paco finished what he was eating, dabbed at the corners of his mouth with a napkin, and then took a sip of champagne.

'Who are we going to bring in?'

'Archer is putting together a deal to bring in Kocsis. They're still working through personal terms but he's confident we can get it over the line in time.'

'Anyone else?'

'No, Rigg's golden rule.'

'Oh hombre,' he said exasperated. 'We need a new six. A wide forward as well as a central striker. A new right back.'

'This is what I've been saying.'

I took him through the shortlist I had proposed to the TSG.

'Linares is just what we need.'

'The problem is Archer and Scooter don't want to hear it. They both want another marquee signing. Anita is the same.'

'They all dance to The Owner's tune, tell him what they think he wants to hear.'

A plate of Galician octopus arrived. Paco served both of us, carefully spooning out a dollop of Alioli on each plate. He ate a piece and then told me how impressed he had been with Zharnell's response to his red card.

'He's a strong kid.'

The media coverage of Zharnell's performance against Aldershot had been merciless. The papers criticised his lifestyle, his love life, and where and how he spent his money, employing coded language and racist dog whistles to tear him down.

We had respected Zharnell's wish and continued to make no reference to his brother's death but a number of people had started to connect the dots on social media and this filtered through to the media coverage and the terraces. Chirk's supporters taunted him early on in his first match back after his one game suspension. It started quietly, just one or two voices as he took a throw in and then grew and grew.

'ZHARNELL LEWIS YOUR BIG BROTHER IS DEAD.
ZHARNELL LEWIS HE WAS STABBED IN THE HEAD.
ZHARNELL LEWIS HE BLED, AND BLED, AND BLED.
ZHARNELL LEWIS YOUR BIG BROTHER IS DEAD.'

I had encouraged Zharnell to talk to a psychologist and it seemed to have helped. He was now feeding off his emotions, determined to prove people wrong.

'JC has to do better with the clearance.'

I closed my eyes and shook my head in frustration. 'I know. He said his legs had gone. You could see he didn't have the spring to get up to it. I've asked De Backer to add vertical and lateral hops into his conditioning programme.'

Paco motioned towards the octopus, offering me the last piece. It was his favourite dish so I shook my head and encouraged him to have it. His smile broadened as he carefully transferred it to his plate.

'You're working them too hard. They had nothing left to give in the final fifteen. We dropped too deep, allowed them to come onto us.'

'It's not new. They've been like this for the past couple of years. The conditioning isn't good enough,' I replied. 'We're working on it.'

'They looked over cooked to me. Too much in their legs. You need to ease off a bit.'

'It's how it is when you're turning a team around. Remember what it was like when you arrived?'

After all his success, the domination he enjoyed, the deep changes he wrought on English football, it was easy to forget how difficult Paco's first couple of seasons were. It had taken time to implement his ideas. Two long years of setbacks and false dawns, when the pundits revelled in his misery. He was doomed to fail in England they cried. He needed to adapt, to play long and direct, change his system. His achievements in Spain were dismissed, explained away. Paco was lucky they said. Fortunate to have been in the right place, at the right time. Any coach could win titles with Kwizera in his team, but Paco couldn't do it without him they sneered. His face was disfigured by the losses. The soft, young features turned sallow and dull. His hair faded to grey. Bags formed under his eyes and then spread out, colonising his cheeks. A scowl replaced the ever-present smile. Rumours circulated about problems in his marriage. That neither he or Isabel had settled in England. But Paco never deviated from his principles. He cleared out the drinkers and the technically deficient. The doubters and the time servers. Brought in gifted technicians and leaders. Players like Bijkerk and Muñoz. And most importantly, he signed a young Azem Valon to strengthen his high line and bring control and influence in the first phase of possession. The transformation was astonishing. The team of flaky losers, the butt of endless jokes, was reinvented as a free-flowing, all conquering, winning machine.

'It takes time. You have to be patient amigo.'

'Time is one of the many things I don't have at the moment.'

Paco finished his champagne and motioned to the waiter who brought us a carafe of red wine.

'Ribera del Duero. One of Bobby's favourites.'

'I remember sharing a bottle with him after the comeback against Atléti.'

'Hombre,' he slapped his thigh and leant forward. 'One of the greatest games of all time. The volley from Fi—'

'And then when Piz scored—'

And then to go on and win La Copa in the Bernabéu.' He raised his glass. 'To Bobby and Johan. Absent friends.'

He took a swig. Then looked at me. 'The look on his face after Ronny's goal against Compostela.'

'Like he'd just seen a ghost.'

'Six or seven fouls. They tripped him, barged him, pulled his shirt, and he just kept going.'

'The level he was on that year was frightening.'

The waiter cleared our plates. Paco exchanged a few words with him. Then spoke to me again.

'Emily came for lunch yesterday.'

Paco was Emily's godfather. Like everything he did, he took the role seriously.

'She can't understand why you don't want to see her.'

'Of course I want to see her.'

'Do you?'

'Yes. But there's so much to do, and she should be revising.'

'She finished her mocks last week.' He paused. Looked at me and then continued.

'I thought this club was my legacy, but everything I built has gone. Family is the only thing that endures. I see that now. I was never there for Ramon. We're fine but there's always a distance. Don't make the same mistake. Spend some time together, re-connect. It'll do you good.'

24

Deadline day. The longest day in football. A day when players, agents, and clubs use the ticking clock to leverage the best possible deal. A day when best laid plans quickly unravel. A day for holding your nerve when everyone around you is losing theirs. When agents, sporting directors, and club secretaries earn their salaries. A day a player can discover out of the blue they are surplus to requirement, a makeweight in other deals, or - if they are lucky - coveted by one of the European superpowers. A day when they can train with one club, speak to a second and end up signing for a third or fourth. When they have to tell their wives and children they are moving home – today - changing countries and schools. A day that began at five am with a call from Anita. As always, she got straight to the point.

'The Kocsis deal is off. We've been gazumped by City.'

'When?'

'Last night. Dave shook hands on it with Kocsis' agent then left Kath at the hotel to do the paperwork while he went out to dinner to celebrate. But Kath is not authorised to sign contracts above thirty million, so they were waiting for Dave to come back. Meanwhile van Meegeren caught wind of it. He knew our car was out the front so he came in via the service entrance and stole the whole thing from under our noses. Kath was sitting there looking at her watch, sipping tea. It was only when van Meegeren left by the front door and gave our driver a big smile and a thumbs up that they realised what was going on.'

'So what now?'

'Dave doesn't have a back up,' Anita replied. 'I've spoken to The Owner and he's agreed to green light your three names. We'll carve it up between us. I'll speak to Senghor's people. Mike is tracking down Borello's brother. You lead the negotiations with Piedmont and sell it to Linares. Kath will take care of the paperwork. Don't try to nickel and dime them. Go in at twenty-one. They'll know you're lowballing but at least you're not insulting them. When you get to twenty-seven tell them you've got another call and put them on hold. Go make a cup of tea, come back, don't apologise, don't say anything, let them restart the process. If you get to thirty-seven hang up and call me. We'll take stock, see where we are with the other puts and takes.'

I arrived at Datchet two hours later to find a group of reporters and cameramen already camped outside the entrance sheltering from the rain under branded golfing umbrellas. Kelly Ajiboye from Sky recognised my car first and flagged me down.

'Nice day for it,' I said after lowering my window. The TV cameras swung into my face.

'Morning Joe. Can you confirm Torinese are in for Ryan Slaney?'

This was true. Torinese were looking to splash the cash and on paper the deal made perfect sense. The Italian champions were into the knockout stages of the European Cup, and unlike every other elite striker in Europe, Slaney was not cup tied. But the club had agreed a deal with Stuttgart for a fee of £120 million, with £90 million upfront and two further installments.

'All I can say is Ryan is still an Athletic player.'

'Will you be bringing anyone in today.'

'You'd need to speak to David Archer about that. Who'd like a tea?'

They all replied gratefully.

'We'll send some out. Have a good day.'

I called Dani Linares at home at seven thirty his time (only players with kids get up before 7 am, even on deadline day). The conversation went well. I reminded him of my philosophy: high press, high line, high energy, using space and positioning to create overloads. I invoked Athletic's history, telling Dani he would be pulling on the same gold and maroon striped shirt as Manchon, Velasco, and of course, David Archer. I told him he would be the cornerstone of the project to revive the club's fortunes. That we needed not just technical ability but character and personality. His winning mentality. I could tell he was interested, really interested, but also wary of making another mistake. After a difficult spell in Italy, his next move had to be a success. His main reservation was the possibility of a change in manager at the end of the season. You can't worry about that, I told him, that's true of every club. Come here. Bring your a-game, and you'll do well.

***

'Why does David not want to call me himself? He's not still crying about the Euros?' said Sergio Fossati, Piedmont's technical director and a two time Seria A winner. He and Archer had history. A series of run-ins (Foassati's excessive celebrations when Archer's penalty struck the crossbar in the Milan derby, Archer's off the ball elbow to the jaw) which came to a head in the quarter-finals of Euro 2004, when in the face of Fossati's roughhouse treatment and incessant needling, Archer allowed his emotions to get the better of him and squared up to the Italian. The two men's heads pressed together momentarily, and then Fossati fell to the floor where he lay clutching his nose and writhing in simulated pain. This was followed by a straight red card, a wink from Fossati to Archer, and Northern Ireland's exit from the tournament.

'It's a busy day.'

'I'm sure it is with all of that money Stuttgart are going to pay you for Ryan Slaney. You tell Davie I still have what's left of his shin pad if he wants it back. Did you know, we called him Signore Stromboli when he played in Italy?'

Everyone knew this but I let Fossati deliver the punchline.

'Because you never knew when he was going to erupt.'

'Something's never change.'

'So I gather. Now I understand you are interested in Dani Linares?'

'Yes, we think it's a good move for everyone. We all get what we need.'

'That as maybe, but you're the third call I have received about Dani this morning and I said the same to the others: he's not for sale. Not after everything we have been through together. The boy is like a son to me.'

I looked down at the script I had drafted and redrafted on my note pad.

'Signore Fossati, you are an important man, and this is a very busy day, so I will get straight to the point. We are willing to pay €21 million up front plus 7 more in add ons. We believe this is a fair price for a player who is still on his way back from a serious injury.'

I pictured Fossati mentally spending the money.

'Maybe in the summer but not now. There's no time to find a replacement. Not for a player of his class. Ball playing deep midfielders do not grow on trees. Besides, he has two years left to run on his contract.'

You can't be afraid of silence in any difficult conversation, you have to use it as a tool. So I did not reply. For thirty, maybe forty, long seconds the phone was quiet. I doodled on my pad, trying to stay calm. I reminded myself not to mention an improved figure until Fossati made a counter offer. Eventually he spoke.

'As you say, it is a busy day and I don't have time for games,' and with that he hung up. There was nothing to be gained by calling Fossati straight back. Instead, I opted to sit tight and wait for him to return to the table. I looked at the social media report, which had been prepared before Archer's bid for Kocsis had been hijacked. The various word clouds and pie charts documented the supporters' frustration with our failure to find a suitable replacement for Slaney. The report also contained screenshots from different social platforms including a lengthy thread by Benedict Moore, an attention seeking radio presenter, castigating the club's transfer policy. He listed the players he would move on and who he would like to see the club sign. It was pie in the sky. Fantasy football at its worst. We would do well to generate half the money from the sales he was advocating. Archer had made the mistake of responding, ridiculing Moore's weight, his performance in *Soccer Aid*, and his number of followers, and then dropped heavy hints about an imminent deal for a proven goal scorer, words that had now come back to haunt him.

I went back over the plan for that morning's training session, made a few final adjustments, and then reviewed the clips from the previous day. Kuipers demanded the ball, hollering at Valon and gesturing towards the turf in front of his feet. He played a slick, first time pass around the corner, and then moved immediately to seek out the space between the lines. He looked a completely different player to the nervous wreck I had inherited a few weeks before. The pricetag, an albatross around his neck for so long, now looked like a fair valuation. Or cheap at twice the price as Terry liked to say. I moved to the next clip. Again, he looked every inch the eighty-five-million-pound player. Arriving late on the edge of the box, he oozed confidence, taking the ball back across his man, twisting one way, and then another, before threading his shot through Jose Costa's open legs into the bottom left-hand corner.

Every player has confidence issues at some stage in their career and the causes are as varied as the symptoms: an honest mistake or bad luck, as in Fabio's case; criticism by the press and pundits; a slow recovery from an injury; the signing of a new player in your position; hostility from your own supporters during a match or afterwards on social media. Some players, sensitive souls like Kuipers, are more susceptible than others. The Dutchman took everything to heart, and not being wanted by Bescond was a new and wholly unenjoyable experience for him. For as long as Kuipers could remember, he was always first on the team sheet. Every coach, all the way back to the under eights, played to his strengths, building teams and game plans around him. And then suddenly he found himself in and out of the side, played out of position, unable to replicate his best form or affect games. He became trapped in a toxic circle of self-doubt, belittling comments from Slaney, and abuse from the fans. He was so scared of making a mistake, of another hammering from the fans, that he no longer looked for space or showed for the ball. A well-meaning, but poorly administered pep talk from Archer only made matters worse. He hauled Kuipers into his office and proceeded to catalogue all of the deficiencies in his game, making unfair comparisons with former teammates who excelled in the position that did not suit the Dutchman. This only served to reinforce his imposter syndrome. On my first day at Datchet, after the meetings with Fabio and Valon, I sat down with Kuipers and told him how important he would be for me, how well suited he was to my philosophy and principles of play. I handed him a blank sheet of the club's letter headed paper with his name and mine printed at the bottom.

'Forget what has happened since you joined,' I said, passing him a pen. 'Forget Bescond, the crowd… all of it. Today is a fresh start. Today I'm signing the best young number eight in Europe. The player who scored seven goals last season, provided nine assists. An attacking midfielder who can take the ball on the half turn and play through the lines. The man who is going to help me turn this club around. You just need to sign and date it at the bottom and then we are done.'

Kuipers looked bemused, but like the good soldier he was, he scribbled on the dotted line. I shook his hand.

'Welcome to Athletic. You are going to enjoy it here.'

Miracles rarely happen in football and I'd be lying if I said this triggered an immediate transformation. Kuipers was still a quiet, shy figure in the dressing room. He still lacked the focus or mental strength to put mistakes behind him. During a match or even a training session, you could almost see his mind whirring, as he overanalysed each mistimed shot or misplaced pass. But over time, positive reinforcement combined with an unbroken run in the side in his favoured position, saw him regain his belief. In those early weeks I gave him more one-to-one attention than any of the other members of the group, sending him clips and comments after each session. It wasn't all praise and soft soap. I highlighted areas for improvement, demanded more of him, but always with the clearest of subtexts: I value and accept you for who you are. I will help you become the best version of yourself. Archer dismissed any suggestion of appointing a sports psychologist ('This lot need tough love not tea and sympathy.') so it fell to me to change

Kuipers' inner narrative. Visualisation had helped other players in the past, so I encouraged him to imagine himself completing passes, short and long, providing assists. Celebrating in front of the Hill End as the fans chanted his name. I gave him a cue to manage his emotions, instructing him to spit on the grass to get the negativity out of his system whenever he felt it creeping back. After the Cheadle game, I joined him in the cryotherapy chamber, and as the temperature plunged, and the blood from our skin was redirected to our organs, I told him he could be the best in the world in his position, making sure the five other players shivering next to us heard. This, more than all the coaching or clips, seem to have the biggest impact on Kuipers. The following week he displayed far greater purpose and intensity in training, as if he finally believed he belonged. He clattered into Valon at full force, urged Zharnell to feed him the ball, and when Mats dug him out, he gave it back with interest. Clip by clip, word by word, confidence was reborn. Kuiper's legs no longer felt like lead when he crossed the line. He no longer suffered from a shortness of breath. He became far more decisive, making better decisions faster. He moved the ball with more speed and greater accuracy, and his numbers (passes in the final third, carries into the penalty box, chances created) all swung in the right direction.

In the next clip, Kuipers anticipated the pass and accelerated towards his man as the ball was played into him. Showing far more aggression, he blocked the pass before it was fully released, and the ball cannoned away towards Zito. I added another caption:

'Love the INTENSITY!'

After thirty minutes there had been no contact from Fossati. I began to think about how to break the news to Anita. I wanted to bring her a solution, not a problem, and so I looked again at the list of players that Xabi and I had identified. Then the phone rang. An Italian number. I smiled to myself and let it ring six or seven times before answering.

'Sergio—'

'HEY MOTHERFUCKER,' blasted the voice on the other end of the phone.

It was Gianluigi Corti – Gianni to his friends and enemies – Dani's agent.

'I hear you're trying to put together a deal for my guy. I'll tell you this just the once. Don't ever try to go around me again. *Ever.* If you do

I'll make you eat your own cojones – which won't be easy with broken fingers and no front teeth.'

Agents are a breed apart, all bluster and bravado. You learn to ignore the posturing and provocation. Besides, he didn't give me a chance to respond.

'I've spoken to Forsatti. He says someone else is in for Dani but that's just bullshit. I refuse to believe there's more than one person in this industry stupid enough not to come to me first,' he said in his rasping, chainsmoker's voice.

Dani had mentioned Gianni. The Italian called him twice a day without fail while he recuperated from his surgery. Each morning a new parcel arrived. Dani showed me the contents of one of his deliveries: The Godfather Part II DVD. Dani's favourite chocolates. Gucci socks - £125 a pair. A vintage copy of Italian Playboy. And a long handwritten letter full of dirty jokes and spelling mistakes.

'Dani wants to make the switch. And what my players want I always - *always* – get them. You feel me? So you and I are going to smoke that limp dick out. How high can you go?'

'We can up our offer to thirty-seven million.'

'I'm not talking about your next offer. I want to know how much you've got if you go all in.'

'I'm not going—'

'THREE SECONDS. You've got three fucking seconds or I'm going to call Ms Fang and tell her you fucking fucked this up. And you don't want that.'

Anita and I hadn't settled on a final figure, it hinged upon whatever we raised from any additional sales, and the fees for the other two players, so I took a gamble.

'Forty-six.'

'Good now you're starting to see how this works. Now one thing you need to know about me is I'm always fucking transparent when it comes to money. Mr fucking glass. You can ask anyone. They may hate my guts but they know they can trust me. So this is how we are going to break the number down. Thirty mill for Piedmont in two instalments. Three for Dani as a signing on fee. Six for Sergio. Three for you and four for Gianni. See what did I tell you, as clear as honey.'

'I can't agree to that.'

'Oh, sure, sure, of course, I forgot, you've got your code of fucking conduct. *Please.* Listen up Bambi. That's how it works. We'll keep yours and Sergio's end off the books. It all comes to my account in

Lichtenstein. We wash it at thirty degrees on a delicates setting and then it works its way back to you via a few small islands somewhere in the Caribbean. Or we can do crypto if you're into that.'

'I don't want any money.

'Wake up Joe. This is football, not Sunday school. We all need a little extra for a rainy day.'

***

Anita was encamped in the war room over at Preston Park with Mike Brooker, Kath Littlewood, the club secretary, and a couple of external lawyers. It took me four attempts to get through to her. I told her about Gianni's fee but glossed over Sergio's kickback. She must have known Gianni was greasing the wheels, but code of conduct or no code of conduct, she chose to look the other way.

'If that's what it takes then so be it. We're making slow progress with the other two,' she said. 'Kaiserslautern are digging in, they know we're getting top dollar for Slaney. And Lat-Am is not awake yet. Mike has WhatsApped La Boca's owner, Borello's agent, and a couple of other people he knows over there but we're not expecting to hear back until late morning.'

'What's the score with the medicals?'

'The team are on standby. We do them over at Mount Alvernia because we don't have our own MRI at Datchet. We're holding five slots between twelve and ten. We typically allow three hours to get it all done and review the medical data from the selling club, but we can do it in two at a push.'

Deadline day training sessions are the hardest of the year. Harder than integrating new signings into the group on the first day of preseason, or Christmas Day when the players and staff just want to be with their families. No one is fully present in the moment. There are too many emotions swirling around the players' heads. Excitement about a new signing who will strengthen the group. Disappointment that a move away has fallen through. Envy of another player's dream move or reported pay deal. The sense of bereavement from the sudden unexpected departure of a close friend. They would much rather be at home following it all on Sky Sports News. While as a coach, you wonder whether one of your best players will be snatched away against your wishes. Or if deals will be closed in time with those players you want to bring in. You can be fielding calls or swapping messages with the owner, the sporting director, agents and players. All of this severely impairs your ability to construct, communicate, and land a clear message with the group while out on the grass. So, in an attempt to hold everyone's attention, I added a new drill based on match play scenarios, pitting seven attackers up against six defenders in one half of the pitch, with four small target goals on the halfway line, and a keeper in a full-sized goal at the other end. The exercise began with a 4 v 2 midfield overload in the centre circle. The midfield four had to play a minimum of three passes to work the ball past the two opposing players. The front three took the ball on the half turn and then attacked the defensive line, with support from overlapping runs from midfield. If the defenders recovered the ball they attacked the unguarded target goals on the counter-attack. The drill worked on a core fundamental for each of the three units: for the defenders, how to hold a compact line, for the midfield, breaking the lines with forward balls under pressure, and for the attackers, how to pin and turn their marker.

We were midway through the session before I heard back from Gianni. He messaged as he spoke, in short, quick-fire bursts.

'We're ON.'

'SG on board.'

'Wants to change the payment schedule to balance books. No biggie.'

'Don't do commercial flights. Have booked a jet. (U R paying)'

'Will give Corriere the exclusive.'

'In LDN by 3.'

I could feel the players and coaching staff staring at me as I replied.

***

Mike Brooker helped himself to two more curled sandwiches from the platter in the centre of the boardroom table. A sullen, hungover Archer opened another can of Coke. Hannington continued with his monologue. The pompous idiot was enjoying his moment in the sun.

'…body fat is exemplary and VO2 is prodigious for someone who has played so little football… He has the blood pressure of a Hummingbird… Eyesight is fine, there's no dental problem, no skeletal problems. There's no trace of EPO or any other growth hormones in his bloods. No sign of any anabolics. No stimulants. No diuretics or masking agents. And he's all clear on recreational drugs.'

Anita gave the speaker phone a look that said 'get on with it.' I glanced up at the TV screen. The reporter outside Darlington's ground did his best to ignore the jostles and comments from the fans crowded around him. One of the teenage lads mimed a blow job. Another, a couple of years younger, waved at the camera. The reporter brought a hand to his ear in an attempt to hear himself speak over the the noise. The cameras cut back to the studio where the presenter battled to maintain a straight face. Next they switched to the other end of the country for an update on the feel good story of the window. Marcel Janvion was on the verge of a shock return to Torquay on loan from Milwaukee United until the end of the season. Here the supporters all wore curly wigs and false black goatees in a tribute to their hero. Two kids, too young to remember his first spell at the club, held up a banner with the words 'second coming'. The ticker tape reported another bit of good business by Macclesfield. Rijvers in for an undisclosed fee. Their third signing of the day and three more than Athletic.

'…wheat intolerance and cut bread out from his diet completely six years ago. Low density cholesterol is very low. HDL cholesterol is high… but that's the good one.' He paused for a moment. 'If it wasn't for the knee I would be dusting down the rubber stamp, but I'm concerned about the Medial Collateral Ligament. The player did OK in the physical tests. Good strength, good flexibility - but we can't judge how it will hold up to a long run of games, playing every three or four days. I'm going to need an expert opinion before signing him off.'

'JFDI,' Brooker mouthed at the speakerphone.

'That's fine Alistair. Please go ahead,' said Anita. 'We're running out of time.'

'Well, therein lies the problem. There are only two consultants in Europe I trust. Susan Greenberg is the best. She's published multiple papers on ligament reconstruction, but City have her on an exclusive retainer today. The same with Arjun Sharma at the Solis Clinic. The earliest either can do is tomorrow lunchtime.'

'There must be someone else,' said an exasperated Brooker.

'You can always find someone who will tell you what you want to hear Michael but if you want advice you can trust it has to be Sue or Arjun.'

Anita speared a tomato and a chunk of avocado with her fork and popped both in her mouth, giving nothing away, and so it fell to me to challenge Hannington.

'The PFA says more than seventy five percent of players Linares' age make a full recovery from this operation.'

'And I've no reason to doubt them. But one in four have long-term issues - Hoyle, Irani, Bruno Serina all come to mind - and there's no telling which camp he will fall into.'

I muted the speaker phone and spoke to Anita. 'I still think we should do this. No deal is without risk.'

Brooker was ominously quiet. The drone of a distant vacuum cleaner reverberated through the corridors of Preston Park. On the TV screen Slaney arrived at Stuggart's training ground. He stopped to sign a few autographs, grinned at the cameras, and then disappeared through the gates.

'Of course you can go ahead, that's your prerogative,' chimed in Hannington, as if he had a bug in the room. 'But look what happened the last time you disregarded my professional judgment.'

The boys had been working harder than before, a lot harder. You could see it in their faces and in the metrics. The sports science team raised a red flag, and Hannington advised me to reduce their load but I kept pushing, spending extra time on the training pitch and setting new goals for their fitness programs. Two days later Jeremie Aubert ruptured his Achilles stretching to win back the ball. He screamed as he hit the ground and lay there writhing in agony. The players rushed to comfort him, all except a smirking Slaney who juggled a ball on his own. The Maradona Seven – both feet, both knees, both shoulders, and then the head – on a loop. Aubert was carried away in tears. The pain and the prospect of rehab too much to bear. The thousand bee stings from the ultrasound. The endless sets of plyometrics, hopping forwards and backwards, left and right, around the clock face. Hours alone in the gym or the pool while the rest of the group worked with the ball, like a kid confined to bed on a sunny day, face pressed to the window as their friends play outside. Valon walked alongside the stretcher holding Aubert's hand. He knew about the long journey that lay ahead. I really felt for the lad. Another season wiped out by injury after he had worked so hard to recover from his ankle problem, contract renewal immediately placed on hold, but when you overhaul a squad's fitness and ramp up the intensity, you are going to lose a few players along the way.

Eventually Anita spoke. 'I'm sorry Joe. Without medical air cover we invalidate our insurance. We'll have to pass.'

25

The sky above Mehrabad airport was a cloudless blue, the sun a flaming yellow ball. Upon stepping out of the jet, we were immediately enveloped by the warm, heavy air. So warm, so heavy, you could feel it brush your cheeks as we descended the steps.

'This is more fucking like it,' said Jose Costa rubbing his hands. Like the rest of the squad, he was thrilled to see some sunshine after months of training outdoors in the wind and cold rain.

'Yeah, bro soak it up,' replied Zharnell from behind his sunglasses.

I looked left and right across the apron at the line of military jets. The warm weather training camp in downtown Tehran was a five-day long publicity stunt for the Iranian authorities and their bid to host the World Cup. But no matter what Em thought ('I can't believe you agreed to this,' she had said with disgust. 'I mean seriously, what were you thinking? You know women are banned from football stadiums?') the extended period of time together was also a golden opportunity to integrate the new signings and forge a sense of togetherness.

We were led across the tarmac into the VIP terminal. Ali Pezeshkzad was at the head of the party, flanked on either side by Rigg and Archer. A short walk through gleaming white corridors and an enclosed glass walkway, took us up and over the stationary aircraft and down into an adjoining hotel where the first of several media events was due to take place. Beneath crystal chandeliers, in an opulently furnished conference room, we met the Minister of Culture, who with his closely cropped beard, smart glasses, and open neck shirt looked far more western than I had expected. In fact I could easily picture him sitting next to Nick Cole around the cabinet table. He walked along the line of players, like a dignitary at a cup final, shaking hands and pausing every now and then to exchange a few words with one of the group. After this he introduced us to a group of smiling school children – all boys – between the ages of eight and twelve, who the minister said, stood to gain the most from a World Cup in Iran. Then the minister, accompanied by Rigg, Archer, and Ali, took his seat on a raised platform at the front of the room. The Union Jack, the Iranian flag, and Athletic's gold and burgundy colours were draped behind the four men. After the minister delivered a short speech in faultless English, Rigg rose to his feet and spoke at length without notes. He was in his element. Quoting Shakespeare and Plato, he thanked the minister for his hospitality, lavished praise on the country's sporting infrastructure, its commitment to using solar energy to deliver a carbon-zero tournament, and urged the football world to think about the huge positive legacy from bringing the World Cup back to the Middle East. Then, to a round of applause from the hand-selected audience, he announced the establishment of Tehran Athletic, a new spoke in Athletic's multi-club wheel. The players, dressed in their blazers and ties, listened dutifully. Senghor, Linares, and Barrolo sat next to each other in the back row. Mike Brooker and I saved the Linares deal, hammering out a loan until the end of the season with the option to make the move permanent. Gianni and Fossati's payments were doubled to smooth the way – Anita deliberately left the room when we reached this stage in the negotiations - and we closed the Borello deal with just minutes to spare after his agent demanded an additional £10,000 a week in wages and an undeserved reward fee.

Once the speeches were out of the way, Archer played head tennis with two of the older children. He played up to the cameras, bending down on both knees at one stage and trapping the ball behind his head between his shoulder blades. I had to hand it to him. The ambassadorial side of the role - posing for the cameras, exchanging gifts and firm handshakes, and generally scattering stardust over the proceedings - was what he did best. Everyone, from the Culture Minister to the school children, wanted a photo with him, and he took it in good grace, stopping at one point on our journey through the airport to pose for a selfie with a young security guard, then a photo with our driver in front of the coach.

From there we were whisked through the city, along streets lined with sycamore trees, to one of the new stadiums built to support the bid, where we held a gentle open training session in front of the media. It was amazing the difference sunshine and a change of scenery made to everyone's mood. The jaded negativity evaporated in the heat, replaced with child like enthusiasm as the players went about their business, laughing and joking in the sunlight, with no Slaney to bring the energy down. Even Terry just had the one complaint.

'I just can't get my head around the time here,' he grumbled as he adjusted his watch. 'Three and a half bleeding hours ahead. What's point of that? Why can't they keep it simple and round up to four?'

Dinner was a relaxed affair in a private room at the hotel. The four newest members of the squad each took it in turns to stand on a chair and sing a song. Xabi cracked jokes, while Archer entertained the players with yet more stories of his sexual exploits. Around 9 o'clock Terry and I left the group to unwind, safe in the knowledge alcohol is strictly forbidden in Iran. Archer, along with Rigg and Scooter, had a top floor penthouse suite and headed back to his room at the same time. I spent an hour studying Letchworth's patterns in defensive transition until I was interrupted by a panicked phone call from Terry.

'I popped my head round the door gaffer, just to check things were all okay, and it's fucking carnage down here. Dave and Bailey, and a few of the other lads are slaughtered.'

I was dumbfounded.

'The nearest bar is over a thousand miles away.'

'Archer has a suitcase full of booze. Looks like he emptied the jet. Most of the lads just had a glass or two but Dave couldn't leave it there. He and Bailey and Javi have been caning champagne, vodka, you name it, and he's been telling the boys one by one what he really thinks of them. It's not pretty.'

I shuddered when I heard this, thinking back to Archer's rant in his office on my first day.

'The hotel staff have turned a blind eye so far but if the police get wind of it we are well and truly fucked.'

'I'll be right there.'

When I entered the room Archer was laying into Rafiq with an expletive riddled assessment of his game and character. Rafiq stood frozen in front of him, not knowing where to look or what to do. Archer was paralytic, but seemed strangely pleased to see me, and it was only when I declined his offer of a drink that he transformed into his fearsome alter ego, a man who could shred a player's belief with just a handful of words. He sloshed some more red wine into his glass, spilling a small scarlet pool on the tablecloth, and then let rip.

'Did you honestly think you could walk in here and turn this lot around? A couple of seasons laying out the cones for Paco, a few years in charge of a club no one's ever heard of doesn't qualify you to play with the big boys, I mean we're not playing Football Manager here son. This is the real fucking deal.'

He looked me up and down. The chiselled features were flushed with alcohol. Envy and resentment blazed in his eyes.

'Face it, you've been found out,' he said savagely. 'Eight games is what we gave you, isn't that right Tel?' A shamefaced Terry looked away and said nothing in reply.

'But it looks like you'll be out of here sooner than that. And I won't lie. I can't fucking wait.'

'Look Dave, it's been a long day, why don't you call it a night hey? said Terry. '

'Call it a night? I'm only getting started.'

He rose to his feet and swayed momentarily, before steadying himself by grasping the tabletop. He leaned forward, speaking now in a stage whisper.

'Psst… and I've got to tell you something son, if you think these three' – he waved an arm in the direction of Linares, Borello, and Senghor who were seated together and looked shell shocked – 'are going to save your skin, you're barking up the wrong tree. They're not fit to pull on the shirt' – he turned to address them – 'no offence lads, few are.' He inhaled yet more red wine.

'Do you know what I told him on his first day?' he said addressing the group. '"Recruitment is my area, keep your neck wound in." But you couldn't help yourself could you? Eh? Well look where it has got you,' Archer said scornfully. 'These boys don't have what it takes.'

Then he took two strides towards me and without warning threw a punch. This wasn't the haymaker he landed on Keith Tomkinson in the cup final. It was a slow, ragged swipe, and easy to avoid, and before I could stop it my balled fist slammed into Archer's stomach, knocking the air out of him. Archer went down hard and lay on the floor gasping and moaning. The players looked on, not knowing what to do. Archer tried to stand up, but his legs buckled, and he lurched in one direction before toppling in the other. He groaned again, raised his head a few inches off the ground and then passed out, leaving us with the task of smuggling one of the world's most recognisable men, a man famous for his drink problem, through a crowded hotel.

The following morning we had another training session, this time at the newly renovated Azadi stadium. We began as usual with box work, then more positioning drills, using a large sack of plastic markers we had brought with us to mark out the grid. After that I mixed things up with two six a side matches, one in either half of the pitch, where the players were forbidden from speaking to force them to raise their heads and improve their awareness of what was going on around them.

Early evening, as temperatures began to fall, we played a friendly behind closed doors against the Iranian champions. Winning is a habit, a muscle that needs to be conditioned, so I fielded our strongest eleven and resisted the temptation to make extensive changes at half-time.

The hosts, familiar with the conditions, and pumped up by the opportunity to play a famous English club, flew out of the traps and scored an early goal. My heart sunk as the ball was deflected past Fabio. Defeat here was unthinkable. But I need not have worried. Without the fans on their back, the boys played with freedom, rotating positions, creating angles and options. Suddenly everything we had been working on for the past four weeks fell into place, and it did not take long for Kuipers to score a nerve calming equaliser. Four more goals followed, each better than the last as Senghor, Barello and Zito ran riot under a Peach Melba sunset. The only negative was the woeful performance by Ali Pezeshkzad, a second half substitute, who struggled to find space or complete his passes. Xabi and I exchanged a concerned look as he failed, yet again, to control a ball played into him at pace. With all the coaching in the world, he was never going to be good enough.

26

The large flag rippled in the hands of the sponsors and competition winners lined up around the centre circle as the anthem reached its climax. The two rows of players clapped and waved to the crowds. The young mascots dressed in replica kits and tracksuit tops smiled and fidgeted. The camera panned up out of the stadium. A white mitre full moon hung low in the sky, so low you could see the acne scars on its face.

'Last chance,' said Terry.

'Three nil to Haarlem. Faas Wilkes to score first, in the twenty third minute,' said Jordan Allen.

'Three one to Haarlem, Wilkes in the sixth minute,' said Xabi.

'Gaffer?

I took a sip of wine. 'Two one to Macclesfield. Maleche in the thirty second minute.'

'Like candy from a baby,' said Terry. He held out his hand. 'Fifty sovs each.' He gathered the notes and placed them on a small plate in the centre of the table.

Dinner was on me. A chance to thank the staff for their support in turning things around. After the difficulties and missed chances in January, we had taken fourteen points from eighteen in February and moved up to seventh in the table. The new additions to the squad and time together in Iran had made a massive difference. Dani Linares settled quickly and transformed the team, policing the area in front of the centre backs and linking play like Makélélé or Busquets. He was comfortable under pressure, always available for the ball, with a first touch like Laudrup, the flicks and angles bending the laws of physics to breaking point. He spotted players' runs before they made them, and completed passes with faultless distribution off both feet.

The impact of Barello and Senghor at the top of the pitch was just as pronounced. The Uruguayan scored on his debut and notched up two more goals and four other goal involvements in the following five games. Along with Senghor and Zito he brought aggression and intensity to the first line of defence, harrying opponents and winning the ball back close to their goal. Valon's Indian Summer had also continued, his form and confidence fully restored. He provided the on-field coaching needed to embed a different playing style, pushing his ageing body and vocal chords to the limit. Reminding the other boys when and where to move, what zones to occupy. Correcting our shape and the distance between the lines. Ensuring we were narrow and compact out of possession and maximising the full height and width of the pitch when we had the ball. Applauding every positive action and urging and cajoling when the level dropped. Alerting teammates to incoming challenges and bellowing instructions at set pieces. He was so hoarse after each game that the sports science team made him gargle warm salt water.

I had persisted with Zharnell at right back and he had proved to be a fast learner. Day after day we worked on the defensive side of his game, improving his positioning and correcting his upright body shape. Now he crouched low when he was in a duel, ready and able to make a sudden move in any direction, and he held his position intelligently when we were set in a defensive block, with his body open so that his heels were perpendicular to the goal line. He scanned across the defensive line and over his shoulder and had become far more decisive and authoritative when handing a runner over to Valon.

The single biggest factor in our revival, however, was the change in mentality. If I'd taught the players one thing, it was the value of winning. To never settle for anything less than three points. To understand the true cost of defeat, and to fight to the very end. To win every ball, every training session, every half. To take ownership and ask themselves: 'what can I do today to improve? How do I ensure we win the next game? And the one after, and the one after that.'

It was important not to get carried away, we were still only in the foothills in the long hard climb towards peak performance, but the building blocks were now in place. And success on the pitch had led to increased influence and access off it. Anita calling late at night to seek a second opinion on proposed coaching appointments at our affiliate clubs, which players to track for the summer window, or my assessment of the performances and prospects of various academy and loan players.

Hawksmoor in Piccadilly was an Art Deco lover's wet dream: Herringbone wooden flooring, oak panelling, and racing green leather seats and booths. Lead-lined windows allowed diners to watch the pedestrians below take their lives in their hands as they crossed Regent Street, weaving between the black cabs and red double decker busses. As well as enjoying a good meal, dinner was also an opportunity to watch Macclesfield, one of our forthcoming opponents, play FC

Haarlem, the Dutch and European champions. It was a duel of contrasting styles and philosophies, two very different strains of football. The Dutch fighter jet, optimised for speed, stealth, and movement, versus the English heavily protected battle tank. Haarlem were everyone's favourite second team. An emblem of the beautiful game, full of quicksilver combinations and attacking intent. A showreel of one touch passing sequences and finishes that lifted you out of your seat. They made the audacious seem routine and the mundane joyful. While for Macclesfield, football was a bloodsport. They dismembered opponents with a sharp-edged midfield diamond and a battering ram of a centre forward. Everything was simple, direct, and premeditated. They sat deep, pressed in synchronised waves, and countered with preset attacking patterns.

Haarlem attacked from the first whistle, moving the ball with a succession of short snappy passes and pushing Macclesfield back into their favoured low defensive block. They looked sharp and in the mood, a storm front of attacking options. It was like watching the sea pound a coastal wall at high tide. Again and again, they rained down upon Macclesfield's goal, but the away side stood firm, repelling the attacks.

'Macclesfield were the first team I saw as a kid. They were playing Lincoln City, my Dad's team. This was when they were still bumping around in the lower divisions,' said Gemma Dando, the club's head of sports science.

After selling their newspapers, the Cromwell sisters had borrowed heavily to acquire Macclesfield. Rather than service the loan themselves, they loaded the debt onto the club, triggering a wave of buy outs as TV revenues surged.

'First game I saw was Spurs against Brighton in 1990. It was Graham Moseley's testimonial. Italia 90 was only a couple of months away but Gazza and Lineker both turned out,' said Kenny Walsh.

Everyone shook their heads in disbelief. The two men who led England to victory in the World Cup, risking injury only weeks before the tournament started to help a fellow pro.

'I was there in the North Stand right behind the goal with my mates from school. I remember Lineker leaning on the front post waiting for a corner to be taken. We were only a few feet away. The older lads behind us giving him a bit of banter, all good humoured, "Leicester reject" stuff like that. Lineker smiling and waving. It was the first and only time I've enjoyed watching Brighton lose.'

'SCHRIVJERS. A QUICK ONE-TWO. HERE'S KLAASSENS. ABIOLA WINS IT BACK.'

'And Gazza bossed it. This was a decent Brighton team - we made it to the play off final the following season - but no one could get near him.'

'That was when he was at the very top of his game,' said Terry, cutting a wedge of rib eye and smearing it in béarnaise sauce. 'He just glided past players, made things happen. On muddy pitches, with zero facking protection.'

We discussed Gascoigne's best goals. Turning Colin Hendry inside out at Wembley, and then celebrating in the dentist's chair. Beating five men as he strolled through Pescara's zona mista. Then Mike Brooker told us about his first game, Forest away to Ajax in the European Cup.

'One of my Dad's mates was a PE teacher and he borrowed the school minibus. We took the ferry from Harwich across to Rotterdam and drove on up to Amsterdam. There was twenty of us squeezed into this rattling old thing with no seatbelts in the back. Clive, one of my Dad's mates, was a big fella and he had these cuts and bruises all over his face after an accident at work. We stopped somewhere for lunch not long after leaving Rotterdam. A nice little place—'

'All tulips, and clogs and bike lanes eh Mike?'

'Yeah, Terry, something like that. Anyway, we walked up to the only bar in the village but the owner saw us coming. He took one look at Clive, who was at the front of the group, and the rest of us behind him in our football shirts, and he dashed to the door, locked it and turned the sign to closed.'

Brooker stared into space for a moment, running through the memories from the trip.

'And then when we got to the ground my Dad got me and a couple of the other kids to hold up this big hand-painted banner to see if we could get on TV.'

'What was the score?' asked Xabi.

'Forrest lost one nil on the night but won two one on aggregate. Viv Anderson was immense. Didn't put a foot wrong all night.'

'MALECHE WANTS A FREEKICK BUT THE REFEREE WAVES PLAY ON. THE COLUMBIAN IS FURIOUS.'

Ricardo Maleche was a card waving, boundary pushing Provocateur. A black belt in mental disintegration. He chipped away at defenders' concentration and discipline. Shoving, kicking, and scratching. Whispering insults. All to trigger an error or a reaction.

'THAT'S GOOD DEFENDING ALAN, REALLY GOOD DEFENDING.'

The camera cut to Lauge Dastrup who was prowling the technical area with his usual aneurysm inducing intensity. His face balled up in anger, cheeks the colour of beetroot, two black bullets for eyes. Urging his players on and haranguing the fourth official. Behind him Macclesfield flaunted their wealth, with half a dozen world class players warming the bench. They each made a point of encouraging their team-mates, applauding every pass or tackle. Dastrup demanded nothing less. During his first game in charge he had watched how the players on the bench reacted when the team missed a chance. Some were visibly frustrated, as they rooted for the team from the sidelines, but the rest showed no reaction, no commitment or togetherness, and were shown the door at the end of the season.

'RIGHT IDEA. HE JUST OVER HIT IT.'

'Hold on. I want to look at this,' I said. 'Rewind. Back a bit, the next phase, here. Look at how awkward Tyreece is when they made him play quickly on his left.'

We watched as the fullback hit a rushed pass straight to an opposing player.

'We need to adjust the first press. Give the centre backs no option but to play to Tyreece and then jump him.'

It wasn't much but it gave us something to work with. A thread to pull at.

'THAT'S A GOOD INTERCEPTION BY WANJIKU, WHO PLAYS IT LONG AIMING TO PICK OUT MALECHE. SCHRIJVERS CLEARS BUT ONLY AS FAR AS OLSEN.'

Maleche backed into Olsen while the Norwegian was in the air, making no attempt to play the ball. We watched it again in slow motion from several angles. Maleche looking over his shoulder and waiting until Olsen was at the height of his jump then moving into him. Haarlem's number eight fell hard, triggering a mushroom cloud of grass cuttings, and Maleche then went to ground, face down, clutching the back of his head.

'He did that on purpose,' said Xabi.

'He did the same thing against Collingham and Darlington. He knows exactly what he's doing.'

'It's so dangerous. He could break someone's neck.'

'Come off it Gem, there's nothing wrong with that,' said Terry. 'He's being smart, using his body to draw the foul.'

The referee kept her cards in her pocket but pointed to the spot, waving away the protests from the Haarlem players who had gathered around her. A smirking Maleche wiped a blade of glass from his forehead and winked at a teammate. He ignored the noise from the crowd, the movement from the keeper on the line, and his own nerves, slamming the ball into the bottom corner. He made it look as simple as shutting a car door. No stuttering steps or waiting for the keeper to move, just picking a spot and trusting his technique.

Dastrup had transformed Macclesfield into confident front runners. Under the Dane, they had dropped only two points from winning positions in two seasons. Shape and organisation remained paramount, even after they scored. There was no deviation from their policy of containment, no rush to push home the advantage. Instead, they sat back, slowed the game down, and dared the opposition to overcommit. The base of the diamond providing protection, the tip ready to spring the counterattack. Dastrup was the first to enter the tunnel at half-time, in a hurry to remind his players that, despite the scoreline, the world remained against them.

'He must need a dump,' said Terry.

Rinus Kohn chatted calmly to one of his assistants as they ambled from the dugout, smiling at his team as they passed. The message was clear: no need to panic we've still got this. The cameras returned to the studio. David Archer, as the caption on the screen reminded us, lifted the trophy three times.

'Let's hear what the oracle has to say,' said Terry.

Archer was dressed in a beautifully cut suit, with a paisley patterned tie and matching handkerchief in his top pocket. He spoke first, stumbling over his words.

'It's been a game… a good game of football… two good teams, different styles… all to play for in the second half.'

'Definitely back on the sauce,' muttered Terry.

Leanne Price, the former England captain, broke down the Maleche incident using slow motion footage to explain how the Macclesfield striker engineered the foul. Archer responded but stumbled again and lost his train of thought. Amir Ghosh the show's anchor completed his sentence for him before they watched the incident from a different angle.

Archer had been even more difficult to work with since our confrontation in Tehran. One moment he would be in what was a good mood by his standards, and we would have a constructive conversation about tactics and individual performances. The next, he would be terse and objectionable. Questions would go unanswered or be met with a pointed question of his own. The smallest thing would spark an angry outburst or a personal attack. You're the fucking coach, he would tell me if I asked him for his opinion. But the reaction would be even worse if I didn't seek his input. And the more games we won, the better the performance levels, the more praise the media lavished on me, the more respect the club's hierarchy afforded me, the worse he became.

The camera's gaze fell back upon Archer who struggled either to remember or pronounce the name of Macclesfield's full back and resorted instead to all manner of verbal contortions ('the left back, the new lad, the kid from Ecuador'). Price cut across Archer and said something smart and insightful about Haarlem's positioning when the ball was recycled, contradicting Archer's rambling comments.

'He won't like that,' said Terry.

Anger flashed in Archer's eyes as if his shins had been raked with metal studs.

'I think you must be watching a different game love. When you've—'

Ghosh leapt in. 'Hold that thought Dave,' he said before turning to face the camera. Archer shot him a death stare. 'We'll be right back after the break with more analysis from Leanne and Dave and all the second half action. Don't go away.'

'Terrible news about Ronnie Clark,' said Mike Brooker topping up Terry's glass.

Clark's family had announced he had been diagnosed with early onset dementia.

'Facking awful. The poor guy's only a few years older than me.'

The Scottish central defender was a mainstay of a fractious, hard-boiled Leeds side that yo-yoed between the second and first division in the late 1970s and early 80s. A mountain of a man, with legs like girders and a hair trigger temper, he was never happier than when playing the man and the ball.

'Did you play against him?' Xabi asked Terry.

'A couple of times. He was some player, always ready to put his body on the line.' Terry looked around the table to check everyone was listening. 'And he was nasty,' he said approvingly. 'I went past him the first time I played against Leeds, and he told me he would split my knee open if I ever did it again. And he facking meant it. And every time I went up for a corner, he lamped me with his elbow.'

I thought of the story of Clark completing a match with a broken leg. Him squaring up to Jim Broadie during the Charity Shield. His blood-stained shirt after the clash of heads when playing for his country. The photo of him holding a cigar and swigging from a can of lager in the Wembley dressing room after winning the FA Cup.

'He would've had a hundred caps in any other era,' Terry continued. 'But Hansen, McLeish, and Willie Miller kept him out of the team.'

'Heading will be out of the game in five maybe ten years' time,' said Gemma.

I had a flashback as she said this to Sunday league football as a kid. The Dad who managed the team yelling at us to head the goal kicks as the heavy wet ball plummeted out of the sky, screaming if we let it bounce first. How your whole head shook if you misjudged it.

'Out of my cold dead hands,' said Terry.

The referee checked her watch, exchanged words with the fourth official, and blew her whistle to kick off the second half.

'GO ON,' shouted Jordan Allen, rising out of his seat. '*YES*.'

'What a goal,' said Xabi, shaking his head. He was right, it was brilliantly worked, a set play straight from kick off. Timmerman, the left wing back, received the ball just inside his half and broke the lines with his body shape. He turned back towards his own goal as if to pass to Haarlem's central defender but at the last moment played a diagonal ball infield to Rynsburger who carried the ball a few yards before picking out Manyang just outside the D. The Sudanese striker played it first time, at pace, between the two centre backs and to the feet of Kovalenko who took two touches. One to control the ball, the second to fire it past the keeper from sixteen yards.

Play continued at a frantic pace for the next fifteen minutes as Haarlem sought to capitalise on the shift in momentum. Twice they manufactured good chances down the left channel. A graphic flashed up on the screen showing that Haarlem had had 78% possession since the start of the second half.

'KROL HAS BEEN SO DYNAMIC FOR THE DUTCH SIDE.'

The waitress cleared away our plates and asked if we had enjoyed our meal.

'Yeah, thanks love,' replied Terry. 'It was proper nice.'

'WAIT A MINUTE. THIS DOESN'T LOOK GOOD.'

Play stopped and the fourth official held up the board. Maleche trudged off the pitch muttering and gesticulating towards his lower abdominal area. Everyone around the table cheered.

'His groin's gone,' said Jordan Allen.

Maleche's replacement clapped his teammate off from the touchline. The two men high-fived with both hands.

'Looks more like his hip flexor to me,' said Gemma. 'There's no way he'll be fit to play against us.'

'LONG BALL PLAYED TOWARDS RAMIRES. BEAUTIFULLY PULLED DOWN.'

Maleche's understudy made an immediate impact. He lifted his right knee up high so that his leg formed a perfect right-angle – like the *Karate Kid's* crane – then cushioned the ball so it fell thirty centimetres in front of him, begging for a half volley. But Ramires didn't trust his left foot and stabbed awkwardly at the ball with the outside of his right. It was an ugly, jerky movement but enough to guide it past the keeper and into the net, and a reminder that the quick thrust of a broken bottle can be just as deadly as any elaborate swordplay.

Ramires raced towards the corner where he slid across the turf on his knees with his tongue stuck out pointing at the cameras. He stood up and embraced the rest of his team. The camera returned to the Haarlem keeper to capture him spitting into his goal and shaking his head in annoyance. The goal triggered an immediate response from Rinus Kohn. He made his final substitution replacing one of the centre backs with a fourth striker and switching to a 1-2-3-5 system. But the blockade continued, restricting Haarlem to half chances and recriminations. We muted the sound as soon as the referee blew time.

'So what do you think? I asked the group around the table. Xabi spoke first.

'We have to attack the diamond. It's the only way.'

He was right. The four central midfielders in Macclesfield's 1-4-1-2-1-2 system dominated the middle third. Their narrow diamond was a road block and supply line, overloading opposing midfield threes and rerouting the ball forwards. Rather than attacking this killing zone head on, we needed to bend it out of shape, exploit the space on either flank.

'It's all about the fullbacks, I said.

I took the glass tumblers for the iced water and arranged them into Macclesfield's formation, with the four points of the diamond at its centre. 'This is Macclesfield and this is Zharnell.' I moved a glass of red wine into zone 10, wide on the right, approaching the halfway line. 'We feed the ball to Zharnell.' I moved the salt cellar from Valon to Zharnell. 'We now have two options. If their left midfielder comes towards Zharnell.' I shifted the tumbler on the left side of the diamond. 'Then Zharnell passes to Kuipers in the space that has been vacated. But if they don't press, then Zharnell can continue down the wing and feed Senghor or Borello.'

'What if the diamond moves to the left as a unit?' said Allen, re-arranging the glasses. 'They protect the space inside the diamond and stop Zharnell from carrying the ball down the wing.'

'Zharnell switches play with a ball out to Mats in zone eleven or twelve,' said Xabi moving the salt cellar to the space that had opened up on the other side of the diamond.

'Exactly. Giving us space and an overload. We also mix it up, with some rotation, to keep them guessing. Zharnell advances up the wing without the ball into zone sixteen.' I moved the glass five metres inside Macclesfield's half. 'And Kuipers drops short to receive the ball from Valon. If Bowen holds his position to cover Zharnell then Kuipers carries the ball into the empty space here.' I pointed to the area to the right of the centre circle, just past the halfway line. 'And then works it forward to Borello or Zito who are in this pocket.' I pointed to the gap between the players at the base and right side of the diamond. 'But, if Bowen tracks the run when Kuipers drops, Kuipesy should still get there first and can play a quick out ball to Zharnell who will be free here.'

'Won't their left back push up and mark Zharnell?'

'No, Dastrup won't let him leave Senghor free,' said Xabi.

'Build it into the drills Terry,' I said. 'We'll use two thirds of the pitch and feed into Valon in zone seven, three or four metres from the centre circle. He works the ball to Zharnell or Mats. But it has to be quick from side to side, one or two touches, no more. The faster we do this the more they have to move, and the harder it becomes for them to maintain their shape.'

27

Before arriving at Preston Park, I did not appreciate how much of my time would be given over to the media and external communication. Pre- and post-match press conferences, often twice a week. Print and broadcast interviews with media outlets from across the world. A profile in *L'Équipe*, an interview in *Marca*, and the constant pieces to camera for Athletic TV and the club's social media channels. Then there was day-to-day issues management. Agreeing a line on the form, fitness, and availability of individual players. Responding to mind games from opposing coaches or comments by the pundits. Messages and phone calls would intrude at every hour of the day or night. Lara was the best in the business, but like Scooter, she had different objectives. Success on the grass was everything to me, but for Lara it was just an input. A stepping stone towards a stronger brand and more followers around the world. My invitation to spend the day with us at Datchet was an attempt to re-calibrate her priorities.

'Alright gaffer? Nice to see you down here Lara, bit out of your way, aren't you?' Terry teased, as he and his heavily ladened tray clattered by.

'You're looking well Terry,' she replied.

Breakfast together was now mandatory for all the players and coaching staff. No exceptions. One or two of the late risers resisted it initially but Valon soon brought them into line, and to breakdown the cliques we encouraged the players to mix up their seating arrangements, doing away with the senior players' table or sitting in units, and ensuring everyone sat next to a different person each morning.

'The gaffer's got me on a new regime,' he said brandishing his tray proudly. 'Omelette, porridge, berries, enough nuts to see a family of squirrels through the winter. No more sausages, no bread. No sugar in my tea.'

He turned sideways to show Lara his slimmer profile.

'What do you think? Not bad huh?'

'Like a new man Terry.'

'Work in progress, Lara, work in progress. You know what they say, if you can pinch more than an inch. Now I gotta go. The only thing worse than a bowl of hot porridge is a bowl of bleeding cold porridge.'

Terry joined the staff and players on the long table we had installed in the centre of the canteen. The clips running on a loop on the video wall behind him highlighted the space either side of Macclesfield's midfield diamond.

'Where were we?' Lara enquired.

'JC's Marca interview.'

'It's going to cause waves I'm afraid.'

'What's he said now?'

They asked him if he ever thought about playing for Barcelona or Madrid and he said 'it's every Spanish kid's dream to pull on the white shirt.'

I groaned. This was going to be a distraction, a four day media sideshow we could do without. The interview was Scooter's idea, to support the club's drive to '*deepen the fanbase on the Iberian peninsula,'* and another example of misaligned objectives.

'You must have seen that one coming?' I replied, annoyed.

'Of course, but it was a young female reporter and JC was trying to impress her, giving good copy rather sticking to the lines to take.'

I looked over at Jose Costa who was laughing and joking with Barollo. I could have throttled him.

'What do we do?'

'Ride it out. Say nothing that will enflame the situation and it will blow over in a few days.'

'What about getting JC to put out a statement or a post on social media?'

'No, it will just give it more legs. The only thing we could do is bring forward the comms on Zito's new contract. Give them something else to talk about.'

'Let's do that. Can you square it with Dave?'

'Leave it with me.'

'Perfect, and I'll tell JC to be more careful next time.'

She handed me her iPad.

'Here's the latest draft of your programme notes, we've incorporated all your changes. The paragraph on Ronnie Clark is a nice touch.'

The staff and players stood and cheered as Fabio walked through the door. The Italian had earned a recall for the forthcoming international break after a series of excellent performances. Lara whipped out her phone to record the scene, as the players struck up a chant of:

'F-A-B-I-O, WE'VE GOT FABIO.'
'F-A-B-I-O, WE'VE GOT FABIO.'
'F-A-B-I-O, ITALY'S NUMBER ONE.'

Fabio and I exchanged fist bumps and a look as he passed. Once he had joined the other players, we took our seats again.

'There's one other thing you need to be aware of,' said Lara lowering her voice to a murmur. 'It's the Lantsov trial.'

The court case had begun a month or so ago and things did not look good for the Russian. I had zero fucking sympathy for him. Every time I read one of the daily updates I asked myself what was he thinking? How could a man who had everything, a wife, two young children, a five-year deal with Athletic, be so reckless, so stupid? Where was the control, the fucking discipline?

'The prosecution are going to disclose that Bailey introduced Vlad to the girl. Apparently, he was sleeping with her sister, on and off. I'm talking to Bailey and his agent later today, see what we can do to get ahead of it. We'll dial down his promotional activity through the club's channels and up his charitable work, but let's face it, he's in for kicking. The press will dredge up all the old stories.'

'Will he have to give evidence?'

'It wouldn't surprise me, although Christ knows, he is the last person you would want to put on the stand.'

She sighed. 'Life would be so much easier if these boys could just keep their dicks in their pants.'

***

'MOVE THE BALL FASTER,' I shouted. We were working on attacking the second six-yard box, the rectangle of space between the penalty spot and the goal area where the majority of goals are scored. It was a drill I picked up from Gerard Houllier. I had written to tell him how much I enjoyed his book *Entraineur: Competence et Passion* and received a handwritten response inviting me to spend a few days observing pre-season training. It was a typically generous gesture. A few weeks later I stood in the shade of the Millennium Pavilion and inhaled history. Ron Yeats, Ian St John, and Roger Hunt. Emelyn Hughes, Kevin Keegan, and John Toshack. Hansen, Souness, Dalgleish. Barnes, Beardsley, Rush. Fowler and McManaman, they all trained on those three pitches. One exactly the same size as Anfield. One shorter and narrower, and the third longer and wider. I watched as

Gerard, the old schoolteacher, wrung every last drop of ability out of his pupils, his words echoing off the granite walls. I wasn't the only spectator. Fans stood on bins to peer over the wall. Kids looked in from the balconies and windows of the nearby tower blocks.

The session was all about creating chances through rapid movement and passing in and around the box. The attacking unit working the ball between them from one side of the box to the other and then playing in a wide forward in the half-space channel. We started with unopposed practice, just five mannequins spaced out along the eighteen yard line and an empty penalty area. One player carried the ball inside from the left wing until he met the mannequin on the corner of the box, where he would check back, so his body faced the centre circle, and play a short angled pass to a teammate in a pocket between the lines. This player would drive towards the goal at a forty five degree angle until he met the second mannequin, where he would turn and feed a third player, who had dropped deep. This player would move the ball a few feet and then play a weighted pass between the fourth and fifth mannequins, behind the defence, and into space for the wide player on the right. His job was to cut it back first time and pick out player one or player two who were now bursting into the second six yard box.

We worked at this for twenty minutes or so, switching flanks and rotating starting positions, and then moved to an opposed set up with Valon and Jose Costa in the box, adding a further two defenders after another ten minutes. Borello looked razor sharp, moving rapidly to occupy the correct positions and fire past Fabio. The Argentine had a tremendous work ethic. Like, Dani and Valon, he treated every moment of training as if it was a cup final, and his attitude and work-rate, the dedication to his art, was infectious and inspired others to new levels.

We stopped for a drinks break. The players chatted about *Love Island* and the darts world championships, poked fun at Bailey's new haircut with its elaborate feather fringe, and teased JC about his latest girlfriend. Zharnell and Bailey tried to persuade Zito to play *Call of Duty* that evening, but the Brazilian politely declined. Valon reminded the group about a forthcoming visit to Wexham Park, the local hospital. Mats tightened his studs. Xabi was stationed on the opposite touchline to spot mistakes and give instructions to the players furthest away from me. My request for him to join the first team coaching staff was the latest flashpoint with Archer, threatening to tip our Cold War into a full blown nuclear conflict. Thankfully, Anita had overridden his objections, declaring that it would be a good experience for Xabi. Like Terry, Xabi's career was ended prematurely by injury. It was pretty much the only thing the two men had in common. For while Terry had no throttle, and was incapable of regulating his most basic of impulses, Xabi had superhuman levels of self-control. And in contrast to Terry's weary, seen-it-all-before air of resignation, Xabi was a giver of time and energy. He lifted the group the same way he lifted weights; tirelessly and with a smile on his face. At thirty-two he was closer to the players in age and mindset and understood their world, their language and motivations, better than any coach I've known. He had that unquantifiable x-factor that drew people to him and made them seek his approval. And when he delivered a tough message, one to one or with the individual units, it was taken as encouragement rather than criticism.

'It was a good laugh last night boss, the boys are buzzing this morning,' Xabi said after bounding over to join me. While performances had improved, I still felt the players had more to give. Too many were just passing through the club, with no knowledge and little interest in its history and traditions. They needed to understand they were part of something bigger than a pay cheque if we were going to unlock their extra discretionary effort. My first idea was a tour of the museum and a talk from the club's historian, a former employee now in his late seventies who maintained the archives. Emily scrunched up her face when I mentioned this to her over dinner. 'History doesn't have to be boring Dad, you know. Why don't you do a pub quiz instead? Make it interesting.'

The format for the evening was based on various TV game shows and I asked the players to prepare the questions for each round. Fabio had edited photos for name the player, concealing faces and identities. Zharnell and Jose had compiled a selection of video clips for what happens next? And Borello gave a star turn in name that chant. Bailey was the MC, cracking jokes and recycling catchphrases from quiz shows that most of the people in the room had never seen.

'How's Rob?' asked Terry.

As well as sheep dipping the squad in the club's history, the quiz was also an opportunity to improve my relationship with the former players who now worked in the media. Rob Meade, Bernard Joffre and a handful of their former teammates all joined us. Rob had swapped tables to keep his distance from Terry. The two men had barely spoken since Paco called time on Rob's career.

'You know Rob, soft skills are not his strong point. But we had a good chat. He likes the direction we're heading in. I told him the lads have taken a battering from the media this year, that we need more positivity. He went off on one. "Too many people in that dressing room feel they're entitled to a living. They can't expect any favours. They need to earn praise, understand what it means to play for Athletic." But at least the line of communication is open. I also had a good conversation with Bernard. He told me, all he wants is for the team to do well. We have his support as long as we continue to move in the right direction.'

28

At the end of every day's training, after he had thawed out from the cryotherapy, I spent an hour with Zito watching videos of the best centre forwards at work. Each session was a masterclass in the art of goal scoring. We studied how Sergio Aguero turned a player, the positions Ian Wright and Robbie Fowler took up during different passages of play, how Klinsmann moved across the defender to meet the ball. The timing of Andy Cole's runs behind the last line. How Lineker moved towards the ball and brought a man with him, and then spun and used his pace to get in behind. I pointed out how Lineker would signal to his teammate on the ball that he was about to spin and make the run. We then moved onto Shevchenko, Stoichkov, Shearer, and Sutton. Rush, Rossi, and Van Nistelroy. Romario, Edmundo, and Ronaldo. Vieri, Del Piero in his final years when he played more direct. We watched the clips over and over again. The first two or three times at normal speed, then in slow motion, freezing the frame or going back to get a better appreciation of the player's body shape, movement or technique.

It was this limitless thirst for knowledge and self-improvement, as much as his natural gifts, that marked Zito out as a special player. After the first few sessions he came armed with clips he wanted to share with me, things he had noticed watching games in the evenings or whilst trawling through YouTube. The previous day's homework was a Dennis Bergkamp compilation. A lot of the clips were from the 1997 – 1998 season when he won the PFA and Football Writers Player of the Year, and alongside Ian Wright, fired Arsenal to their league and cup double. I had asked Zito to analyse Bergkamp's movement.

'How did you get on?'

'Good boss. Top player. Muito inteligente, no?'

'You would have loved playing alongside him. What did you notice?'

'Runs he make, he find space between lines. He…' Zito turned to Xabi who had joined us. 'Como voce diz cai fundo?'

'Drops deep.'

'Sim. He drop deep, he link play.'

'Anything else?'

'He stand still.'

I smiled, 'go on.'

'He no follow ball. He stand still. Other players move, he take space.'

'Exactly. It's natural. You want to show the fans you care, to make things happen, but sometimes the smart play is to stand still and see what develops. I want you to really think about this.'

'Sem problemas.'

I played him a recording of a one v one from training that morning.

'Watch as you approach the goal.' I slowed it down. 'Can you see how you're waiting for the keeper to move?' Zito nodded. 'You have to remember you're in charge in this situation, the keeper is reacting to you, not the other way. You need to be decisive. You decide where and when to move the keeper. Got it?'

'Sim, OK.'

'Look at how Michael Owen does it.'

We watched a series of clips of Owen outsmarting the keeper one on one, the year he won the Ballon d'Or.

'Can you see how he suckers them in? If you watch closely you'll see he tricks the keeper – look here – into thinking he's over hit the ball, and so the keeper moves out thinking he is the favourite to get there first. And then Owen uses his speed to beat him to it and work the angle. Let's take another look.'

We watched it again. 'I want you to work on this.'

'I try. I practise.'

Next, just for the fun of it, I showed him England's third goal against Holland at Euro 96. A power surge propelling Gascoigne, with his peroxide buzz cut and barrel chest, past two static defenders, and then the cut back with the outside edge of his right boot. Sheringham the grand master, always three moves ahead, shaped to shoot first time, but what was this? The cutest of square balls rolled across the box to the unmarked Shearer in his baggy white shirt with the oversized number nine in antifreeze blue on the back, and he never missed from there.

***

Psychology is as important as technical development for a young player making the step up into the first team. My job in those early weeks was to ensure the fear of failure did not creep in. I've seen it happen before. Strikers, really good strikers, who miss an easy chance and then disappear. Passing when they should shoot, no longer making the right runs or making themselves available. Driven by the logic of fear: 'no one can blame me for missing if I don't have the ball'.

I kept telling Zito not to be afraid to miss, reminding him that even the very best, the golden boot winners, will always miss more than they score. It's the courage to go again - to deal with your emotions when the crowd are on your back and a teammate is laying into you for not passing - that separates the good from the great. To reinforce this message, I made a point of applauding misses, suppressing any signs of frustration or negative body language. Each day I gave Zito a video of an important goal by a top-class striker along with the forgotten misses and half chances by the same player from earlier passages of play.

After Zito left I dropped by the performance analysis office to go over Darlington's pass start locations when they enter the box. The clips indicated that much of their chance creation came from the left side of the pitch, zones 12 and 18, especially when they were set up in a 1-4-2-3-1, but I wanted to check if the data backed this up.

Sophie, Xabi's PhD student, was hunched over a MacBook, her face lit by the glow from the screen. The carcasses of two kiwi fruit lay on a plate on her desk next to a hydration tracking water bottle. We first met a week or so after the under 23's match. Xabi brought her to my office in Datchet where she told me about her background (playing chess and poker to pay her way through college, a first in physics and applied mathematics, a year studying data science at Caltech). She spoke passionately about her research. After impressing me with the rigour and ambition of her work, I asked Sophie to develop a blueprint for how the club could move from being a laggard to a leader in analytics and artificial intelligence. The scope of the project was much broader than just performance analysis, it also included the use of data and AI in scouting, recruitment, conditioning, and training. We had agreed Sophie would look at best practice in European football and what we could learn from the use of analytics in other ball sports, especially baseball and basketball, as well as Formula One and cycling. One early idea she had already sketched out was to use artificial intelligence to tailor the size of the playing space for small sided games based on individual real match scenarios. None of this would help me win games in the short term but I wanted to show Anita and The Owner I was more than just a stop gap and had the drive and imagination to turn the club around.

'Where are the others?' I asked looking round the empty office.

'Five-a-side with the sports science mob.'

'You not invited?'

She gave me a thin, patient smile.

'I wanted to work on this.'

She pointed to a string of code, white letters and digits on a black background.

'What is it?'

'A pattern recognition algorithm. It's part of my thesis.'

She explained how the software used event data – passes, shots, tackles – and player movement data to predict how an average player would act in any given scenario.

'This is what it looks like.'

Sophie switched from the code to an animated bird's eye view of a pitch. Coloured dots, each with their own number, represented the two sets of players. Athletic in Burgundy and Gold, the unnamed opposing team in blue.

'These are our defensive motion patterns against Letchworth.' The four - one defeat in mid-December was one of Bescond's final games in charge.

'What's that?' I pointed to a grey dot attached to the Athletic centre back by a line. The line expanded and contracted, like a fast twitch muscle fibre, as the two dots moved around the final third.

'That's the ghost. It simulates the movements and actions of the average centre back in our division.'

The ghost shadowed its digital twin, occupying a similar space, and then moved in a different direction to track the run of an opposing player as its doppelgänger moved to press the ball carrier.

'The idea is you can assess and quantify the impact of a player's decision-making and actions and benchmark this against what the average player in their position would do. Here you can see how Jose follows the ball rather than his man in the build-up to the second goal. As a result, the likelihood of Athletic conceding from this possession increases from 34% to 62%.'

She pointed to the figures in the top right corner of the screen.

'What about an actual team rather than an average player? Could we predict how City would respond if we progressed the ball in a certain area?'

She paused for a second.

'That wasn't the intention, but in principle, sure, why not. We can give the team we want to profile its own vector and then the model will mimic the team's characteristics and playing style.'

'That's where it will have the most benefit.'

The coloured dots started the phase of play again, with Jose doomed to repeat the same mistake.

'Can you have more than one ghost at a time?'

'Yes. It's still in the sandbox phase, so I'm limiting myself to a maximum of six ghosts in any scenario, but in theory you could have twenty-two.'

'How long have you been working on this?'

'Almost three years on the algo but I didn't have access to the tracking data until I started here. I had to manually plot player positions and movements using YouTube. So my data was dirty, no better than guesswork. It gave me enough to test and refine the model but you couldn't trust what it was telling you.'

She rubbed her hands.

'But now I've got the first team tracking data it starts to become meaningful.'

'When will it be ready?'

'It depends on how quickly I can sort out the modelling errors. Maybe another two or three months.'

I didn't have that long.

'What would it take to have something usable in three weeks?'

She laughed. 'Time dilation.'

'There must be a way to speed it up. What do you need?'

She took a glug of water while she thought about it.

'There is one thing. If I could speak to Dionysus' data science team in the Valley. They've been doing lots of cool stuff on deep imitation learning and neural networks, how to model complex behaviour.'

'Anyone in particular?'

'Liu Deng. She's a rockstar. The Messi of analytics. The first person to train an algorithm to detect lung cancer.'

'I'll talk to Anita. Get you on a call with her.'

29

The dressing room at Thorpe Lane was the stuff of legend. Mustard brown walls, a colour chosen specifically to make visiting players feel tired or unwell. Clothes hooks placed high up the wall to stretch and place extra pressure on calves and achilles. The naked strip light blinking on and off, just as it had when Athletic played here the previous year and the season before that. A long rectangular counter in the middle of the room prevented the seated players from making eye contact during team talks. Laid out on top was an inviting selection of the worst foods you can eat before a game. Bowls of wholewheat pasta. Granola bars. A salad loaded with avocado. Plates of cheese. Slow to digest, they could all lead to cramps or nausea during exercise. All of this was the work of Roger Kabila, Darlington's coach, who with his pathological will to win, had transformed the club from entertaining lightweights into a team of hard running warriors. Over successive windows, he had patched up the holes in defence and injected a play-on-the-edge physicality into the front two lines. Ibrahim Dabonne, Darlington's captain and midfield centrifuge, linked the three units. He wasn't an attacking midfielder or defensive holding midfielder. He was a throwback. A box to box, cover-every-blade-of-grass-midfielder built in the image of Robson and Keane. They called the Ivorian the extra man, because he did the work of two. A split personality, he could mix muscle with flair, create and destroy. Break up play, then carry the ball forward or play line piercing passes. Dani Linares was relishing the chance to benchmark himself against the best. All week there was an extra bite in his tackles as we practiced defensive transitions and overloads in small-sided games of 1v2, 2v2, and 3v2.

Time spent cultivating the media had continued to pay dividends. In the week running up to the game there was a lot of positive commentary on the progress the team had made since my appointment. *Monday Night Football* took an in-depth look at our shape and fluid systems ('He's a coach who focuses more on positioning than players' positions'), how we progress the ball through the thirds, the level of organisation and togetherness. Jimmy Carol referred to me as a 'top, top coach'. Mark Robinson agreed, using on-screen graphics to highlight the dramatic improvement in various key performance indicators: distance covered, chances created, number of defensive actions against the ball. And to my delight, an article in *The Guardian* ('The Prince of Positional Play') described me as the rightful heir to Lobanovsky, Michels, and Cruyff, while Rob Meade called for the club to make my appointment permanent in his *Mail on Sunday* column.

Just before we left the dressing room Valon took Zharnell to one side. He placed one hand on the youngster's shoulder and said 'Nothing down our side today, you here me? We win every duel, every second ball, every tackle.'

The players all averted their gaze as we passed under the famous sign on our way to the pitch, apart from Borello who took a wad of gum out of his mouth and planted it in the middle of the crest. He then turned and winked at the Darlington players filing out next to him, triggering a scuffle in front of the cameras. After Valon pulled the players apart, I apologised to Kabila and his staff, but secretly I was pleased. It showed the boys were not cowed by history or reputations and were ready for the fight.

We came into the match in good form after back to back wins against Walton and away to Northolt in the West London Derby. Borello lit up both games with his all-round performances. He lifted the entire team, demanding the highest standards and leading by example. Senghor had also found his feet. He linked up exceptionally well with Kuipers and Zharnell, giving us more balance and far greater penetration on the right side of the pitch. As instructed, they rotated their positions on the three points of the triangle, taking it in turns to hold the width, occupy the half-space and play off the last defender's shoulder, creating space and chances for each other with their patterns and movements and chasing the ball down in unison. The two results were worth far more than the six points on the board, because success breeds success. You could see it in the way the boys started the game. The courage they showed in maintaining a high line. The willingness to play through the press and commit bodies forward after every midfield turnover. The work rate out of possession. We disrupted Darlington's build up play with an aggressive 4-3-3 zonal press built on wide pressing traps. The front three of Zito, Borello, and Senghor, stayed narrow and pressed in tandem with Kuipers, barricading the passing lanes into central midfield. When the ball was diverted wide, we moved fast to overwhelm the wide player. Eight of our outfield players intercepted the ball at least once in the first forty-five minutes, and Dani was immense, completing all of his twenty-three passes.

Fabio also continued his improved run of form. He imposed his authority early on in the game by coming off his line and through a crowd of players to claim a high ball and played without fear, sweeping behind our high line. In the thirty sixth minute he collected a loose cross in the six-yard box. With a quickness of mind and feet, he sprinted to the edge of the area, bent his knee and bowled underarm. The ball bypassed the first and second press and reached Borello on the edge of the centre circle via three skimming low bounces. Two red shirts closed him down, but Borello wriggled free, shielding the ball with his body and avoiding the turnover. A burst of speed and a shift in body weight took him past Adam Ripley, leaving the last man in his jet stream. The centre back, off-balance and stumbling forwards, caught hold of Borello's shirt with an outstretched arm, pulling it away from his back, but the Argentine was too quick, his core too strong, and he wrenched the fabric from Ripley's grasp as he hurtled towards the goal. Doncaster's keeper made himself big, like a cobra protecting its eggs, but the stand-off was short lived, Borello drawing first, with an ice cool finish through Guomundsson's legs. Fabio threw back his head and roared, while Doncaster's players argued among themselves about who was to blame.

The message at half-time was simple: don't deviate from the plan no matter what they throw at you in the second half. Keep your shape, stay compact, maintain the intensity. We watched just the one short clip, more out of habit than necessity, spoke again about the threat from Jack Cox, and then I sent them out a few minutes early. As we walked past the home dressing room, we could hear Roger Kabila shouting at his players, his voice wobbling out of control as he cranked the hairdryer up to the highest setting.

'…AND YOU FUCKING LEAVE SOMETHING ON HIM.'

When play resumed a few moments later, Kabila paid the boys a huge compliment, abandoning his favoured system and switching to 1-4-4-2 out of possession. Darlington flew at us from kick off, like a guard dog lunging at an intruder, playing with far greater aggression and intensity. Energised by Kabila's rant and with an additional man in midfield, they regained control of the middle third, dishing out reducers to Borello and Dani. We struggled to replicate the tempo and rhythm of the first half in the face of this onslaught. Our movement was sluggish. Passes went sideways or astray, and Kuipers and Dani were both sacked in the middle third as we relinquished possession and momentum.

'I don't like this one facking bit,' said Terry.

'They're playing right through us. We need to change it up,' said Xabi.

'We need to facking get into them,' replied Terry unwrapping another stick of gum.

When the ball went out of play near the the technical area I passed a message to the forward line, telling them to sit ten metres deeper to increase our presence in the middle third. Darlington's wide midfielders moved inside in response, re-opening the wide spaces for Zharnell and Mats. A few moments later Borello was fouled again, the fourth time since the break, as the Darlington players took it in turns to kick and trip him, targeting his stronger right leg. Each individual offence was carefully calibrated to stop short of a booking and because they stuck to a rota, no one player was punished for persistent fouling. I protested to the fourth official, but he just waved me away.

Jack Cox made another intelligent run, darting across our back line and taking two of our defenders out of the game by dragging José into a less valuable zone. Cox was the perfect example of the difference a good coach can make. When he arrived at the club he liked to hover on the shoulder and blindside of the last defender, always looking for the ball in behind but under Kabila he had become a more complete player. He had learnt to work the channels and hold up and link play, feeding the other forwards and overlapping midfielders with flicked passes and balls around the corner. Now he pulled out wide in the transition to create a passing angle or to overload and isolate a fullback. His separation movement was more dynamic and less predictable. He would throw off his tail with sudden changes in direction, doubling back upon himself. And he worked far harder out of possession, his total pressures out numbering his actions with the ball in some games.

Dani slipped the ball through a gap in the lines, like a seamstress threading a needle. Borello took it on the half turn but before he could carry the ball towards goal, Ripley slammed into him with the force of a runaway truck. It wasn't a bad tackle, it wasn't a tackle of any kind. It was a full blooded kick at Borello's planted right leg, just above the ankle. We heard the bone crack from the bench, and could tell by the reactions from both sets of players - the frantic signals to the bench, the heads held in hands - that it was serious. Ripley tried to apologise as Borello lay twitching on the ground, but Valon and Jose shoved him away. After a lengthy delay, while the medical teams from both clubs worked to immobilise the fractured bone and save the limb, Borello was lifted delicately onto a stretcher and carried off the pitch. By now both legs were covered by a blanket but after the match Zito, the first player to reach him, told us that Borello's ankle was facing in the wrong direction with his fibula poking through his sock. As he approached the entrance to the tunnel, Borello tore off his oxygen mask and shouted angrily in Spanish at the cameraman who had moved in for a closer view.

I looked at our players while the ground staff washed the blood away from the turf. It had hit them hard. Jose Costa was in tears. Valon and Zharnell stared at the ground. Dani held his face, which was drained of all colour. Zito retched into a bag by the bench. What happened next was predictable, but I felt powerless to stop it. First Darlington equalised, Dabonne firing home a second ball from the edge of the box. Then in injury time, Cox scored a left footed half volley on the turn, making him the first Darlington player to score twenty or more goals in three consecutive seasons since Sergio Olmos. The worse thing was the players didn't seem to care. They marched off the pitch at the end like hollowed out zombies.

The post-match interview is an important moment in the week. A platform to speak to the fans (including The Owner) direct without any filter. A chance to put results into context, to point to the bigger picture. To deflect blame where necessary or send a coded message to the players and set the agenda for the week ahead. But that afternoon I just wanted to get away from the ground, get away from football. The broadcaster, however, insisted, reminding Lara of league rules, and so with my blood still pumping from a run in with one of Darlington's coaches in the tunnel, I squeezed into the cramped broadcast room. Jerry Ryan and his camera man were there already. Ryan was a one-man good cop, bad cop routine, always starting with a gentle question to warm up and avoid a car crash of curt, monosyllabic responses, then as your guard started to slip, he would move to searching questions about the major talking points.

'Thanks for coming out and doing this Joe, I know it's been a rough day,' said Ryan, as the cameraman adjusted the lights. 'We'll do three or four questions and then leave it there. I'll start by asking you how long you think Borello will be out for and then about your thoughts on the tackle. Have you seen the replay?'

I nodded.

'Good,' he said. 'It was a shocker.'

Showing you he was on your side before going on air was another of Jerry's tactics. He turned to the cameraman to check the microphone, then put a finger to his ear.

'Yes, he's here, we're good to go. Don't worry, will do.' He turned back to face me and mouthed 'twenty seconds.'

I gently bit down on my tongue to moisten my throat.

'Ten seconds. Five, four, three, two… How is Borello Joe?'

'It's bad… one of the worst injuries I've seen.'

'Any idea how long he will be out for?'

'It's far too soon to say…' Ryan nodded his head while I spoke, encouraging me to continue. '…let's see how the operation goes.'

'I don't know if you've had a chance to see the replay but the team in the studio all agree it was clumsy rather than—.'

'It was deliberate.'

'I know you are upset Joe but—.'

'It was deliberate. They took it in turns to kick him until they hurt him. So don't tell me they didn't want this to happen. They knew what they were doing with the rotational fouling, all targeting his right ankle.'

'That's a serious accusation—.'

'It's a serious offence. What they did was criminal. And if that boy doesn't play again, it'll be on their consciences.'

I moved to leave. Ryan took the hint and handed back to the studio. As I opened the door, he reached across to shake my hand. He was happy. The clip would lead the bulletins and echo across social media.

'That was great Joe. Good on you for calling them out. See you next time.'

30

The Owner was a collector, a harvester of celebrities. He groomed them from an early age, catching singers, actors or artists as they broke through. Sending a case of champagne from his vineyard to congratulate a number one song, a strong performance at the box office or the opening of a new exhibition. Dolling out invitations for weekends in the Hamptons or skiing in Verbier. Tickets to join him in the box for the Monte Carlo Masters or court-side for the Lakers. The VIP area at Burning Man or front row at New York Fashion Week. He stood in the centre circle of the room holding court, dressed in his home strip: black Megadeth t-shirt, skinny jeans, and white Nike Air Jordans. The same outfit he wore whenever in public. Lord Rigg, the water carrier, maintained a steady flow of introductions. The Governor of the Bank of England. The US ambassador to London. Several cabinet ministers, cap in hand, seeking private investment in government projects, or a seat on the firm's European advisory board after the election. They hung on his every word, laughed on cue at his punchlines.

In the corner an ageing rock star swapped anecdotes with a member of the royal family. Two famous actresses pretended to be pleased to bump into each other. A reality TV star shivered and shimmered in a revealing dress, an outfit chosen for the benefit of the photographers outside. Trays of champagne cocktails and intricate Dim Sum – lobster and Prunier Caviar, Wagyu beef with black garlic – floated by.

On a raised stage at the far end of the room two robots took it in turns to outdo each other with their breakdancing routines. A squadron of micro drones, each with their own LED light, hovered above, changing their position and the colours of the lights in time to the music. Anita circulated the room, collecting cards and smiles, never spending more than three minutes with any one guest. She played with her head up, scanning the room, always looking for the next target. Picking her way through the crowd. Air kisses to greet people, a pat on the arm or shoulder as she moved on. A friendly wave and an 'I'll talk to you later!' to those of less immediate interest.

I was on duty, there to make small talk with commercial partners and other guests. Lara had provided a set of suggested talking points.

Messages to convey about our community investment activities, the literacy programme and after school clubs. Funding for food banks across London and grassroots football in Africa and India. A separate, longer document detailed the answers to give if asked about things we didn't want to discuss. Inflation busting increases in the price of season tickets. Accusations of child labour or modern slavery in our merchandise supply chain. The convictions of two former youth coaches for child abuse. The death threats sent to Neelie de Bie after she sent off Rafiq the previous season. Any suggestion we were profiting from misery with the club's online gambling service. On page two, sandwiched between the lines to take on the Iranian investment and the proposed European super league, was a short reactive statement on my future at the club:

'The board is pleased with the recent results and performances under the current interim head coach. We have no plans to announce the appointment of a permanent head coach at this time.'

I mingled with the guests, enjoying the novelty of being one of the least famous people in the room. As always, everyone I spoke to had a view on my tactics and selection decisions and the boys' performances. Bjorn Fernandez, the Olympic taekwondo champion, congratulated me on taking a tough line with Bailey who had not started for the first team since his under 23 antics. The CEO of one of our sponsors, a balding Glaswegian who I met at the drinks reception on my first day, greeted me like an old friend and heaped praise upon Kuipers for the way he had adjusted to the false nine role since Borello's injury. The Belgian had the game intelligence required to link play and pull defensive systems apart with his movement. Our second goal a few days before was a perfect example. Kuipers dropped deep and took a central defender with him and Zito moving inside and along the defensive line to attack the vacated space. I listened politely and answered questions, citing various performance metrics, but in truth my mind was elsewhere. We had three matches in six days, so I needed to rotate a couple of players for the Toxteth game and figure out how to nullify their attacking patterns. Rather than stretch the pitch, Toxteth's inverted wingers cut inside, running onto long diagonal balls from midfield and overloading the centre backs in the zone in front of the penalty area. It presented a tactical dilemma. Should we play an extra pivot and accept the reduction in forward passing options when we had the ball? Or bring one of the fullbacks inside and restrict our progression upfield? Or be brave and keep our usual shape and trust that we could deal with the problem at source by pressing high and denying supply to the forward line?

I glanced at my phone. It was still goalless at Dyke Road where Tiverton were cashing in their game in hand and looking to move five points clear of us in fourth place. Xabi was watching the game with some of the younger players and sending regular updates. Tiverton had started slowly, hampered by the suspension of their eight and an injury to one of their forwards in the warmup, and neither side had had a shot on target in the first twenty-five minutes.

Around nine o'clock The Owner hopped up onto the stage and gave a short speech congratulating Manisha Wall on her Oscar and name-checking several of his other guests. With this the curtains parted, and Rosa Sharp stepped out onto the stage in a white dress, her hair died blonde and cut short. The Owner feigned surprise and then gave the singer a hug, lifting her high heels off the ground. She sat down at the piano and played a few keys and then turned to the audience. My phone buzzed. Against all odds, Goole had taken the lead. A comedy of errors according to Xabi.

'This is an old one, a song about jealousy and infidelity.'

'My favourite,' said The Owner, placing one hand across his heart.

'Just because you're paranoid doesn't mean they're not cheating on you.

'He says he loves me but I know it's not true.'

Sharp's voice had the purity of a cleanly struck shot, the grace and beauty of a Cruyff turn. After the final bars died away she slumped forward, as if performing the song had exorcised her from its control. After a long pause she stood up. She silenced the applause with a finger to her scarlet lips, and began to sing Happy Birthday, edging closer and closer to The Owner at the side of the stage. It was a supercharged performance, breathless and coy. High notes held long, eye lids fluttered. At the end she cradled his face in her hands and gave him a long slow kiss. I took the opportunity to lose my marker, a young Irish actor, promising to give him a guided tour of Datchet at the end of the season. As I slalomed through the crowd, like Barnes at the Maracaná, it dawned on me that the only guests I knew, were people I didn't want to speak to. I stopped to admire one of the paintings on the wall and found myself sucked into the artist's world. The silhouette of a hot air balloon hung in the morning sky, like a ball stood up at the back post. Beneath it a landscape the colour of sandpaper stretched towards the sea at low tide.

'It's exquisite isn't it?' said a voice behind me. I turned around. She was late thirties, maybe early forties, with dark hair and eyes the colour of Minstrels. She wore a black dress, tailored to display slender arms and legs, and a large diamond ring on her ring finger. I was lost for words. She smiled playfully. 'The balloon is a metaphor for the ego.'

I was so far out of my depth; I couldn't see the shore. I leaned towards the painting to get a closer view and buy some time.

'Who painted it?' was the best I could come up with.

'Michael Andrews. He was a contemporary of Freud and Bacon. As you can see, his work is as strong, stronger than theirs, but he never had the same profile and he's largely forgotten these days. It was one of the first pieces I ever bought. Chris asked me to find something special for his wedding anniversary.'

After introducing herself as Carla, she explained that her gallery specialised in curating art collections for the super-rich. She divided her time between acquiring works by established artists in auctions around the world and talent spotting the next generation. Tracking down rare works and arranging installation or restoration. Managing loans and exhibitions.

'Where did you find it?'

'This was a coup,' she smiled. 'His work rarely ever surfaces on the market. A friend of a friend put me in touch with a Swiss industrialist with a liquidity problem. He wanted a quick sale and didn't want his shareholders or competitors to hear about it. So, I bought this and moved a few other pieces for him.'

We spoke for a long time, the room and the people around us fading away, like when you apply one of those blurred backgrounds in a Zoom call. She grew up in Barcelona and we switched from English to Catalan, and back again, as we compared notes on our favourite places in the City. She told me about her battle with cancer, how she had caught it early. About the friend from her support group – a woman in her early thirties with three young children – who wasn't so fortunate. How she had sought to assuage what she described as survivor's guilt by fundraising for cancer charities.

'I wouldn't wish it on anyone. But…' She laughed at herself. '…I'm an optimist, always looking for the positive, and the past year has given me clarity. Made me reassess my goals, the people in my life. What it means to be fulfilled.'

Eventually there was a lull in the conversation, a natural time for us to go our separate ways, but I didn't want to break the spell, or lose her to another guest. I searched for something, anything, to say. The noise around us grew, puncturing our bubble. Over Carla's shoulder, I saw a magician perform a card trick to gasps from the crowd around him. Then we both spoke at the same time.

'It was very nice to talk to you—'

'—I'm thinking of buying a painting for my daughter's birthday, it's her eighteenth,' I blurted.

'What sort of things does she like?'

I dredged a few names up from the depths of my memory.

'Chagall, Rothko, Miro. We used to go to the Miro museum a lot when we lived in Barcelona. When the weather was good, we'd swim in the Olympic diving pool in Montjuic—.'

'I love that place. Watching the synchronised swimming team rehearse and the views across the city.'

'We'd go every week then wander down to the museum.'

She gazed at the painting and bit her lip, as if she was considering a major decision, then looked back at me, her smile turned up to full beam.

'Why don't you drop by my gallery one evening? I could help you pick out a piece.'

'Thanks. I'd like that.'

My phone went into a spasm in my pocket. I pulled it out, hoping to see that Goole had doubled their lead. Carla saw my frown.

'Bad news?'

'Tiverton have equalised.'

She leant in close to watch the clip. Her hair smelt of almonds and her shoulder touched my arm, the warmth from her skin radiating through my sleeve. The goal was all about Jacobsen's movement. The Norwegian striker stood just past the halfway line, offside and disinterested, as Tiverton's left-back and pivot exchanged passes in zone four. Kyle Mackey, who was on loan from Raith Rovers, changed things up, bending a pass between two players into a pocket midway between the centre circle and the touch line. The Goole defender over-committed, going to ground too easily, and was beaten by Benkirane's clipped first touch into space. The Frenchman carried the ball forward twenty-five metres, moving at speed, then cut inside. Meanwhile, Jacobsen allowed the two retreating central defenders to pass him, then tracked the defensive line, curving his run just before the ball was played to remain onside without sacrificing speed or momentum. He met the through ball without breaking stride and shot first time, finding a gap at the near post.

'The keeper will be disappointed when he sees that again,' Carla said with a smile, as if she had spent her life surrounded by footballers. With hindsight, I should have made the connection then. Before I could reply, she noticed Charlie Laker heading our way. He had commandeered a tray of canapés and was balancing it on one hand.

'I should circulate.' She handed me her card. 'Call me.'

I watched her glide away.

'Fuck me,' said Laker in my ear. 'Just look at her. The one signing Dave got right.'

He laughed at the look of surprise which must have flashed across my face and then coughed, wafting ashtray breath my way.

'Don't tell me you didn't know? Where have you been living? Outer fucking Mongolia?'

I turned to walk off but Laker caught me by the elbow.

'Come on Joe you won't get anywhere in this business if you hold grudges.'

Laker had always been too busy running his car dealership to take any interest in football, until that is, he saw the opportunity to make money. Towards the end of the 1997 – 1998 season, he was asked by Nicky Morris, his neighbour, to help him negotiate a pay rise. Morris earned six thousand pounds a week at Kettering United and wanted a two-thousand-pound increase to bring him in line with the other senior players. When they sat down with Marcus Rivers the club's owner, Laker deliberately avoided mentioning any figure. Instead, he outlined fictitious approaches Morris had received from two other clubs. Rivers gave a deep sigh and then listed the costs the club faced. Repairs to the West Stand roof. Increased rental for the use of the training ground. An unpaid tax bill. The best he could do was thirteen thousand. Laker and Morris were speechless. Rivers mis-interpreted the stunned silence and panicked, raising his offer to fifteen thousand. Now, most people would have quit there – Laker and Morris were so far ahead they were past the finishing line, showered, changed, and having a cold drink in the bar – but Laker could spot an opportunity. He placed an envelope his wife had asked him to post face down on the desk, telling Rivers it was a transfer request. They left the office ten minutes later with a nineteen thousand a week contract and a new car to be purchased from Laker's dealership.

I shook my arm free. Laker had laid into me on social media after I dropped Javier Varallo ('Who does this turd think he is benching the greatest right back of all time? Where's he been for the last 20 years. #NotFitToTieHisLaces.') The insults escalated over the following weeks as I successfully eased his player out of the side.

'It's never personal with me Joe,' said Laker. 'I'm like a barrister, just looking out for my clients' best interests. And I want to help you get your next job.'

'I'm happy where I am.'

'Enough of the take it one game at a time bollocks. You need to be thinking three moves ahead.' He swallowed a Dim Sum and belched. 'Got anything lined up?'

I didn't reply.

'You know there's zero fucking chance you'll be at Athletic next season, don't you? They're lining up Wyszkowska. That's football my friend. You take the cheque and move on. I can get you a job in Spain or Germany, or you can sit tight, do some TV work, and wait for someone to get the bullet in England. You'll be back in the saddle by Christmas.'

'I already have an agent.'

'You've got a brother, not an agent. And word to the wise Joe. Loyalty is a fantastic quality in a dog. But if you want to maximise your potential you need to grow up, ditch the sentiment, be ruthless. You wouldn't pick your brother to play in goal, or to operate on a player, so why trust him with your future? He didn't get you this job, and he won't get you the next one. You need someone who can open doors, pull strings. How many owners does your brother know? I'm godfather to Carlo Vinci's daughter. Was best man at Julio Abastos' wedding. I holiday with TK Crawford and his family. Go to the Monaco Grand Prix with the Cromwells every year. I provide Wallace with all his girls, Liang with all his pills. These guys owe me so many favours I have to employ someone just to write them all down.'

Rigg appeared from nowhere to rescue me. He was sporting a smoky grey suit and the ever-present deep tan. His striped tie was fastened with the sort of knot they only teach you at Sandhurst or Eton.

'You look well Cecil,' said Laker, trying to provoke a reaction, but it just bounced off Rigg like a free kick driven into the wall.

'Thank you Charlie. Just back from a Parliamentary fact-finding trip to Mauritius. All business you understand. Furthering relations between allies,' he said with a smirk. 'Do you mind if I steal Joe?'

'Be my guest Cecil. We're all done. Think about what I said Joe.'

Rigg steered me away. As soon as we were out of earshot he murmured 'I can't stand that bottom feeding leech. If I had my way we'd sever all ties. Ortega as well. The problem is they have us over a barrel and they know it.'

'He says you're bringing in Wyszkowska.'

'The king over water?' Rigg snorted. 'Never trust an agent Joe, you should know that. They're always working an angle.'

Only when I replayed the conversation later, did it dawn on me that this was a politician's classic, non-denial denial.

'Radzi is dying to meet you. He's a season ticket holder.'

Radzi Ncube was the BBC's political editor.

'In the Hill End,' I replied. Rigg raised an eyebrow.

'Full marks Joe. Good to see you've done your homework.'

Unlike Rigg, I had read Lara's briefing paper.

'He's over there,' he motioned with his head towards The Owner who was in conversation with two men. One was tall and lean, a cyclist or a runner, the other a red-faced coronary time bomb. The Owner's hands moved fast, as if he was directing traffic. Beyond him, in the shadow of one of the trees that stretched up to the glass roof, Carla was speaking to one of The Owner's army of bankers. I watched enviously as she laughed at his jokes.

'Who's the other guy?'

'That's Henry Ackerman. He chairs the digital, media and sport select committee, so naturally, he doesn't like football or big tech.'

'Why's he here then?'

Rigg laughed.

'Why are they all here? Word of warning he loves to grill people. Some poor chap from a betting firm keeled over after appearing before his committee last year. So don't be surprised if he gives you a hard time.'

As we passed through the crowd, Rigg greeted various guests and I caught fragments of different conversations:

'…it's not bad, you can tell they've made an effort because it's DC, but nothing compares to the Emirates lounge in Dubai.'

'…I've got this fab place on Hyde Park Corner, twenty sixth floor, views to die for. If you'd like we could…'

'...social media is twentieth first century tobacco. We'll all pay the price in years to come.'

The Owner stood facing his two guests in a small tight cluster as if they were waiting for a corner to be whipped in. Ncube saw me first.

'Here he is, the man who turned our season around!'

He shook my hand and then insisted on taking a selfie with his arm around my shoulder. Ackerman, meanwhile, carried on speaking to The Owner. Judging by the vintage malt in his hand, he was quite at ease fraternising with the enemy.

"...the problem is everyone knows the oversight board is just window-dressing. If you want it to be credible you need to—'

Rigg interrupted him.

'Joe, have you met. Henry? One of the three most influential men in Westminster. The scourge of underprepared Ministers and over-reaching corporates. This is the man who forced Axion to back down on data roaming charges last year and who shone a light on problem gambling.'

Ackerman did not respond to Rigg's flattery. There was a hardness about him. An absence of compassion or empathy. I had seen his sort before. A bed was made and therefore had to be laid in. The son was liable for the sins of the father.

'Henry, this is Joe Hendricks. Athletic's head coach – you might have heard of them, they're a popular football team,' he teased.

'Good to meet you Mr Hendricks. I'm afraid football is not my thing. I've always regarded it as little more than social control, opioids for the masses. There'd be blood on the streets without it of course and I have to visit Vetch bloody Lane every four or five years—'

'Just before an election,' said Rigg.

'Quite, some of us have to answer to the public Robert. I stand in the centre ring and do the raffle. But the stench of inequity makes me ill. How can someone who kicks a ball for a living be paid thousands of times more than a nurse or a teacher? It's what happens when you don't regulate a market.'

'Why shouldn't a hard-working lad from a working-class background get the going rate?' asked Ncube. 'Success in football is purely based on merit. There's no short cuts, it all comes down to talent and hard work. No middle-class parents using their contacts to line up an unpaid internship. It's why a kid from an estate in Liverpool has more chance of making it than a kid who goes to Eton.'

'I agree,' The Owner said. 'I can't think of another industry or profession that's created more working-class millionaires in this country in the past twenty years.'

My phone twitched again. Goole had retaken the lead. At the same time an alert flashed up on The Owner's watch. He gave me a hug and then bellowed 'CHAMPAGNE.'

'Who scored?' asked Ncube pulling out his phone.

'Torelli,' I replied.

'Ah man, I told Dave to bring him in but he and Gonzalo insisted we sign Slaney,' said The Owner re-writing history.

'How long left?'

'Twenty-five minutes plus time added on.'

'You know, I've always thought that Prime Ministers and football managers are very similar.'

'In what way Radzi?' asked Rigg, playing along.

'They are both at the mercy of events beyond their control, and both depend upon a fickle public while dealing with a hostile media. They know what they need to do to build long-term success but are rarely given the time to do it. The average life expectancy of a premier league manager is what, twelve to eighteen months? Most governments are behind in the polls after a short honeymoon period. So they end up chasing short term results, ducking tough decisions, courting popularity. Only a few very talented coaches or political leaders are able to defy the rules of gravity, and even then, their careers always end in failure.'

***

My car was parked outside, rain drops rebounding off the roof. The street was silent, with no sign of light or life coming from any of the other properties. The security gates of the house opposite were clad with hoardings. The garden of the neighbouring mansion, a house worth more than Stuttgart paid for Slaney, was overgrown. Rex broke the bad news before could I fasten the seatbelt.

'Tiverton have equalised. Yasar bundled it in after a long throw.'

I had no right to be disappointed - Tiverton would beat Goole at home eight or nine times out of ten - but they had been so close to dropping all three points.

'It's the hope that's the killer,' Rex muttered.

I caught up on my emails as we listened to the final five minutes of the game. I deleted messages from two agents without looking at them, replied to Lara to confirm the changes to my programme notes, and thanked the sports science team for the rapid progress Olivera was making in recovering from his torn quad. Next I scanned Mike Brooker's weekly report. He was concerned that our loan players in Poland and Belgium were not getting enough game time and suggested we recall both. The commentator's voice rose with excitement as Tiverton took a ninety sixth minute corner.

'…IT'S DEACON… and Baedeker clears with the last touch of the game.'

A motorbike swerved to avoid a deep puddle, forcing the car in front - a big Mercedes with passive aggressive brake lights - to brake sharply.

'The Tiverton players are crowding around Mike Willis, I'm not sure what they're protesting about.'

'They're claiming there was a handball,' added the co-commentator.

'The referee Mike Willis is speaking to the video assistant… he's going to check the monitor.'

Outside the rain moved up through the gears. Streetlights and neon shop fronts polluted the night sky. Across the road, an elderly couple carrying a large laundry bag between them were struck by a tidal wave from a passing bus. The woman looked at her husband and they both laughed.

'…he's pointing to the spot… HE'S GIVEN A PENALTY.'

I opened a short message from Rob Meade. 'You're on. Let's stick it to them.'

I sent a short response to Rob to thank him.

'In comes Case… AND HE SCORES!' A WINNER AFTER THE WHISTLE WAS BLOWN.'

I kicked the back of the seat in front of me.

'Jammy bastards,' groaned Rex.

Like the rubbernecking driver who slows down to inspect a pileup, I couldn't resist taking a look at the penalty. The first thing I saw when I opened X, however, was Archer stroking his own ego.

'23 years ago. What a night. HALA MADRID.'

Below this was a video of one of his trademark Belfast Turns. A slo-mo close up of Archer dragging the ball back behind his right leg with his left sole, screening it from the two defenders with his body, followed by a second drag back to complete the 360 degree spin, and then the twenty five yard slide pass assist for Xavier Xaltier. It was beautiful but Christ, he was such a needy narcissist.

31

Paco invited me out to his place in Begur a week or so after we clinched our third title in Spain. Since the divorce it was like a second home to me. We sat on the wide terrace overlooking the coastal path worn into the rocks and the crescent of honeycomb sand. Beyond the beach the languid water stretched out from the bay to meet the sky. Paco's wife Isabel was nowhere to be seen, which was unusual. Normally she would greet me with a cold drink and a kiss on both cheeks. Tell stories about her week. Tease Paco about forgetting their anniversary again. Hum old pop songs. According to Paco she was visiting relatives in Córdoba, but something didn't feel right. I wondered if they were going through another rough patch.

Our two previous titles had been won at a canter, but this had been a long gruelling season for the players and staff and their families. The new head coach in Madrid had hounded us every inch of the way. We felt like fugitives, chased from town to town, constantly looking over our shoulders to see Rui Fernandes and his posse of well drilled men bearing down on us. They became stronger and stronger as the season went on, gaining ground every time we stumbled, eating away the eight-point lead we had accumulated so easily in the first half of the season, and taking the contest right down to the wire.

Until then I had not appreciated how much Fernandes' attritional mind games and the constant media pressure, the carping and the second guessing, the endless speculation, had taken out of Paco. He looked old and tired, emotionally spent. The first hint came when the referee called time on the season. Paco shed tears of relief not joy as we embraced on the touch line. His celebrations with the players were strangely muted, as if he would rather be anywhere else. He gave a short, terse post-match interview, after which you would have been forgiven for thinking he had lost the title rather than won his third in four years, then retired to his office alone.

Paco poured us each a glass of Verdejo, taking great care to ensure we both received the same amount, then gave me a sad, half empty smile.

'Listen hombre, I have some news. I wanted you to hear it first.'

Immediately I thought of Isabel and said to myself 'please, *please*, don't let it be divorce.' He gazed out to sea for a moment, as if he was steeling himself, then looked back at me. 'I'm stepping down.' I felt my stomach drop, my heart rush, as he delivered this bombshell.

'We'll inform the boys tomorrow, after the parade.'

'Why?' was the only response I could muster.

'I need a break, time to recharge, to reconnect with my family. I've become a stranger to them this past year. And I'm done with the god damn goldfish bowl. Isabel and the kids should not have to put up with it any longer. I've spoken to the President. He didn't try to talk me out of it. Maybe I would have stayed another year if he had but I've taken the club as far as I can. It's time for a new voice, fresh ideas.'

I could see that the prospect of this conversation had added to the strain upon Paco so I tried to listen to what he had to say, to nod and smile sympathetically in the right places but my brain was a goalmouth scramble as questions ricocheted around my mind. Who would succeed Paco? Could anyone replicate his incredible run of success? How would the players react? And most of all, what does this mean for me? I spared Paco this last question.

'What are you going to do?'

He gestured towards his yacht which was moored in the mouth of the cove.

'Fish for a few weeks. Then we are going to spend six months in LA, after that we'll see…'

Paco was the best communicator I had ever seen, a man who commanded the attention of the dressing room, always knew the right thing to say, so it pained me to see him so subdued. I began to understand how much it had cost him to hold things together and carry us over the line. He turned again to the sea, seeking whatever comfort or inspiration it could offer. For a moment or two we sat in silence. A warm breeze rustled through the pine trees and rippled across my face. Paco shifted in his seat, took a gulp of his wine, and then ripped off the bandage.

'Talamantes is coming in and bringing his own team. There won't be a spot for you.'

I felt my face burn, my stomach lurch again, as everything I had worked for went up in flames.

'I'm sorry Amigo. I wish there was another way but trust me, you'll be fine. After what we have achieved there will be lots of opportunities for you.'

'A change will do me good,' I said, trying to alleviate his guilt.

'I can put in some calls.'

I dearly wanted – needed – this but couldn't allow it. Paco had to look after himself.

'It's OK boss. Leave it to me. Something will come up.'

32

Zito wheeled away, arms outstretched in Careca's classic aeroplane celebration, a private message to his grandad watching five thousand miles away in Belo Horizonte. It was the Brazilian's fourth goal in six games, a downward header that reared up off the turf and found the space between City's keeper and the raised, forlorn boot of the defender on the line. Terry gave me a bear hug and then bounced along the touchline.

'Take that you motherfuckers,' Xabi screamed in the direction of City's bench and then launched himself into a chest bump with Jordan Allen, while our fans took great pleasure in witnessing the mighty fall.

TWO ONE, AND YOU'VE LOST THE LEAGUE.
TWO ONE, AND YOU'VE LOST THE LEAGUE.
TWO ONE, AND YOU'VE LOST THE LEAGUE.
TWO ONE, *AND YOU'VE LOST THE LEAGUE.*

I gestured frantically at the players, urging them to stay focused, to keep their shape. Lothar Steck slumped back into his seat in the dugout, took a swig of water, shouted something in German, and then threw the bottle to the ground in disgust. The champions' title was slipping from their grasp. On paper it was a very difficult match up for us. City played with a similar brand of possession based attacking football but were stronger in almost every position. It was like sparring with your shadow. They looked familiar, moved in recognisable ways, anticipated your every action. For the past two seasons they had slashed through defences and shattered records en route to back-to-back titles. This, however, had been a difficult campaign. Injuries to key players and the mental exhaustion of chasing down successive titles had taken their toll. There was no defiance from their players after Zito scored. In fact, they looked relieved to shed the burden of being the front runner, to slip back into the chasing pack, and allow another club to become the target, the team against which every side raises their game. Freed from the expectations of their manager, Steck's hectoring and cajoling no longer able to stoke the flames of their depleted ambition. To not have to go again.

Like us, City, rearranged themselves into a front five during the second phase of play with one player occupying each of the five vertical zones. Two inside forwards operated in the most advanced positions, each pinning a centre back and fullback by taking a position in one of the half space channels. A third striker, the midpoint of the M shaped attacking formation, linked play from a deeper position between them, taking passes from midfield on the half turn, while wingbacks pushed up high and wide on either side. And they defended high up the pitch, with two split centre backs situated on the halfway line. Short passes and small distances between each player reduced the risk of a counterattack, and tactical fouls took care of any players who beat the press and threatened to carry the ball forward. The fouls themselves, the clipped heels and trips, looked inconsequential and because they took place in the opposition half there was never any danger of a red card for denying a goal scoring opportunity. This happened several times a game and it gave me something to work with. The plan was to highlight City's reliance on tactical fouls in the days leading up to the game and force the referee to take action. Which is where Rob Meade came in.

He kicked off a media offensive with a column headlined 'Death by a thousand trips'. His ghostwriter captured it perfectly. For City, the tactical foul was exactly that, a fundamental tactic, a central plank of their game plan, and it was killing the game. A bar chart showed how City had committed far more tactical fouls than any other team in the division over the past three seasons. Four annotated photos illustrated the clever fouls City's midfielders would use to stop a counterattack. One paragraph stood out.

'As a midfielder myself, I appreciate the dark arts, but this has gone too far. Alessandro Michaelis is constantly breaking down attacking moves, many of which would lead to a certain goal scoring chance. But because he's higher up the pitch, never the last man, and always apologises to the ref, he's rarely punished. It's time for referees to take a tougher stance and for the authorities to consider rule changes. I'd like to see an automatic yellow card for a deliberate attempt to break down a counterattack.'

Bernard Joffre shared the article in social media, likening City's tactical fouls to financial doping, and calling for the introduction of a sin bin. Other former pro's and pundits weighed in, offering different views. Some said it's nothing new, but the majority called for tighter rules to favour the attacking side. The article was a major talking point in the lunchtime media conferences and it had rattled Lothar Steck. There was none of the usual easy charm or friendly chitchat from the

City coach. Instead, he treated the press to a mini meltdown, accusing them of tarnishing his players' achievements, and then stormed out.

When you have your foot on your opponent's throat, as I always tell my players, you have to keep pushing. And so, the next morning we stamped down hard. I asked Sophie to calculate how many goals had been denied by City's tactical fouls. It was not a scientific figure, but that's what made it so powerful – no one could prove it either way. We gave the data to Rob who passed it off as his own work on his weekly TV show, using video analysis of City's fouls in recent matches to point to the 'stolen goals'. The story rumbled on through the weekend, ahead of the Sunday teatime kick off.

City, in their canary yellow shirts, started strongly, zipping the ball around with high tempo one touch passes, like a pinball wizard in the zone. Everything revolved around Ben Lynch, a running number ten, who smuggled the ball through the lines with the strength and balance that comes from a low centre of gravity. It was a season of restitution and rehabilitation for the young attacking midfielder after two disastrous World Cup qualifying matches the previous summer. First, he been pilloried for refusing to sing the national anthem, shouted down by the tabloids when he claimed to be both a Republican and a patriot. Then he was vilified for a moment of immaturity and ill-discipline in the second game. A stupid, petulant elbow to the ribs of the Slovenian captain which cost England a penalty and any remaining chances of qualifying for the tournament. He shrugged off the burnt effigies. The bullets and dog shit sent to him through the post. Tuned out from the taunts from the crowd about his wife and young daughter. Sucked up all of the bile and recycled it into self-motivating energy.

Midway through the first half Lynch darted inside from the right wing. He took the ball past Jose Costa with his first touch on the edge of the D, duped Fabio with a look towards the far post, and then ripped the ball in hard and low at the front post. City attacked again, a few minutes after the re-start, Lynch weaving past Mats and pulling the ball back from the byline. Valon reacted first, stretching to prod the ball clear. Dani played a quicksilver one-two in the jaws of City's high press - textbook Rondo - to release Kuipers. As the Belgian sped towards the halfway line, Alessandro Michaelis tapped his ankle, sending Kuipers sprawling. The referee produced an immediate yellow card for City's pivot, as if he had been waiting to put a stamp on the game. City reset their defence and the freekick came to nothing.

We spent the next twenty minutes camped out in our half. It was another immense performance by Valon. Time and again he stepped in to intercept the ball or break down dangerous attacking moves. Then in first half injury time, Michaelis mis-timed a tackle on the greasy surface, catching Zito's shin. Steck threw his arms in the air and then wagged his finger.

'No, no, no. There's nothing there.'

I couldn't help myself.

'He's got to go,' I said to the fourth official.

'You fucking stay out of this,' screamed Steck.

The crowd reacted immediately.

'OFF, OFF, OFF
OFF, OFF, OFF.'

Thirty metres or more away, the referee, oblivious to the heat and noise on the touchline, brandished his card to cheers from the crowd.

'That was never a yellow. Not even close,' continued Steck.

We struggled to make our advantage count in the first twenty minutes of the second half. City's defensive line was an unbreachable barrier, but as with all solids, there was more space than mass and the boys kept probing away, like a safe cracker turning the dials, until the tumblers fall into place. A cute no-look reverse pass from Reece Hughes to the near post, one touch from Zito to fillet their centre back, and then the lightest of side foot finishes. Roared on by the crowd, we pushed for the winner. Lifting the supporters out of their seats with a frenzy of attacking football. Each shot or half chance greeted by a louder cheer. In the eighty-first minute Valon strode forward to join the attack, his blood coagulating, clots spreading through his veins he was so high up the pitch. Unable to find a pass he shot from twenty-seven yards. The ball went through the keeper rather than past him, soaring between his outstretched arms at Mach 2, and then collided with the honeycomb of small white hexagons.

For the City fans the long journey home began with the walk of shame. Darting up the aisles of steep concrete steps in twos and threes, pelted with half-time food wrappers and taunts of 'CHEERIO, CHEERIO, CHEERIO' from our fans in the neighbouring section. The three points kept us in fifth place and for once I enjoyed the post-match interviews. That evening, after I had completed my analysis and written up my notes, I texted Valon to tell him:

'You're the best fucking defender in the world.'

33

Archer's day in court was an unmitigated disaster, the worst own goal since Sandy Brown's leaping header in the 1969 Merseyside Derby. It started well enough, with an appearance before the cameras on the steps outside the Court, Archer sporting a new three piece suit bought especially for the occasion. And he read the oath loud and clearly, delivering the lines as if he was filming one of his commercials. He also did a fine job in speaking up for Vladimir Lantsov, describing how they first met in Madrid when Archer was coming to the end of his career and Lantsov was breaking through. The two men shared the same agent and socialised regularly. Archer swore he had never seen Lantsov drink more than the occasional glass of wine and scoffed at the idea of him taking cocaine. 'There's no way he could run one hundred metres in under twelve seconds on drugs, he said. 'Besides, we test the players all the time.'

Lantsov was a devoted husband and family man Archer continued, locking eyes with each and every member of the jury, before moving onto the clincher: Lantsov's charity work. Like Archer, Lantsov was a UNICEF ambassador, and had paid for the construction of more than thirty floodlit all weather football pitches for orphanages and children's homes across Russia. So far, so good. But then the proceedings changed ends, as the prosecuting counsel rose to his feet and set about shredding Archer's character and credibility as a witness. Revelling in the media attention, he reminded the jury of Archer's transgressions over the years. The drinking, the adultery, the on and off field altercations. He painted a portrait of a vain bully, a sexist misogynist who could not be trusted around women. And like countless opposition players over the years, he targeted Archer's hair trigger temper, seeking to provoke a reaction. To gasps from the jury, he even repeated the strongly denied, but ever so plausible rumour that Archer racially abused a teammate at half time back in 2003.

Court cases, unlike football matches, are not televised. There's no spider cam or touchline close-ups. Which was a shame, because I would have dearly loved to have watched Archer's face turn puce, his eyes narrow. The slow gulps of air as he fought to prevent a meltdown, and then succumbed to the inner anger.

'I don't have to sit here and listen to this shit from you, you jumped up fucking twat,' he snarled. 'What makes you think you can speak to Davie Archer like that? Eh? What have you ever done?' he continued as the judge's gavel struck the wooden bench.

'You'll never know what it's like to live your life in a fucking goldfish bowl. To have every waking moment live tweeted or filmed on some stranger's phone. To have women throw themselves at you *every single* time you go out for a quiet drink. Do you not think footballers are human? Course we are. If you were surrounded by temptation all the fucking time, wouldn't you crack every now and then? Of course you would, look at the size of that fucking gut.'

The prosecuting barrister remained quiet as Archer did his job for him.

'That there is a good man but none of you'll be happy until he's fucking topped himself, will you? I mean for Christ sake, if he's guilty, we all are.'

'Order, order. Mr Archer, I will not tell you again,' cried the judge struggling to make himself heard. 'I will not have that language in my court.'

'I'll say what I fucking well like, you hear me?' Archer replied, underlining his words with a blast of the death stare.

'ORDER. You are one more expletive away from a night in custody. Now unless the prosecution has any further questions I suggest we leave it there.'

And then, just when Archer thought things could not get any worse, as he raised his chin for yet more photos outside the court, a carton of cold chicken soup was thrown in his face and dripped down his new suit.

34

If you want players to take ownership on the pitch you have to treat them as adults off it. So in my first week I asked the boys to define the rules and behaviours they believed an elite set of athletes should be governed by. They spent an hour discussing it without any input from me or the coaching staff and agreed a list of offences: being late for training or medical appointments, exceeding body composition targets, phones ringing during meetings. Wearing outdoor shoes in the dressing room or flip flops for meals. Non-attendance at home matches by unselected players. Valon policed the system with zeal and creativity. Punishments were tailored to fit the offender not the crime. Bailey was required to wear clothes bought only from the supermarket. Mats was asked to alight from his high horse and clean the boots of the academy trainees. Reece Hughes had to recite a Shakespearean sonnet in front of all the staff and players. So the group were delighted when the big man arrived almost an hour late for training, buckling up his GPS vest as he ran out to join us on the practice pitch. He had a half-moon shaped bruise under his left eye and stubble the length of Astro turf. The players halted their agility drill and formed a guard of honour, two lines of twelve, for Valon to walk through. Fabio stood at the end consulting an invisible clipboard.

'Ah, Señor Azem, so very nice of you to join us. I'm afraid this is gonna cost you.'

Another glance at the clipboard.

'Your punishment for this serious misdemeanour is to sing to Peggy, to *serenade* her.'

The players clapped and whistled their approval. Peggy, a popular member of the canteen staff, made no secret about having a soft spot for Valon, regularly adding his favourite Balkan dishes to the menu.

'And the song is…' Fabio turned over a couple of pages on his imaginary clipboard. '…You've lost that loving feeling.'

Valon groaned and shook his head but before he could protest Bailey chipped in, mimicking the Bosnian's catchphrase.

'If you can't do the time…'

The rest of the players joined chorused:

'…don't do the crime.'

***

Valon came to see me later that afternoon. His fingertips were black from signing shirts with a permanent marker and the bruise below his eye had already turned a darker shade of purple. Whatever had struck him, Ana's fist or a flying object, had hit him hard. He took a deep breath.

'I'm sorry about this morning boss. I thought it would get easier once we brought the girls home, but it's so tough right now. Ana's up every night. If she is not feeding one, she is feeding the other or changing nappies. She's not getting any sleep. Marko is terrible, he's used to having Ana to himself during the day, and Tomas is really struggling with his reading. They all need more from me, more than I can give.'

I told him not to be too hard on himself. That it was a big adjustment. 'Yeah, we're moving from man marking to zonal,' he replied without a smile.

'Are you getting much sleep?'

'That's part of the problem. I've been sleeping with noise canceling headphones in the guest wing. Ana snapped when I came down this morning. Screaming at me that I'm not pulling my weight and she can't do it on her own. She said I have had my time, now I have to choose between her and the kids or football.'

His voice trailed away as he said this. I resisted the temptation to fill the silence, telling myself he needed to unload.

'She has said it before but this time she means it.'

Neither of us said anything for a minute or more. Eventually Valon spoke again.

'I've had one family taken away from me. I will not lose another but what am I going to do all day? I need targets and goals, to be working towards something. You know what I mean?'

'Believe me I do.'

I told him that my wife had set me a similar ultimatum a decade ago after another weekend on her own with Emily in the small apartment off Avenida Pedralbes. That I chose football, telling myself it was the best decision for all three of us.

'It's a decision I have never regretted but it came with a big price tag.'

'That's why I think Milan could be good for us. A fresh start.' He gestured towards the raindrops slaloming down the windowpane.

'Better weather. And Ana's sister is only an hour away. I think we'll all be happier there.'

'Maybe, but Ana needs help right now. Have you spoken to player liaison?'

He shook his head.

'Talk to Helen. See if she can find someone.'

'Ana won't like that boss. She's too proud.'

'Then you need to convince her.'

'I'll give it a shot.'

There was no putting it off for any longer. I told Valon he was out of the squad for the trip to Wallsend the following evening. He made it easy for me, accepting the decision with good grace.

'It's okay boss, I get it.' He repeated my motto: 'Standards are everything.'

I really didn't want to lose Valon. It would be a tough, physical battle, trial by long ball, and we needed our leaders on the pitch. But he left me with no choice. Favouritism is corrosive. It eats away at team spirit. Each player needs to know they will be held to the same standards, no matter who they are, or what they've done for the club.

'We'll tell the press you picked up a minor knock in training.'

'OK.'

'You won't travel with us either. I want you to spend the evening with Ana. Figure out how to make things work. Just don't go out anywhere. We can do without those headlines.'

As Sir Bobby once said to me, being a coach is about more than just tactics and selection decisions, training and systems. You have to care for your players, carry their weight. Help them with their problems off the pitch and equip them to be their best on it. And while this didn't come naturally to me - it was a learned behaviour, acquired through repetition and observation - it's no coincidence that most other elite coaches in the game right now have extraordinary levels of emotional intelligence.

'Thanks boss.'

'You can tell Ana you talked me into giving you the evening off.'

'No,' he laughed, the light returning to his eyes. 'She'd never believe that.'

35

Loakes Park, or Ice Station Zebra as Terry liked to call it, was the highest ground in the league and the coldest. The wind-swept stadium with its mock Tudor façade and sloping pitch (the goal in front of the two-tiered North stand was six foot three inches higher than the goal at the other end) had a powerful hold over Athletic. In the past four visits we had scraped just the solitary point. Dripping with talent, Athletic had always been the better side, but could never match Wallsend's spirit, cope with the hostility of the crowd or the next level shithousery. From the ambush on arrival, the reinforced windows tested by a hailstorm of golf balls and fireworks, to the cranked up heating in the dressing room, you knew you were in for a fight. The players also had to deal with the ghost of Matty Harper. A radio pundit for the evening, it was Harper's first return to the ground since a patella shattering lunge terminated his career days before his twenty second birthday. He swung by our sweat box of a dressing room before the game, still smiling and limping after three operations.

But we broke the spell that wet blustery evening, with a season defining performance. We withstood the barrage of long balls and the psychotic rain, thousands of cold needles attacking the players from every direction. Matched Wallsend's aggression and returned it with interest. Zharnell receiving his first booking since the red card against Aldershot for a challenge that left Wallsend's centre back writhing on the floor clutching his ankle. Dani Linares slit Wallsend's underbelly open for the first goal with the quick and casual precision of a veteran surgeon. His driven pass from just inside our half took four players out of the game. A second goal followed six minutes later. Jiri Bezek, Valon's replacement for the evening, rose high to meet Zharnell's outswinging corner, to the delight of the rest of the squad who rushed to congratulate him. There was no easing off, as the boys sought to fully exorcise the past. We forced Wallsend to run up and down the hill for another hour, pursuing shadows. Pounded their back line until it broke and broke again.

Tim Proctor, Wallsend's long serving coach, looked straight ahead as he brushed past me at the final whistle. Proctor embodied and embedded Wallsend's winning ugly mentality. He was upset with not just the result but also the repudiation of his ideas. His assistants shook hands grudgingly, muttering 'well done' and 'congratulations' through clenched teeth as they sped towards the tunnel. I blocked the path of one to make him say it properly. Next, I congratulated the boys, hugging Bezek. He broke the embrace and gave me a rueful smile, knowing that he would be back on the bench for the following game.

'Enjoy the moment Jiri. This is what it's all about,' I said clapping him on the shoulder.

We gravitated towards the two thousand or so Athletic supporters who were held back while the home fans slinked away. Fabio and Dani, stripped to the waist, led the group. There is something special about away fans. The willingness to clock up the miles when the best they can realistically expect is often no more than a gutted-out draw. Laser pens shone in their faces. Doused by plastic bottles full of urine, flung at them while the stewards turn a blind eye. Ticket costs jacked up by price gouging hosts. Restricted views. They suck it all up and never stop singing. It's a small cadre of loyalists. The diehards who go without a summer holiday in order to fund the trips throughout the season, topped up by a smattering of displaced fans who live locally, and those who tick off a new ground once or twice a year. A travelling caravan, scarves displayed in car windows, saluting each other in service stations. Stopping to help a fellow traveller change a tyre on the hard shoulder. Catching two or three trains and getting back home in the early hours. They share a deep collective memory of standout performances and flawed refereeing decisions. The last-minute winner against Collingham, Valon's thumping header under the lights at Manor Road. The red card and disallowed goal that cost Athletic two points against United back in '06. You quickly start to recognise their faces, even their voices.

They had been terrific that evening, chanting my name for minutes on end, and so I wanted to give something back. As we leant across the hoardings to pose for selfies, a teenage kid, decked out in leisure wear and yet to grow into his out of proportion frame, beckoned me over. You could see how much it mattered to him. I handed his phone to Fabio, gave the kid my gold and burgundy scarf and draped my arm around his shoulder.

'My bro's are gonna be green.'

'Let's give them a call.'

'Wot now?'

'Why not?'

'Wicked.'

I chatted to the kid's friends for a couple of minutes, then someone else's Dad, who was recovering from a heart bypass. After that a conversation in Spanish with un abuelo in Valencia about Benitez's title winning side and Pablo Aimar's brilliant goal against Liverpool. Then a new chant started up, to the tune of a seventies pop song.

'GIVE JOE, GIVE JOE, GIVE JOE THE JOBBBB.
WONT SOMEBODY PLEASE, GIVE HIM THE JOB.
GIVE JOE, GIVE JOE, GIVE JOE THE JOBBBB.
PULL YOUR FINGER OUT AND GIVE HIM THE JOB.'

The volume grew as more and more fans joined in. Back in the dressing room the boys laughed and jeered as a stony-faced Proctor gave a short uncooperative post-match interview. He sought to divert attention from his team's poor performance by questioning a refereeing decision in the build-up to the first goal. Once he had finished speaking, Zharnell turned up the stereo and the other players clapped and cheered as he danced. An extra loud cheer went up as Xabi entered the room. The players and staff all began to chant his name. Earlier that evening, as the coach made slow progress on the final mile to the ground, passing through clouds of smoke, the windows rattling from the impact of the incoming fire, Xabi walked the length of the aisle. Standing tall, he demanded that the players look him in the eye, telling them one by one that the noise outside was just a reflection of how much they feared us. He expected us to win, he insisted, and when we did, he would dye his hair gold and red.

Xabi leapt up onto the bench and placed a finger to his lips. The shouts and cheers slowly died away. He made us all wait, the crowd nestling in the palm of his hands. Finally, he spoke quietly.

'Open the door Jiri. I want them to hear this.'

Then he shouted suddenly, making everyone jump.

'WHAT DID I FUCKING TELL YOU?'

He slapped his hand on the wall behind him.

'WHAT DID I FUCKING TELL YOU?'

'THOSE PUSSIES THOUGHT THEY COULD INTIMIDATE YOU, BULLY YOU. NOT A FUCKING CHANCE. YOU MY COMPACHOS, YOU'VE GOT BALLS OF STEEL.' He was screaming now. 'SO FUCK THEIR PISS POOR FIRST TOUCHES. THEIR LONG BALLS AND LOW BLOCK. FUCK THEM.' He took a breath. 'FUCK PROCTOR FOR HIS LACK OF CLASS. ALL

BULLSHIT EXCUSES AND NO HANDSHAKES. HE GOT A PROPER SCHOOLING TODAY.'

He had gone too far now. Proctor would use this against us next season. Replay Xabi's speech word for word every day in the run-up to the game. But next season would take care of itself, all that mattered now was the next three games. Xabi dabbed at the sweat on his forehead with his fingers.

'AND FUCK THIS STINKING EXCUSE OF A DRESSING ROOM. DID THEY REALLY THINK TURNING THE HEAT UP WOULD STOP YOU FROM IMPOSING YOUR GAME? FUUUUUUUCK THEM.'

He motioned to Jiri to close the door.

'Now I seem to remember making some sort of promise,' he said quietly, producing two bottles from his pockets. The sound of cheers and laughter filled the small hot room again. 'Any volunteers?'

***

The coach wound its way through the Chilterns back to London. Yellow streaks from the motorway lights flashed by. The boys posted updates on social media, played on their handheld games consoles, or watched movies on their iPads. Mats, as always, had his head in a book (The rise and fall of the Holy Roman Empire). Zharnell practised Spanish. He jabbed at the screen on his tablet and murmured phrases to himself, frowning at each incorrect translation. Zito sat at the back on his own FaceTimeing his parents. Xabi, with his newly dyed hair, hopped from seat to seat to show the players a clip and get their own feedback on their performance, while I studied the videos of our next opponents. A few of the boys messaged Valon on the group chat but I was pleased to see he didn't respond. 'Looks like Vallo and the missus have had an early night,' said Terry with a wink.

I gazed through the window at the dim outline of the hills and reflected on a perfect evening. Another goal for Zito, who continued to grow and improve at a ferocious pace. Another clean sheet. Confidence and spirit within the group now sky high. And crucially, the gamble to leave Valon at home, to put the team before the individual, had not backfired.

36

'I heard Ann and Lara, who else is on?' asked Alastair Richards, the club's director of security.

'Hey Alastair—'

'...David's here,' said Archer cutting across Scooter from his hotel room in Madrid.

'...it's Scooter.'

'Joe's on.'

Moonlight slanted through a gap in the curtains, forming a silver pool on the floorboards. I switched my phone to speaker and took a swig of water from the glass on the bedside table.

'Thanks for scrambling. The Crisis Steering Group - to be known as the CSG from now on - is quorate. Lord Rigg is unable to join so Scooter has full delegated authority as per item 1:6 of the club's major incident management policy.'

Like a reserve keeper who starts the cup final after an injury in the warmup, Richards was thrilled to have a real crisis to manage after all the war gaming and desk top exercises.

'We'll begin with a Sit Rep based on intel from the blue light services. No interruptions please. I'll take questions at the end.'

Carla slipped out of bed. I took in the geometry of her body as she dressed. The curve of her breasts, the triangle between her thighs.

'At 23:52 Thames Valley police received a 999 call...' Richards was now competing with the sound of traffic and gusts of wind. Who, I wondered was out at three am? Archer returning from a bender? Scooter swapping beds?

'...from Aze... Can everyone go on mute. Thanks. From Azem Valon's house in Virginia Water. Officers arrived at the property four minutes later and found a serious crime scene.'

A slight pause to let it sink in.

'Valon and Ana were both rushed to hospital with multiple stab wounds and are in a critical condition.'

'Oh my god,' said Carla loudly, raising her hands to her face in shock.

'Two other men - IC1s, late 20s - were also found at the scene with multiple injuries. I'll spare you the full list but it includes a broken jaw, two broken kneecaps, several broken ribs, concussion, and stab wounds. There are unconfirmed reports that a third man fled the scene. The intruders were professionals. No ID, chemicals to destroy forensic evidence, and a printout of a recent planning application with details on the layout of the house and the security system. That's all we have so far. I'll now take any questions.'

The background noise returned as Anita spoke.

'Will they be OK?'

'Valon is still in surgery, he's lost a lot of blood. It's touch and go. Ana should pull through.'

'Jesus Christ,' said Carla. She sat down on the edge of the bed next to me. Her face drained of all colour.

'What hospital are they in?' asked Anita.

'Wexham Park.'

'And what do we know about the team operating on him?'

Richards must have been expecting this question. His answer was crisp and precise, as if he was reading from notes.

'He's in good hands. The lead surgeon is very experienced. Two spells in Camp Bastion in Afghanistan and then nine years working in the trauma unit in St Thomas's before moving out of London a few years ago. She's written several papers on how to apply battlefield medicine and treatment to the NHS. Received an MBE last year.'

'Speak to Hannington, get his views on the quality of after care and whether we need to arrange a transfer.'

'Of course, I'll ring him first thing.'

'*Tomorrow*? No, I want him at the hospital now to liaise with the medical team and give us a full assessment. You wake him the fuck up.'

Richards asked one of his team to take care of this. Archer spoke next.

'Does our insurance cover this?'

I looked at Carla and wondered what went through her mind when she heard her husband's voice.

'All players are covered for all eventualities,' said Anita. 'We'll receive a figure based on his market value if he is unable to play again.'

'Why didn't he travel with the squad?' asked Scooter.

I brought my finger to my lips. Carla nodded and I then unmuted the phone and explained the situation.

'I told you not to drop him. If you had listened to me we would still have a fucking centre back,' said Archer.

This was not true. While he had been quick to point out the downsides of resting Valon, Archer had stopped short of advising me to reverse the decision.

'Now's not the time to be second-guessing past decisions. The only thing we should be thinking about is how to manage this situation,' snapped Anita. 'Let's talk comms. Lara, thoughts?'

'Someone in the police will sell the story, they always do, so we don't have much time. I'll circulate draft statements for the two main scenarios. Please mark up any edits in tracked changes. And let's be quick. I want to get on the front foot and brief a few friendly journalists before it blows up. I suggest Scooter does a very short piece to camera for Athletic TV in the next half hour, thoughts and prayers etcetera, and then we'll do separate print and broadcast media conferences at nine am with updates via our social channels as soon as any new information emerges.'

'I'll do the video and the pressers,' I said. 'He's my player.'

'Agreed,' said Scooter.

'And I'll need as much detail as you've got to share on background. The more we feed them, the less likely they are to bite us,' Lara added.

'Stay on at the end,' said Richards.

'Will do. And one last thing,' said Lara. 'I recommend we hold a blood donation drive at Preston Park on Saturday, get the fans to show their solidarity and ensure something good comes of this mess.'

'Fantastic idea,' said Scooter. 'Think of the photos with the players first in line.'

Anita, usually so buttoned up and corporate, was the first to show any humanity.

'Enough of the stunts, where are the children?'

Richards was thrown by this. 'I'm not sure… maybe the police station.'

'I want you to find out exactly where they are and then get Helen to take them back to her house. Make sure they've got food, clothes, toys. Whatever they need.

37

I took one last look around the empty apartment before locking the door and heading down to the double-parked car in the street below. I did not have many possessions, and most of what I did have, the signed shirts and video tapes of old games, was still boxed up, so it had not taken long to pack. I waved to the truck driver who was waiting impatiently with his crates of soft drinks for me to move. He responded with another long angry blast of his horn. Nothing is ever a rush in Italy I thought to myself, until you hold up the traffic. I turned the ignition and the engine spluttered to life.

The move to Racing Club Roma had been a mistake from which it was hard to salvage many positives, but disappointment from failure was tempered by the new possibilities that lay ahead, and the long drive up the hamstring of Italy, past Ancona, Rimini and Ravenna, and then down through Slovenia and into Croatia, provided fresh perspective and time for reflection.

With hindsight I had taken the position for all the wrong reasons, seduced by the club's history and a significant pay increase, and had not given nearly enough thought to the head coach's philosophy. It was a mistake I told myself I would not make again. Alberto Manente resented my appointment, which had been made against his wishes, and didn't care who knew. I was excluded from meetings and belittled in front of the players. Input was rejected or taken as an insult. I received no credit for the team's success, only blame for our defeats. Worst of all, the slow, ponderous, defensive football was an anathema to everything Johan and Paco had taught me. Our first conversation set the the tone. Despite being fluent in English, Manente insisted on speaking in Italian, even as I grasped, painfully for the correct words, and stumbled over my verb endings. He refused to outline my responsibilities. When pressed he scowled and threw up his arms. In fact he only spoke twenty words of English to me the whole time we were together, after I suggested I could provide more input and assistance.

'Titles in three different countries.' He held up three fingers as he said this. 'The day I need your help is the day they put me in the ground.'

By the time I reached the outskirts of Venice, I was so cold from the air con that my forearms were pimpled with goosebumps. The sign for Udine on the overhead gantry reminded me of Santagostino's late winner against the run of play. Manente and I celebrated like brothers in the technical area, caught up in the emotion of the moment, and as we boarded the bus, he slapped me on the back, only for the familiar frostiness to return the following day.

Quitting was not an option, so I stuck it out until the end of the season, hoping that things would improve or Manente would leave, and then I received the call from Hadjuk's sporting director that would change everything. I first met Horst when he was studying for his coaching badges. The fresh faced, blond haired friendly giant from Essen was part of a steady stream of aspiring young coaches who spent a few days observing Paco and his staff at work on the training ground. Always grateful for the opportunities that Johan and Paco gave me, I tried to pay the favour forward whenever possible. Over a long dinner in Poblé Sec I explained Paco's game ideas and shared my insights and anecdotes from working alongside the great man, first as a performance analyst and then as a coaching assistant. We traded ideas on tactics and game plans, drills and conditioning. Thrashed out a starting eleven of the best players under twenty from across Europe.

Ten years later, Horst had been brought in by Hadjuk's new owners to overhaul the club's football operations. Installing a new head coach, someone who could take Hadjuk to the next level, was one of his early priorities and he was keen for me to meet with their owner. He either anticipated my scepticism or heard it in my voice.

'Ja, ja, I know, we are a small club in a little league, but you will get the chance to build something here the right way, just like we said all those years ago. No politics. No bullshit. And you get to be the main man.'

This final point got me thinking. Making the step up to head coach was hard, very hard, and it certainly wasn't going to happen where I was working. Most clubs wanted someone with experience rather than take a chance on a junior member of the coaching staff. I still had reservations, but as Horst told me he would cover the cost of flights and accommodation, I thought to myself, what do you have to lose?

The owner, Goran Perković wanted the candidates to be under no illusion about the club they would be joining or the scale of the challenge they would be undertaking, so he gave me a tour of the stadium himself, highlighting everything that was broken or needed to be improved as we went. We stopped when we reached the dressing room, which like dressing rooms all over the world, smelt of stale sweat, damp showers, and a trace of Deep Heat. Perković asked a question which convinced me this was the right move.

'What would it take to turn this club into champions?'

He was not, I quickly came to learn, interested in vanity signings or the fringe benefits of owning a football club. For Perković it was all about one thing. Winning. I may have struggled with my Italian grammar but this was a language I could understand.

'Money, time, and players who are willing to work and learn.'

'I can give you the first and the third. As for time, in my experience, it is both a blessing and a curse.'

Perković had come up the hard way. He made his first million by the time he was twenty-six after selling his family pizzeria to a property developer. From there he branched out into haulage, nightclubs, and pornography.

'It will take three years to build the squad, embed the mentality and the—'

'You'll get two years. No more.'

38

Valon's knife wounds, the lacerations to his stomach, chest, arms, and legs, were too deep, too severe, and the big man died on the operating table shortly after we finished the crisis management call. His funeral took place in Sarajevo on a dry and dusty April afternoon. The coffin, draped in the Bosnian flag, was escorted back from London by three fighter jets and then carried through the city on the back of an open bed truck. The procession crawled through streets lined with mourners on its way to the famous old mosque. A phalanx of police motorbikes led the way. Anita, Rigg, Scooter, Archer, and I travelled in one blackened minivan. Fabio, Mats and several other members of the group followed behind us. Carla was in the third vehicle along with a handful of other wives and girlfriends. We had not exchanged any words at the airport or on the jet, just the one involuntary and quickly suppressed half smile as she passed down the aisle, and I longed to be with her alone.

The Bosnian government had declared a day of national mourning and judging by the crush of people on both sides of the road, the entire country had turned out to pay their respects. Tears rolled down the faces of men and women of all ages. Small children, dressed in their smartest clothes, perched on top of their parents' shoulders. Flower petals thrown from the crowd fluttered on a light breeze and gathered on the windscreen. Helicopters buzzed above us, tracing our slow progress.

It had been a difficult, draining week since Valon's death. Bedside conversations at the hospital with Ana. Meeting after meeting to discuss the funeral arrangements. Media interviews on behalf of the family. And Bromsgrove had resisted any suggestion of postponing our fixture, knowing that the boys were in pieces, until Rigg reminded them that their owner's visa was up for renewal, and he had friends in the *highest of fucking places.* Training had continued, if only to maintain conditioning and a semblance of normality. But it had been hard work. A few of the boys threw themselves into the sessions, anything to take their minds off other matters, but the majority didn't want to be there. Fabio and Mats had taken it particularly hard. They lived in the same private gated community as Valon on the outskirts of Windsor and their families socialised together, taking it in turns to host dinner parties or screenings of away games. They shared the same Pilates instructor and drove into London together to visit the museums and galleries, Fabio at the wheel of a luxury, twenty seat Mercedes-Benz minibus. Even Xabi, normally so good at lifting the players, was quiet and subdued. Terry had been worse. Flying off the handle at the smallest thing. And results had gone against us at the weekend. Collingham and Tiverton both won, widening the gap to fourth place.

Scooter oblivious to the mood, chatted breezily about the city's history and strategic importance to the Ottoman Empire. By the time we reached the riverbank, he was reading from his phone about the assassination of Archduke Franz Ferdinand, the heir to the Austro-Hungarian Empire, and the man whose death triggered the First World War.

'Seven assassins, all members of the Black Hand secret society, were positioned along the route. The first two stood outside the Mostar Café but lost their nerve when the motorcade reached them. So it fell to the next man, a dude by the name of Čabrinović. He pitched his bomb but it bounced off the back of the Archduke's car and blew up the vehicle behind it. Čabrinović took a cyanide pill and jumped into the river, but the crowd dragged him out and kicked his butt. When they reached the town hall, one of Ferdinand's flunkies lambasted the Governor of Bosnia, demanding to know why he had not arranged a military guard for the heir to the throne.' Scooter chuckled to himself. 'Get this… and the Governor replied, "do you think Sarajevo is full of assassins?"'

We passed yet another banner with a photo of Valon's face. I thought again about my decision to send him home, telling myself for the umpteenth time that he would not have wanted it any other way.

'It was here,' Scooter cried excitedly as we reached the Latin Bridge. 'This was where it happened. After giving a speech at the town hall, Ferdinand decided to visit those wounded by the bomb in hospital. But the motorcade took a wrong turn, just there,' he said, leaning across me to point out the window. 'They tried to turn around, but Ferdinand's car stalled and Principe, who was standing nearby, stepped onto the running board and shot the Archduke and his wife at point blank range—'

'And the rest is history,' said Rigg dryly.

The column of black vehicles proceeded along the quayside and crossed the Emperor's Bridge. Down below us life continued as normal. A river cruiser slid by. Teenagers splashed and swam in the shallows, batting a small ball between them with their hands, lunging and diving to prevent it from falling into the water. Peels of laughter wound their way up to us. Eventually we reached the Mosque and joined the long queue for the entrance. I barely registered the Minaret stretching up to sky or the red stain on the ground in front of us.

'What's that?' asked Anita.

I looked more closely at the scars and pock marks in the concrete filled with red paint or resin.

'It's a Sarajevo Rose,' replied Scooter, resuming his role as a tour guide. 'There's hundreds across the City. They mark the spot where people were killed by the blast from a mortar shell during the civil war.'

A look of disdain flashed across Anita's face.

'They really need to move on,' she muttered.

Rigg couldn't help himself. 'Those who fail to learn from history are condemned to—'

'There's Jorge,' said Anita interrupting him. 'I must have a word.' And with that she was gone.

The chairman drew alongside me as the queue shuffled forward again.

'Good news. It's all systems go after your meeting yesterday. Well done.'

I had woken to the news that the club was on the verge of extending my contract. In this industry, this world of perpetual rumour and speculation, it is the kind of chatter you get all the time and I would have dismissed it instantly if it was not for one thing. A senior club source, code reserved exclusively for the chairman or when Lara briefed the media on his behalf, was quoted as saying the board would sit down with The Owner at the end of the month to finalise the situation. *The Telegraph* had learned - always *learned*, never *been told* - I would be given a four year contract and a greater say in recruitment decisions. On the short drive to work my mind flitted between next season's targets and the importance of lifting a trophy. The players we would need to bring in. How to make the most of the pre-season training block. And for once I looked forward to my early morning meeting with Archer.

Rigg was waiting in my office after training, reading what looked like a contract. Slanting sunlight through the window projected his silhouette onto the white board. It was the first and only time I ever saw Rigg in Datchet, and away from his usual comfort zone of the boardroom or the Pall Mall members club he seemed strangely diminished. He gathered the papers and turned them face down as soon as I entered the room. He removed his reading glasses, placed them in his jacket pocket, and stood to greet me enthusiastically.

'Dear, boy! So good to see you. And how are the troops? Bearing up? Splendid.'

As was often the way with Rigg, the conversation was one sided. He told me Ana had accepted his offer of alternative accommodation when she left hospital and counselling for her two eldest children. He listed the new measures the security team had introduced to safeguard the players against copycat crimes (perimeter alarms, anti-climb paint, bullet proof panic rooms) and then lavished praise on me.

'You have done a first-class job Joe, truly outstanding. You know I said to Anita only yesterday, that hiring you was the single best decision we've made this year. She agreed. And we're both immensely grateful for how you have helped us steer the club through these choppy waters.'

Then he alluded to the morning's news.

'Obviously, I can't speak for The Owner but let's just say I'm not expecting to do any press conferences this summer.'

Rigg let this last remark hang in the air for a moment or two and then with the flattery and inducements out of the way, he got down to business.

'There's something we need you to do for us. It is a rather delicate matter.'

He brought his hands together and gave me a long meaningful look over his steepled fingers.

'There's a bit of a hitch with the insurance company. You know what those sharks are like, do anything to get off the hook, and they've got it into their heads that Azem was planning to leave at the end of the season, which massively depresses the value of the payout. Now of course we all know that Azem intended to stay, and a three-year deal had been agreed. It seems like a lifetime ago now, but if you remember, the plan was to do the big reveal after the Wallsend game, until events, sadly, got in the way.'

Credit where it's due. Rigg was an elite liar, one of the very best in the game, with a technique honed through years of practice, capable of beating any polygraph. First he convinced himself, then others. He kept his eyes locked on mine. The pitch and volume of his voice remained consistent. He did not blink or fidget or roll his lips back.

'The good news is, under English law you don't need a written contract - verbal agreement is sufficient - and Azem agreed terms in his discussions with various club executives. We just need you to vouch for this and everything will go swimmingly.'

'What do you mean?'

'Their chap wants to speak to you, David, Anita, and myself. It's just a formality, the man has a job to do. He also wants to understand why Azem did not travel with the squad that evening. Now we know it was due to a minor injury but there have been rumours in some quarters, totally wide of the mark of course, that he missed the game for disciplinary reasons. Our conscientious friend has pointed out that if this was the case then his firm are not required to stump up. Naturally we've assured him it was purely down to a question of match fitness. The trouble is there are no records from the medical team, one can only assume they got lost in all the drama, and Dr H is a bit of a stickler, as you know, for detail and process. So you need to explain that Azem missed the match as a precaution.'

'You're asking me to lie?'

Rigg threw his hands up in horror. He seemed genuinely offended.

'You ought to know me well enough by now Joe. I would never - *never* - dream of doing that.' A pause. Another meaningful look over the fingers.

'No, we all have our version of the truth, and you absolutely must tell yours. I'm just asking you to think about the calibre of players we could sign with that money. We're talking the best part of one hundred million pounds here.'

Like the coach who instinctively senses whether a player needs an arm around the shoulder or a boot up the backside, Rigg knew which buttons to press.

'When do you want me to meet him?'

'Tomorrow afternoon at Preston Park.'

He stood and put his papers away in his briefcase.

'We won't forget this Joe.'

We passed through a low archway into a tiled courtyard with a fountain where we washed our hands and feet before entering the prayer hall. The room was silent. Music and conversation, strictly forbidden. The men knelt on prayer mats in rows at the front, the women grouped together at the back. While we waited for the service to begin, I counted four Ballon d'or winners and seven heads of state. Two Wimbledon champions and multiple Olympic medalists.

Valon's teammates from the national side carried his coffin dressed in their blue and white tracksuits. They set the casket down in front of the Imam and joined the mourners in the front row. The Iman stood with his back to us and began to pray. Much of the funeral prayer was silence itself, with occasional words spoken aloud in Arabic. The only noise was the sound of sobbing and the faint buzz of the helicopters above. My mind returned again to the game at the weekend, and how best to replace the irreplaceable. Valon wasn't just the spine of the team; he was the beating heart. The gatekeeper and the conductor. Breaking the first press with short tidy passes to Dani. Carrying the ball forward and stepping up to provide an extra dimension in midfield when teams sat off us. His loss was an engine failure mid-flight, but football has no time or respect for excuses. The conveyor belt of games keeps coming at you. Good managers adapt and survive, the very best find a way to turn events to their advantage. Jiri Bezek's performance against Wallsend confirmed what I suspected. He was strong in the tackle and the air, and relished the physical battle, trading kicks and elbows with their burly striker, but Bezek was no catalyst. He was hard wired to pump it long, not build play. Unfortunately, we had few alternatives. Apart from Jose Costa, Bezek was the only fit centre back in the first team squad, and none of the academy players were ready to step up. So, I called Shan into my office the day before we flew to Sarajevo. The young kid from Guiyang had everything I value in a player: fantastic technique, with a near faultless first touch, ferocious pace - over both short and long distances - an abundance of energy, and a high tactical IQ. But he was competing for a spot with Linares and Kuipers and so I had rationed his minutes, limiting him to eight appearances as a substitute and just the two starts. He came on in the final ten or fifteen minutes and helped us control the end game, operating comfortably within the system with a pass completion rate of 89%. Shan looked stunned when I informed him he was starting alongside Jose Costa at the weekend.

'Don't worry, I'm not looking for a traditional centre back. I want you to bring the ball out, draw the press, and once you've played the pass keep moving forward. Mats will tuck inside to cover and Dani will move to a wider area creating space for you to receive the pass here.' I pointed to the pockets of space between the first and second lines of pressure on the tactical board.

'You play it forwards, quickly, and then go again, moving higher up the pitch, giving us an overload in every phase. No one will pick you up, and if they do, you'll open space for someone else.'

'Yes boss,' Shan replied but he seemed unsure, thinking no doubt, about the challenge of containing the rapier quick movement and attacking intent of Bromsgrove's front three. We spent the best part of an hour going through the opposition analysis and discussing what he had to do. The importance of staying narrow and compact out off possession. Which zones to move to during the first phase of build up. To anticipate and step in rather than go to ground, and rely on his pace to recover if beaten by the first touch. To use his upper body strength to win aerial duels by levering their forwards out of the optimal attacking positions. Who to mark at set pieces.

'Xabi has some more clips to show you,' I told him. 'Relax, you've got this.'

The Imam finished the prayer, and then in a break from tradition, turned to face the funeral party and the cameras behind us and delivered a short eulogy, switching from Arabic to English. The old man had presence. Stagecraft. He used the acoustics of the domed ceiling to amplify his voice. The wrinkles in his face to project his emotions. Like a player who feints in one direction and then moves in the other, he varied the pace and tone of his words. He spoke about Valon's childhood. How his life had been scarred by hatred and violence. Valon and his mother and sisters seeking sanctuary in Sarajevo after his father and brother were rounded up with the other men from the village, escaping one hell only to enter another.

'Azem was there that day in Dobrinja when the shells landed on the football pitch and in the crowd. He watched friends and neighbours die.'

He told the story of the family's move to Marseille.

'Azem worked as a kitchen porter in one of the hotels down by the port, rising early to work before school, and late into the evening after football training. He worked fast with a knife, chopping and peeling vegetables. He washed pots and pans, scrubbed the kitchen surfaces.'

And learnt how to swear in French.

'One of the chefs looked after Azem, made sure he always had a good hot meal before he returned home. And when he heard Azem was taking three buses to travel to training he persuaded his wife to give him a lift. Azem never forgot this kindness. When he joined

Athletic he didn't buy an expensive car or a big house. Instead he used his first pay cheques to help his old friend open his own restaurant.'

I couldn't believe Carla was sat only metres away and yet I couldn't see or speak to her, let alone run my hand over her smooth, scented skin. Now I knew how Archer felt. To want something so bad and not be able to have it. And like Archer I was jealous to the point of blistering anger. I craved the time and proximity to Carla that he scorned. Was furious that he rather than I could hand her a cup of coffee every morning. Watch as she dried her long dark hair. Hold her hand in public. Be the one she shared a new work of art with. I could not bear to be in his presence and yet once a day or more I had to sit down and look him in the eye and talk football as if nothing had changed. And the thought of the two of them entwined together in bed or under the shower, Archer inside her, Carla making those low moans, made me physically hurt.

Carla had told me she was not ready to leave him. That she did not have the strength to deal with the circus and the media fall out ('Let's keep things as they are for now.') So when this jealousy was at its most destructive, part of me wanted to force the issue. For Archer to criticise Carla, so I could defend her. Point out how fortunate and foolish he was. Or to tell him straight out that I loved her. I began to fantasise about him falling ill or having a fatal accident. I even wondered if we could swap. To offer to give up the job if he walked away from his marriage. But I didn't dare for fear he would say yes, and I would not be able to go through with it.

'...he was always devout. A man of great faith. A faith that sheltered him in the darkest times, kept him rooted when he became successful.'

The Imam's words reminded me of Valon's request to adjust our training schedule to take account of Ramadan. Like all Muslims, Valon and Rafiq could not eat or drink between the hours of sunrise and sunset during the Holy Month, so we agreed that the two men could switch their gym and cardio sessions to begin at four in the morning, and the catering team took it in turns to get up early and serve a specially designed breakfast just before five. The other boys agreed among themselves to bring the main session forward by a couple of hours, an act of unity and togetherness that would have been unthinkable a few months before.

'...and just as he never forgot those who helped him along the way, Azem will live on in our hearts and in our memories,' said the Imam with a final flourish.

After the burial I gathered the players together.

'I don't know about you, but I need a drink.'

The boys looked surprised but didn't protest. Our drivers conferred briefly and then we set off towards the Old Town, leaving Anita, Rigg, Archer and the others to glad-hand the dignitaries. By now, the crowd lining the streets had begun to disperse, laughing and chatting, as they made their way home. The sea of people parted and then reformed behind us, pointing and staring at the tinted windows, banging good humouredly on the roof.

'He's given them one last great performance,' said Mats bitterly.

The bar was empty apart from a small group of men in their sixties or seventies hunched over a backgammon board. A TV in the corner replayed the Imam's speech. The barman welcomed us with a flicker of recognition and a solemn nod of the head, and gestured for us to sit wherever we liked. The men barely looked up from their game as we pushed two tables together at the back of the room. The TV switched from the Imam to footage of Valon's casket being lowered into the open grave, his head pointing towards Mecca. The barman glanced our way, saw the pain in the players' faces, and turned it off.

Once everyone had a drink in their hand I raised my glass.

'To Vallo the best player you could hope to work with, the best man you could hope to call your friend.'

'To Vallo,' the boys replied.

No coaching manual or seminar prepares you for picking up a group of players after the violent death of their leader. I talked it through with Xabi and Terry and asked Lara for her thoughts, but nothing they suggested felt right. In the end, I sought advice from a grief counsellor, a former army chaplain and a veteran of Helmand and Basra. He told me grief is like an IED lurking beside the road waiting to ambush you. Some days the blast leaves no more than a scratch or a dent in your armour, others it tears right through you.

'Their maximum effort is discretionary, you know that you've read the books,' he said to me. I nodded my agreement. 'Only they can decide if they're willing to give it their all after everything they've been through. Honesty and empowerment are the only way.'

I put down my glass. Cleared my throat. The boys looked on, waiting for me to speak. The distance between us had never felt greater.

'This can go one of two ways now. The season ends here, or we find a way to finish the job. I'm not going to insult you with any bullshit about honoring Vallo out on the pitch. The question you have to ask yourselves is whether you want to play football after what's just happened.' I looked around the table.

'And there's no wrong answer.'

Kuipers stared at the table. Zharnell took a sip of his Diet Coke. Jose Costa dabbed at a tear. Mats glanced at the others and then began to speak. I cut him off.

'It's too soon to decide. Give it a day or two and then come tell me what it's going to be.'

A tray of shot glasses arrived. A gift from the backgammon players, the barman explained. We turned to thank them, and they raised their own glasses in salute. The back draft from the sweet, peachy spirit swept down my throat, and blazed away within my chest. Mats told the story about when he arrived at the club. Valon took him out for dinner on his first evening, and when he heard Mats was staying in a hotel on his own, insisted he come stay with him and Ana. Every night for six weeks the two men watched football from around the world. Low scoring contests in Italy and bad tempered South American matches. Dutch Cup ties and Spanish league games. They analysed tactics and systems. Identified defensive vulnerabilities and mapped out what they would do to tighten up.

'I would have been lost without him,' Mats said with a sad smile.

I beckoned the waiter over and ordered two bottles of wine for us and whatever the backgammon players wanted.

Jose Costa gave a deep sigh.

'He learnt Spanish when I joined. Made me write down a playbook of instructions in Spanish.'

Dani looked puzzled.

'Why didn't you use English?'

'Vallo thought I would react quicker if we spoke in my native language.'

I passed around the glasses of wine. Everyone accepted one, apart from Zharnell who stuck to his soft drink.

'God that's good,' said Dani Linares after taking a sip. 'I can't remember the last time I had a drink.' He took another careful sip, savoring the taste.

'You'll never believe what happened earlier. Macclesfield's technical director tried to tap me up. Said I was a Macclesfield player in an Athletic shirt.'

'Motherfucker,' said Fabio.

'What did you say?' Zharnell asked.

'That I'm here to bury my friend and he can go fuck himself,' Dani replied.

Zharnell wept as he revealed Valon had appeared at his home the morning after his disastrous performance against Aldershot.

'We drove out to Virginia Water—'

'The big man loved it there,' said Fabio.

'We went for a long walk around the lake. V stopping every now and then to talk to the dog walkers, the guy on the coffee stand, you know what he's like…' Zharnell's voice broke as he caught himself using the wrong tense. '…never happier than when he was befriending strangers. When we got back to the car park this young mum was losing her shit. She'd locked her kid and her phone in the car and was hysterical. The kid was screaming. V calmed them both down. Started pulling faces, animal impressions, you name it anything to make the kid laugh. The woman couldn't afford breakdown cover, so Valon called them up and paid for it there and then. We waited for over an hour for them to arrive. By this point he'd made a puppet out of one of his socks. Kept attacking me and himself with it. The kid couldn't get enough.'

We reminisced about famous victories. The times Valon laid his body on the line. Fabio spoke about the lock out against Lisbon in the semi-final of the European Cup, one of Valon's most dominant performances.

'He had Schulze and Bouderbala in his pocket that night. They didn't get a sniff.'

Mats relived the towering header against Merton to clinch Athletic's last title.

'He told me to block Faisal and he would do the rest.'

Two of the old men began to bang on the table top, hammering out a rhythm. A few moments later their companions started to sing a sad, plaintive song. Mats pushed back his seat and wandered over. Fabio joined him, nodding his head in time to the beat. Soon we were all on our feet. More drinks and singing followed. At some point, late into the evening, the barman beckoned us through to a back room. Candles flickered in the gloom casting light on a long wooden table lined with plates and glasses. Once we were seated, food arrived. Miniature beef kebabs, served with onions, cream and freshly baked flatbread. Spinach and feta burek. Bowls of tomato and cucumber salad. After serving us the bar owner's son took a picture of the assembled group. His father scolded the boy, demanding he hand over his phone. Mats, who was seated next to him, whispered in his ear. The man protested but Mats persisted, placing his hands together in front of his chest, as if to pray. He asked for his son's name and their postal address so we could send the boy a signed shirt. Eventually the bar owner relented and provided the details, speaking fast and then slow. Mats laughed at his own failure to understand and passed his phone to the blushing teenager so he could tap it in himself.

I discussed Bosnian and Yugoslavian football with my neighbour, a heavyset man with sad, sorrowful eyes and the worn, calloused hands of a carpenter. We replayed the win over Spain in the 1990 World Cup. Dragan Stojkovic dummying a volley at the far post, then bringing the ball under control and inside the defender in one beautiful motion. Bemoaned the three missed penalties in the shootout against Argentina in the next round, after Yugoslavia had played for ninety minutes with ten men. He then went further back in time, retelling the story of the 1968 European Championships. I indulged him, pretending not to have heard it before. He described in minute, romanticised detail, how Yugoslavia beat West Germany and England, the World Cup finalists from two years before, along with France en-route to the final against Italy in Rome. How Italy owed their place in the final to a coin toss in the dressing room after a goalless draw against the Soviet Union. Italy's captain Giacinto Facchetti correctly calling tails. He let out a short, bitter laugh as he described how Yugoslavia opened the scoring in the final and passed up several golden opportunities to extend their lead before Angelo Domenghini's free kick rescued the home side with ten minutes to go. The game finished level after extra time and rather than settle this match with another flip of a coin, the two teams returned to the Stadio Olimpico two days later, with the Italians winning the replay.

After this I only remember fragments of the rest of the evening. More wine, endless plates of food. A heated disagreement between Mats and Jose Costa over who made the greatest Athletic XI of all time. Kuipers falling asleep at the table. A raucous walk back through the dark cobbled streets in search of our hotel. Dani playing keepie uppie with an empty can. Stopping somewhere for yet another drink. Jose Costa disappearing with two girls he met in the bar and returning later with a sheepish grin on his face. Stumbling around my hotel room, colliding with a chair and a floor lamp. Breaking the agreed rules and calling Carla to tell her I wanted to be with her all the time. Carla, who must have been alone, crying down the phone, saying she wanted the same thing. And then falling into a deep, troubled sleep as the room span around me.

39

Grierson pulled up a wide-angle freeze frame from one of Bury's recent matches.

'Look how narrow the front three are. They stay central, constantly swapping positions, leaving space for the fullbacks.'

Bury's fullbacks were their main creative outlet. The pair played high and wide, enabling the wide forwards to move inside and overload the centre backs. Nilton's delivery was especially effective. The left back played the ball quick and early, bending it around opposing defenders and into the danger zone, and had already contributed nine assists that season. While Cohen, his counterpart on the opposite flank, preferred to use his pace to run onto balls played into space, or receive on the turn, and carry the ball before cutting it back to their eight around the D.

Grierson switched to another still image.

'You can see how both of Flixton's fullbacks have been sucked inside to support the centre backs, leaving all this space for Nilton and Cohen.'

In our pre-meet, Grierson had suggested we switch to a low block and try to shut Bury out. Terry agreed, but containment is futile against a team like Bury, you have to be brave and take the battle to them.

I took over from Grierson.

'Next slide.'

The heat map showing Bury's chance creation was replaced with a graphic of a 1-3-2-5 formation with names against each of the eleven dots.

'If we sit back for ninety minutes and allow them to play their game there's only going to be one outcome. We've got be brave and proactive. Play with high tempo. They'll be tired from the trip to Athens, so we go at them from the beginning. Push Nilton and Cohen back up the pitch and make them suffer. Next slide.'

'Without the ball we defend in 1-4-3-3 keeping the usual shape and high line. If you play at the same level as the weekend, you'll cause them all kinds of problems.'

In the end, I didn't have a further conversation with the boys after our evening in Sarajevo. They returned to training two days later and let their feet do the talking. The intensity, the snap in their tackles, told me all I needed to know: they still wanted to compete, still needed to win. Our first game back was an emotionally charged two nil win away to Bromsgrove, a result which kept us in touching distance of fourth place. The two captains led the players out carrying a banner with a photo of Valon and Ana. The Athletic supporters in the away end cranked up the noise:

'Super, Super Aze;
Super, Super Aze;
Super, Super Aze;
Super Azem Val-on.'

Within a few seconds the home fans seated near to them joined in. The words spread around the ground, like when a trail of spilt petrol is set alight in the movies, growing louder and louder, until all 82,000 voices were chanting as one. The most powerful, most emotionally charged moment I have experienced in a football ground. Eventually the noise subsided, fading away as quickly as it started, and the game began. There was sixty seconds of applause in the fourth minute - Valon's shirt number – and the boys surfed the wave of emotion, taking all their pain and anger out on Bromsgrove's defensive line.

As we wrapped up the analysis meeting, Fabio called out:

'I spotted something Boss. Vieler always goes with a shorter wall on free kicks. He leaves half a metre space on the side he covers so his view is not blocked and then just before the ball is hit he takes a sidestep to give him an extra split second to reach the ball over the wall.'

'Grierson, give us some clips. Play them through in real-time and then again at half-rate.'

'Two seconds. What camera angle?'

'Behind the goal.'

We watched the montage.

'Look, watch him here,' said Fabio pointing excitedly at the screen.

And sure enough, Vieler moved to his left a split second before the ball was struck, stealing a yard and playing the odds - nine times out of ten the ball goes over or around the wall.

'Fabio's right. You can see there, he's putting all his weight on his leading foot with the early step, which makes it hard to change direction and dive the other way,' said Xabi.

'You hit hard and flat into the top corner on the side he's standing. Take him by surprise, no?' said Dani.

'Great work Fabio. Dani, Zito, practice shooting for that spot. And then when you're done let's film you hitting over and around the wall and put it out as a behind the scenes video. Make sure Bury's analysts see it. Right boys, let's get out on the grass.'

40

Over at the High Court, it took the twelve men and women of the jury a little under two hours to reach a unanimous verdict in the Crown's case against Vladimir Lantsov. The judge read out the verdicts (guilty, guilty, guilty), admonished Lantsov for a complete lack of remorse and for abusing his status ('wealthy individuals like you and Mr Archer need to understand you are not above the law'), before handing down a nine year prison sentence. It was then, and only then, that the Russian showed any emotion, blowing kisses to his mum and sister in the public gallery as he was led away.

The players, Lantsov's teammates for just a matter of weeks, did not mention him once in training the following day. Archer also kept a low profile, opting to be abroad on the day the verdict was delivered. During a conference call with The Owner that evening Rigg, Lara and Anita all agreed we needed to 'throw a dead cat on the table.' It wasn't until two days later, during another maddening meeting with Hannington, that I found out what they meant by this.

'He continues to make reasonable progress physically,' said Hannington. 'With a fair wind we should be able to introduce ball work in eight to ten weeks, but I have to say I'm increasingly concerned from a psychological perspective. He is still in a dark, dark place. Long night of the soul and all that.'

Borello had no family or friends in the UK and continued to struggle with his English. After physio each day, one of the drivers would drop him back to an empty house in the Berkshire countryside where he had far too much of what injured footballers need the least. Time on their hands to think. Long evenings alone to ask himself, over and over, whether he would play again, and if so whether he would still have the explosive first five yards or the ability to make sudden changes in direction. Whether he would be able to regain a spot in a lineup that was winning without him. To dwell on the fact that he would miss the World Cup just as he was breaking through to the national team. To brood on what he would do to Ripley if he ever came across him again on a football pitch. To replay revenge fantasies, kneeling beside Ripley as he writhed in pain after two feet to the knee and saying to him 'how do you fucking like that?' Words, Borello reminded himself, he must learn in English.

'There's still too much anger. Too much self pity. It doesn't make for a good recovery.'

Borello's whole identity had changed and he found himself defined by a traumatic injury rather than his talent and achievements on the field.

'It's been hard for the lad. How's his alcohol intake? Still OK?'

Borello had his blood tested every two days.

'Yes, it's unchanged, but we are having to manage his meds carefully. Twice in the past week he has asked us to up the dose.' Hannington hesitated for a second. I looked at his face, lined from the strain of having to continually cover his arse.

'And I gather he has now started to pay for female company.'

One of the player liaison officers had introduced Borello to an escort agency which was popular among London based players. From the little I had heard, they were very good at what they did, catered for all tastes, and were very discreet, taking pride in the fact that none of their clients ever ended up in the papers.

'How he spends his money is none of our business.'

Hannington pursed his lips in that pompous way of his.

'You know that's not true. I feel I simply must bring it to the Chairman's attention.'

The breaking news caption flashed across the TV screen as Hannington said this.

WYSZKOWSKA APPOINTED ATHLETIC HEAD COACH

Hannington saw the expression on my face and turned to look at the screen. The presenter stood in front of a large video wall. To her right was a photo of Lukasz Wyszkowska, to her left the Athletic Club Crest. I unmuted the TV.

'*Big, big breaking news. Sky Sports sources have confirmed Lukasz Wyszkowska is set to be unveiled as the new Athletic head coach later today. The fifty nine year old, who has been out of the game since leaving Freiburg last summer, will be reunited with David Archer, who will join him in the dugout as assistant head co*ach.'

The photo on the screen was replaced with old footage of a training session in Munich. Wyszkowska had a ball under one arm, the other was wrapped around Archer's shoulders.

'I'm very sorry Joe,' said Hannington. The usual smug condescension was replaced with genuine sympathy, which made it only worse. 'When did you find out?'

'There's no news yet on what this means for Joe Hendricks.'

I muted the TV and forced a smile.

'We've been planning it for a couple of weeks,' I lied.

***

I met Wyszkowska at a coaching conference years before. He delivered a thoughtful presentation on the importance of Zone Fourteen, outlining how over 80% of France's assists in Euro 2000 came from the golden square in front of the penalty area. He had the best slides of any of the speakers, with detailed graphics highlighting the vertical movements of the French players on and off the ball in this zone. How wide players would attack the space vacated by the central striker. Wyszkowska built his career on this analysis, using a pair of defensive midfielders to clampdown on any build up in central areas, conceding just thirteen goals en route to the first of his two back-to-back German league titles. Five good seasons followed in Italy, where his safety first, low block was fully appreciated, but success had become a stranger to the Pole in recent years. First there was a difficult spell in Spain, a poisoned chalice of a rebuild he should never have accepted, which exposed the limitations in his methods and character. Then a multi-car pile-up in Paris. After that, Wyszkowska had all but exhausted the limited pool of elite European clubs. And apart from one unhappy short lived second spell in Bavaria, none of his former employers would countenance a return - too many bridges had been burnt, too many grudges nursed. And Wyszkowska was temperamentally unsuited to the part-time nature of international football. So, he moved down a rung on the ladder, accepting roles with second tier clubs in Italy and Germany, lifting minor domestic trophies with both teams.

I introduced myself to him during the coffee break and asked about specific tactical decisions. The use of a false ten in the Rome Derby. The adjustment after twenty minutes in his first Clásico. How he had accommodated Gallina, Varalda, and Kowalski in the same side. He couldn't have been more different to his prickly, cross-the-road-to-pick-a-fight public persona. He sketched out diagrams on paper torn from a leather-bound pocketbook. Listened patiently while I outlined my ideas on passing angles, the use of third man runs and the up, back and through combination, before he explained why he favoured a more direct, vertical approach. This was when Wyszkowska was at his very peak. Before the game moved on and left him behind, like an ageing fullback puffing and panting in the slipstream of a spring heeled forward. Before the breakdown in relations with his players in Bologna.

The landmark legal decision finding him and the club guilty of constructive dismissal for freezing out Vandereycken in his first week in charge, *por encourager les autres*, as Vandereycken's lawyer said on the steps of the court.

Rigg's secretary called twenty minutes later. With her drawn out vowels and haughty disdain, she had the air of a minor Royal. One who had married into the family and had to work doubly hard at the elitism. The Chairman needed to see me right away she explained. The camera crews and photographers were already assembled as we drove out of Datchet – Looking back, I can only assume they had been tipped off. Flashbulbs lit up the interior of the car like fireworks on a cold November night, as the reporters crowded close to the windows, shouting their questions for the benefit of the cameras rather than in expectation of an answer.

'WHAT DO YOU MAKE OF THE NEWS JOE?'

'JOE, JOE, WHAT'S YOUR NEXT MOVE?'

'HAVE YOU GOT A MESSAGE FOR THE FANS?'

Rex took pleasure in running over the toes of one of the reporters before speeding away.

The meeting took place in the same room as the interview a few months before. It was a warmer day. The distant gongs of Big Ben drifted across the park and in through the open window. Rigg apologised for making me travel in from Datchet ('I prefer not to leave Zone One if I can help it') and then brazened it out. He glossed over the media reports and skated around our conversation after Valon's death.

'I wanted you to hear it from us first,' he said without blinking, the words rolling off his tongue with the ease and conviction of a man who spent years lying for a living.

'We'll be announcing Lukasz Wyszkowska's appointment later today as our new Head Coach. On behalf of The Owner and everyone at the club I want to thank you for your service.'

It was as if he was reading from one of those letters Downing Street publishes after a Cabinet Minister is forced to resign. Empty cliché, followed empty cliché: it was a difficult decision, taken in the best interests of the club. I was a true professional. He had nothing but respect for the way I had conducted myself.

'As a token of our appreciation, we have decided to increase your performance bonus by twenty percent if we finish in the top four.'

He paused, waiting for a thank you, and then continued after reading the room.

'We want to keep you in the Athletic family. There's an opening in Sydney, a real project for you to sink your teeth into.'

It was a cynical, empty gesture. An attempt to make me the villain by tabling an offer he knew I would refuse. Until then I had kept my emotions in check but suddenly, I felt the anger bubbling away deep inside me, rising up my throat. I opened my mouth to take a breath and it gushed out.

'I'm not moving to fucking Australia.'

Rigg looked upset.

'Don't rush to make a decision. It's an incredible lifestyle out there, with none of the pressure or nonsense you have to deal with here. You can rent a place down by the harbour. Go out for dinner and no one will ever know who you are.'

I looked at the portrait of Churchill. He glowered right back as if to say 'don't take this crap.'

'We're on the verge of something special, you've seen how we been playing. Why throw all that away for the sake of a name?'

'Come on Joe, this is Athletic, we were *always* going to go for a name. You must've known that. Don't let it affect you. You are four games away from becoming rich, very rich, and the journey doesn't end there. Another job will follow and another one after that. Go and gain some more experience, build your CV, the door will always be open for you to return in the future.'

He handed me a sheet of paper.

'Here's the press release. We don't want to unsettle the players, so we'll keep it tight and clean. No interviews with Lukasz until the end of the season, no comments from me, The Owner or Dave beyond what's in the release. And then we've got a full script and Q&A for you to work from tomorrow.'

It occurred to me then that Lara must have known this was coming, and yet she had given nothing away when we met the previous day to discuss the mid-week media conference. She spent fifteen minutes taking me through the talking points about various players' fitness, our forthcoming opponents, and the latest set of reactive lines to take on Valon, in the knowledge that the reporters would only want to talk about one thing.

'As you can see, we are fulsome in our praise for what you have achieved in your short time with the club. We want this to look good for you and us.'

I read the release carefully.

Athletic appoint Lukasz Wyszkowska

We are delighted to confirm the appointment of Lukasz Wyszkowska as new Athletic Head Coach from 15th May, subject to work visa requirements. Wyszkowska has signed a two-year contract with the option of an extension.

Commenting on the appointment Lord Rigg, Athletic's Chairman, said 'Lukasz is one of the most accomplished managers in world football. A serial winner who has won titles and trophies wherever he has gone. He will return the club to the level the fans rightly demand.'

Lukasz Wyszkowska said: 'I'm thrilled to be appointed and can't wait to get started. There is so much potential in the dressing room and in the academy.'

I scanned down the page to my quote.

Joe Hendricks, interim Head Coach, said: 'It has been a privilege to wear the Athletic badge and a wonderful learning experience. I am very grateful to the players, the staff, the owner, and the fans for all their support. I welcome Lukasz's appointment and wish him every success. But the job's not done yet and I will be focused 100% on winning our remaining games.'

I passed the sheet of paper back to him.

'Change it so it reads "the fans, the staff, the owner, and most of all, the players" and add in "I'm proud of the improvement in the team's performances".'

When I opened my front door that evening I was greeted by the sound of pulsing electronic music and the smell of roast chicken. Emily's trainers had been kicked off in the hallway, and her gym bag and jacket dumped at the bottom of the stairs. I found her in the kitchen pouring batter into a muffin tin. The tell-tale detritus of a chef who prefers to cook than clean lay scattered across the kitchen island. A milk carton without its lid. A dusting of flour. Vegetable peelings and eggs shells piled high on a chopping board next to a jar of gravy granules. The ransacked cutlery draw only partially closed. Pots and pans bathing in a sink of greeny, grey water.

She turned down the music and gave me a hug.

'Your stereo is unbelievable.'

'I didn't know I had one. What are you doing here?'

'I didn't want you eating on your own tonight, and I knew you wouldn't want to go out.' She pointed to the kitchen counter. 'Take a seat. Dinner will be ready in twenty-five minutes. I'm doing a roast. Stuffing, Yorkshire Puds, the works.'

I kissed her on the forehead and blinked away the tears.

'Vino?' she said holding up an uncorked bottle of white burgundy. 'Bill picked it out.'

Bill was Emily's step-dad, a man who knew his wine.

'Then I should definitely give it a go.'

She poured two glasses.

'Bill said not to serve it too cold.'

'Well he would know.'

'Rough day?'

'I've had better. But this makes it all worthwhile.'

Dinner tasted every bit as good as it smelt. The chicken dissolving on my tongue on contact. The roast potatoes crispy on the outside and fluffy on the inside. We discussed the book she was reading, Javier Medina's latest movie, her ever changing plans for the long summer break. Anything but football. Em asked me to tell her stories about my Interrailing trip. She couldn't believe I visited the Bernabéu but not The Prada.

'How about an internship at Dionysus?'

'I'm not interested in working for *Big Tech*.' She pronounced these last two words as if they were a pejorative. 'All that money swilling around, all that brainpower, and what do they do with it? Create another get rich quick app that no one needs. Meanwhile, every thirty seconds, a kid dies from pneumonia somewhere in the world.' She topped up her wine glass.

'Whatever I do this summer has to mean something.'

'Like what?'

'I want to do voluntary work, VSO or something like that. Bill knows someone who runs a program in Cambodia. We're having a chat with her next week.'

We caught up on her driving lessons: she was getting closer to the kerb with her parallel parking, she'd perfected the emergency stop, but roundabouts in general, and the Hanger Lane gyratory in particular, were still a problem. Eventually, while plating up a chocolate and pear tart – shop bought she said, as if it was a confession - Emily broached the subject of life after Athletic.

'What do you do next?'

'Beat Bury and Tiverton and finish fourth.'

Emily rolled her eyes in mock frustration.

'You know what I mean. After you leave?'

'We'll see what's out there. It's got to be the right move, with the right conditions for success. Get it wrong and I could be back looking for another job in a matter of months but with a question mark against my name. So I won't jump on the first train that pulls into the station.'

'Cream?'

'Go on, just a drop. The problem is, you never know how long you might have to wait for the next train or whether it will be any better. And there are always loads of good people out of work, looking to get back in the game, and the longer you leave it, the harder it is.'

'Have you spoken to Uncle D?'

'He called earlier. He'll start to put some feelers out.'

'Oh by the way, before I forget,' she leapt up and grabbed something off the shelf above the sink.

'I found this on the bathroom floor.' She held up a gold earring. 'Anything you want to tell me?'

'Well, it's not mine if that's what you're thinking. When are they picking you up?'

'Nine thirty.'

'Plenty of time to clear up then.'

While I scrubbed the muffin tin, removing every last stubborn fleck of Yorkshire Pudding from each of the small metallic sink holes, I reflected on a difficult afternoon. I returned to Datchet after speaking to Rigg, crossing the picket line of reporters one more time. Again the flashbulbs flooded the interior of the car with harsh, white light. 'Get a proper fucking job,' growled Rex as we edged our way past them. The players had all left for the day, apart from Borello, who was in the gym making slow progress on the long uncertain road to recovery. We exchanged a few words and then he continued with his exercises under Kenny Walsh's close supervision, grimacing with pain as he flexed his knee a few extra degrees.

I messaged the rest of the boys in WhatsApp to tell them that nothing had changed. Our goals and approach, our remaining fixtures, the points we needed to amass, all remained the same. The players echoed this sentiment in their responses, but I knew that their concentration would be scrambled, their minds switching inevitably to next season and the question of where they would fit, if at all, in Wyszkowska's plans. Other messages followed. Zharnell sent a photo of me standing in the technical area clapping my hands to urge the players on along with a red heart emoji. Mats promised a proper send-off with a team dinner at the end of the season. Kuipers sent a selfie of the two of us celebrating in the dressing room after the win against City.

I tried to reach Darryl but each time I called it went straight to voicemail. I trawled through my messages. There were far fewer than when my appointment was announced in January, so it didn't take long to reach the short WhatsApp from Laker.

'No fucking tears. This is an opportunity. Let me help you seize it.'

I called Darryl again. Still no response. Frustrated, I messaged Laker. He replied immediately.

'I'm in the Antibes with the Fonsecas. Will call at midnight your time. Chin UP.'

Xabi came to see me after finishing a session with the under 20's. He flopped down into the seat. I looked at the grass stains on his knee and shins, the pulsing veins on his temple.

'Been letting off steam?'

He gave me the grimmest of smiles. I had never seen him so low.

'Let's just say I reminded them of the level we expect from them.'

He gave a deep, troubled sigh. Shook his head.

'This is a travesty. A fucking stitch up. Where have they been for the last couple of months? Can't they see how you've got them playing again?

'It's football.'

'It's insane.'

'You'll get used to it.'

'No, I'm done with this place. I'm coming with you.'

I could see he meant this and so I tried to talk him out of doing anything rash.

'I've no idea where I'll end up yet. You need to sit tight.'

'I can't work for someone or something I don't believe in. Low block, low possession. Management by fear. That's not me. And anyway, he and Archer won't want me. They'll squeeze me out.'

'You don't know that. Anita loves you—'

'She used to love you.'

'That's different. Athletic is in your blood. They'll want the continuity.'

'No, no, no,' he said becoming more agitated. 'I can't do it.'

'You can't win every game four nil. Sometimes you have to suffer, grind it out. Wyszkowska will be gone within eighteen months. You know what he's like.'

Xabi wasn't convinced with this and mentioned the prospect of Archer succeeding Wyszkowska.

'Look I could be out of the game for six to twelve months. Can you handle being away from the training ground for that long?'

He sat back, bit his lip, and folded his hands in his lap.

'You take something from everyone you work with, the good and the bad. So you have to play this one with your head. Make yourself invaluable. Keep your options open.'

Sky Sports News repeated Dan Stevens reaction to Wyszkowska's appointment on the screen behind Xabi's shoulder. The former Athletic utility player was speaking into a laptop from his home in Berkshire. He was wearing an open necked shirt and Apple AirPods. His square face and greying hair framed by the soft colours and clean lines of his tastefully decorated living room. In the top right-hand corner of the picture – the camera strategically placed, no doubt, for just this reason – sat a cluster of trophies on a blonde wooden shelf.

'Have you spoken to Anita?'

'No, she sent a message. She's in the States.'

The timing of Anita's trip to California was no coincidence. Once the order to remove a coach had been given, she liked to distance herself as much as possible from the blood letting.

'What did she say?'

'It was all warm words and soft soap: it's not you, it's us. Whoever hires you next will be lucky to have you.'

I wondered how many of my predecessors had received an identical message.

Terry thundered into the room. If it hadn't been for that day's news, I would have assumed he had lost on the horses again. ('I backed another bleeding donkey gaffer.')

'They've really mugged themselves off with this one,' he said angrily. 'Christ knows what the boys will make of it.'

'Have you heard anything?'

'Not much gaffer, just that his nibs is coming over for the game on Sunday and has asked for access to all the performance data.'

Together we watched Archer drive out through the gold and burgundy gates at the back of Preston Park and stop to speak to the media. He leant out of the car window towards the cameras and thrusted microphones. He was sporting a new look. Hair cut short and serious. Black framed spectacles - it was the first time any of us had seen him wearing glasses - a sober, dark suit and crisp white shirt. I turned up the volume to hear what he had to say. Gone was the shouting and screaming. The bullying and the insults. In its place was David Archer, suburban bank manager, speaking more in sorrow than anger, as he ever so gently twisted the knife.

'No I don't think it's harsh. The lad's done OK but he was only ever a stopgap to the end of the season, what they used to call a ferryman when I was in Italy. Lukasz is on a different level altogether.'

The reporters fired questions at him, speaking over each other.

'This club must be challenging for titles next season. The supporters and the board wouldn't expect anything less.'

'That didn't take long.'

Terry was right. You had to admire how swiftly Archer had moved to destabilise his mentor, setting expectations Wyszkowska could never live up to.

'...of course we'll look to back Lukasz in the market. I'll sit down with him in a few weeks. Work out who we bring in and who to move on.'

Archer toyed with the reporters, retreating back inside the car and then leaning out again to answer another question.

'The Owner asked me to help and of course I said yes. I just want to serve the club I love,' he said piously, smiling for the cameras.

'He's like the facking moon landings,' Terry scoffed.

Xabi and I both stared at him.

'A total fucking fake.'

It was only later that evening, after Bill had picked Emily up and given me a sympathetic squeeze of the shoulder and one of his infuriating smiles, after I had watched all the footage on Sky Sports News again (Wyszkowska running down the touchline to celebrate one of his league titles, my car passing through the barrier of photographers like a convicted prisoner being taken away from court) and combed through the commentary and analysis online, after I replied to the last of the messages, that I allowed myself to let it all out. To release the strain from having to hold everything together. I sat hunched up on the bed and sobbed uncontrollably, my body shaking at the thought of all the public and private humiliations I had endured, heaving at the prospect of having to put the mask back on the following day and tough it out again. The team meetings, press conferences, handshakes on the touchline for weeks to come. I've no idea, even now, of how long this lasted. It may only have been a few minutes but it felt like hours. I pounded a pillow repeatedly, hurled the remote control against the wall, the plastic splintering into pieces. Much of the anger dissipated with this final violent act. I changed and went downstairs to the gym, sweated out the emotion and alcohol on the rowing machine, and then showered and prepared for my call with Laker. In the bathroom I stared into the misted mirror and sought to convince myself this was the beginning, not the end. That good things would follow. Reminded myself you can't be in football if you're not willing to accept setbacks and defeats, but the words I had used to pick up deflated players over the years felt empty and hollow.

41

Bury tore into us with their power tool football, sawing through our splintered lines. There was a lot at stake for both sides. A draw would clinch the title for Bury, their first in over two decades, whilst we needed to match or better Tiverton's result away to Eccles to keep our hopes of finishing fourth alive. Butenandt, the King of assists, shook off his tail, drifted into space, and cushioned a pass - unselfish as ever - to Aziz who struck it cleanly through Fabio's legs. The game should have been over by half-time, but Fabio kept us alive, blocking the ball with his knees and chest and parrying a powerful close-range header with an incredible reflex save.

I sent on Jiri Bezek and switched to a back five in the thirty ninth minute to staunch the bleeding. A chastening acknowledgement, according to Doug Molloy in his match report, that the overthinking gamble of playing Shan at centre back had exploded in my face.

'Fuck,' said Terry, kicking a water bottle.

'What?'

'Tiverton have scored.'

The news quickly spread around the stadium and the Bury fans taunted our supporters, chanting one nil to Tiverton.

Looking around the silent dressing room I could see the boys were beaten mentally, emotionally depleted. The win against Bromsgrove and the positive energy it generated, ancient history. I gave them a minute or two to wallow, to see if anyone would speak up, and when they didn't I let rip, slamming a locker door shut so hard it broke the latch.

'WHO THE FUCK WAS THAT OUT THERE? BECAUSE IT WASN'T THE TEAM I KNOW. THE TEAM I KNOW DOESN'T GO DOWN WITHOUT A FIGHT. THE TEAM I KNOW PLAYS WITH MORE AGGRESSION, MORE SPIRIT, MORE UNITY.'

I paused for a second, surveyed the room.

'And do you know what?' I said lowering my voice. 'These guys are running on empty – right Terry?'

'Yeah gaffer. There's no way they can keep that up for ninety minutes. Not after the other night.'

'So attack them with and without the ball.'

I slammed the locker door again.

'And if we lose, we lose, fine I can live with that, but we play the game our way. That's all I'm asking for.'

The bell on the away dressing room wall, the old brass bell which had called time on team talks by Bill Nicholson and Bob Paisley, Howard Kendall and Brian Clough, and countless other managers down the years, began to ring. I clapped my hands.

'Now get out there and play our way.'

The dressing room theatrics had the desired effect. The boys looked energised in the first fifteen minutes of the second half, moving the ball at a faster tempo, and playing it forwards not sideways. The interval had also broken Bury's rhythm. They struggled to match our energy, to find their level as Dani exerted control, forming triangles with Zharnell and Kuipers and bringing Zito, a bored bystander in the first half, into the game.

The shift in possession and momentum enabled Shan to venture further forward. He passed and carried the ball through the first wave of Bury's press, triggering movement in their midfield line by cooly shaping to pass in one direction, then sending the ball the opposite way to a teammate in open space.

Preben Povlson, Bury's Danish head coach, sat zen-like on his haunches at the edge of the technical area, the bald patch on his crown that he tried so hard to hide from the cameras visible to all the supporters in the stand behind him. Suddenly he sprang up, screaming and waving his arms, veins bulging, palms slicing through the air.

'YOU'RE TOO FUCKING DEEP

DON'T LET THEM COME ON TO YOU.

Ango. PUSH UP. *UP.*'

Like me, Povlson could sense a goal was coming. He returned to the dugout, spoke briefly to his assistant, and then signalled to Patrick Olufemi to get ready to go on. Olufemi unzipped his top, tightened his laces, spat out his gum, and then ambled over to the half way line where the fourth official was preparing the board. The veteran Nigerian, one of a handful of players to win the league with two different clubs, was still stretching his suspect hamstring when Zito darted into the box and hammered Shan's through ball in at the near post. Game on.

Olufemi's first meaningful contribution seven minutes after the restart was to rear-end Kuipers as he received a third man pass near the D, giving us a chance to test Fabio's theory. In the slow-motion replay you can see Vieler split step like a tennis player receiving serve just before Dani strikes the ball. He took a stride to his left, then once he had processed the flight of the ball, pushed back in the opposite direction, losing purchase for a split second, then threw himself to the right, the ball grazing his fingertips as it flew into the net. Fabio went berserk, running to celebrate with the coaching staff and analysts, grabbing Valon's shirt and holding it up to the camera screaming:

'FOR YOU VALLO, FOR YOU MY BROTHER.'

The lead, however, was illusory, a brief, worthless moment in time. Alfie Ellwood leveled the score within a minute of the restart. Showing the flexibility of a downhill skier, he stretched to control and manipulate a low, fast deflected pass between Shan's legs with one caress, then ran beyond him to side foot past Fabio from just inside the area. With results elsewhere, Bury were now champions and the gap to fourth place had widened to four insurmountable points with one match to come. Play continued at a ferocious pace, an end-to-end exchange of shots and pressure as both sides sought in vain to apply the killer blow. The scoreline remained symmetrical with ten minutes to go, but as the time ran out the two teams' ambitions began to diverge. Preben Povlson and his players were happy to settle for a point and the title that came with it. They dug in to protect what they had, rather than push for more, and Povlson made his final change, sacrificing one of his front three for an extra defensive midfielder. Butenandt trudged off slowly, applauding all four corners of the ground, and stopping to remove his shin pads, anything to run the clock down.

We pushed higher and higher up the pitch, seeking to capitalise on the frayed nerves and misplaced passes. Senghor conjured a chance out of nothing, his dipping, swerving effort kissing the frame of the goal. Two half chances followed, then in the eighty seventh minute pressure and fatigue combined to scramble Alistair Brown's decision making. Bury's left back felled Zito as he passed him in the box. The Scottish international wagged his finger vigorously in the direction of the referee.

'Stonewall,' said Terry confidently. 'He's left the ref no facking choice.'

As Terry said, it was an open and shut case and the referee didn't hesitate. He blew his whistle, waved away the protests and pointed at the spot.

'Yes,' I said under my breath. Terry and Xabi exchanged high fives. Zito accepted the congratulations and then retrieved the ball and handed it to Dani. The Spaniard assumed responsibility for penalties when Slaney left and had yet to miss one. The crowd howled their displeasure. The fans in the section behind the dugout sensed the title was slipping through their fingers again for the second season in a row. Dani bounced the ball while we waited for the video review to be completed. The checks were taking a long time for what should have been a formality.

'I don't facking like this,' growled Terry.

'Must be something in the build-up,' I replied.

Xabi spoke to one of the analysts up on the gantry via his headset. 'Fuck… Yeah, we thought so… Thanks.' He turned to us. 'They're looking at whether Shan fouled Zelich.'

And with that the referee drew a rectangle in the air with his fingers.

'Here we go,' groaned Terry.

The referee strode over to the pitch side monitor and studied the replay for what felt like an eternity. Finally, he turned and marched back onto the pitch.

'He's not gonna give it.'

After a few paces the referee again waved his hands in the air, this time to signal he had overturned his original decision. The crowd roared their approval. Play resumed and we continued to push Bury back towards their box, searching for the goal we needed to keep our season alive.

The fourth official held up the board to indicate three minutes of additional time. I remonstrated with her, pointing out to no avail, the delay for the video checks and the treatment for a clash of heads early in the half. Time moves doubly fast when you are chasing a goal, chasing a game. Goal kicks, duels, turnovers. A half chance, a substitution. Another half chance. The ball pumped high into the stands, and then kept in the corner. It all flashed by as the minutes and seconds slipped through our fingers. A section of the crowd cheered loudly and prematurely after they mistook the desperate whistle from one fan for full time. And then a few moments later it was all over. We shared a point, a point that meant everything to Bury, and nothing to us. The crowd erupted. Supporters who were biting their fingers or could not bring themselves to look a few seconds before, now embraced each other. Thrilled to witness Bury's restoration, their return after twenty-three years, to the apex of the football pyramid. They punched the air and sung the names of their heroes. I noticed a couple in their mid-fifties hugging each other, both with tears in their eyes. A dad lifted his young daughter onto his shoulders to give her a better view. The chants rang out:

CAMPIONE, CAMPIONE, OLE, OLE, OLE.

It's always incredibly difficult to be an onlooker, a spectator of another team's sporting achievements. Povlson and his players would go down in history, remembered and revered for bringing the glory days back. Me and my group would be a footnote at best. The opponent who gave Bury a scare but fell short of fourth place. Rather than let it reinforce a sense of inferiority or inadequacy, you have to use these moments. Take the memory and lock it away. Truly believe that this is what you yourself are working towards. So, I did not allow the boys to quickly slink away. I made them stay out on the pitch to congratulate the champions one by one. To absorb the winning feeling. I offered my congratulations to Povlson. He had enough class and empathy to momentarily reign in the celebrations. He was one of the few people on the planet who knew how I felt. Who had suffered the crushing pain that comes from falling just short. Bury finished second the previous year with a points total that would have won the title in any other season. He picked his team up, found a way to go again.

'Wow, football, huh? What a fucking game,' he said shaking his head in disbelief. He pulled me into the tightest of bear hugs and spoke into my ear.

'I meant what I said in the presser. You've done an unbelievable job. They've made a massive mistake—.'

Povlson was peeled off me by two of his senior players, disbelief and joy carved into their faces. He threw his arms around them and the three men pogoed on the spot. Out on the grass. Oriali and Younes gave thanks to their respective gods. Their teammates hugged each other and blew kisses to family and friends in the stands. I saw one player on his knees. He plucked several blades of grass and placed them in his mouth. Donny Swift, the last remaining homegrown player wept openly.

I walked onto the pitch and told the players one by one that it wasn't meant to be, but they should be proud of their performance in the second half. Shan was devastated. He sat on the ground near the penalty area in front of the North Stand. I walked towards him, stopping to exchange a few quick words with a couple of the Bury players, and ignoring the camera tracking my movements from a few paces away. I started to think about what I would say in the flash interview and the media conference that followed. It would be important to stress how much we had achieved, how far the club had progressed in a short space of time. To remind them that we would be second if the league had started on my first game in charge. I helped Shan to his feet, placed a hand on either shoulder and looked him in the eye. He started to apologise for the equalising goal, but I cut him off.

'No defender, not Valon or anyone else, could have stopped him. Sometimes you just have to put your hands up and say too good. But listen, I have no regrets, you were outstanding, you caused them so many problems.'

His response was drowned out by a huge roar from our fans. I spun around and looked towards our bench. Xabi was staring at his tablet in disbelief. He caught my eye and gave me the thumbs up. Tiverton had conceded a late, late equaliser deep in injury time. They remained within reach, three points clear but with inferior goal difference. I punched the air and shook Shan with excitement.

'We can still fucking do this.'

42

'Shall I be mother?' Laker asked, mimicking Rigg's plummy tones.

'Be my guest.'

He threaded his large meaty fingers through the handle of the teapot and poured Earl Grey into two delicate cups. He was wearing a white velour tracksuit with green trim. The sleeves were pushed up on both arms to reveal a Rolex and a lime-coloured Apple Watch. With everything that had happened, it seemed like a lifetime since we had last spoken. The late-night call on the evening of Archer's victory was a one-sided monologue. Laker outlined my options, which were limited, reminded me that this could and would change fast, and promised we would sit down with his PR agency to discuss how to boost my marketability, just as soon as I signed on the dotted line. I came to realise that Laker was far more discreet than people gave him credit for. Yes, there were the photos of him dining with players and club executives, but these were only ever taken at a time and place of his choosing. Just as news or speculation about possible deals only surfaced when it was to his client's advantage. He even operated a network of safe houses. A string of properties across Europe where he and his players could sit down with possible suitors away from camera phones and prying eyes. Which was how we found ourselves in the conservatory of a large country pile somewhere in the Surrey Hills. A sun-drenched room filled with wicker furniture and green leafed pot plants. Laker slid a Manila envelope across the table.

'Here's the contract.'

I flicked through the pages of densely worded text. With all the double negatives and impenetrable legalese, I could have been committing to anything. Laker read my mind.

'Relax,' he said with a wave of his hand. 'I'm not gonna brow beat you into signing your life away. Get someone to go through it. It's all legit.'

I reached the section on fees.

'You found the important bit.'

'What's this here?' I pointed to the clause headed 'reward fee'.

'Simples. Every time you buy one of my boys, you'll receive two percent of the fee. Total fee including add ons that is.'

'I only ever sign players who fit my profile.'

'I wouldn't expect anything less. Of course, the very best players - all ages, all prices, in every position - are on my books. I find it makes sense to work with trusted partners. But we can red line that bit if it makes you feel better.'

I was surprised with how amenable he was, and it must have shown in my face. Laker laughed then coughed. It took him a few seconds to get his breath back.

'Look man. I'm not some fucking despot. You're in the driving seat and I want you to be able to sleep at night.'

To show he meant it, he took the contract and ran two lines through the relevant section with his pen and then handed it back to me.

'Like I tell all my clients. I'm here for you. The tail doesn't wag the fucking dog and that's why I'm the best in the business. Now come on Joe live a little. Have one of these beauties. They're freshly baked.' He waved a plate of scones in my face.

'No?' He raised one eyebrow. 'Your loss my friend.'

He took two and sliced both down the middle.

'I can never remember if it's cream or jam first, so I do one of each. That way I know I'm right half of the time, which is more than I can say about Cecil and those other muppets running the show at Preston Park. Sipping champagne while the club goes down the Swanee.'

He spread a thick layer of cream onto the second scone.

'Tell me what you're looking for. What does the dream move looks like?'

'I want a proper project. Something I can sink my teeth into—. '

'Fuck the project my friend. Fuck. The. Project. You need a springboard not a sinkhole. Here's my plan for you: we get you back in with a top ten club. Two seasons, three at the most, we'll move you up a rung. You do well there, go deep in Europe or challenge for the title, and you'll be in with a shout for City or Bury. Sounds good right?'

Laker had built up a head of steam and there was no stopping him now.

'And you can't afford to disappear over the summer. You have to stay front of mind. My guys will help you build your social profile. You'll do a press interview every week and a masterclass video with *Coaches Voice*. The tactics you used to beat City. A podcast with *Training Ground Guru*, plus an article for *Elite Soccer* on one of your drills. And we'll get you on the telly for el coppa del mondo. We're tight with ITV's production company.'

'TV is not for me.'

'You gotta play the game my friend. Owners are like fucking goldfish. Do you think any of them will remember you in three months' time? They'll all be looking at the latest shiny thing. Fuck it's hot in here, it's like a sodding green house.'

He unzipped his hooded top and draped it over the back of one of the empty wicker chairs. Sweat patches had begun to form beneath his arm pits.

'That's better.'

Laker looked at me.

'How's your brother with all of this?'

As expected, Darryl had taken the news badly, screaming about backstabbing betrayal. Claiming he had lined up exploratory talks with clubs in Croatia and Belgium and telling me to never come near him or his wife and kids again.

'He's demanding a severance payment and a percentage of all future income.'

'Has he lawyered up?'

'Yes.'

Laker blew out air.

'Family and business is like pizza and pineapple. The two just don't go together. Send me a copy of your contract. We'll go through it with a toothcomb. Chip away at it until falls apart.'

'There's nothing written down. He's my brother.'

He gave me a pitying look.

'All the more reason.'

He studied my body language for a moment then spoke again, showing surprising empathy.

'There's no place for guilt or any emotion here Joe. You don't owe him or anyone else a living. Darryl needs to make his own way in life. And, you know what, he'll feel better when he does it on his own and the two of you can go back to being brothers.'

43

The evening at the cinema was Xabi's idea. A spot of team building and a chance to take the group's mind off the game at the weekend. Many of the players regularly attended movie premieres – another perk of playing for a London club - but it was the first time for Emily and me, and in fact, I couldn't remember the last time I had set foot in a cinema. Em loved every part of the experience. Photographs on the red carpet under swooping searchlights. Complimentary drinks and finger food. Not knowing whether to say hello to the instantly recognisable faces as we made our way to our seats. Locking our phones away in a secure pouch to prevent illicit recordings. The Q&A with the director and cast members who stood obligingly at the front of the auditorium before the screening began. The way everyone remained seated for the entire credits at the end and clapped and cheered when a friend or family member's name appeared on screen. To my surprise, I found I also enjoyed myself. I had forgotten how comforting it is to sit in the dark, cut off from the rest of the world, and lose yourself in the giant screen and booming surround sound. To be alone, and at the same time, part of a crowd that laughs and gasps together. Only once or twice did I find my mind returning to the starting eleven for the weekend and the question marks around Dani's availability after he rolled his ankle in training.

The cinema was built around the same time as Preston Park, and after the screening we stood in the marble floored foyer, with its domed ceiling and large gilt mirrors, and chatted amongst ourselves. The wives of the senior players assumed a similar status to their partners, monopolising the conversation. The news that Carla had left Archer was the main topic of discussion.

'Good for her,' said Luciana, Fabio's wife. 'No one should have to take what he's put her through. All the lying and cheating. Hitting on her friends, her own *sister*, while she was being treated for cancer.'

'She should have done it years ago,' replied Ingrid Kuipers.

Archer had begged Carla to reconsider. He promised to change, to undergo counselling. He enlisted the support of their shared history. How happy they had been in Madrid. The trips to Dubai and Ibiza. Christmas in New York. And when this didn't work, he turned nasty, promising to leak intimate photos and videos. While Carla fended off these threats and entreaties, her newly appointed PR agency issued a short statement about the couple's many happy years together and how they would always be there for each other, words that Carla neither wrote or believed. The agency also provided selected journalists with additional background information, including details about Carla's illness the previous year, something she had managed to keep private and was against sharing. Lara, who was advising Carla in an informal capacity - retribution for the countless leaks and internal power struggles - insisted. ('They always punish the woman in these situations. This makes you bullet proof.') The agency also provided the reporters with a list of Archer's transgressions over the years. Here Carla drew the line, insisting they only highlight details that were already in the public domain. This was more than sufficient. A lengthy document chronicled Archer's relationships with various teammates' wives. His one-night stands with Las Vegas showgirls and Spanish reality TV stars. The time he was caught parked up, trousers around his ankles, a hooker busy at work, somewhere near *El Retiro*. And much, much more. For a man consumed by his own image, it was a crushing blow. All meetings were cancelled, and his X handle – usually so garrulous - fell silent, as Archer disappeared from view.

Carla was also keeping a low profile. Her lawyers had warned her that as well as the media, private investigators working on her husband's behalf would rummage through every aspect of her life. Steal her bins. Hack her emails and voicemails. Trail her movements. For this reason, we had agreed not to meet up until after the final game of the season. The last time I had seen her, we laid in bed after we made love and discussed going away together over the summer, somewhere quiet where nobody would recognise us she said wistfully.

'He tried it on with me a few months ago,' Dekker's girlfriend Keeley confided, trying to break the stranglehold on the conversation. 'I told him what Thomas would do to him if he laid a finger on me,' she said, stroking her boyfriend's toned bicep. Dekker seemed stunned to hear this. He looked around the room as if expecting to see Archer sipping cocktails with the other celebrities.

'You should've told me.'

'It was nothing hon, I didn't want to cause any trouble,' said Keeley realising she had said the wrong thing, that Dekker would not rest until Archer had been made to pay.

'He either came onto you or he didn't,' said Dekker angrily. 'Which was it?'

'Look at Jose with Rosa Sharp,' said Conchita Linares in an attempt to bail her friend out. 'They're getting on like a house on fire.'

Across the other side of the foyer, the singer - dressed all in black, her hair lacquered back – rested her hand on Jose Costa's arm and laughed at whatever he had said. Only then did I place the voice on the movie's haunting theme song.

'That's going to cost me. JC bet me he could get her number,' said Zharnell.

'Oh hell,' said Mats. 'We are never going to hear the end of it.'

44

'This is the third and final message.' I paused and looked around the room. The boys were silent, hanging on every word. 'All I'll say is that I've translated it from its original language.'

It was the sixty million pound match. Ninety minutes to determine who would play in Europe's biggest club competition the following season. In the week running up to the game I had asked each of the players' parents to write a short message and I read out three just before we left the dressing room, omitting any details that might give away the identity of the player.

'Hello my boy, my son. I can't believe I've not told you this before but sometimes these things are easier to write down than to say out loud. I want you to know that your mum and me are so proud of everything you have achieved. Every day I see the kids playing in the street with your name on their shirt. It brings tears to my eyes. When people stop me to talk about your performance or a moment in a match my heart bursts with pride. I know how you live for the game, how hard you worked to get where you are, how much of your childhood you had to give up. How you backed yourself when others doubted you. I also know you have made mistakes, learnt from them, and become a better man. This moment is yours. Enjoy it. Love Dad.'

None of the boys said anything and for a moment I worried had misjudged the mood but then Kuipers, a man of few words, stood up and broke the silence.

'Let's fucking do this,' he said clapping his hands.

There was a chorus of agreement.

'Let's go, let's go, let's go,' Zharnell shouted.

'First ten minutes.'

Too good to go down, not good enough to break the big six stranglehold, Tiverton had been stuck in mid-table purgatory for the past ten years or more. But a season of transition for Macclesfield and Collingham and Athletic's difficulties had artificially inflated their standing in the table. Their recruitment policy had been to hoover up players from big clubs across Europe. But this was not a team of winners. These were the weak links, the passengers carried by former teammates, or the lightweights who played above themselves when surrounded by great players but could not do it elsewhere. It did not make for a strong team identity, but Don Hoyle had worked wonders, moulding these offcuts into a well drilled, hard to beat, counter-punching machine. Their success was founded upon a heavily fortified low block, three centre backs staying narrow and compact and denying any space behind, and speed in attacking transitions.

Hoyle had resurrected Remi Toussant's career, reconfiguring the ponytailed Frenchman from a discarded left back into an authoritative number six, and turned Ricky Abimbola into a twenty goal a season striker, drawing upon his own experience to mentor him in the art of finishing. After combing the internet Kyle Fernsby had found an interview with L'Équipe where Abimbola had spoken about how Hoyle had instructed him to be more single minded, to make a beeline for the penalty area rather than spend time outside the box.

Our plan was simple. Start fast, disorientate Tiverton with our movement and tempo, and fire up the crowd. For Tiverton it was a question of doing what they did best: sit deep, defend the box, disrupt our rhythm, and wait for the chance to break. To pounce on a misplaced pass, a slip, or a player who dwelt too long on the ball.

The tunnel leading from the dressing room to the pitch at Preston Park is more air raid shelter than sporting arena. A long narrow concrete corridor with barely enough room for the two lines of players to file out without brushing each other's shoulders, the taller players having to stoop every couple of metres to avoid heading the light fittings. The officials in their emerald shirts held us up, squeezing past the players to check their boots and studs. Zharnell fiddled with his socks. Senghor cracked jokes with a couple of the mascots. One of the Tiverton players wiped his sweaty palms on his shorts, another scratched his arse. Rafiq murmured a quiet prayer, face and index fingers pointing to the ceiling. Kuipers and Dani blanked the friendly greetings from former teammates. Shan ran through his breathing exercises, while Jose Costa tilted his head towards one shoulder and then the other. Fabio, always the last to leave the dressing room, adjusted his ponytail one more time. And then we were moving again, a conga of tattoos and sculpted hair marching out to the beat of the vibrations from the stand above.

We were greeted by clouds of red chalk dust from the lit flares, a blizzard of gold and maroon confetti, the stamping of feet on the old wooden floors, and a drumbeat of 'ATHLETIC, ATHLETIC, ATHLETIC.'

This is what it would've felt like to have been a gladiator. To go over the top into no man's land. The announcer ran through the teams, the crowd cheering each name, reserving extra decibels for Fabio, Zharnell, Shan, Dani, and Zito. Then the supporters unleashed the big bazooka. A two-minute, spine tingling, a Capella version of *We carry each other.*

The boys started fast, like a wheel-spinning getaway car, any nerves left behind when they crossed the line. We stress-tested Tiverton's midfield with quick-fire passing and shape shifting movement and their centre couldn't hold. Kuipers manufactured the first of three chances in the opening ten minutes with a sly no look angled pass to pick out Zito. The shot was cleanly struck but straight at the keeper. Zharnell then cracked open their shell with two clever deliveries from the right. The first a cross to an on rushing Zito at the far post, the second playing in Rafiq. A fingertip save and an outstretched right boot from Raoul Lopez denying both.

The players and the crowd fed off each other. The snap in the tackle and the high tempo passing and movement energising the fans, and the sound waves from the stands inspiring even greater levels of effort and desire from the team. Don Hoyle paced around the technical area, hands in pockets, fresh worry lines forming on his forehead. Another chance followed, Kuipers connecting with the post. Their central defender took no chances, hoofing the rebound into the crowd. A bullet-headed man in his fifties rose to his feet, shoved his neighbour out of the way, and met the ball with a high looping header, sending it back down towards the touch line. He milked the applause, doffing an invisible hat and taking a bow.

Mats played a short pass to Kuipers just inside our half, but for once his first touch was heavy and Lewis Walker was quick to react, seizing the ball and driving forward into the space between Dani and Jose Costa. Walker scored only eleven goals in his three years with Athletic before moving to Tiverton the previous summer and you could hear the crowd thinking aloud '*Relax*. It's only Lewis.'

Jose knew Walker wanted to engineer a one v one with Fabio, so he stood off, moving backwards towards the eighteen-yard line at speed, taking care not to commit himself. Walker looked for support, but his teammates lagged far behind, so he shot from distance, with placement rather than power and the ball arced over Fabio, brushing the underside of the crossbar on its way in. Goals, especially first goals, change games and you could see the effect immediately from kick-off as all twenty-two players processed the same harsh truth: Athletic need to score twice now. Momentum is the slipperiest of eels. Once it escapes your grip it's tough to recapture, and the boys were wilting. The fast start, the heat, the mental stress, and the scoreline all taking their toll. We wouldn't win the game in the remaining ten minutes before half-time, but we could easily lose it. When the ball went out of play on the other side of the pitch, I called Zharnell over.

'Tell the boys to stay calm, keep their shape. There's no need to panic. We've plenty of time to turn this around but we *cannot* let them score again. Keep moving the ball. Go.'

Then I whistled with my fingers. 'HEY DANI. OUTSIDE. PLAY IT OUTSIDE.'

Another whistle. My eyes locked with Kuiper's. I clapped my hands in encouragement.

At half-time the lads couldn't get off quick enough. Fabio unwrapped a new pair of gloves, a long-standing tradition. The physio team examined the strapping on Dani's ankle and re-taped Zharnell's feet. I looked around the room at the gloomy faces and negative body language and sensed the players needed reassurance not a rollicking.

'The first half is gone, forget about it. The plan hasn't changed. You bring your a-game in the next forty-five and you've still got this. Trust me. You score one and this lot will fold.'

The stadium was quiet at the beginning of the second-half. I thought we had cured the crowd's defeatism, but it was just in remission, lurking beneath the surface, waiting for its moment. Groans of frustration and angry swearing accompanied every missed pass or turn over in possession. And despite my words at halftime, panic took hold of the players, as everything we had worked for started to slide away. The boys tried to force it, shooting from distance or low percentage angles, shots that flew over or harmlessly wide. They rushed and squandered the one or two good opportunities we carved out, ratcheting the stress levels up further. The old negative behaviour, the recriminations and blame game, returned. Rafiq threw his arms up in the air in frustration after Senghor snatched at a shot. Mats swore at Jose Costa for a stray pass. Jose shouted back angrily, telling him to work harder to find space.

We missed Valon's influence and authority, his vocal presence, but leadership comes in different guises, and Dani grew as the others shrank. He still had the nerve to make himself available, to go at Tiverton's midfield line with the ball at his feet. To attempt the low percentage pass and risk the backlash from the crowd or his teammates. He hauled us back into the game with just under twenty minutes to go with a perfectly weighted pass behind Tiverton's right back for Zito to run onto. The Brazilian played the ball inside to Zharnell who struck a half volley across the keeper and into the far corner.

The goal brought the crowd back from the dead like a defibrillator to the chest. A roar reverberated around the stadium, engulfing the coaching staff in the technical area. Xabi bumped chests with Terry, then waved his arms to whip the crowd up into an even greater frenzy. I turned and faced the supporters, knees bent, feet planted wide, tightly curled fists held out in front of me.

'COME ONNNNNNNNNNNNN,' I screamed.

The goal and the re-vitalised atmosphere in the stadium lifted the players, triggering our best passage of play since the opening fifteen minutes. We played with aggression and courage, monopolising possession and snatching the ball back like a jealous toddler whenever we lost it. Isolating their fullbacks and peppering the box with crosses and cutbacks.

In the seventy ninth minute Kyle Mackey T-boned Kuipers. It was a needless, petulant challenge. Hotheaded retribution for a late tackle a minute earlier. The referee took out his foam canister, sprayed a mark just outside the box in the left channel facing the goal, and placed the ball on it. He paced ten yards and drew a line for the wall to stand behind. Dani and Mats stood over the ball, discussing who would take it and whether to shoot for goal or clip a short, angled ball into the box for Senghor and Jose Costa to attack. Luiz Silva, Tiverton's six, sidled up to Dani, put his hand on his shoulder and whispered something unpleasant about his younger sister in his ear. Mats shoved the Bolivian hard in the chest. Silva laughed and goaded Dani again, elaborating in lurid detail on what he and his teammates would like to do to her and then mimed a sex act as one of his teammates led him away. Dani remained impassive. He squeezed the ball and then replaced it on the foam dot. He took seven steps back and stood sideways on, almost ninety degrees to the goal, hands out in front of him, breathing deeply to slow his heart rate and calm his nerves. Tiverton's keeper directed his five-man wall into position, shielding the left side of the goal. The ground fell quiet, like Centre Court on Championship point. The whistle blew, Dani took two more deep breaths and then took his first step with his non-striking left foot, followed by five more steps. He planted his left foot next to the ball and then pushed his right leg back into an extreme take back to generate maximum power. As his foot made contact - around five on a clock face - Dani wrapped his boot around the ball to create anti-clockwise spin, and twisted his upper torso violently so his chest was facing the goal, generating extra power and additional spin. The rest was all pure physics, Newton's third law and Magnus Force. As the shot flew towards the goal the spin forced the air around the right side of the ball to move faster than the air around the left side. The difference in air speed generated pressure on the right side of the ball, creating the bend, and the ball curled around the wall and into the top left corner. Again, the noise was deafening, as if we were standing on a runway as a jet took off above us.

Hoyle responded immediately, replacing a centre back and one of his pivots with two attacking players and switching to a 1-2-1-4-3 set up. They lay siege to our goal straight from kickoff, taking the fight to us in the ten final and most important minutes of the season. The joy and relief of scoring a late goal had affected our players. The boys looked skittish, their concentration scrambled by the emotions. Rather than seeing the game out, they wished the time away, dipping too soon for the finishing line. They allowed Tiverton to push our defensive line back to the penalty area. They glanced up at the clock every time the ball went out of play. I shouted at them to move higher up the pitch, to keep playing our way.

'We're too passive,' said Xabi anxiously.

'Yeah, we need to do something,' said Terry shoving yet another stick of gum in his mouth.

Lewis Walker peeled away from Jose Costa, dropping deep to receive a long diagonal crossfield pass. He took one touch and then slipped a clever ball into the corridor of space between Mats and Jose. The overlapping fullback cut infield and drove the ball towards the far post where it was met with a diving header which flew past Fabio and rippled the net.

'Facking hell,' groaned Terry.

The away fans cheered. Hoyle and his coaching team leapt into the air. I felt a horrible sinking feeling deep within my stomach. Pins and needles up the back of my neck. My knees felt weak. After everything we had been through, to lose it now, like this was unbearable. And then their supporters fell silent, and the home crowd jolted back to life, laughing and jeering at the Tiverton fans. A wave of relief passed through me while Hoyle held his head in his hands, a snapshot of frustration and despair, as we all realised the shot had struck the side netting.

'I can't take much more of this,' said Terry.

The wave of pressure continued to force us back as the fourth official held up the board indicating seven minutes of stoppage time.

'Fuck's sake,' said Xabi.

'There's no facking way it's seven minutes,' said Terry pointing at his stopwatch.

The minutes and seconds limped by, wheezing and pausing for a rest like an old man climbing a flight of stairs. The whistles from the crowd grew louder and louder, home advantage turned against us as the supporters' anxiety infected the players.

And then it happened.

Shan beat Walker to a knock down on the edge of our box and hooked it clear with his weaker left foot. The ball fell to Dani in zone seven, close to the centre circle. He controlled it with his first touch and shaped to turn but was bundled to the floor by Duarte Cabrita who came through the back of him and stole the ball. The referee waved play on, ignoring our appeals and the outrage from the crowd. Cabrita accelerated towards and then past Mats, who brought the Portuguese number eight down with a late, tired looking challenge. The Tiverton players gathered around the referee, protesting about Mat's foul, while the crowd booed and howled abuse. A confrontation broke out between Jose Costa and Tiverton's central midfielder. I bellowed at Dani and Rafiq from the edge of the technical area, telling them to restore order.

Mats stood in front of the ball while Fabio organised the wall, and then retreated ten yards. It was a clever free kick, stood up at the back post but with not much pace. Time stood still as the ball hung in the air. Jose Costa, not for the first time, was guilty of watching his man rather than the ball, whilst Shan was deceived by the slower flight of the ball and jumped too soon, giving Jacobsen a free header in plenty of space seven yards out. Jacobsen leapt high and adjusted his body in mid-flight to attack the ball. He stuck his arms out in front of him and then pulled them in sharply to produce maximum leverage for his neck muscles and compensate for the lack of power in the delivery. He thrust his head forward and connected with the ball at the peak of his jump. The powerful header was angled downwards and back across the goal to make it harder for Fabio. The ball thudded into the aluminium post, triggering the mother of all goalmouth scrambles, as it ricocheted around the six-yard box. Fabio lost his balance and his bearings and stumbled back behind the goal line. Tiverton's left sided attacker dug the ball out from the melee and drilled it towards the goal. Zharnell reacted quickly, blocking the shot with his outstretched left shin, whilst keeping his hands behind his back. The ball cannoned off Jose and fell to Dani near the edge of our box who let it run across his body, buying himself a split second to see Shan sprint past him. Dani needed no invitation. He slipped a pass between two Tiverton players and into the path of Shan's run with inch perfect placement. The beautifully judged combination of power, angle, and spin delivered the ball to Shan's correct foot so that he could control and move it forward without breaking stride. Shan advanced quickly into the open space taking a series of big touches with the lower part of his boot, just below the laces, and pumping his arms like pistons, elbows bent at exactly ninety degrees. He kept his eyes down for the first twenty-five metres and then lifted his head as he achieved top end speed.

Optimising pace within the group was an early priority when I arrived at the club. Working with Darren Crawford, a former two hundred metre runner turned sprint coach, we went back to first principles, correcting flaws in the players' technique and developing key muscle groups. We measured and adjusted each boy's stride length. Remedied Zharnell's tendency to land on his heel rather than his front foot. Turbo charged acceleration over the first crucial five metres by strengthening their glutes through multiple sets of lunges and squats with weights. Boosted their power with cone, speed ladder, and hill sprint drills. Then graduated to what Terry nicknamed Killer. The players sprinted from the goal line to the edge of the box, jogged back to the six-yard line, laughing and joking, then turned and sprinted to the halfway line. They jogged back to the eighteen-yard line and then sprinted seventy-nine yards to the penalty area at the other end of the pitch, turned and jogged back to the halfway line, gasping for air, Bailey always bringing up the rear. They sprinted to the six-yard box, turned and jogged to the edge of the area, their muscles screaming, lungs burning, turned and sprinted to the goal line, Zito, Zharnell, and Shan vying for first place. Crawford taught the boys that sprint speed comes from the arms, not the legs. Explained to them that they needed to relax and not tense their shoulder muscles. To keep their hands unclenched. Shan was the second fastest in the squad with a personal best peak speed of 22.07 miles per hour. He raced towards Tiverton's last man who was hovering near the centre circle. The covering defender hesitated for a split second and then started to back off. Shan feigned to the right and then took an explosive step to the left, pushed the ball into the open space behind the stranded defender and left him for dead.

'Bury it,' screamed Terry as Shan bore down on the goal.

In any one v one with a goalkeeper the advantage is always with the attacking player, but Lopez was smart and played the percentages. Rather than rush out and give Shan the opportunity to go around him or lift the ball over him, Lopez hung back and dared Shan to pick a corner. He bent his left knee, stretched out his right leg and spread his arms diagonally above his head to reduce the angle and the size of the target that Shan had to work with. By now Shan had reached the outskirts of the penalty area and Lopez was scanning his face, his body shape, looking for any sign of his intentions. The keeper made a quick movement to his right, showing Shan the near post. Shan shaped to shoot, drawing back his left foot and lifting his right arm, but pulled out of the motion at the very last moment, flicking the ball to the left with the outside of his boot and then hitting it hard, opting for power not placement. It was a fierce short-range effort, struck hard and true, but Lopez read the feint and the shot was at a good height for the Chilean number one. The ball slammed into the tips of his index and ring fingers, changed course, collided with the inside of the post and rebounded into the white polyethylene net. It was Shan's first goal in English football. Unaccustomed to celebrating, he froze for a second, unsure what to do, and then the emotions took hold. He raced towards the Milton Road Stand where his family were seated in the lower tier, tearing his shirt off as he ran and whirling it above his head. He sidestepped a fan who had jumped onto the pitch, brushed past a second pitch invader, and vaulted onto the top of the hoarding. He stood there blowing kisses to his mum and dad, while the fans embraced him and took selfies. It was this image that bounced around social media and was splashed over the back pages the following morning underneath the same headline:

Shan-pions league.

The final few moments raced by as the boys confidently recycled the ball, each pass greeted by cheers of 'Ole' from the crowd. The Tiverton players slumped to the ground at full time clutching their heads in their hands. I walked onto the pitch, hugged Zharnell, Shan, Fabio, and Zito. Helped Lewis Walker to his feet. He wiped the sweat from his forehead but disappointment and defeat remained etched across his face. I told him there was always next season. He forced a smile. We both knew it wasn't true. This was high tide for Tiverton, a once in a generation opportunity to break the stranglehold of the big four. City, Bury, Athletic, and Macclesfield would regroup and bring in new players over the summer. Tiverton's standout performers, maybe even Hoyle himself, would be lured away. Football, as is its way, punishing those who don't take their chances.

The hour after the match was a blur of noise and activity. A lap of honor with the players, scarves draped around their necks by jubilant fans. Kuipers wearing an oversized hat. Mats and Fabio holding hands with their kids, Senghor carrying his baby. Borello hobbling on crutches. Zito FaceTiming his parents. A one-sided conversation with The Owner, who delivered a long rambling assessment of the players' performances and then walked me through the hodgepodge of players on his wish list for the summer window. A begrudging well done from Archer. An awkward embrace with Anita. A succession of interviews with TV channels from around the world, each asking about my plans. Jerry Ryan attempted to put words in my mouth, coaxing me to bad mouth Archer or Rigg, like a witness-leading lawyer. I refused to take the bait, repeating the pre-agreed lines and heaping praise on the players and The Owner. As Laker's PR agency suggested, I went out of my way to praise the standard of football in the Bundesliga, La Liga, and Seria A in my interviews with the German, Spanish, and Italian media, signalling my willingness to relocate.

The rush from winning is always short lived, especially when compared to the lingering pain of defeat, and I felt numb, hollowed out, as I approached the tunnel for the last time. I came to a halt in front of the West Stand. I looked up into the sea of faces, saw the assortment of lifelong season ticket holders and fair-weather supporters. People from all places, all races. The well-heeled and the rough around the edges, and everything in between. Groups of guys in their teens or twenties, middle aged blokes all dressed in replica shirts, maroon and gold stripes from every era. Pensioners, mums and dads with their kids. More women than people often assume. All singing, all waving the flags we'd left on their seats before the game. After they had finished singing Borello's name, they turned their attention to me.

'JOE, JOE, GIVE US A WAVE.
JOE, JOE GIVE US A WAVE.'

I smiled and gave them a thumbs up.

Rigg clapped his hand on my shoulder.

'They're so fickle and yet so predictable,' he said with his hand over his mouth. 'Calling for your head on a spike one moment, venerating you the next. And to think we give these plebs the vote.'

His cynicism and disdain for the supporters and what the game meant to them was one thing I would not miss.

'It's their club, not yours, not mine. They'll still be here long after we're both gone.'

He snorted.

'That's what they all like to think, and it's important we maintain the illusion. Throw them some red meat every now and then, a new signing or two, a change in coach, but they're called spectators for a reason. We could change the name of the stadium tomorrow, sell it from under their feet. Join a new league, because we're the change makers, the ones who'll leave a legacy.'

Before I could respond, Xabi pulled me away for another selfie. This time just the two of us. He draped one arm over my shoulder and adjusted my position so that the scoreboard behind us was visible in the shot. Next, he called over the players and took a photo of me with each of them, one by one. Dani was the last up. The Spaniard was overjoyed at the prospect of European football. The two previous seasons he had watched his colleagues play in Europe, first from his hospital bed, then from the bench. Now he could look forward to floodlit duels in Madrid and Milan. After placing a hand on his breast to signal his love to the fans, he turned to me. Speaking in his slow deliberate way he said:

'I'll never forget the chance you gave me, how you believed in me when everyone else had written me off.'

I pulled Dani into a close embrace and thanked him for raising standards and leading the turnaround in our performances. By now the emotions were too much for me. I slapped Dani on the back, hugged Borello and Shan, turned to take a final look at the stadium, high fived the hands dangling down over the tunnel wall and headed inside.

About the Author

Steven Bartholomew lives in Surrey, England with his wife and daughters. He is the author of several short stories including *The Great Resignation, Friends in Politics*, and *Accidents Will Happen. The Half Turn* is his first novel.

Acknowledgments

Like most football fans, I'm an armchair coach with no experience of working in the pressure cooker of modern football. Research and background from a variety of sources was therefore invaluable. In particular, I'm indebted to Coaches' Voice and Training Ground Guru. For anyone who wishes to deepen their knowledge of the game, I cannot recommend their articles, videos or podcasts enough. The same is true with Elite Soccer which provides training ground drills from the world's most forward thinking coaches.

I tried to resist the temptation to read autobiographies or biographies of famous football managers and largely succeeded. The only exceptions were Quiet Leadership by Carlo Ancelotti, and Pep Guardiola: The Evolution by Marti Perarnau, which provide great insights into the methods and mindsets of two very different coaches, both of whom I admire enormously.

For as long as I can remember, I have enjoyed reading about football in local and national newspapers, and interviews and feature articles in The Athletic, The Guardian, The Times, The Daily Telegraph, The New York Times, The Daily Mail, The Manchester Evening News, and The Independent all helped with my research. The following were especially useful:

Vulnerable channels and 20 zones: the tactics behind Guardiola's title win, by Jonathan Wilson, The Guardian, April 2018

Liverpool's Pep Lijnders: Our identity is intensity. It comes back in every drill, by Arthur Renard, The Guardian, December 2019

How Mikel Arteta learned the Pep Guardiola way at Manchester City, by Pol Ballús and Lu Martín, The Guardian, December 2019

In search of Dieguito, by Martin Amis, The Guardian, April 2004

Kieran Trippier the 'defensive animal' trusted totally by Gareth Southgate, by David Hytner, The Guardian, June 2021

What are Man City? Premier League champions, the greatest team ever and a 'sportswashing instrument' of a foreign state, by Miguel Delaney, The Independent, August 2019

Man City manager Pep Guardiola sent goalkeeper message ahead of next season, by Daniel Murphy, Manchester Evening News, March 2020

Be Quick Press High, Cut Back: How to score in the Champions League, by Rory Smith, New York Times, August 2020

The Greatness of Pep Guardiola in a blade of grass, by Rory Smith, New York Times, April 2018

How data and some breathtaking soccer brought Liverpool to the cusp of glory, by Bruce Schoenfeld, New York Times, May 2019

How to scout a football team, by Murad Ahmed, The Financial Times, November 2018

Intensity is one of football's favourite buzzwords – but what does it mean? by Sarah Shephard, The Athletic, October 2022

How Liverpool have evolved: Thiago in the left half-space and more cutbacks like City, by John Muller, The Athletic, May 2022

Mino Raiola, the superagent loved by football's biggest stars, by James Horncastle, The Athletic, May 2022

Being a footballer during Ramadan, by Carl Anka, The Athletic, April 2021

Lampard's Chelsea sacking: Tension with Marina, unhappy players and secret job offers, by Simon Johnson, The Athletic, January 2021

What it's like to play for Ralf Rangnick: The eight-second rule, cognitive training and huge focus on nutrition, by Oliver Kay and Raphael Honigstein, The Athletic, December 2021

How Txiki Begiristain became one of the most influential men in football, by Sam Lee, The Athletic, April 2020

Dan Ashworth interview: England, B teams, homegrown quotas and making Brighton a top-10 Premier League club, Andy Naylor, The Athletic, February 2020

'Jurgen surprises me every day. His brain works differently to other people' – Exclusive interview with Klopp's No 2 Pep Lijnders, by James Pearce, The Athletic, January 2020

Mikel Arteta lived alone with tactical diagrams on the walls: what lies behind the eyes of Arsenal's new manager by Daniel Taylor, David Ornstein, and James McNicholas, The Athletic, Dec 2020

The church that Cruyff built, by Steven Scragg, The Athletic, October 2019

Various blogs, magazines, and websites were also helpful:

How do you measure a player's character before signing them? by Alistair Magowan, BBC, January 2013

The World at Their Feet: How Footballers Look After the Tools of Their Trade, by Tom Williams, Bleacher Report, July 2018

Tactical Analysis: Positional Play, Breaking the lines, August 2020

Recommendations for hamstring injury prevention in elite football: translating research into practice, by Matthew Buckthorpe, Steve Wright, Stewart Bruce-Low, Gianni Nanni, Thomas Sturdy, Aleksander Stephan Gross, Laura Bowen, Bill Styles, Stefano Della Villa, Michael Davison, Mo Gimpel, British Journal of Sports Medicine, April 2019

This is the 7-step process an elite football club uses when signing a new superstar, by Alan Dawson, Business Insider, 2017

Data-Driven Ghosting using Deep Imitation Learning, by Hoang M. Le, Peter Carr, Yisong, and Patrick Luce, California Institute of Technology, Disney Research and STATS LLC, March 2017

Pep Guardiola's Positional Grid: A Cognitive Roadmap for Players by Coach Dibernardo (an extract from Dibernardo's book published on his website)

How Fit is an Elite Footballer? by Thomas Reynolds, Coach Web, June 2016

Attacking the midfield diamond, by Julen Lopetegui, Elite Soccer, July 2020

Why playing out from the back has brought mixed results for Premier League clubs, by Stewart Robson, ESPN, September 2019

Frank Lampard's intensity and one big difference - Behind the scenes in Chelsea training, by Scott Trotter, Football London, October 2019

Behind the scenes at Arsenal's Player Performance Centre, Unai Emery's £30m base of operations, by Scott Trotter, Football London, August 2018

Tactics Part 2 The Low Block, by Tris Burke, Football News, 2021

Header goal analysis in League 2, by Leo, Football Performance Analysis, February 2019

Guardiola's 16-point blueprint for dominance - his methods, management and tactics, by Andrew Murray, Four Four Two, August 2016

Johan Cruyff: The player, the coach, the legacy, by Ben Clark, Four Four Two, March, 2016

What really goes on behind the scenes of a big football transfer, by Daniel Geey, GQ, January 2019

Guardiola's Class, by David Garcia, It's just a sport, November 2018

Pep Guardiola Team Culture Story, by Keep it on the deck, April 2019

The half-spaces, by SCI Sports, April 2016

Manchester United's "Boxes" Soccer Drill, by Soccer Training Info, June 2019

Pep Guardiola's positional patterns of play training, by Soccer Tutor.com

Tactical Theory: Set-Pieces, by Steve Beregi, Spielverlagerun.de, December 2019

Analysis: How a high-pressing game works in football, by Zain Mahmood, Sportskeeda, June 2014

RB Leipzig principles of play under Julian Nagelsmann, by Tactics and Technique

The Kidnap of Alfredo Di Stéfano, by Daniel Edwards, These Football Times, April 2015

Pep Guardiola's positional play and zone rules that have helped Manchester City dominate the Premier League, Tim Palmer Football, December 2017

Bayern Munich: Positional play in possession under Hansi Flick, by Carl Elsik, Total Football Analysis, June 2020

Tim Walter at VfB Stuttgart, by Cameron Meighan, Total Football Analysis, 2020

A day in the life of a Championship footballer, by Simon Austin, Training Ground Guru, April 2017

The Physics of the One Goal You Won't See at the World Cup, by Robbie Gonzalez, Wired, June 2018

On X (AKA Twitter) there is a whole community of talented football analysts and coaches who share their analysis, insights, and data visualisations. Again, if you wish to learn more about the game I strongly encourage you to follow people like:

@EricLaurie; @CañoFootball; @FMAnalysis; @pythaginboots; @timpalmerftbl; @AlbionAnalytics; @nomifooty; @CarlonCarpenter; @GoalAnalysis; @FTStands; @UtdArena; @xGPhilosophy; @JamiescottUV; @Gegenpressing91; @VenkyReddevil; @amonizfootball; @CamH__; @AFHStewart; @BetweenThe Posts; @TacticalThinker

Following these accounts not only made me look at the game differently, but also helped me learn the language of modern football.

Wikipedia was of great help, in particular, for the history of football stadiums and the section on Didi and 1950s Brazilian side. As were certain videos on YouTube, for example the Tifo Football and Coaches' Voice channels, along with The Guardian Football podcast, The Gary Neville podcast, and the High Performance podcast, especially the episode with Rio Ferdinand.

Big thanks to Kate, Chloe, and Mia, and to my parents Graham and Barbara Bartholomew. To Keith and Karolina at Michael Terence Publishing and early readers Simon Lloyd, Steve Brooks, Nick Bartholomew, Dan Bridge, Nick McCurtin, Neal McCormick, Martin Day, Shaun Marin, Tim Redgate, Anil Mistry, Scott Vosper and Andy Corrigan.

Available worldwide online
and from all good bookstores

Printed in Great Britain
by Amazon